'No,' Claire said. 'Leave me alone, or I shall scream.'

'I don't think you will,' he said carefully. He looked up and down the road. 'Listen. People may come asking questions. They've been to see Geoffrey already. So-called Security people, from inside the Government.'

'I don't believe it –'

'Oh yes they have. You ask •Geoffrey. We know,' he said. 'We watch. You ought to make sure that Mr Powers stays on the right side. And keeps his mouth shut, like you.'

'Please tell me what it's about,' she asked desperately.

'None of your business. Don't worry, Mrs Powers. And stay away from Billy Vane. No harm will come to you as long as you keep mum. Mum's the word, as they say.' He even laughed, a little throaty rattle. 'Because if you don't –'

'Don't what?' she asked feebly.

'If you say anything, anything at all, you or Mr Powers, that damages our prospects . . .'

'What prospects?'

'Don't be stupid now, please. I'm talking about the next Prime Minister.' He took his hands from his pockets and showed clenched fists. 'You keep quiet, Mrs Powers, or someone could be cut up rough.'

*Also by Matthew Hunter
and available from
Mandarin Paperbacks*

The Kremlin Armoury

MATTHEW HUNTER

The Gibraltar Factor

Mandarin

A Mandarin Paperback

THE GIBRALTAR FACTOR

First published in Great Britain 1991
by William Heinemann Ltd
This edition published 1992
by Mandarin Paperbacks
Michelin House, 81 Fulham Road, London SW3 6RB

Mandarin is an imprint of the Octopus Publishing Group,
a division of Reed International Books Limited

Reprinted 1995

Copyright © 1991 Matthew Hunter

A CIP catalogue record for this title
is available from the British Library

ISBN 0 7493 0623 8

Printed and bound in Great Britain
by HarperCollins Manufacturing, Glasgow

Par 403j. CIA : appropriations; expenditures.

(a) Notwithstanding any other provisions of law, sums made available to the Agency by appropriation or otherwise may be expended for purposes necessary to carry out its functions, including (1) personal services, including personal services without regard to limitations on types of persons to be employed . . . (2) supplies, equipment, and personal and contractual services otherwise authorized by law and regulations, when approved by the Director.

Central Intelligence Agency Act of 1949

Prologue

The NVA hit them in the early evening — cool, unusual for Saigon — just as he had the kids ready, lined up for the chopper, a splinter of machine gun bullets blasting into the mud and bamboo and corrugated shacks of the orphanage.

Melrose fanned out the Marine unit.

NVA commandos, creeping out of the jungle, out of the earth, shooting at their own people. He sweated in his flak jacket, crouched in the admin building with the little po-faced Sister.

'Stay there, lady.'

He saw the flames coming from the other side of the river where they'd burned the USAID godown.

'Sneaky bastards. Okay, okay, Sis. Don't worry.'

His orders were to get the kids out. Jake Melrose would do just that. One chopper, big CH 53C, two trips — one for the kids, one for the Marines, getting the hell out, back down the coast to Vung Tau.

Rattattattattattattatta . . .

Answering fire from the heavier Marine guns.

Melrose grinned. 'That'll keep the gooks down.' He wiped the sweat from his eyes. The firing died, the NVA melting away as quickly as they'd come.

The young POL–2 beside him was shivering, and it wasn't cold.

'Shit. They don't wait,' Melrose said.

Brendan Wallace lifted his head, saw the tall Marine lieutenant uncoiling from the chipped wall where they'd crouched in the dirt and go ambling across the courtyard to cheer up the Marine patrol. His men. His boys.

Out there in the yard, within the walls of the orphanage compound, the big Boeing Vertol was getting ready to move.

The lieutenant watched his unit take up their covering positions in case the gooks came back. Sweat-soaked, no drinking water, all of them shaken. Training paid at times like that, he told himself.

1

'Okay?'

'Okay, boss,' they said.

'Let's get the kids in.'

The Sister was urging them to hurry, hurry out of the communal shelter: a crocodile of thong-footed, bare-legged, doe-eyed, almond-faced kids. Abandoned kids. He hated what war did. He hated this part of his trade.

The junior CIA man was now in a blue funk.

'How . . . long . . . we gonna wait here?'

Melrose glanced at his face, a sensitive, large-boned face streaked with dirt. A bush shirt stained like batik. A young, smart-ass ex-Harvard Intelligence jerk, on a familiarization run, Melrose felt sympathy for him.

'Couple of hours turnround.'

'Jesus,' Brendan Wallace said.

The CH 53C was setting its engines into a primal howl, dust blowing round the vortex. It looked like some great insect standing there in the courtyard. Beyond the orphanage was the clearing and then the trees. Beyond the trees the road, now firmly in the NVA hands. These were late days in 'Nam, as they all knew. The crew clamped on their football helmets and gave thumbs up.

'Go. Go. Go,' Melrose said to the kids.

The crocodile broke into a run and surged towards the ladder up to the helicopter cabin. From high to their right the support Phantoms came swooping in, trying to hit some fucking impossible shifting jungle target, Melrose thought. And when they had gone the gooks would come back again. But they would have two clear hours, maybe three. His orders were to get the kids out.

They scrambled up the ladder like ants. Seventy-five kids. Almost instantly the chopper began to gyrate and tremble. The tail gunner crouched over the open rear door, just to make sure.

And then the guy from Saigon was running. Running, sweating, cursing, screaming across the compound after the kids, and clawing at the ladder as the crew tried to haul it aboard.

'Wait. Wait for me. Christ.'

Then Lieutenant Jake Melrose got very angry. He hurled across the compound, grabbed the civilian's shirt, pulled him back off the ladder, shouting under the whirlybird downdraught.

2

'No, you fucking don't. This is the kids' trip.'

He pulled Wallace back in his arms, saw him pop-eyed with panic, jabbering with bush fright.

'I wanna go. I wanna go.'

'Sure. An' I got orders to take you, safe 'n sound.'

Wallace flailed out helplessly in the lieutenant's strong grip. And Melrose was grinning at him, the thin head under the helmet like some Indian totem.

'Lemme go.'

'Next time, kiddo.'

He pulled Wallace back and loaded the last five kids, then made a windmill with his arms. 'Go. Go. Go.' The chopper began to rise, and he saw the wide-eyed faces, neither scared nor impassive, but human, wondering. Then it was above them, a light in its belly blinking, and they caught the whirlpool from the massive rotors.

The chopper rose and banked, almost as if reluctant to leave the safety of the clearing for the flight over the treetops down to the coast.

'Jesus Christ. You bastard,' Wallace cried. He levered himself away from the lieutenant, aware that the men had seen him shit himself.

'That's okay,' Melrose yelled. 'Your turn next time.'

Maybe Wallace should have gone. Could have gone in with the kids, but Melrose was in charge of the unit. You had to lead by example, Number One rule in the book.

The chopper was over the trees, setting course along the road, across the green web of jungle towards the safety of base.

Inside, the kids would be muffling their ears against the head-splitting roar and the draught from the open tail door.

One thousand feet up, he reckoned.

Big clumsy whirlybird.

And then it fell.

Oh Jesus. Oh Christ.

He hadn't seen a rocket, hadn't seen anything hit it, just the thing falling heavily, nose down, the tail rotor splintering, pitching and rolling and plummeting, like a huge dark stone, into the trees, maybe a mile away.

Then an explosion.

Then smoke. Black, oily, funereal smoke.

Melrose took off his helmet. He felt cold, colder than he'd ever been

3

in his whole goddam life. He tried to pray, forgetting every rule in the book. A Sister of Mercy and eighty orphan kids, and a mercy mission crew.

Wallace walked outside and stood by the wall and was sick.

The smoke grew thicker and thicker.

'Get your asshole back inside,' Melrose yelled. He ran towards the opening. Sergeant Papriski was shouting at them from the edge of the compound to get their fucking heads down.

Wallace was shaking. He just stood there and cried.

Melrose reached him just as the lone NVA rearguard opened up, spraying lead along the wall from his foxhole on the edge of the clearing. Reached him and screamed obscenities and pulled him back into cover as the platoon returned fire.

Wallace was looking at him like he was some sort of hero.

'You saved my life. Twice,' he said.

1

'Jake. Got a job for ya.'

Melrose had been killing time on contract, checking out Embassy security in various European capitals, so the London trip was no problem. But when he flew in, Wallace had been curiously cagey, sitting in a room with chunky furniture like in some *New Yorker* cartoon. A secretary brought a jug of coffee.

'Jake! It's so good to see ya. Jake, you look fighting fit.' Wallace's hand was soft and warm.

'Yeah,' Melrose said. 'How about you, Brendan?'

'Great.' Wallace passed the coffee and parked his buttocks on the end of the desk, next to the picture of Angie when she was younger.

Brendan Wallace's eyes belied the middle-aged body. There was nothing bland about them: with his pale, hawk-like face he reminded some people of T. S. Eliot, but not Jake Melrose, whose idea of poetry was a night out with the boys. To Jake he was someone he'd rescued way back in 'Nam, when they thought they could plan their future.

'You still looking for work?' An enquiry from a one-time buddy who was almost embarrassed at having done so much better.

'Sure thing.'

'Jake, you willing to sniff out a bone for me? Little hunch of mine, political stuff, outside the Firm's routine.'

Melrose smiled. Wallace knew damned well; knew that he was not on strength. So far as Melrose was concerned this was just a personal assignment, a favour from Brendan Wallace who had brought him over from Paris and wanted it kept private.

He sat down and waited.

5

'Ever been to Madrid?' Wallace tipped in a sachet of Milko vegetable oil and sipped his coffee.

'Nope. I ain't ever been there,' Melrose said. 'Not on my list.'

Wallace moved his feet, rubbing his jaw and peering between the slats on the window of the office in Grosvenor Square.

'But maybe you could go? Nose around a bit . . .'

'I guess so.' He grinned. 'You know me, Brendan.'

'Right, Jake. I don't forget. And right now I got worries,' Wallace said. 'Guy has come to us with a story about a ten-mile-high Brit. It may be crap. I don't know.'

'So?'

'Well. This guy drops a name, then wants a meeting out of town. Maybe he isn't sure. Maybe he's shit-scared.'

'The contact Brit?'

Wallace said. 'That's the boy. And it ain't like him, I know. We've had dealings before.'

What did they want him to do about it, Melrose wondered. Wallace was a clever bastard.

'I want somebody I can trust to keep his head screwed on. You with me, Jake?' Wallace levered himself from the desk, even lowered his voice. 'He wants to talk about Godber.'

'Freddie Godber?' British Secretary of State for Defence. Jake Melrose searched back in his mind. Godber was one of the previous contenders for No 10 Downing Street. Self-made, ambitious as hell. Now that the Government was shaky, trailing behind in the polls, the right wing was again suggesting that he should tilt at the crown.

'Right.'

'Why should this Brit guy come to us?'

'He wants some cash, Jake. Kind of a personal injection.'

Melrose waited, at attention, yet relaxed.

'Okay. What for?'

Wallace was staring at him, wondering if he was too rigid; but Melrose was available, in Europe, a freelance. Jake, retired from the Marine Corps five years now, a brush-top of greying hair, a lean face and coat-hanger shoulders. A veteran in mufti, and, hell, he could be tough. And discreet.

'Disclosures,' Wallace said. 'Won't say exactly what. You got to meet him for that. An informer. A Brit, ex-SAS. How about taking him on?'

'Okay by me. So long as the Firm pays expenses.'

Wallace nodded, referring to a notepad on his desk.

'You speak Spanish, Jake?'

''Fraid not, Brendan.'

Wallace shrugged. The bifocals, as he bent down to read the notes, made him seem awkward. But Melrose knew he had been Chief of Station in Beirut and Berlin before his appointment to London. He appreciated the fact that Wallace had called him in on the sort of job that didn't need regular files.

'So. Okay. This guy has come with a story about some scheme by Godber, involving Spain. Listen. We got bases there, Jake. We don't want any trouble. Strip the guts out of it, Jake.'

Melrose's eyes were steady. He didn't give a shit who, a job was a job if it paid.

'Who is he, Brendan?'

'Name of Vane. Billy Vane.'

2

Three weeks earlier, a staff car had sped out of Belfast down the Crumlin Road, making for Aldergrove airport, and the special flight back across the Irish Sea. Armed escort along the road and in front, three men plus driver inside as they headed into open country, on a cold spring evening.

The Rt. Hon. Freddie Godber allowed himself a sigh of relief. Another duty tour over, to the one place he hated with its unsolvable questions and endless sectarian killings, the one place that dragged him down, him and the Army, associating his name with that graveyard of political ambitions. Over the dark back of the head of his private secretary, Geoffrey Powers, sitting in front and equally glad to get out, he could see the wipers snaking away at the rain. And bow-tied young Peter Brocklehurst, his political agent, wedged in beside him, in the other corner of the car, next to the despatch box, was handing him the latest papers. Headlines of the doom and disaster, economic and political, awaiting him when he flew home to London.

Godber sank back on the velour seats of the bomb-proofed Rover saloon. It wasn't the way that things should be. When the last power struggle for the Premiership had occurred his campaign team begged him not to cry off. Melanie, his wife, had said so, and she was invariably right. And Oliphant and Mayfield, those disaffected elder statesmen who had lost out in the Cabinet reshuffle. Politics was a dirty game, and everyone had urged him to mix it but at that time some vestigial sense of decency or nervousness or insecurity in his origins had caused him to stand aside. It was a mistake, Brocklehurst kept whispering to him, that he must not make again.

His mind went back to his beginnings. Small town, small time son of a family doctor, it hadn't stopped him making a pile in property speculation in the Eighties, enough to be one of the wealthiest men in the House. It hadn't stopped him marrying Melanie, the daughter of old money, the landed end of the Party, whose father had served under Winston. It hadn't stopped his own ambition, and if that wasn't enough he had a track record and a profile, first in business then politics, at Environment, the Foreign Office and now the Ministry of Defence. Friends in the country and in the Commons. And a Government that needed a new broom, not just the uninspiring nonentity who was the compromise candidate at present in the chair.

It was almost as if young Brocklehurst, as his PR adviser, had the same treacherous reflection. Two minds with a single thought. The Minister caught his eye and smiled.

'You've got to make a bid for the Leadership,' Brocklehurst said. 'You've got to make a challenge now. Now. Otherwise

8

you'll sink with the ship. You don't want it to go down with all hands, do you?' Brocklehurst twisted his round ad-man face across towards Godber until the Minister could see the pores in his skin, and the calculating brown eyes of his media guru. Another one of Melanie's favourites. He spoke softly so that Powers couldn't hear.

Godber's lips pouted. He watched the small houses slide past on the road out to the airport. More trouble in the Falls Road. A Land Rover blown up near Newry, with gruesome pictures in the Belfast papers. And the London nationals were full of speculation about the Government's prospects, most of them featuring his name but suggesting he had no Departmental power base. At the time of the Gulf business he had been shunted sideways into Defence to clean up the mess. Savings, savings, savings, that was now the name of the game, in London and Washington. He thrust the rubbish away, back onto Brocklehurst's lap, and dusted his pin-stripe suit. The mane of dark wavy hair was only just flecked with grey, but his face reflected uncertainty. Freddie Godber's ambition was tempered with a native caution instilled by a frugal start and confirmed by a second-tier school.

'It's too risky to put myself up from Defence, in the middle of the review of commitments . . .'

'You're wrong, Freddie,' Brocklehurst said. 'Defence is as good as anywhere. You're sitting on a winner. Full credit for the defence cuts. Management efficiency. Now stepping forward to run the country.' There was only one business motto in his political agent's mind, and that was that power made money. The politician knew that, and knew it would profit them both if he made it to the top, with Brocklehurst installed as head of the Press machine in No. 10. They read each other's minds like books.

Godber smiled.

'Peter, you're over the top as usual.' A coup d'état? A joke.

'No. I've just got a gut instinct. About timing. And this fellow I mentioned could provide the ammunition.' He leaned across to Godber again. 'Look, I think you should at least listen to what he has to say.'

Again, Godber said 'No'.

Powers's ears were cocked like triggers, but to Godber, looking at the back of his head, he seemed not to be there. Was he listening, the Minister wondered for a moment, and then dismissed it. Powers was a man of straw, a cipher, one of those human automatons thrown up by the civil service machine, not even Godber's own appointment. His sights would be limited to two or three rungs up the ladder, enough money for an extension to his damn house in Wimbledon and an inflation-proof pension. If Brocklehurst chose to have a political conversation with a Cabinet Minister who directly employed him, that was out of a private secretary's hands.

'You've got to make a move. A signal,' Brocklehurst persisted.

Godber flapped the briefcase shut. 'Defence cuts weaken my position.'

'No, they don't. You've done a marvellous job. A management job on the Army. You've only got to make your case.'

They were out in the fields, cattle and potatoes and cabbages.

'Don't preach to me.'

But Brocklehurst could see he was worried. Chances were slipping away.

They entered the airport approach and Godber glimpsed the RAF executive jet loading up on the apron as he was whisked away into the security lounge. A young captain saluted, an Army detail guarded the door, along with the RUC. The Army took care of its own and the salute was vigorous. Godber felt pleased.

An RUC Special Branch man with an iron face handed him a late report, which Powers intercepted.

'Read it on the plane, Minister,' the young man said. Godber had to remember that he was there. He had almost forgotten how self-effacing Powers was, thin, bleached, used to speaking in whispers. His Principal Private Secretary seemed to Godber to exude whatever was the opposite of human warmth: a career civil servant too concerned about his preferment to want to venture opinions.

'All right.' He turned to the liaison people. 'Let's go.'

But there was a temporary hitch. A flustered Air Force flight lieutenant came in to explain that they had a small blip on one of the engine checks. Fifteen, maybe twenty minutes, while they ran it through again, just to make sure. Would he mind waiting?

He would have to, Godber said, unused to being held up. 'I'll have some refreshments brought in.'

The Secretary of State for Defence, Brocklehurst and Powers reseated themselves in the biscuit-coloured room, stretched out on moquette chairs more suitable to a saloon bar.

The flight lieutenant returned and said something to Brocklehurst, who turned again to the Minister.

'He happens to be here again. I think you'd find it worthwhile.'

Godber was tired. Frustrated. Angry and missing Melanie.

'I suppose so . . .'

When the man came through the door, blue-suited and correct, he realized that he knew him by sight from those closed briefings in Lisburn involving Intelligence, the RUC and Army Undercover Ops. The hidden side of Government, as opposed to the public face.

'Landsdowne,' Brocklehurst said, introducing them. 'Colin Landsdowne.'

'Just five minutes, Minister,' Landsdowne said. 'That's all I want.' He was middle-aged but already white-haired and nearly bald, so that a silver stubble grew round the sides of his head like grass in a sharp frost. An oval, anonymous face with pale blue eyes. Suspicious eyes, Godber thought, confirmed by the line of the mouth. A soft Antrim accent.

Godber nodded.

Landsdowne was holding a copy of the *Sun* with its shrieking political headlines, 'Down They Go' – the Government, that was, in the opinion polls. He smiled with a pall-bearer's sympathy.

'I'm an Orangeman, born and bred. We're all behind you, sir.'

Godber was not there to be flattered.

11

'What do you want?'

Landsdowne drew up a chair, close as a father confessor, leaning over the coffee table and pushing the teacups aside. He had the short neck and rubicund complexion of an open-air man, and wrists as strong as a boxer's.

'There's a lot of us rooting for you – '

'I'm in a hurry, please . . .'

'I won't keep you, sir. It's just that I know how to work a trick or two. The B-Special Police. Para-military. I was in them. After that, covert ops here, reporting directly to the GOC, Land Forces,' he said proudly, confirming his credentials.

The room was sound-proofed. Artificially quiet.

Godber looked across at Brocklehurst, who motioned him to wait. Powers said, 'Excuse me,' and went outside for a moment, as if to the lavatory.

'You should make a bid,' Landsdowne whispered. 'Just like Mr Brocklehurst suggests. What I'm saying is that I could fix you up with a winner. Something that would put the skids under the rest of 'em.' He didn't need to refer to Godber's rivals in the Cabinet.

In spite of himself, Godber smiled.

'How?'

'Remember the Falklands . . .'

'Different times, different problems,' Godber said. 'Leave the politics to me.'

But Landsdowne would not shut up.

'Listen, I'm telling you, sir. I could fix you up with a cause. An opportunity. A threat that you could respond to. That's all you'd have to do. Seriously. Show 'em what you've done for Defence. The Rapid Deployment Force.' He seemed to be fascinated by Godber's position. 'Put the UK on top.'

'That's ridiculous,' Godber replied.

'No, it's not. I have my contacts,' Landsdowne said, 'with a certain lady in Madrid.'

The Secretary of State had heard these stories before. Any politician was fair game for propositions from undercover people with ambition or chips on their shoulders. He tried to get rid of the man.

But Landsdowne was persistent. 'I'm referring to Julia Maria Villalba, Countess of the Asturias,' he said softly. 'The daughter of Vidal Eduardo Villalba, Franco's last right-hand man.'

Godber rose. It was just as Brocklehurst had told him, privately, over dinner at his Worcestershire home. A threat could be 'arranged', at a price.

'I'm not prepared to discuss that sort of thing.'

He held out his hand, which Landsdowne took with enthusiasm.

'You will. I'm sure you will.'

Brocklehurst showed him out and, standing outside in the corridor, Landsdowne added, 'Make it clear to him, Peter, that it wouldn't be Government-to-Government stuff. That's not the way I work. And it wouldn't entail any risk . . .'

Brocklehurst handed him over to the security guard and went back to the VIP room where Godber was sitting alone.

The Secretary of State looked up and said 'Madman' as the agent closed the door.

Brocklehurst said, 'Not really. Plenty of people in Spain would like to see pressure on us. All you would need to do is stand up and be counted when that happens . . .'

Godber's face was enigmatic as he smiled. It was only when the door opened again and Geoffrey Powers slid back that the political agent also for a moment wondered if he had overheard anything, while they were in the corridor and Powers in the lavatory. A look at that cold face reassured him. Brocklehurst was not to know that Powers had shared a study at Wellington with Billy Vane. Billy, the little romancer who had taken to calling on Claire Powers in the long nights when Geoffrey was working, and who was due to have dinner with them both on the following day.

As the private jet took off, Geoffrey Powers was interested to see that Godber was deep in thought. And it never crossed the Minister's mind that Powers could be more than a yes-man who would do what he was told and above all keep his own counsel.

3

Billy Vane was waiting at the bar of The Prince of Wales hotel in Hereford when Melrose first saw him; at 7.45 p.m. the place was scarcely busy, just pleasantly full.

'Look for a Brit about 5 foot 10 inches, around 170 pounds, fair-haired guy with brown suede shoes. Single. Loner. Says he'll be carrying a trench-raincoat, whatever that is. And reading *The Independent*. You got that? It used to be *The Times*,' Wallace had said with a grin.

'Why can't he come to London?' Melrose had asked.

'Because the guy runs a recruitment agency, ex-SAS men, based in Hereford,' Wallace had replied, blowing cigar smoke. 'With a private calling code. You want Billy personal, you have to ask for Uncle William, like he's two different people.'

'Why Hereford?' Melrose had queried.

'Because he works there. Tough bastards train round there. Anyways, historic city. One of those big cathedrals. You should go visit.' These days Wallace prided himself on his culture. He spoke bad French and good German and belonged to several book clubs.

'Yeah.' Melrose sounded unconvinced.

'I've said that you'll be coming,' Wallace repeated, 'tomorrow evening. You can get down there for that.'

'I'll pick up a car,' Melrose said. 'How do I find him?'

'He says he'll meet you in your hotel. In the bar. The Prince of Wales down by the river. Seven o'clock. Think you can make that?' These days Brendan Wallace was so urbane, so successful, you would think he was in charge of the world, but Melrose always remembered that the way the dice fell was unknown.

'How far is it?'

14

'One hundred fifty maybe. Miles. Say three hours on the road.'

'Okay. No problem.'

But he had forgotten the roads. By the time he got there he had been held up twice, in a long queue round Oxford and roadworks near Cheltenham. He had to hustle from Tewkesbury and even so he was late; threequarters of an hour late, drinking time for Billy Vane in the bar.

Melrose was thin, tall, dressed in a sand-coloured lightweight suit, a bit too light for May, reinforced by a pale blue sweater. Vane was perched on a bar stool talking to a stray business woman. Two senior citizens drank up their beer and left; half-a-dozen youngsters in the opposite corner were giggling at a joke. There was Muzak from a speaker somewhere.

Vane was drinking that lukewarm pump-handle beer and telling the passing woman some funny story, concentrating on her eyes. He recognized the stranger at once and Melrose saw his back stiffen. He looked at the Yank with suspicion, and Melrose thought 'Uncle William' but did not say so.

'I'm Jake,' the American said. 'Jake Melrose. Sorry I been delayed, coming from London.'

'Yes. A pity.' Vane nodded but did not shake hands. It upset him to have been left standing, wasting his time. If it hadn't been for a later engagement, he would already have left. And this guy wasn't what he had imagined.

'It's a big country,' Vane said.

Melrose thought he was taking the piss, as they said, but he couldn't be sure. He half-smiled, his eyes widening, the creases at the corner like scars.

'Beg pardon?' he said.

Jesus, Billy Vane thought as he tapped on the bar. This bloke is out of a Western. Vane's hands were slim and delicate, as he motioned to the barman.

'What'll you have?'

'Tomato juice,' Melrose said.

Billy Vane ordered, with another half for himself, then suggested they moved. The business woman said she'd powder her nose, then must be going. Melrose noticed she was young-ish and pretty and wore a ring.

The hotel was down by the meadows opposite the cathedral and Vane led Melrose outside. It was one of those late spring evenings with the horsechestnuts coming into flower, pink and white, and the long grass of the watermeadows flecked with buttercups.

There was a small patio, a flagstoned terrace overlooking the river. A man walked a dog on the towpath, two scullers eased with the tide. It was all so laid back that it seemed stupid to Melrose to discuss a deal out there. He stared at Vane while they waited for the woman to return.

Melrose said, 'I hear you got some information?'

Billy Vane grinned. 'That's the ticket. At the right price.'

'Price ain't my business. Leastways, not here.' Melrose waved his hand at the bar behind them. He feared the woman would come back too soon.

'Well then, you'd better get clearance,' Vane said. 'I'm available in the office tomorrow.'

Melrose did not make friends like that, but he kept on.

'Who's the lady?'

Vane seemed to look straight through him as he stroked his chin.

'Look, why don't you mind your own . . .'

Melrose never did find out what he should mind, because the young woman was there again. Her eyes appraised him coolly.

'Jake here has come down from London for a spot of busi-ness,' Vane said to her. His hair was as neat as if he'd just been to the barbers, his fawn raincoat was immaculate. He was a snappy dresser, in the style that got up Melrose's nose: grey trousers and desert bootees – brothel creepers. Confident of his inbuilt superiority, like a Cheshire cat. Why the fuck had Wallace asked Jake to take him on? But of course he knew. He knew why Brendan felt a debt, after nearly twenty years, which he repaid by trust.

'Really?' The woman picked up her coat and said she must

16

be going. He watched Vane escort her to the door as if she was Marilyn Monroe.

'Look,' Melrose muttered. 'I prefer to talk business some place else.' Vane had confused him.

'Okay by me,' Vane said, drinking up. 'I've got to go in five minutes. 'Nother day tomorrow.'

Melrose found himself embarrassed. 'Sorry I made it so late.' He didn't feel like confiding in Vane, he wanted time to think him over. The younger man's clear eyes seemed to be concealing his thoughts.

'Suit yourself,' Vane said. He finished the second beer and pulled out a business card. 'I could sell the story elsewhere but I thought maybe you guys would like to know first, given the way you nose about.'

What the hell did that mean, Melrose wondered, standing on the river terrace. A breeze began to ruffle Vane's light brown hair, leaving Melrose untouched.

'I'll think about it,' he said, freezing.

'Call me tomorrow if you decide . . .'

'What time?' Melrose asked, loathing this potential partner. He would go through the motions, but only for Brendan's sake.

Vane shrugged. 'Eleven? It's in the middle of town.'

Reluctantly Melrose agreed, and as Vane got up to leave, squeezing past the American, Jake noticed the limp, slight but perceptible.

'You invalided from the military?'

Vane turned round like a cat. For a second there was a flush of anger, or frustration, or shame, then it was as quickly smothered.

'Don't you worry about that, old man,' he said. 'Spot of bother in the South Atlantic.'

Melrose saw that he had gone too far. 'Pardon me,' he said. He had been around at that time too, working his butt as the Galaxy C5s supplied spares via Ascencion. Maybe they had something in common, after all.

Melrose was pondering that discussion later that evening over

17

something called gooseberry crumble and a half-pint of lager. The restaurant was nearly empty and the lager just as warm as he expected. Maybe he should have had English beer but that would taste like a rubber mattress. The kind of thing Vane drank.

With their first meeting behind him Melrose felt strangely unenthused. The last thing he wanted was to buy from a guy like that. Didn't like the look in his eyes. How could these people seem so fucking superior? He'd seen too many of them lacking the will to get moving. He must tell Wallace what he thought.

Billy Vane. So where was he off to now? Some other assignment? The Agency jobs Jake had been on, courtesy of Brendan Wallace, often had this kind of pattern, starting slow, doodling round in circles, picking up people like Vane. Sure, it would be like that. It always was.

Jake Melrose finished his coffee and wandered through the hotel: potted plants, a couple of clerics in dog collars, businessmen in a huddle drinking Scotch on a settee. These characters puzzled him as he walked past. Like a being from another world, he saw them as a different race. An earthman on an alien planet. Aw, come on Jake, he told himself, ease up. Go for a walk someplace.

4

'But could it conceivably work? How could it bloody well come off without a hitch?' Freddie Godber had asked Brocklehurst several times over the next few days.

And Brocklehurst always gave the same reply. 'Fortune favours the brave.'

'What the hell does that mean?' Godber swung round and smiled, aware of the political options narrowing as they took stock at the weekend in the constituency offices in Worcester, a shop front just off the High Street, with Godber's official picture in a blue frame in the window. He had finished his 'surgery' and was in a positive mood, hands thrust in the side pockets of the expensive suit.

Encouraged, Peter Brocklehurst had to wait until the secretary stopped fussing, and they got rid of the local Party chairman. He closed the door.

'Good session, Freddie. You've got them all cheering for you. Tremendous popular appeal.'

Godber frowned. He didn't like Brocklehurst's presumption in calling him Freddie, he didn't like the way he plotted. And yet . . . and yet . . . you couldn't get media coverage by going round kissing babies and helping old women across roads. Given the slide in the polls the Party had to have a fresh leader, and he must be in with a chance. He hadn't been tainted by holding the Exchequer, or Trade, or Home. He hadn't given away Hong Kong. He'd kept his nose clean in Northern Ireland, where poor bloody Quennell got the aggro as the Secretary of State. He'd kept the tanks in Germany and set up the new commands and cost-efficiency centres. Now that they were really worried about the effect of defence cuts, the professionals could be relied on to sing to his tune. The Army, Navy, Airforce men.

He had sounded them out, one by one, in quiet corners during his official visits. And so had Brocklehurst. But by Christ it had to be quiet. His soundings within the Party had been similarly discreet.

Brocklehurst said, 'Whisky?' and he nodded.

They sipped the drink in silence for a while, then the younger man said, 'Well?'

'Well, what?'

'Have you thought about what Landsdowne could do? Fixing up something in Spain . . .'

'It would be too damned risky,' he said again.

'Nothing venture, nothing have.' Brocklehurst jumped from his chair. 'Two Para are spoiling for a fight. I had a word with the Colonel while we were down at Andover.'

Godber winced at this young pup with the cuff-links and PR talk thinking that you could run politics like one of the

19

Saatchi campaigns for which he'd been responsible, launch a piece of bravado like a new brand of chocolate. What did they know about life, Godber reflected, this new and classless breed that had come out of the universities in recent years, interested in power and money. He wasn't even sure where the man had gone to school, only that he lived in Hampstead with some Italian model. But Godber knew that Brocklehurst intended to climb to influence on his political back, by helping him to Number 10. And he had the sneaking feeling that he needed him, a feeling almost of admiration for this manipulator who might in the end be right.

It kept them in harness together but it didn't mean he trusted Brocklehurst. Godber crossed to a filing cabinet and pulled out a sheaf of letters, which he flapped up and down.

'You see these? Pledges of backbench support. I'm not risking my future on any crack-brained piece of Jingo.'

Brocklehurst refilled the glasses without being asked.

'I wouldn't put too much faith in your friends,' he said. 'A lot of 'em are fair-weather sailors. They need to be sure you can win this time.'

Godber brushed an imaginary hair from his suit and began to pick up his things. The car would be outside now to run him back to Melanie at Lower Broome for lunch. He would need to confide in her, to take her views.

'Look,' he said. 'Get it out of your head that I'm in favour of setting up the Spaniards so that I can don a flak jacket, jump down off a chopper and wave the Union Jack.'

Brocklehurst grinned.

'Marvellous photo opportunity. You'd look terrific. Upstage that wimp in Number 10 from the start. You've got to create a vacancy before you can fill it.'

Godber smouldered, but couldn't conceal his interest. In the Britain of the Nineties, politics were increasingly influenced by what would go down well with the media, now that they televised Parliament, and he was good on the box.

'And who sets up the Spanish?'

'No problem. Landsdowne has all the contacts.'

'With a crowd of superannuated fascists? You must be joking.'

'Judging by her photographs, the Countess is not exactly superannuated.'

'Right. So you fix it all up with a woman?'

Brocklehurst picked up the whisky bottle and set it aside under the Thatcher photograph.

'Better that way,' he said. 'They are more likely to get things done.' He grinned.

But Godber shook his head.

'And what if war breaks out? A shooting war? People killed. We don't want another Gulf scenario.'

'It won't. It'll all be planned. Just a threat.'

'Famous talk. It's not like persuading people to buy a new washing powder. It's asking the military to set up a phoney confrontation.'

'For real, as far as they're concerned.'

'That makes it worse . . .'

'No. Better. It makes it look genuine.'

Brocklehurst accompanied him to the door.

'Have a good weekend, Freddie.'

'Go and sleep it off,' Godber said as he walked out to the Jaguar, with the police car waiting behind. He turned to the political agent.

'Look. This thing has got to be kept quiet. Even the idea, half-baked as it is. If anything crept out, it could ruin me and ruin you. As for that Ulster madman, Landsdowne . . .'

'Don't worry. Landsdowne will take care of your back. He has his own means . . .'

'He's an idiot.'

'He's not an idiot, Freddie. He's a patriotic extremist who wants to see you on the throne and not some wimp manoeuvred there by Central Office after three ballots.'

They stood for a moment on the steps in the sunshine, looking at the High Street traffic. A few people recognized the tall man with the dark, Byronic hair and paused for a moment to stare.

'You see,' Brocklehurst said. 'You need a cause, and they

would all be behind you. Tremendous pressure of public opinion on the Party.'

'I'll think about it,' Godber replied, returning a wave as he got into the car.

He dined the following week with the Inner Circle, in Pratts club off St James's. Coal fire in the grate, discreet service at the table reserved for Winston long ago in the alcove in the basement. A meeting place for conspirators, Godber thought. Smoke-filled back rooms still had their place in politics, and one part of him thrilled to it.

A flunkey took him downstairs. 'Lovely evening, sir.'

'Quite beautiful.' Godber sniffed the air. He appreciated these obsequious touches, the smell of warm money, privilege, the bastions of the Establishment, all the more because they were not quite his by right. He had climbed up the pole without getting too greasy, and it pleased him. Now they were all waiting, the ones on whom he needed to rely: Wainwright, the Chief Whip, Drumblane, leader in the Upper House, Oliphant and Mayfield now on the back benches but lately of the Cabinet, Pickering the chairman of the '22 committee, Burke from the supporters' club. The plotters, the Guy Fawkes men.

They rose as he came in and then resumed places hastily so as not to make it obvious, but of course it was patently clear to the old hands, the others who were dining there. Godber knew the tongues were wagging, just like the press speculation, and for Christ's sake why should he mind. This, after all, was politics, the contaminating mistress.

He greeted them all in turn, carefully, not effusively. The Party never liked show. They concentrated on small talk, then on the food, roast pheasant with club claret. Freddie Godber felt much better, and as he began to relax – the company of friends, he thought – his eyes roved over their faces. Wainwright was the one to watch, playing a double game – what was the old Cold War word, 'a double agent'? – he was both 'in' with the PM, marshalling the Government troops, and sizing up the runners for the next succession. No, Wainwright was not to be trusted, however much Drumblane said so. Poor old Duggie Drumblane, the umpteenth earl, with a brain of pure sorbet, but such a damned good chap. Bertie Oliphant and Terry Mayfield were Freddie's men through and through, no doubt about that after the way they had been treated. Godber smiled at Oliphant now and saw the gleam of shark's teeth in the salmon-coloured face. Oliphant at sixty-three was too old for the leadership, and too heavy in girth, but he would make damned sure it would go to the right kind of man. That left Burke, Freddie's long-time supporter, good old Burkey, blue-suited and looking as always like a senior police inspector with that sparse greying hair – God, how the lack of hair hurt some people in this televisual era – and Philip Pickering. Pickering of course was the key, the absolute fucking key, Godber decided, a spider at the heart of the '22 web. Grey in dress and mien, a watery, watered down man – how the hell did you get adopted with a personality like a sponge, let alone chair the Backbench Committee, something to do with the Peter Principle, Godber decided – Pickering had to be won over. He concentrated on Pickering as he ate a crème caramel.

'Philip. We're going to dip the Election unless something happens . . .'

And Pickering agreed. He rubbed his grey jaws.

'I was hoping for a decent Budget.'

But that hope had been disappointed, as they all knew. A few tax cuts, next to nothing. A hike in the mortgage rate to help stem a tottering pound. A thoroughly confused economy.

'The last bloody straw,' Burke said.

Oliphant was elder statesman.

'Something has to be done.' He reminded Freddie Godber of the Duke of Windsor as Prince of Wales with the South Wales miners fifty-odd years before. A famous, and useless, phrase, usually uttered by those who didn't have a clue.

But Freddie had. That afternoon, handling Questions in the Commons, he had shown he was good; motivated, at the top – and they congratulated him.

'What we need is your kind of fire . . .'

'Set-em-alight, Freddie,' Burke added on cue, and Godber hung his head modestly, just for a second.

'The image has gone wrong,' Wainwright said cautiously.

'I agree. We've managed to give the impression of being a load of shits.'

'Too much self-interest.'

Not without cause, Godber thought privately. Most politicians were greedy sharks, nothing much wrong in that. Greed was a basic drive, but it had to be directed, regulated, organized: the economy needed a new hand on the tiller. And to get there he had to work from where he was, his power base in the MoD. Not, they might think, the best, but in young Brocklehurst's view they were wrong and Freddie was increasingly coming round to agree.

Oliphant was turning to him.

'Well, Freddie, what would you do?'

Now was his moment. And the Rt. Hon. Frederick Godber, MP, Secretary of State for Defence, knew exactly what he had to say.

'Think back,' he urged. 'How did we win last time?'

'By pulling out the stops. Economic boom – '

'And bust.' Godber was leading them through. There was not much chance of a repetition this time round.

'And before that, in the Eighties?'

Pickering was staring at him. Pickering had an inkling perhaps. Pickering was a bastard.

'We won a bloody war,' Burke said.

Godber smiled.

Drumblane had roused himself from contemplating the table: he tended to drink too much, a feature which Godber despised.

'We can't have another Falklands . . .'

'No, of course not,' though looking at Oliphant and Wainwright he seemed to see lights in their eyes. These old ex-Army men. Godber paused for effect. 'I don't think it's necessary. But when you have a rough time at home and want to get the peasants to back you, you know the best thing to do?'

Burkey nodded.

'Start waving the flag,' he said.

'Precisely,' Godber agreed. And who should be there holding the flag: none other than the Rt. Hon Freddie, who could cut a fine figure in a camouflage jacket, or jumping down the steps of a jet.

But Oliphant was full of gloom. 'The trouble is, Freddie, there's nowhere to wave the damned flag. Hong Kong's a running sore, and God help us messing in Cyprus or rotten little Belize.' He sighed and ordered more brandies. 'I think those days are gone, Freddie. What would you want to conquer – the Isle of Man?'

Freddie Godber threw back his head, that famous and lordly gesture.

And laughed.

5

Jake Melrose was wandering into the city, past the pinkish façade of the cathedral church. Downtown Hereford was dead, nine thirty on a May evening. A few teenagers mooned on the benches, the flowerbeds were littered with paper, women waited for buses back to the outlying estates. Only the pubs seemed open, but Melrose didn't fancy more drink. He took alcohol in moderation, knowing it was bad for fitness, and fitness was all important when you were still in the field and turning forty. It worried him sometimes, age. Where was it going to end, how much longer could he keep in commission, one job after another. Leastways he was set up now for the best part of a year with the Eastern Europe property check, before Wallace had called him over. Lucky maybe, now that the world was calmer, apart from the Arabs and Chinese, since jobs in Europe were scarce. Could be he should learn Arabic or something, but he was crap at languages, had chickened out of school too early. Made good in the Marine Corps.

From the Halls of Montezuma to the Shores of Tripoli: a great life if you kept good.

He marched ahead into what they called High Town, and picked up the familiar smell of hay and dung, a cattle market the other side of the centre. Melrose was okay with animals. They didn't cause trouble. He had learned to ride horses and when he had quit the Corps had thought about moving West. Cattle in the Dakotas or maybe Montana like in the Marlboro ads; but that was a Hollywood dream. The Agency was for real, looking for guys like him, willing to chance their arm. Field operatives, single and straight, combat-trained and loyal. Melrose had followed his nose, just as he did now. The cattle had gone away, the market had closed hours before but some of the garbage remained. Covered sheds and open-air pens. They had swept up the piles of shit and hosed down the concrete standing, but you could still smell the animals.

Melrose walked on. He walked past deserted stalls where goose feathers swirled. He'd seen markets all over the world, from Texas State fairs to the side streets of Macao and Hong Kong, from sheep hurdles in Iraq, when the Firm was passing covert munitions to Saddam Hussein, to fish auctions in Japan. And now England, this buttoned-up little country.

He wandered down a narrow passageway between two sets of railings thinking what he'd offer to Vane. He stuck one leg on the piping and leaned a while. Get alongside of Vane, Brendan Wallace had said, perched on that desk in London. What was the phrase he had used? 'Billy has got hold of something.' Melrose frowned. Wallace was a smart guy, so Vane must be on to some deal. What about MI5; or maybe they already knew? He broke open a stick of gum and chewed it slowly, watching the paper flutter like a broken rotorblade. The Brits were always a puzzle.

Melrose changed position, leaning on the rail and wondering how he should put things. Uncle William. How much should he offer, how much would Vane admit? All that Wallace had said was that Vane was linked with Godber. Something was cooking in Spain. Were there no goddam Spanish experts in Wallace's command? Experts on Spain? Drugs, or crime, or whatever? He couldn't see why Wallace had specially wanted him. Well, let it roll. Another day on expenses.

He stood up and scraped his shoes. The alley was narrow, ill-lit, and the metal pens gleamed dully from a single light on the corner. Time to be going back, time for an early night. He walked towards the far end and saw the four big shadows moving closer: guys in black gear, leathers and plastic leggings, bikers who had appeared at the end of the pens, three abreast and one behind, vaguely threatening. Melrose was walking towards them and there was no going back, not unless he wanted to run.

He stopped there to let them pass. Four big guys, he could see them clearly now, who looked as if they lived rough: two shaved heads, two pony tails. Menacing. Except these guys would be British, and saying 'Sorry'.

He stood and watched them and realized that they meant trouble: one to four, four big bikers in leathers. It was growing dark by the side of the cattle pens and Melrose felt for the railing, leaning back against it. The smell of hay and cattle shit. The four guys swaggered towards him. Swagger was the word, he felt; the bums had been drinking. The leader showed a tattooed arm where he had cut the sleeves out of his jacket. Heavy guys in their twenties, bulging with muscle. Big deal. He watched them as they lurched forward in the narrow space between the pens. The biggest guy had a root vegetable face straight out of the soil. Melrose stood six foot one but this guy must have been bigger, six foot two, round as a drum.

'You bastard,' he said sniffing, swaying in the wind, eyeball to eyeball with Melrose.

Melrose ignored him but his fists tightened. The others came up and hemmed him in.

'Keep your nose out, curly,' the big guy challenged.

'Say that again.'

Instead Melrose got a push on the shoulder, a knee coming in at the groin. Melrose hit him on the mouth; not quite hard enough but drawing blood. He felt the teeth rattle as his fist went in.

'Jesus Christ, you bastard,' the big guy said and aimed a

27

counterblow, but Melrose was too smart and jumped aside. They pinned him against the railings.

'Get the fucker,' the big guy shouted. Melrose could sense them moving rather than waiting to see, as he ducked instinctively. Don't run, don't let them get behind. There was an arm round his neck, but he brought his leg up and kicked. The grip relaxed but the leader was calling, 'Hey, hey, Mister, you're heading for big trouble.'

Don't let them get behind you, Melrose thought. He could feel the steel bars of the cattle pen rigid behind him.

A blow into his ribs lurched him against the bars, then another one into his chest wall. The big fellow was the problem, his frothing, blood-streaked mouth inches away from his own.

'You fucking sod, keep out,' the giant hissed.

Melrose punched his way out by ramming his head into the big man's gut. Melrose had a head like a bullet, hard bone with plenty of gristle. That left a space between them. He kicked out at another one who was holding on to his neck and got him in the nuts.

Now, he told himself. Now. Down the track before they recovered. But one of them put out a leg and Melrose stumbled. On his knees they were hammering his head and ribs, and he could see the pain, a tunnel lined with white stars and occasional flashes of lightning. He fought back, scrambling away, realized the fence was behind, with a two-foot gap in the piping. He turned somehow and slipped through. They were big and drunk and less agile. He could hear them swearing and cursing.

'That's enough. Leave him alone.'

'No way,' the big guy said. 'He done my mouth in.' He spat out blood and saliva.

Melrose picked himself up. Rows of animal pens, one after the other, each closed off by gates. An obstacle course. The four faces loomed above him, clambering over the barriers, too heavy to slide through. He looked for a weapon, or friends.

'Hold it, boys . . .' he began.

'Fuck you,' they roared, one by one dropping beside him.

28

They were rolling inside the pen now, the big one trying to crush him, and Melrose kicked again, hands grasping the scalp, pulling back the pony tail. No way the others could get him if he kept it close, one to one. But the big guy knew that too, and pulled off. Melrose was lying on the ground, his head on a pile of straw, bleeding from cuts on his cheek, breath coming in handfuls. He could see the world going round in a crazy carousel of pig pens and stars and one leaning street lamp up there on a wall bracket.

'Get out,' a voice said, coming from nowhere, calm with a hard edge.

Billy Vane had decided that it was time to be counted. Whatever his misgivings, this guy was genuine, locked in a fight to the end. They had misread him, whoever they were, whoever it was they were after. It might have been Billy Vane: he had seen them outside the hotel when he said goodbye to the woman, but perhaps that had confused them, looking for a man on his own. Anyway, time to move in, before there was serious damage.

Melrose saw him drop from the sky: Billy Vane, whirling a four-foot stave like some Samurai warrior, round and round. A crack sent the big guy to his knees, another one hammered him into the ground. They tried to duck, but Vane caught another one of the skinheads and Melrose saw him go down.

'Okay. Come on, Jake boy,' Vane roared.

The big guy was doubled up, two others began to scramble up and over the pen, sent on their way by Vane, who seemed to enjoy it. The big guy had collapsed like tarpaulin, and one skinhead was stretched out in the corner.

Vane stepped over them and helped Melrose to his feet.

'You all right?'

'Thanks,' Melrose said, unsteadily. He clung to the railings and took in air. His own head was still on up there, connected to his backbone, but the going was tough. It didn't seem to respond too well to questions.

Vane stood over the big man and prodded him with a

bootee. The biker's face in the shadows looked like something dug up.

'You could do with a wash and brush-up, old man,' Vane said. And then to Melrose, 'Let's go.'

He unlatched the gate of the pen and helped Melrose through. The skinhead with the bad head was moaning in a corner, the big guy nursed his guts. The other two had run.

Melrose found himself being led, supported, helped to the end of the pens, where the alley opened out. Street lights, a road, and passing cars. He saw the bikers' motorcycles, left in a heap. Lit windows in a nearby pub. People on their way home, but no one had wanted to know about the fight in the market.

Except Vane. Billy Vane who had followed him around as if he did not trust him.

Melrose was feeling his bruises.

'Do you want a doctor, old man?' Vane asked.

The American shook his head. 'I'm okay. How the hell d'you get here?'

'Just a hunch, old boy. Wondered what you were up to.'

'Come on. What kind of hunch?'

Vane said. 'Here's the car.'

Melrose saw a grey shape, small windows, like a beached submarine.

'What exactly is this?'

'It's a Bristol,' Vane said. 'Not many of 'em around.'

Melrose wiped a hand across his mouth. The hand still felt shaky.

'I mean those guys,' he said. 'How come you were there like the Cavalry?'

'I had a warning of trouble. I came back to find you.'

'Don't give me that.'

'Well, tell the truth, a telephone call that they would be looking for trouble. I went back to warn you. Then saw you pitch in. Thought you might need a hand.'

'How about telling the cops?'

Vane considered this, as if it were a new idea.

'You want to nail them?'

30

'Damned near tried to kill me.'

'I wouldn't be so sure. Probably more like a warning.'

'Warning of what?'

Vane somehow looked uneasy under these sodium lights. Or maybe Jake's head just hurt.

'Talk business tomorrow,' he said.

The big car accelerated and nosed through the sleepy traffic of Commercial Road, past the railway station and up the tree-lined thoroughfare of Aylstone Hill, heading out of the city.

'Hell's teeth, where we going?' Melrose said from the back. The trees were a blur of fresh green.

'Don't worry,' Vane shouted over his shoulder, driving with concentration. 'Spot of R and R.'

It was like some kind of kidnap. Melrose cursed himself for letting it happen, for having to be rescued. Now he would owe Vane something. They were shooting past suburban houses and down towards river meadows, soft and shadowy in the dark. Vane cornered round a medieval-looking bridge and flashed the car up an incline, into the rolling agriculture of the hills, orchards and tight little gardens, neat cottagey houses, town overspill thinning to country livings, a village called Coombe something glimpsed on a leaning signpost, then down a gravelled lane and full stop before a small square white stone house with a slate roof.

'Home,' Vane said. 'Let's have you.'

A girl was helping him out, a girl who seemed to have been waiting, had come to the car door, saw him and gasped, but asked no questions – a looker, with dark auburn well-cut hair, in smart pants and a neat little jacket top, blazer style.

'My God,' she said. 'What's happened?'

'Don't worry,' Vane said. 'Just grab hold of his arm.'

Melrose's legs were wobbling, but he kept his shoulders rigid though it hurt him to breathe. His ribs ached like crazy and there were cuts on his cheek.

'Get him inside,' Vane said.

Inside was full of sleep, brasses and settled furnishings that had grown old with the house. And a fax machine in the corner.

'I bought it complete,' Vane said. 'Except the fax.'

Melrose's mouth felt sore, but his square old bucket head was still firmly screwed on.

The girl began to help him upstairs. 'Two up, two down,' she said.

Melrose was eased on to a bed. The girl was taking off his jacket. Vane dragged off his shoes and pulled up his shirt.

'Easy now,' Vane muttered. 'Let's have a dekko at the ribs.'

As the shirt came away they saw red weals on the flesh where the boots had gone in. The girl came back with hot water, flannels and towels. She wiped the blood from Jake's face and held the flannel like a compress to his swollen cheekbone.

'I'm Claire,' she said. And as she smiled her face lit up.

'Good job they missed the eye,' Vane muttered. 'Otherwise you'd have had a shiner, old boy. As it is you needn't worry.'

'They were lousy shots.' He grimaced as the pain hit him and bit his lips to stop the fire.

'Who were they?' Claire asked. Melrose had the feeling that she felt bad about what had happened.

Billy Vane laughed. 'You get these oddballs about. Motorbike junkies pulling off the M5.'

The girl looked at him thoughtfully, with an amused concern. Melrose knew she didn't believe it.

'Such bastards,' she said.

'Don't worry,' Vane counselled again.

But Melrose was worrying, worrying why it had happened, as he glanced round the room. He was lying on a white coverlet in a whitewashed cell with beams up to the ceiling. A pot of primulas set in a saucer on a big chest of drawers, two wheel-back chairs, a man-sized wardrobe.

'I'm okay,' he said. 'Ouch.' Then 'Jesus,' as the pain hit him.

Claire finished her sponging and dried him deftly, competent and sympathetic, and he liked her for not asking more questions.

'Lie back,' she said. 'I'll ring for a doctor.'

'I'm okay,' Melrose repeated. 'They didn't dust me over.' Not as much as in Saigon in '74 when he'd been twenty-six. All these years later he reckoned he should be older and wiser, but what in the name of Christ was he doing on some fancy bedspread in an English country cottage? Jake was a country boy, born Appeldoren, Wisconsin. Cold as hell in the winters, so he joined the Marines. No feel for this kind of set-up.

'Jeez,' he said. 'My head's rolling.'

'You get some kip, old man,' Vane grinned, covering him with a cellular blanket. 'Best sleep it off. Let me take care of things.'

He slipped out of the door.

Melrose had almost dozed off when Claire returned with some coffee and a slug of Courvoisier in a balloon glass. He gulped them thankfully. The brandy seemed to dull the aches, and he brushed aside the Anadin.

'Where is this place?' he growled, struggling to get up.

'Come on. Rest up.' She looked at him and smiled.

'Where the hell am I?'

Claire sat on the bed and helped him to coffee. 'It's what Billy calls his pad. Ten miles outside Hereford. A little village by the Lugg. A bit of peace and quiet.'

'Those bastards weren't peace and quiet.'

'Billy doesn't want to call the police.'

He looked at her: she was smart and sweet. Attractive. He liked the sound of her voice. She wasn't one of those girls who said 'Hullo' and then left you out in the cold.

'Don't you think that's kinda strange?'

She hesitated. 'Maybe not in Billy's position.'

Vane happened to look in and picked up the suggestion.

'They've learnt their lesson,' he said. There was a gleam in his eye.

'How d'you manage to get there on call?'

'Told you. I was looking for you,' Vane said smoothly. 'I got the feeling those guys might duff you up.'

'You or me?'

33

'You should have talked to me. Then you wouldn't have hung around.'

'Yeah?' Had Vane really been following him?

'Yup. No sweat, old man.'

'Where'd you been?' Melrose muttered. Something about this smooth-haired almost fragile-looking Brit still made him uneasy.

'Met my friend, brought her here. Then came back to check on you.'

'Check on me?'

'You're a suspicious bastard,' Vane complained.

'Christ.' Melrose flopped back on the bed. 'So are you.'

Claire was offering some kind of embrocation for the bruises. It smelled like crushed nettles. 'You'd better stay here and sleep it off.'

'I'm okay,' he said. 'I got a hotel. The Prince of Wales.'

'I'll phone them and cancel the room. You stay here. Billy's got two bedrooms,' she said.

She read Melrose's mind, which was wondering about her relationship with Billy Vane.

'Don't worry about me,' she said. 'Billy's going to run me back.' As if to reassure him. Something in her attitude told him she was glad of the excuse.

Chivalrously, Melrose added, 'Don't want to put you out, ma'am.'

She smiled. Claire had got herself into an awkward spot and this gave her one way out.

'Honestly. I've got to go.' Vane was looking at her hard. 'I've got a place booked.'

'Pretty late now to check in. You going far?' Melrose said from the bed, feeling stiffer with every movement.

She shook her head, laughing at Vane. 'Not far.'

Vane handed him another glass of brandy. 'Sleep it off here, old man. That should do you. Not to worry.'

Melrose was tired, dog tired. The voices and faces above him drifted on and off.

'Mustn't be a nuisance,' he said slowly.

'That's okay. I'll just run Claire home.' Melrose had the

34

feeling that now he had appeared Vane also wanted to get Claire away, right out of his enquiries.

'Home?' Melrose muttered.

'Well, part of the way, old girl,' Vane grinned.

'The White Horse Country Club,' Claire said.

6

When he woke up they were gone. The little house was empty and it was dark. Melrose looked at his watch and saw he had slept for an hour. It was now nearly midnight. He was stretched out on the bed and felt a damned sight better. His head was clear and most of the aggro had gone. Apart from a swollen mouth even the pain was less, in fact it was not too bad, give or take a few bruises which still squealed when he touched them. He breathed in and out slowly, relaxing, then tensing, flight checking his muscles, lying prone on the bed.

He stripped back the coverlet and slowly stood up. Surprisingly, he was ready for take-off. Felt pretty good again. He grinned to himself: a survivor, they said. But this was Vane's room, in Billy Vane's house; the guy who had approached Wallace and the CIA. A crazy little place, a bit like a monk's cell. He touched the whitewashed walls as if not sure they were real, and left a mark on the plaster from the grease on his fingers. And he wanted the bathroom.

Gingerly, he moved to the door, then found he could walk firmly and swing his arms, knowledge that reassured him. There was a connecting passage between the two upstairs rooms but nothing that looked like a pan. He called out downstairs.

'Hi there?'

The house was silent apart from a ticking clock, but he called again to make sure.

'Hi. Anybody home?'

Vane and the girl had gone. Who the hell was Claire anyway, the woman who had been waiting for Billy, as if she was intending to spend the night there and then had been only too pleased to slip away?

Melrose began to go downstairs, holding on to the rope rail that curved round with the staircase. He had hardly noticed the room below when he came in, but now he saw a big open kitchen with a square table in the middle, the remains of a bottle of wine, some covered dishes with cheese and cold meat. It was dark and a little chilly, and he found an electric fire and switched it on, together with the hanging light that pulled down over the table. Somebody had left a book there, a paperback copy of Steinbeck's *The Grapes of Wrath*.

He went to the fridge, found a plastic carton of orange juice and poured himself a large glass. Sitting with his elbows on the table, drinking the juice, he began to feel much better. He picked up the book and thumbed through it. Steinbeck. He'd heard of the guy but never read him, something to do with a family trek from Oklahoma to California, according to the blurb. It could wait; but he saw the little gold ownership tag, a label inside the front cover. 'Geoffrey and Claire Powers. Wimbledon.' No wonder Vane had said he was only taking her part way. He stored the names away for reference. And then he noticed the telephone standing on a ledge in the window.

Goddammit, Melrose thought, I could give Brendan Wallace a piece of my mind. Wallace had gotten him into this mess and he ought to report the attack. Get Brendan to check out what had caused Vane to shadow him, if that part of the story was true, and why he hadn't wanted the cops in, and who the girl might be.

Melrose dialled Wallace's personal number. Wallace had told him to contact, any time. Brendan would be at home with his wife in that big apartment overlooking Regent's Park – St John's Wood it was called. And serve the son of a bitch right if Jake disturbed his slumbers.

The phone seemed to ring a long time but he persisted, thinking back as he did so to the chance that had brought them together, years ago, when they both thought they knew where they were going. The only difference now was that Wallace still believed it.

'Who is it?' a woman's voice asked. Melrose didn't recognize it. Angie, or some other dame. Anyways, he wanted Brendan: his relationship with Wallace was purely business, not social. Wallace had commissioned him, and he was now reporting that things had started to screw up.

'Is Brendan there?'

The woman didn't answer. He sensed suspicion at the other end. And hostility, and tears.

'I'd like a word with Brendan Wallace.'

'Who's that calling?' Melrose had the feeling that some guy was with her, listening.

'Jake Melrose.'

'Leave your number and we'll call you back . . .' She didn't appear to know him and was clearly on edge.

Then the phone seemed to be snatched from her hand and another voice, hoarse with anxiety, whispered, 'Who's there? Who is that?'

'Jake Melrose,' he said again. 'Had some business with Brendan. Pardon the late hour, ma'am. Got something to check over.'

There was a long silence. Voices. A strangulated sigh.

The first voice came back. 'Say your name again, please.'

'Melrose. Hey, what the hell's going on?' he asked, leaning against the windowsill, cradling the phone on his shoulder.

He heard the two women talking. A man said something like 'Go on.'

The second woman said slowly, disbelievingly, 'They've . . . just . . . told me . . . Brendan is . . . dead.' Her voice diminished into a whisper. For a moment he did not understand.

'Dead?' Melrose held the instrument as if it was telling lies. Wallace couldn't be dead. Not now, after all this time. Wallace had bought his life at Nang Dong, and the bonus price was five more kids.

'Jesus, no. He can't be . . .'

37

'I'm Angie Wallace.' she stammered. 'I am . . . I was . . .'

'Honey, hear me. I was talking to him yesterday. What the hell has happened?' he said. Not in a jungle clearing. Not in Bangkok or Beirut, but there in London. Wallace might have chickened once, but he had toughed it out later in some of the worst spots, and he never forgot Jake. Melrose shook his head.

'Sweet Jesus. How did it happen?' he asked. He had to know.

'Stabbed . . .' she sobbed. 'He was just out there running. Jogging in the Park. Regent's Park. Apparently they stopped him . . . to ask the time or something. There was some kind of mugging.' She shrieked down the telephone. 'How in God's name did they think they were gonna rob a man in a sweat suit? Not even a dollar on him? Tell me that, will you?'

Melrose felt the jinx at his elbow. The jinx between him and Wallace. He felt the ground was dangerous. It made the little cottage seem sinister as if the walls were closing in. He wasn't afraid, he was angry, angry inside himself.

'I just don't know, Mrs Wallace.'

'They got him. They got him,' she kept on saying.

'How, for Christ's sake, honey, how?'

'With a knife in the back. They found him in a pool of blood.'

Melrose said 'Dear God and Jesus Christ.' He remembered that day at the orphanage. Wallace had been in rough corners – Vietnam where the chopper went down, the Philippines, Iran when the Shah fell. He was an anti-Commie, and anti-Ayatollahs. Berlin. Beirut. If some bastards were out to get him they had a soft target in London, an easy meat post where the security was less. Now Wallace was dead and it was all too soon on top of Jake's own commission. Maybe that was a coincidence; maybe not. Melrose's minor bruises suddenly seemed irrelevant.

Wallace dead, Melrose himself attacked, and he did not trust Billy Vane. Why, why, why, he asked himself.

Melrose could hear her waiting, waiting for him to say something as if it was his move, and there was nothing to say.

38

'Mrs Wallace? Angie. God that's terrible. Real bad.' Not Brendan. Surely not Brendan. 'You got the Ambassador alerted?'

'I got everybody. The Ambassador. The Agency. The British. The Security Officer.'

'Okay, Mrs Wallace, you got to get some rest. You keep your head down,' he said. It was all he could think of to say.

'Where are you?' she asked again.

He had to look at the name scribbled beside the telephone number. 'Some place called Coombe Whitbourne.'

'Jake. Listen. There's a man called Pallett in charge of the investigation at the Embassy. Chris Pallett. You know him? He's here. Says he wants to talk . . .'

'Yeah. Put him on.'

Her voice faded away and he heard Pallett come on the line. Chris Pallett, another young sprig that he'd known way back in Saigon, when they had the world at their feet, or thought they had, and Melrose had been attached to Mission Intelligence.

Pallett said, 'Jake, what's cooking?'

Briefly Melrose told him, but Pallett hardly seemed to hear.

'Jake, you'd better get your ass back here. Fast as you can.'

'But I got to see this guy Vane.'

'Fuck Vane,' Pallett said. 'You get your hide back here before there's any more trouble.'

'I got an appointment . . .'

'Now,' Pallett said. 'Starting tonight.'

'Because of what's happened to Brendan?'

'Because I say so.'

Billy Vane would have to wait, he thought.

'Nobody know who did it?'

'Not yet. The police, they suspect it's an A-rab. Somebody out of Beirut.'

Chris Pallett was another smart guy sitting all day at a desk, but Brendan Wallace had asked Jake a favour. A kind of deal. A contract. And Jake would go through with it, when he knew what it was.

'Okay. Tell Angie I'm coming straight back.'

7

The Speaker called the Emergency Statement and the Rt. Hon. Freddie Godber, Her Majesty's Secretary of State for Defence, stood at the despatch box, confidently scanning his papers. He was conscious of the stir of interest on the green benches behind him, as well as opposite. Some of the well-heeled squires on his own side would not have shed tears at a gaffe, but his pinstriped figure was immaculate and his voice was firm. The way that he tilted his head carried a kind of arrogance, a self-assurance that many found comforting. He had the House of Commons eating out of his hand.

'There is no reason to suppose the death of a member of the US Embassy's staff was other than an unpremeditated act. The police are investigating. I am confident that the perpetrators of this terrible deed will be brought to justice. I offer my deepest sympathy to Mrs Wallace.'

Atwood was on his feet for the supplementary, flipping back his white hair.

'But . . . ah . . . is it not a fact that Mr Wallace was a member of the CIA? In fact, in charge of its London operations?'

'That is a matter for the US Government,' Godber said smoothly.

But Atwood persisted, in that whining Black Country voice, scenting a cover-up.

'Does the Minister mean that he is not concerned?'

'Terrorism,' somebody said. One of Freddie's friends told him to shut up.

'I have no further comment to make,' Godber said firmly, and the House moved on to the next business.

Liar, thought the young man in the officials' box, a young man with black hair combed carefully above the tight-lipped face, not a comfortable face to live with, one that mixed efficiency with a certain compressed cynicism around the eyes. Dark blue eyes. A Welsh face, Godber had long ago decided when Powers was appointed to his Private Office. A career man, a climber, somebody who would see the inside and keep his mouth shut. To look at: a young professional, thin-faced, almost repressed, but also, looking closer, with a kind of fierce interest as he followed Godber's responses. 'Liar,' Geoffrey Powers whispered. Keith Bramley, Godber's assistant private secretary, sitting next to him in the narrow pew, wondered at the tone of his voice.

The two officials came down the steps from the box and waited at the back of the Chair, but Godber did not appear. He was enjoying the limelight, while listening to the PM's defence of the Government's record. MPs who thought that they knew him would say he was testing the temperature of his own support in the House as the Party's popularity slumped.

'I'm going back to the office,' Bramley said. 'What did you mean about Freddie?' A junior official, still intrigued by these jousts in the Commons.

The intensity in Geoffrey Powers's face surprised him: a zealot with a religious conviction that he was right, sanctimonious, obsessive, as if he had stumbled on a version of the truth privately printed for him.

'Wallace was murdered by arrangement,' Powers said. 'Somebody tipped them off about his movements.'

'How do you know?'

Powers gave a thin smile.

'Freddie thinks so. I can always tell.'

'Rubbish.'

'Suit yourself.' There was a look of self-satisfaction in Powers's eyes, as if he was in on a secret.

But Bramley did not believe in the conspiracy theory of Government. The Messenger was telling them to move, and they came out to find the policeman who stood in the corridor waiting to hand them a note.

'Got to go,' Bramley said, promptly dismissing the matter. 'Old Henry wants to see me.'

But anyone watching Powers as he reorganized his briefcase and waited behind for the Minister would have seen more than cynicism in his face. They would have seen suspicion and naked envy. For Godber was everything that Powers would never dare: the self-made millionaire, the quick-footed politician, caricatured as the next leader, standing for anything, according to one of his much-quoted phrases, if there was a market for it.

'The CIA,' Freddie Godber once said, 'is like a foreign state, with missions everywhere. They need to be kept under control.'

Geoffrey Powers walked back to the Secretary of State's room in the House of Commons, a subdued room in brown and green: light oak furniture and Victorian pseudo-Gothic windows. He did not knock but sidled in so quietly that Freddie Godber didn't glance up from his papers until he was standing there. The Minister finished signing his letters, flipped them in the red box and closed the lid.

'Ha!' he said. Off with the half glasses that he refused to wear in public. 'What did you think of that?'

'A shambles,' Powers said. He'd found it better never to mince his words. They liked an appearance of frankness, the politicians. They thought they were frank themselves.

Godber raised his head to look at his Principal Private Secretary. A leonine head, he liked to think, subverted by the cartoonists who appreciated the Byronic hair and the handsome dark eyes. He slipped the spectacles carefully into his breast pocket and concealed them with a silk handkerchief.

'What makes you say that?' He felt in a tolerant mood after having played with the House, side-stepped the awkward question about that American diplomat, put down the ancient Atwood, boosted his fan club's morale, the backbenchers who saw in him their true leader, and been firm in front of the cameras. If only the Party would turn to him before the next

42

Election they would be home and dry, he thought. He was the natural inheritor. He assumed Powers would agree.

It was rare that they had a chance to exchange confidences like this, with no one else present. Normally nothing was said without a third party record, and life was too busy anyway to chit-chat with mere officials. He saved gossip for the Carlton Club, and the drinks after the '22 Committee. But that afternoon he felt good, almost self-indulgent. He stretched his long frame in the well-pressed suit – grey with a broad white chalk stripe, slightly vulgarian, just as the papers liked, and it also showed up well on TV – and invited the younger man's comments.

Powers glanced at his watch. The last thing he wanted was a private conversation with a Cabinet Minister whom he directly served. It wasn't his way at all. He was burningly self-effacing. Cautious, sallow, used to speaking in whispers and sometimes in clever asides which set people's nerves on edge. Godber rather despised him, suspecting he took out resentments on his cute little wife, who probably didn't get much of the sexual action. Godber liked to think of that; it deferred the ageing process, and Powers was one of those people who would probably be unable to sweat in a Turkish bath.

'Why a shambles?' The Minister repeated the question, concerned for a moment that Powers had detected some flaw in his Commons performance.

'Well,' Powers said, 'I didn't like the way they tried to spoil your statement.'

A flicker of anxiety showed in Freddie Godber's face.

'You mean it didn't get across?'

What he meant was across on camera. He knew he mesmerized the House, but they were still learning these television techniques, and the bloody cameras always got you face-on, with some fool's knees in the background or, worse still, a glimpse of belly.

'Oh, no, Secretary of State.' Powers was quick to cover up. 'I just thought they were a shambles. The Opposition.'

Sycophantic bastard, Godber thought, looking at the PPS. In the six months they had been together he had found him

43

clever, priggish, cold and calculating; unlikeable but efficient. It didn't matter to Godber if he had a devious mind, a blinkered mind, as long as he did the work and the whole private office hummed like a Rolls Royce. What he needed was hard work and loyalty. From everyone. Freddie Godber had made his name as chairman and chief executive of Armed Services plc. He snapped the red box shut and turned the key. Nodded.

'I agree.'

Powers picked up the despatch box and followed him to the door. These stupid boxes, he thought, another lunatic leftover from the era of Gladstone. If you wanted a foolproof case for confidential papers, the last thing you would have invented was a wooden box in red leather. But Godber loved them, and so did most of the others, the Cabinet Ministers he met. They looked good, you flashed them around and hoped to be Chancellor of the Exchequer. They were a status symbol.

'If I may say so you came across very well,' Powers said.

Godber strode down the corridors of power, conscious that they were looking at him as they passed, they, the messengers and clerks, wandering Members, deputations to other Ministers – for it was a busy time, with plenty of pressure – him, Frederick Bryant Godber, the PM-in-waiting. It made him feel pretty good.

And Geoffrey Powers, scuttling behind, drawn along in his wake, was not clear what made Godber so confident but increasingly of the view that he was up to something. He caught up with the Secretary of State as they stepped into Speaker's Court and waited for the big Jaguar to manoeuvre across.

'Minister?' he said quietly.

Godber smiled. 'Yes?'

'That bit about the American. Wallace. Was he really murdered because of something going on?'

Godber stood on the steps, bouncing up and down on his toes, breathing the afternoon air.

He wondered if the little ponce could be trusted to keep his own counsel, suddenly recalling the conversation with

Landsdowne that Powers might have overheard, while they waited at Belfast airport.

'It doesn't do to ask,' he said.

The Secretary of State was busy that Thursday, trying to clear the decks for a weekend away at the manor house he'd bought in Worcestershire. The château, he liked to call it, for it gave a sense of droit de seigneur. But privilege had to be paid for and there were papers to kill: the new draft of the Defence White Paper, slimming down the three services now that the Soviet Empire was on the blink. Godber was secretly uneasy, and so were the Chiefs of Staff, but he had learnt to swim with the tide.

Back in his own room in the MoD he received Air Chief Marshal Sir Michael Letwine and General Sir Gervase Taylor, Chief of the General Staff. They came in with the Perm Sec, earnest, balding Henry Burton, the hardcore of the Financial Planning Group.

Freddie Godber waved them in and led the way to his armchairs, around the hinged coffee table. Nobody held meetings any more, he sometimes said, they just talked over drinks.

The Minister sat down first, knowing by the look on their faces that there was anxiety to come. Powers had made himself scarce and young Bramley was taking the note.

'Tea? Coffee and biscuits?'

Godber always enjoyed the formalities, as if this was some Mad Hatter's party. A girl brought the tray in at once, the lady-in-waiting: he always preferred female messengers and this one was really quite pretty. Freddie with his public face smiled his 'best looking man in the Government' smile and offered Jaffa cakes.

Sir Michael Letwine shook his head. No crumbs on the uniform.

'Well, gentlemen?' Godber enquired.

The ACM was quick to the point.

'You've seen the latest draft, Secretary of State?'

Godber agreed that he had.

'It would be ruinous,' Letwine warned. 'Fifteen billion pounds lost over the next five years.'

'Saved,' Godber interjected.

'We simply can't agree, sir,' Taylor added, springing to support the Air Force. 'It means we axe four battalions, two out of Germany under the CFE Treaty, and big cuts everywhere else. And cancelling tank replacements. We shall have to demobilize 30,000 trained men, disband two armoured regiments, slim down the artillery, pull out of the Rhine bases. All on top of the problems caused by the Gulf.'

Godber nodded. 'It's not what I want,' he said. 'God knows we needed them in the Gulf; but it's what has been decided. The PM and the Cabinet.' They fall in like dummies, he thought, and his had been a lone voice at the end of the table.

'It seriously weakens our position in Northern Ireland. Our ability to police Ulster.'

'I know. I know.' Godber poured himself more tea out of the white and gold pot. They didn't have to tell him, but Letwine wouldn't let go. Much to Godber's discomfiture the ACM elaborated.

'It means closing Support Command. Cancelling the Eurofighter, closing ten RAF stations, cutting four RAF squadrons. We shall no longer be able to upgrade our air defences.'

'How many men?' Godber asked, already knowing the figures.

'Twenty-three thousand,' Letwine replied. 'We'd have to defend the Empire with 70,000 airmen.'

We haven't got a fucking Empire, Godber thought, but let it pass. It was a kind of joke. He rose and looked out of the window, leaving them sitting there, always a disconcerting reaction. Godber was good at tactics.

A tug with two barges of rubbish was sliding past on the Thames, together with four pleasure cruisers. One tug, four bloody tourist boats, he thought. The wide boys who run those take half the money on board, no taxes, winter in the West Indies. Make more than a Cabinet Minister. Thank God he had something more to rely on than the miserable salary.

'And how many two-stars have we got? I'll tell you, gentlemen. One hundred and eighty-seven officers above the rank of major-general, AVM or rear-admiral. It will also be necessary to shake out some of those.'

He heard the silence but did not turn round. Whose side was he on, they were thinking, who's bloody side. Secretary of State for Run-Down.

Godber swung round and smiled, theatrically posed, legs braced, back to the Thames.

'All right. I understand. Perfectly understand.' He walked over to the desk and slapped his hand on the draft copy of the White Paper. 'A dog's breakfast, gentlemen. A dog's breakfast, which is what you get from panic when the economy is – ah, overheated – and the Government wants to save money. That's what it's all about, eh, Henry?'

Burton came in on cue. Christ, old Henry, he could play on them like a squeeze-box, giving him background accompaniment. 'That, and the Russian collapse. We have to accept changed times.'

Godber nodded.

'But you mustn't underestimate the IRA.'

'Or the continuing tension in the Middle East. Islamic fundamentalism,' Letwine said. 'Gorbachev's undoing in Asia.'

'Of course. Of course.' Godber strode back and sat down again in the central chair, poised and confident. His foot stretched out and tapped the coffee table. He leaned forward conspiratorially.

'Now, listen, gentlemen. I understand. And just at the moment there's damn all that I can do about it, short of resigning. And that won't help you or me. But I know it's a short-sighted policy. Michael, Gervase – ' he used their Christian names for the first time and he could see they were pleased – 'I know that, and just possibly certain events could prove me right.'

They looked at him. It couldn't be he was backing down, cancelling the cuts? That was beyond his power. But they knew as well as he did that emasculating the services meant cutting off one of the balls of the Minister in charge. The Secretary of State. Godber needed a power base, and the

47

services would have to supply it. For one crazy moment, General Taylor wondered if he contemplated a palace revolution, a coup de main, but quickly dismissed the thought. This was not quite Ceausescu's Romania. No, Godber was surely hinting at something else.

'There are circumstances in which the defence run-down could be reversed,' Godber said. 'But they would need certain precise operations, and your absolute support.' He smiled across to young Bramley, the new APS, who stopped taking notes.

'How?' Letwine asked.

Godber smiled even more broadly, the arrogant head thrown back, the neck arched and full of power. He also knew these two wouldn't go along with dirty tricks.

'That would be telling,' he said.

8

Jake Melrose made up his mind not to wait for Billy Vane. He wanted to get back to London before the Brits returned to whatever it was that Vane was up to in that gingerbread cottage.

He put down the telephone and circulated, first through the two upstairs bedrooms, making sure there was nobody there, hidden in some closet or up in the little loft. He even stood on a chair to prise open the trapdoor at the top of the stairs, and poked his head into cobwebs and junk. He moved downstairs, a creaking wooden staircase through to the kitchen one way, then the bathroom and some kind of outhouse, through the other to the main room-cum-office with the fax and a photocopier. The VDU was unplugged, and he found nothing in the drawers, not even a telephone book. That bastard Vane must have locked away all his business stuff in the two filing cabinets standing over in one corner.

Melrose stared through the window, with Brendan Wallace

on his mind. It was a moonlit night and he would have seen them coming if they drove back up the lane. There was a small front garden with one of those little wooden fences you saw round picture-book cottages, a couple of wind-blown roses, some bushes, a wheelbarrow upside down. It didn't look used. It didn't look as if Vane was much in residence, except when bedding that girl. But why wasn't she upstairs; he'd seen no feminine things, none of that scented bric-à-brac that intrigued him in most women's bedrooms. No lingerie, no ladies' clothes. Come to that, only a couple of suits, three or four pairs of men's shoes. Maybe Vane wasn't there much. Maybe the bastard didn't live there but just used it as a cover. Okay, get out, Jake. And Jake was moving so fast he forgot about the bruised head and the pain in the ribs. What was a bit of pain anyway, after pain in the mind. The memories he had to live with. That 'Nam crash and his own wife's death. And now Wallace's. Cut it out, Jake, he said to himself. Get the hell out of here before that guy comes back.

White Horse Country Club, that's where she said he was taking her. White Horse Country Club. Christ, he'd been stupid. Perhaps the dame was in partnership, some kind of undercover job. Well, he could check Billy out, but next time it would be on his terms. He wasn't waiting around. The downstairs clock struck one a.m., a grandfather clock, like in some Agatha Christie movie. These people were weird.

Jake Melrose went outside, pulling the door behind him, glancing around. Nobody moved in the shadows. He opened the little front gate and set off down the lane. His car was ten miles away, in the car park of the hotel.

Vane missed him by an hour. Somehow he wasn't surprised. It was almost as if they had willed it between them. He delayed running Claire back until the Yank was asleep, and then dallied on the way, pulled the car into a lay-by.

'No,' she said. 'Billy, no. It wouldn't be right. You promised you would book me in. I gave Geoffrey the address.'

He grinned. 'Sure. But you're too nice for Geoffrey.' His arm was round her neck and then her shoulders, then lower on her breasts. She ought not to have enjoyed it, but she did. It was fun to feel wanted.

Claire let him have two minutes. She felt bad enough about it anyway: something starting out as a giggle and ending up getting serious.

'Billy. No. That's enough.'

Vane didn't say anything, concentrating on kissing. Women liked the all-out approach late at night in big cars eight times out of ten, in his experience.

She pushed him away, embarrassed, excited, humiliated, all at the same time. When she wanted to stop, she stopped. She hadn't gone in for this kind of thing, not since she married, and now Billy was testing her.

'Please Billy, I can't. Be reasonable . . .' Pulling things back in place. 'Billy, I can't have an affair with you. This is simply a friendly relationship, is that clear? I'm not being unfaithful to Geoffrey. Find some other bird, but this one's not for the woodshed. Understand, Billy?'

He tried another tack, smiling smoothly. 'As your "friend and comforter" . . .'

'No you're not,' she said, combing fingers through her hair. 'You're bloody well not.' She gave him a peck on the cheek, just to make up. 'Listen, Billy, I know your track record. Leave me alone, Billy. You booked me into the Country Club. I want to get back there.'

Billy Vane sighed and pulled away. Even he could see merit in easing off. Given the circumstances in which the Yank had turned up, the less Melrose saw of Claire the better. And Vane also admired her. How she had pulled in Geoffrey he would never know, but there must have been something there once.

'Maybe you're right, honey bun.'

'I know I am,' She wasn't sure how serious he was but one thing was for real, she was married to Geoffrey, had been since a student crush had resolved itself in catching him and petered out in a career.

'Claire?'

'Yes?'

50

He never mixed duty and pleasure. If she wanted duty she could have it.

'What do you make of that American character?'

She looked out of the car window: a lay-by full of plastic bags, overflowing wastebins, detritus. Couldn't he find a better place to try his luck? Brave but insensitive under the old school tie, that was young Billy Vane. What sort of school liaison, she wondered, wishing she knew more about him, had thrown him in with Geoffrey? Wellington was death he said, expelled for drinking and gambling, short-service commission, switch to the SAS, get yourself in a few scrapes, then set up on your own. That was Billy Boy. A right tough little friend, but he had charm and she liked him, including the way he had dealt with those four bums in the market, when they jumped on the Yank.

'I think he's okay,' she said. 'Straight.'

Vane tapped his hands on the wheel.

'I don't know. He's not what I expected. Not smart enough.'

'Hadn't you better get back there and see how he's getting on?'

Billy Vane grinned and patted her on the thigh.

'All in good time. Give him a chance to recover.'

'It strikes me he won't take long. Pretty hard-bitten customer.'

Vane nodded thoughtfully. 'Combat veteran. Vietnam. Ex-US Marines.'

'A bit like you,' she said. 'What did he get thrown out for?'

'I don't think he did. Just came to the end of his time. Then worked for the CIA.'

'Still does?'

'Still does.'

Claire said, 'Come on, get rolling. I'm going to be late checking in.'

Vane restarted the big old car. The bucket seats were worn with age.

'It's like being in a hearse in this thing,' she said. It seemed to shut them in, smelling of hot oil and leather.

51

'It's a valuable machine,' he told her. 'A Bristol 603, Series V. Not many of 'em around.'

'Like you,' she said. 'A bit archaic.'

'Thanks.' He put his foot down on the pedal and the machine lurched forward. 'And, like me, in good condition. Fully reconditioned.'

'Then you don't need servicing . . .'

But Vane was back on duty, his mind on other matters as they hummed through the centre of Hereford and on the road towards Hay. The roads dwindled into lanes, the lanes full of ancient white cottages and slate-roofed farms. Vane drove on to the Country Club and pulled up outside the main building. He looked a little disappointed.

She smiled. 'I'm sorry, Billy. But that's the way it should be . . .'

But Vane wasn't thinking about that. He came back to the American.

'I'm not sure whether to trust that chap. That Clint Eastwood.'

She was suddenly serious. 'Look, Billy. I wish you'd forget these rumours. It's nothing to do with us. It could all be Geoffrey's imagination.'

'He hasn't got imagination. And it's my bread and butter.'

'Don't go causing trouble.'

'You know me.' He gave her a goodnight kiss.

9

Melrose got a lift from a trucker moving potatoes to Hereford, then drove back to London in the early morning, straight to the Embassy in Grosvenor Square. Anybody could see there was a flap on, from the police cars outside the stockade to the tense air inside the building.

Chris Pallett was in the Control and Supervision Room when Jake tracked him down, sitting in there with half-a-dozen

thrusting faces, all young and eager. Melrose remembered
Chris Pallett from his 'Nam days, when both had been in
Intelligence. Like some other guys blooded there, he'd traded
on the experience and made his name since, while Jake – well,
Jake was doing the rounds, still looking for something.

Pallett was behind one of those pressed steel desks big
enough for dining four, eating a hamburger and slurping
coffee.

'Hi, Jake. What you want now?'

Melrose didn't pause to sit. He'd come a long way since last
night, badly needed a shave and they saw the cut on his
cheek.

'How'd that happen?'

'Told you. Had a brush with some biker guys.'

Pallett seemed too tired to understand. 'Have some coffee?
Siddown. Where exactly you been?' He was a Special Assistant
put on to finding the facts out, a lined, still yellow-haired
man, a bit like an ageing pop star, a guise adopted post-'Nam
as if to make up for his youth, and stuck to twenty years on.
Pushing forty-four, it made him in fact seem younger than the
experience of Jake Melrose.

'Hereford,' Jake said. 'Brendan wanted me to meet this guy.
A Brit called Vane.'

'Yeah. Listen, Jake. What did he ask you to do?'

'Talk to Vane about Spain. Some story involving the Brits
that Vane's got wind of and says he wants to sell.'

Pallett wrinkled his nose.

'You see him? This guy Vane?'

'I saw him. Cocky little bastard with a dame in tow. I got
jumped by these guys in an alley and – presto – Captain
Marvel was there, zap, pow with a stick, and whisked me off
to his pad. A kind of Red Riding Hood cottage someplace
outside the town. But the girl didn't sleep there.' He fingered
the cut on his cheek. 'And I was pretty slugged, so I guess
that I dozed off. When I woke up they were gone. I phoned
Brendan at home to check things out, and then I heard about
this.'

Pallett's eyes glittered.

'Yeah. This. Somebody got their own back.'

One of the others, an Information Officer, said, 'We don't have any proof, Chris.'

Pallett shat on him from the roof. 'Don't give me that bullshit. Two guys jumped him in Regent's Park. Put a knife in his back. Two guys who knew he was coming. Maybe they waited for years but they sure got him.'

'Jesus Christ,' Melrose said. 'I knew Brendan a long time.'

'Yeah. He was the best, but they got him, just six months from going home. We got a special unit on the appraisal, and the Brits have called in their Anti-Terrorist Squad.'

In the end Melrose sat down and took one of the coffee beakers.

'You reckon it could be because of what this guy Vane was telling him?'

Pallett shook his head.

'I doubt that, Jake. Problem is we can't be sure.'

'Maybe I could have found out,' Jake said, 'but you dragged me back here first.' He wasn't too keen on Pallett.

Pallett stretched back in his chair, so far back that his head hit the wall.

'Well, whatever Vane passed on to Brendan, nobody else here knows . . .'

'No record?' Melrose was puzzled. Brendan Wallace, old Brendan, had been a meticulous man, recording, docketing, filing. That's how he'd made the grade way above a non-paper man.

Pallett swung back in his chair.

'No sir. Sweet Fanny Adams. We don't even know what he asked you . . .' Pallett waved at his team. 'Any of us.'

'Okay,' Melrose sipped the coffee as if it was some devil's brew. 'Well, all he said to me was there was a ten-mile-high Brit, and this guy Vane wanted to sell us some story involving Spain.'

'A ten-mile-high Brit? Who the hell is that, Jake, when I'm awake?'

'Freddie Godber, the Secretary of State for Defence.' And contender for the Premiership.

54

'Psshit.'

One of the youngsters answered a telephone on the left of the desk, covering it with his hand.

'It's the police. They've had a phone call saying it was the Said Hamid group. Revenge killing for his time in Beirut among the oppressors.'

Pallett made a wry face. 'Okay. Get the details. Tell 'em I'll call back after conference.' He looked at the expectant faces.

'Said Hamid gang. Claiming responsibility.'

'You believe that?' Melrose asked.

Pallett tipped his head back again, staring at the ceiling, which was low, patterned with plastic light squares. He made no further comment, listening as one of the juniors came out with a string of facts.

'We know that group pretty well, sir. Shi'ites. Training camp in the Beqa'a. Claimed responsibility for that run of car bombs in Paris.'

For a moment they reminded Melrose of free-range chickens, all clucking away; then Pallett said, 'Brendan was involved with the hostages deal. The Said Hamid resented the pressure put on them. They wanted to hang out for thirty million dollars, would you believe it? Maybe they thought he had tricked them.'

'How long has Brendan been in London?'

'Three years.'

'That's a mighty long time to wait before taking revenge,' Melrose said.

'Jake, you don't know these people. They'll wait for ever. They're not Christians, Jake, like you or me.' He bit back from calling them animals.

Melrose said, 'Look, Chris, what more can I do? I went there because Brendan said so. I met this guy. I can go back again. See him tomorrow. Ask him what his story is. How much am I authorized to pay?'

Pallett screwed up his eyes.

'Jesus. Up to five grand, I guess, if it seems worthwhile. But start off at two.'

'Dollars?'

55

'Pounds, Jake. We are in England now.' He held up his hand. 'But before you go charging off, Jake, check it out with British Security. I'll give you the name in MI5.'

Melrose climbed to his feet as quick as a man of twenty, a man who kept in mint condition. Nodded.

'Who do I report to afterwards?' He implied that it shouldn't be Pallett, pride made that personally difficult, reporting to a former junior, and Pallett understood.

'I'm on special assignment till we get this thing cleared up. I guess you'd better talk to Harry Leibermann the DCM. Know him?'

Melrose shook his head.

'Well, he's a great guy. You'll love him. He'll give you any help you need.' His tone of voice seemed to say 'and that ain't going to be too much'. The interview was over; as far as Pallett was going.

At at door Melrose paused.

'Usual rates still apply?'

Pallett grinned. The poor bastard was on contract.

'Yeah. Sure. Usual rates and conditions. And mind the extras.'

10

Freddie Godber summoned Brocklehurst to him later that day. They arranged to meet over lunch at Langan's in order to circumvent Powers: a constituency discussion between the Secretary of State and his political agent. Godber was increasingly nervous about whom he could trust, and in a grim temper, made worse by the fact that Melanie had gone back home to Lower Broome from their London apartment in St Ermin's Court.

He ordered a hurried meal at a quiet corner table in the brasserie, and Brocklehurst read his unease, ambition competing with the fear that he might throw and lose. The shaded lamps cast a roseate glow on the Minister's distinguished features.

'Listen, Peter. There's been some kind of leak. This whole thing has got to stop.' He waved away the good wishes of a passing junior Minister hell bent on impressing a contact. 'Got to stop. I'm not putting my career on the line or my head on the block for the sake of some hare-brained adventure over a piece of rock. A piece of rock that we still own.'

'What's happened?'

Godber breathed in. 'I've had a call from the Cabinet Office security head. Fellow called Commodore Frewin. All very nice and cosy, but he started asking questions. They've been reading the tea leaves.'

'What about?'

'What do you damned well think?' Godber recovered his composure and poured out glasses of wine. 'Had I heard the story that the Spaniards were planning an occupation of Gib, a kind of pre-emptive strike now that there's no real garrison, and that maybe we – I – were somehow conniving at it, for political purposes . . .'

Brocklehurst looked around. Busy busy conversations in the restaurant filled with expense accounts.

'What did you say?'

'What d'you expect me to say? I told him No. Utter rubbish. I wouldn't entertain it. Pointed out that the papers were digging about for a crisis involving the leadership.'

'Good.' Brocklehurst's well-fed face reflected the satisfaction of a marketing man who saw a campaign just launched.

'Good? Frewin reports to the PM.' That bastard who had upstaged him and got the job he coveted.

'Okay. Fine. Interesting he should bother. So now you're in the clear.' Brocklehurst had the PR man's ability to turn everything to advantage.

'Don't be so damned complacent, Peter. I don't want a false move.' Caution ate into him at times like this, inbred and inconsistent: that was how he had lost before.

'Did you ask where the leak came from?'

'I asked all right. Some lineshooter in Grosvenor Square.

According to Frewin a tip-off from the CIA.' The Yanks could be country cousins on security matters, the Minister reflected.

'Pshew. It's nothing to do with the Yanks.'

'The Americans have a bloody great machine that has to spend its time doing something. According to Frewin this CIA man said the original rumour came via that chap Wallace. Then Wallace got a knife in the back.' In Godber's experience, communications were close, but sometimes difficult.

'I'll just have coffee, I think,' the younger man said, surprisingly abstemious for once.

'Look, Peter. I know the game that you and Landsdowne want me to play. I'm not taking chances like that.'

Brocklehurst was looking at him with the kind of face that sold credit cards in the TV ads: young-old, sympathetic, wise and confiding.

'Then you'll never make Number 10. I have to say so, as a marketing man. Look, Freddie. Everything's going for you. The Party's crying out for a saviour. A charismatic leader. All that you've got to do is to stand up and be counted. Put yourself on the front page, rallying the troops.'

Godber calmed down. He sensed that some of those troops were watching him across the crowded room.

'Are you still in touch with Landsdowne?'

Brocklehurst blinked and smiled. 'Of course. I want you to win, Freddie.'

'I could sack you, Peter.'

'But you won't. I believe in you, Freddie.'

The waiter brought them coffee, then Godber said, 'I had a word in private with old Bertie Oliphant this morning. Asked him to come across. Even so the Private Office must be wondering what's up.'

'So?' Oliphant represented the old guard, money and land, the right wing. If he could muster the backbenchers in support of another bid, Godber would be halfway home when the Leadership ballot was forced.

'Well, Bertie agreed with me. No risks.' He had also urged Godber to grab headlines with a suitable move, to create a kind of momentum, but the Secretary of State kept that to himself.

Brocklehurst's lips parted in derision. 'Look where that line got him. Bertie's a has-been, yesterday's man. Consoling himself on whisky. This is now, Freddie. We can do a deal with the Spics.'

'I don't believe in deals,' Godber said, hesitating. 'And please don't call them Spics. Especially if by deals you mean selling people down the river.'

'Oh, come on, Freddie. What about Hong Kong? That was a much bigger deal. And you went along. You could have stood out on that one but you didn't.'

'If I had I would have left the Cabinet.'

Brocklehurst shrugged. 'I'm telling you, if you're going to win the nomination you've got to come off the fence, and show your mettle.'

Godber was swinging back but still unconvinced. It was interesting, Brocklehurst observed, that a man so clear-headed on decisions about other people, management decisions involving thousands of men, was paralysed like a rabbit confronted by a ferret when they concerned his own future. Brocklehurst leaned closer.

'These are uncertain times. Ripe for exploitation. Use Colin Landsdowne. He'll do the setting up and none of it will stick to you. These Spaniards are ready for a deal.'

'And if it goes wrong?' The contender for the throne still could not bring himself to risk his political future on one throw.

'It won't. But if it does, Landsdowne's expendable. Your name won't be attached.'

'I don't want deals.' Godber was looking around as if he planned to escape but the attraction of a quick strike for the top prize still held him there.

'I don't want covert operations.'

'You do, Freddie. You must. You've got to come out waving the flag, big and strong, within the next couple of weeks. Big telly speech this weekend. Then respond to external threat.'

He traced a line on the tablecloth with his index finger. 'Classic power politics move.'

'Don't tell me how – '

'How to get over on TV? That's part of my job, Freddie. You're okay.' Brocklehurst leaned back and inspected the restaurant, where well-fed businessmen were signing their credit slips and looking across. 'They're interested in you, Freddie. Stand up and be counted.'

'What about this chap Frewin, and his tip off from the Yanks?'

'Forget Frewin. Our Security boys haven't exactly covered themselves in glory in recent years. You've stonewalled him, haven't you? As for the Yanks, don't worry.' Brocklehurst lowered his voice conspiratorially. 'Landsdowne is pretty sure he knows how they got involved. A guy called Vane. And he's been warned off.'

'Vane? Where did he get hold of things?'

'That we're still checking on.'

The Minister thought about that, and about the death of Wallace, and wondered if there was a tie-in.

'As far as we know there is no direct connection, but Landsdowne is checking that too.'

'This Landsdowne . . . He wouldn't . . . let us down?'

'Calm down, Freddie. He's a friend. Let him take care of the odds. All you've got to do is give him the starting orders.'

Godber looked at his watch. 'I've got to go,' he said, and took his car back to Whitehall.

As befitted a private secretary, Geoffrey Powers watched him return, and reminded him of the afternoon's engagements. He thought Godber seemed distracted, for once not his urbane self. He had the look of a politician screwing himself up to a decision. Something that was now or never.

Somebody's whispering, Godber thought. Somebody has already leaked. Looking at Powers's thin face he could not believe it was him, nor, if he had asked, would Powers have known it himself.

Brocklehurst went through to Landsdowne from a call-box in Horseferry Road.

'Colin, be careful. Our chum Billy Boy is selling out. And I'm not sure how far we can trust Powers.'

The Irishman's voice was as cold as a freezer.

'I know. I know. I'm keeping an eye on him. And on young Master Powers.'

Brocklehurst for once urged caution. There had been a death already.

'Colin. Keep your hands clean.'

'It's not my hands I'm worried about,' Landsdowne said. 'It's young Master Geoffrey's conscience.' There had been other cases where civil servants had known more than they should, and spilled the beans.

'Don't start threatening him . . .'

'Threatening? I'm suggesting we should deal him in.'

11

Melrose had business in London, next stop St John's Wood, before he got back to Vane. St John's Wood, that was the address that Chris Pallett had given him although there was no damned wood, only the trees in the Park, Regent's Park where Brendan had bought it. A Victorian house with steps and a great portico, far too big for modern living, far too big for Angie Wallace, except that she wasn't paying, and she had the first floor apartment.

There was a policeman outside, a young copper in uniform who asked him what his business was.

'Embassy. CD,' Melrose said, showing him the calling card. The policeman saluted and walked away, leaving him standing on the steps. A beanpole with square shoulders, Melrose was stamped on the barrel 'ex-US Marine Corps stock', and always would be.

There was an armed guard behind the heavy front door,

who stared as he was led to a drawing room on the first floor, where a tearful Filipino maid knocked and introduced him.

Two women sat in the room, a big room with a fireplace, marble surround, oil painting of mountains, photographs on a piano, chintzy chairs, thick carpet. Overseas issue decor. Angie was in a black dress, a cocktail number really, plain with a simple gold brooch. She was sitting dry-eyed on one side of the central settees, comforted by the woman who had first answered his call. Barbara something, an analyst with the Embassy who was standing by an old friend. Melrose glanced at the photographs. There were two kids apparently, he remembered Brendan talking about them one night in the bar of the Orient Hotel in Beirut, when they were all much younger.

He crossed the room and took Angie's hand and found her trembling, a dignified, guarded face coming to terms with loss, with swept-back wheat-coloured hair showing grey at the roots. A good woman, he thought, stable and diplomatic, who had served Brendan well and failed to reap the rewards, the longed-for retirement in Florida, or wherever they had planned to go. Brendan had gone down working, and perhaps that was the best way.

She looked at him, and said slowly, 'I feared it would happen, Jake. I always feared it.'

'No way. It was just terrible luck. God, I'm sorry.'

'It was always on the cards. After Brendan's time in Beirut. Those bastards, they never forget . . .'

'You reckon?' he said, and kissed her gently, until she seemed to calm down. Jake with this forty-year-old, holding and kissing her like she was some sort of mother, and he'd been a bad boy. But, Jesus wept, he had saved Brendan, the bells in his mind ringing, the chopper getting ready to lift with the kids nearly twenty years ago and Brendan screaming in his ear, 'Let's get the hell out, for fuck's sake, those are fuckin' Commies in the trees.'

'Shut up,' Melrose had said, but Wallace had been scrambling aboard.

Melrose had pulled him back, pulled him right off the ladder and shouted in his face. Substituted five more kids. He could see to this very day the young Marine corporal grinning, and the face of the pilot.

'Get back there and shut up. No Reds are coming in. Let's get the goddam kids out. They won't have a chance here.'

And Brendan Wallace whimpering, 'I got to go. I got to go.'

'You go back when I say so.' Melrose had been in command then, and Wallace along for the ride.

Whish . . . Whish . . . Whish. They had been sending stuff in, the NVA, right over the Marine position and Melrose and Papriski and Sausage-Dog and the rest of them were running for cover.

'Get moving,' he'd said to the pilot. 'Get the hell out of here.' And watched refugee kids, poor little orphan bastards, scramble aboard and the whirlybird hit the sky, rise to a thousand feet and waver, and go down in the trees . . .

Melrose blanked out his mind, holding on to Angie Wallace now. She didn't know that, and he would never tell her. Otherwise there would have been no distinguished career, no dramas of negotiation, top-of-the-world headlines, in Beirut. Okay, so Wallace had got over it, maybe had even persuaded himself that the thing never happened, but not Jake Melrose, no sir. Nearly twenty years on he still shuddered.

'Brendan,' she whispered. 'He was a wonderful husband.'

'Angie. Sure thing. Brendan was a great guy.'

Angie was sobbing now, and Barbara saying, 'Hey there, hey there, baby, don't cry. Come and sit over by me,' and patting the diplomatic issuee settee like it was some kind of rose bed.

'I told him not to go on that goddam jogging on his own.'

'You can't read the future,' he said.

'But he would try to keep fit. He wasn't scared of nothing.'

'No, honey, I know. He was just great.'

He sat on and tried to give comfort, a straight-backed Marine man who hadn't known what it was to break a marriage bond of this length. With his Mary it had been six months, and an equally useless end. Angie Wallace was a trooper, he told himself. She was grieving. Maybe someday, somewhere, some female would grieve for him, a kid from the back streets who had seen the Marine ads and joined them to escape the winters in Wisconsin? Life had been pretty robust for twenty years in the Corps, and he never did pause until his time for discharge. Maybe he should have stood down then, gone into farming or something, where he could lean on a fence and watch the cattle, but the streak of adventure was there, and the Government had knocked at the door one day when he was at San Diego and put him back on the payroll.

It's been a long time, he thought, since Brendan and I started out. Brendan hadn't forgotten, and nor would Jake.

Angie was drinking some tea supplied by the Filipino maid.

'They're looking for him . . .' she said in a shaky voice.

'Who's that, honey? Who are they looking for?' Jake said gently.

'An Arab guy. Hook nose and blue tracksuit. There was a British couple who reported he ran right past them, coming away from Brendan. They found Brendan on the path, underneath a big tree. The police say this man was waiting, maybe with another guy.'

'Ambushed?'

'He was jumped from behind. Knifed right through the heart. Brendan never had a chance . . .' Angie was collapsing again, her posture gone, her chin line dissolving as if her face was melting. Then she sniffed and looked up.

'There, there, Angie kid. Don't distress yourself,' Barbara said. 'What did you want, Mr. Melrose?'

Jake said, 'He asked me to do a job. Brendan. Only three days ago.'

Angie was drying her tears. She looked up sharply.

'Brendan asked you?'

'He brought me over from Paris. Talked about something in Spain. It's not in the book,' he said. 'Chris Pallett doesn't know why. It was one of Brendan's hunches.' He added softly, 'Brendan tell you anything, Angie?'

She snuffled and shook her head.

'I guess she ought to rest,' Barbara said. Christ, some women didn't seem to realize that men wanted to help and offer sympathy. Melrose thought back to the days when they'd been young together, the Saigon Hilton crowd, and starting their careers, Wallace and Melrose and Pallett. Some of them made it big, Jake thought, and others just rode on the wagon wherever it happened to go. Yet after all his efforts Brendan had bought it first, whatever it was that was coming to them all in time.

'I'm sorry, Angie,' he said. 'I just had to be sure. We got to try every angle.'

She looked at him with sore eyes, puffed up and red from crying.

'Brendan didn't even tell me that you were coming.'

'No. Well. I guess I wouldn't expect that. I got this place in Paris. I work from there.'

She stared at him. She didn't know him that well. They'd met half a dozen times, the last couple of them in Washington when Jake was posted there and Brendan held a reunion. Brendan had asked him along and Jake had gone. Maybe twice in Bangkok before that, after the collapse, when Wallace had got big and invited Angie out to stay in the US compound. Even in those post-'Nam days Wallace had been convinced about how he was going to make it; maybe he never learned, anymore than he learned in Vietnam. Wallace was one of those guys who stood on the parapet and shouted 'Look at me, you bastards', shit-scared at the same time. He always believed in his luck, something, in the light of experience, Melrose had concluded was chancy.

'He didn't say anything . . . anything about a British guy called Vane? Billy Vane?'

Angie Wallace stopped at the reference. She sat up and remembered, the years of training, of taking in names and numbers, other people's washing, coming to the fore. Even her face seemed to brighten.

'Vane?'

'Yeah. Billy Vane.'

She searched her memory. 'No, I don't think so. There was a guy telephoned couple of times the evening that Brendan was killed. But he didn't give a name.'

Melrose sank back into the cushioned settee. 'What sort of accent?'

'Well . . . British, I guess. Kind of soft spoken.'

'Did he say what he wanted?'

She shook her head. 'He just said he wanted to speak to Brendan. He didn't give a message.'

'Uh huh. How'd he get the call number? You ain't in the book.'

She thought about that. 'I don't know, Jake. I thought he must have had it official, to phone here. Just like you did. Brendan used the house a lot. He said it was safer than the office.' She began to cry again. Melrose had that feeling of being in a foreign country that was familiar but strange.

'Come on, sweetie.' Barbara offered a Kleenex.

'Listen,' Melrose said. 'Brendan asked me to do a job, take up a contact with this Billy Vane. I met him yesterday, then somebody tried to turn me over and Vane rode to the rescue. Then when I call, you say that Brendan is dead. I reckon that's too neat. Too damned neat. Real life just ain't like that.'

Angie Wallace rubbed her nose in the Kleenex.

'What are you going to do?' she asked.

Jake Melrose stood up. Sunshine slanted across the photographs on the piano. Two fine kids back home someplace.

'Find out about this guy Vane,' he said. 'That's what Brendan would have wanted.'

12

It didn't work quite that way: instead Vane found out about him, via Chris Pallett, the investigator on the Wallace murder. Pallett called up Melrose over breakfast in his room at the Holiday Inn, Bayswater.

'Jake. How are ya?'

'Figure I'm in pretty good shape.'

'Swell. Swell. Now listen. We've had this Vane guy call us direct again.'

Melrose sat on the settee and switched off the breakfast TV. These standard hotel rooms, with just enough of America to remind him he wasn't home: the sanitized bathroom, squeaky-clear air conditioning and no pay-slot for the porn channel. He was drinking orange juice.

'Billy Vane?' That guy made him uneasy. What kind of game was he playing?

'Right. Said you had a date but you backed off.'

There were other things, Jake had been weighing up, that maybe he needed to attend to first, like getting back to Paris and picking up on the Security job. Contract work was okay, you could make your own times, swoop down on the Embassies and USIS offices without any goddam notice, but you had to cover the ground and he had the whole of East Europe, from Poland to Bucharest, to fit in before 1 October. A regular job. Sometimes it worried him that he'd not even fixed up with Wallace some kind of extension if the Vane story was real. Shit, no time to tell Pallett now.

'What'd he want?'

'He said where the hell did you go? Said you should have met him, Jake.'

'Christ, Chris. Who pulled me back to London? Anyways it was no big deal. Just some crazy rumour that he was trying to sell.'

Maybe he should tell Billy Vane to stuff his story, and get moving to Warsaw. The US Embassy there had a new Consulate in Cracow, and they wanted him to check it out. That meant five days away, two travelling, three looking around at the electronic equipment, the locks, the windows, the strong-room. Could he afford that time, then come back for Billy V.?

'Jake. You still there? Listen. He's coming to see you.'

'Yeah. I'm here.' Put down the breakfast tray, cradle the telephone, get up and look out of the window. That big grey machine outside, some fifteen-year-old rust-bucket with a shape like a soap dish. Vane's Bristol 603 with the walnut fascia and mountain-bike tyres. Melrose grinned to himself and held back in the shadows. If Vane was that keen, why the hell didn't he march in?

'Chris? How'd he get my number?'

'I gave him the hotel.'

'What the hell for?'

You never did that sort of thing, not with an agent, even a guy on contract. Next rule in the book: never disclose your base. He began to chew Chris Pallett off. The man might be big cheese now, Special Assistant status, working with Scotland Yard, reporting straight to Langley, but he had no goddam right . . .

'Okay. Okay, Jake. Keep your hair on. He says he wants to see you, Jake. We want you to see him. So we tell him where you hang out, right? Before you start rushing off.'

'Thanks a lot.'

Melrose went back to the chair, replaced the telephone, picked up the coffee jug. Poland would have to wait, and so would Billy Vane.

He let Vane stew for a while, looking out of the window every ten minutes or so. The poor bastard could sweat inside there in all that leather and walnut, listening to a hand-tuned radio. It gave Jake a small satisfaction, and his lean face twisted into a private grin.

At ten o'clock he walked down, across the streaming traffic of the Bayswater Road, along towards the Bristol, which was pulled in under some plane trees, big trees with soft green leaves not yet deadened by fumes. As he neared it he saw the heavy car was empty, and passed by without stopping, into Kensington Gardens. He was walking towards the Serpentine: a few early boaters, some kids, one or two nannies with prams. He paused to watch the ducks.

The voice beside him was Vane's. Billy Vane appeared from nowhere, like some NVA patrol, out of the bushes.

'You ran off on me, Melrose.'

Jake swung round to see the smooth-cheeked face, the Momma's boy complexion. Billy Vane was dressed in a tweed jacket and well-cut grey slacks, highly polished brown shoes, his hair slicked back and neat.

Melrose was three inches taller and somehow more substantial. This guy was a lightweight, a film extra in a British movie.

'What are you bugging me for?'

'I'm not bugging you, old man. Just wanted an early word.' The wide eyes looked at him coolly. 'Let's walk,' Vane said, not much enthused by the Yank either.

They strolled along the shoreline of the artificial lake, watching some kids who were fooling with a couple of row-boats. I don't know whether I like this country or not, Melrose thought. Some parts of it are fine – like spring on the water inside a London park, a spring without menace – but then you get cunts like this Brit, who think you owe them a living. And some bastard knocks off Brendan Wallace.

'Why didn't you come inside the hotel?' Melrose demanded. 'You knew where I was.' Courtesy of Chris Pallett, blowing any kind of security. Good old, safe old London, where Brendan got a knife in the back, and this Billy guy could go strangle himself with an old school tie.

'You and I need to be careful,' Vane said with that air of superior knowledge which made Melrose nearly gag. 'I guessed you'd come out some time. Gave it a little while.'

Two hours, poor sucker, Jake thought.

'Yeah? So who's coming after me? An' if they are, why don't they pick us off now?'

Vane tossed a pebble into the water and stood to assess the ripples.

'Maybe they will, Jake. I just wanted to warn you. That little punch-up in Hereford . . . it wasn't an accident.'

'You warning me?' Melrose swung round and confronted him.

The neat little Brit smiled; his eyes seemed icy blue, as sharp as needles.

'I came to tell you to lay off.'

'Lay off what?'

Vane put his hands in the pockets of the expensive – looking tweed. Melrose wondered if he carried a gun.

69

'I wouldn't stick your nose in. If you don't mind my saying so, you're not the man for this one.'

Melrose swore. It was like insulting the flag to tell Jake Melrose he wasn't up to scratch. No bum Brit ex-officer was going to get away with that.

'You tell me what I'm not supposed to see, and I'll tell you, buddy, whether or not it's my business.'

Vane just smiled.

Melrose was heated up. He had a knee-jerk reaction in situations like that; for one brief moment he contemplated disturbing the ducks by up-ending Vane in the lake.

'Okay. Listen to me, Billy Boy. I was told to contact you. Not the other way round. Two days later the guy who told me, bought it.'

Vane looked around. Kids, elderly ladies, a nanny with a pram pushing the next generation of the British Establishment. Or a little Arab. Nobody they could see was remotely interested. 'Let's move on,' he said. 'Would you like a cup of tea?' They neared the café by the Serpentine bridge.

Melrose shook his head. He looked like a kind of eagle, Vane suddenly thought, an eagle with grey feathers; pretty ruffled.

They were circling round the Park under the trees in Rotten Row, then back to where he'd left the car.

'You were going to talk to me in Hereford,' Melrose said.

'Yup. And you didn't have authority to make an offer. We had a date, next day.'

'That was before those bastards jumped me.' Melrose remembered how Vane had appeared, almost too neatly. He gave a nod in the Britisher's direction. Vane was nervous enough of trouble to have gone back into town to warn him, or so he said.

'Look,' Melrose asked. 'Let's get this straight. You got a story or haven't you?'

'Buy you a beer?' Vane said, trying to be friendly.

'No, thanks.'

Vane sighed. His eyes were light, china blue, and unusually large. When he concentrated he seemed unable to blink, which

70

gave him a staring quality, but his manners never deserted him.

'I have to say, old chap, that I've decided it's not a story for you.'

'You contacted the US Embassy. Brendan Wallace. You asked to speak to someone outside the diplomatic network.'

Vane agreed. 'Yup. That's correct. But I hadn't got it right then. Just a rumour. I'm not selling now.'

'Not selling? Who says I'm going to buy?'

Billy Vane brushed an imaginary hair from the immaculate tailoring. 'Oh, you'd buy all right. If you knew what I do.'

'Look. Don't try playing crap with me.' He looked like Dirty Harry. 'What's going to happen in Spain?'

'Spain?' Vane said. 'Don't you worry about Spain, old man. I'm sorry you were troubled. Those guys in Hereford – they were a warning I'd heed. They didn't get there by chance. Listen, Jake, why do you think I'm careful about seeing you today? Why do you reckon I didn't rush in to greet you? If what I think is right we could be marked already, you and I. My advice is you keep your head down. Leave the dirty work to me. I'm a qualified professional in that game.'

Ex-SAS thug, Melrose thought.

Innocently he asked, 'You tell me what the game is first. Then I'll decide.'

Billy Vane shook his head. They had nearly walked round the Park, perambulating quite fast, and every now and then Billy Boy turned round to stare.

'I think we're okay,' he breathed.

Melrose said. 'One last time. You in the market for telling me something or not?'

A kid bounced a ball out of control towards them. Vane picked it up and threw it back, a long, low, accurate throw. He smiled that ruthless smile.

'Maybe when I started I was. I knew Brendan Wallace a little. Too bad he's gone. As of now I'm not playing. Not with you. Not anyone. Have you got that?'

Melrose said, 'What'd you want to trouble me for, if that's all you got to say?'

71

There was no smile this time. Billy Vane seemed to tighten up, as if a spring wound through him, the same kind of innate tension with which he'd smashed up those bikers.

'No. Not quite all, sport. One more thing. I don't want you messing with me. And I don't want you reporting about my lady friend in Hereford. Do I make myself understood?'

'Claire? I thought she was great.'

Billy Vane coloured. 'Forget it, Jake. She was just an old flame from way back. You got that, Jake? She's not relevant. And I don't want you being clever.'

And Melrose nodded. He nodded and said, 'Okay.'

In this game there was more than one devious bastard.

13

Melrose walked on to Hyde Park Corner and along the canyon that was Regent Street, then down Grosvenor Square to the Embassy reference library, quiet in the lunch hour with just a local with glasses minding the desk.

'I want to trace a girl,' he said. 'Name of Powers. Claire Powers.'

She looked at him as if she was thinking, 'Man, you're pushing your luck.'

'Any particular label?'

'Label?' This tall guy with the kind of face that could have been carved from wood.

'Like Miss or Mrs or Lady something? You know.'

'Oh. Sure. Well. I guess she could be Mrs.'

What did he know about the girl, except that she had a wedding ring when he met her with Vane. She didn't look Vane's sort. No way, not with that open face. And then there was the name tag in *The Grapes of Wrath*. 'Geoffrey and Claire Powers, Wimbledon', it had said.

The counter clerk smiled.

'Well. There's the London telephone directory.' She heaved

up the right volume. 'That's if she's in London.' She began
turning the pages. 'An awful lot of Powers, C. Many women
don't put in their first names these days so it's difficult to tell
which are female.'

'Okay. Hold on.' Vane had been in the Army and now he
was working freelance. He had some information that one
time he was going to disclose. Now where would that come
from, Melrose wondered.

'You got the British Diplomatic list? And the Army list. And
the Civil Service list?'

'Right here,' she said.

He took them to one of the tables under the window which
looked out over the square. It was a few minutes' work to
check out the three Powers in the Diplomatic. In the Army
list there was only a lieutenant-colonel. He turned to the olive-
green cover of the Home list. Thicker, plenty of Powers there,
in the Inland Revenue, the Scottish Office, the Directorate at
Kew Gardens. And at the MoD. Melrose began to sit up.

'The Rt. Hon. Frederick B. Godber, PC, MP, Secretary of
State for Defence. Private Secretary (G5) G. R. Powers.'

'Got it,' he said aloud, so that the girl looked up.

'You found what you wanted?'

Melrose sobered down. 'Maybe,' he said. 'And thanks.'

He walked up two flights of stairs, along to Chris Pallett's
ops room, but the door was locked. The crew were all out to
lunch but a young secretary came from the opposite room.

'Can I help you?' she asked cautiously, a stringy girl with a
short skirt and bony knees, nearly as tall as Melrose. Jesus,
why did they make 'em like that?

He said, 'I just want to make a call.'

'You on the staff?' she asked.

He showed her his ID. 'Jake Melrose. Special Assistant.'
Signed by Brendan Wallace.

She nodded. 'Come this way,' and he followed her into an
office where the machines were dead: VDUs on the desk tops,
a fax and photocopier, several printers. 'This is the general
registry for my section,' she said. 'Would you like a coffee?'

73

She pointed to the telephones and produced a polystyrene cup.

He dialled the number in the CS book. Defence – (why did they spell it different?) Ministry of, Main Building, Whitehall. He asked for the Minister's office.

'Which Minister?'

Jesus. 'Freddie Godber,' he said. 'The Secretary of State. The number one guy.'

'One moment, sir.'

They were putting him through. Some junior clerk on the line. He said, 'Like to speak to Mrs Powers.'

'Mrs Powers? Mrs Powers doesn't work here.'

'Oh. I'm sorry. Have I got the wrong number?'

The clerk was trying to be helpful. These bloody polite Brits. 'Geoffrey Powers is the Secretary of State's Principal Private Secretary.'

'Ah. Right. Of course.'

'But he's out to lunch at present. Can I give him a message?'

'Well,' Melrose said, 'I have a kind of personal message. For Mrs Powers.'

'Oh.' He could feel the clerk beginning to realize that this was something fishy, beginning to clam up.

'Yeah. Mrs Claire Powers, that right?'

The clerk was back-pedalling fast.

'I think you had better try her at home.'

'Right on. Can you give me her number?'

'I'm afraid, sir, that we are not allowed to disclose personal information. I suggest you give me your number and I'll get Mr Powers to ring you back.'

'Okay.' He said, and read off the file number of the reference sheet on the desk. It dealt with maternity allowances.

He turned to find the girl watching him from the end of the room. She wasn't leaving him alone. She looked the kind of woman for whom implants were invented. He grinned at her.

'Where you from?'

'Utah.'

'Utah!'

'You know it? Little place called Salt Lake City.'

'Sure,' he said, 'and thanks for the coffee.'

She seemed disappointed. A Goddam Mormon, he thought.

He went back to the library and asked again for the telephone books. Several Powers, G., but no guarantee that Geoffrey would be listed. Next thing was to trace Powers, and thus the girl, but it was more difficult than you might think, finding out where someone lived via the jangling telephones of the MoD. And anyway he'd played that card: maybe they'd already rung the phoney number he'd given and begun to smell a rat. He looked at the long list of names, and counted seven Powers, G., but only three G.R.s.

He walked outside into the sunshine, found a newsagent to give him change for the price of a magazine, and a call-box at the corner of Mount Street. It was broken. Shit. He walked on towards Berkeley Square, no nightingales around, only a mêlée of traffic. Where were the guys in top hats and white ties now? Replaced by office girls eating their sandwiches under the plane trees. Another call-box just off New Bond Street, with a Yuppie and a briefcase inside it. He waited till the man came out.

'Sorry,' the man said.

'You're welcome.'

Melrose shut himself in among the stale air and old MacDonald's cartons, and began to dial the G.R.s.

On one there was no reply.

On two a woman answered. Elderly and rather confused. No Claire Powers there, she said.

On three there was a growly male, who said he'd got a wrong number, mate.

He walked on, between slow-moving traffic, down Dover Street into Piccadilly. Hell. So near yet so far, but the more he thought about Billy Vane's warning, the more he wanted to talk to her. The question was how. Maybe he should ring the MoD again, get hold of Powers himself, pretend to be some old pal, but that wouldn't be so easy, especially if she's not been to the States. Anyway, they'd be alerted by that earlier call. Okay. What about Welfare then? That was a ploy that he'd used once, tracking down that poor bastard who later hanged himself, an FS5 in Bonn, checking out he lived with a gay who'd come in from East Berlin. Welfare were soft, they'd give anything away if it caused a moment's happiness, a friendship renewed. So it was a possibility, but give it time: get the wrong message over and the MoD would put up the fences.

He found himself drifting on, across Piccadilly Circus and heading into Leicester Square, still wrestling with the problem of how to trace a girl he'd met once, a girl who might tell him more than that tight-assed Brit. He knew the name, he knew the area, and the rest should have been easy but Powers was clearly ex-directory, given the job he was in – if Jake was right, that was, in reckoning Claire was his wife, and whatever had set Billy Vane alight had come out from Godber that way.

Another library. Westminster Central Reference, just off the busy square. A counter. Another girl, pushing forty this time, an unmade-up, thoughtful face.

'Can I help you, sir?'

'Well. I guess I'm looking for an address.'

'Do you know the name, sir?'

'Sure. Mr and Mrs G. Powers. G. R. Powers. In Wimbledon.'

'Have you tried the telephone directory?'

'They don't seem to be in there.'

'Ah. Then you do know the road?'

'No. That's the problem,' he said. 'I only know the name. What do I do?'

'Well . . .' She thought for a moment. 'I'm afraid it may be a long haul. But you could get it from the Electoral Register.'

'Yeah. Where's that? You got one?'

'We only keep them here for the Borough of Westminster, sir. But I'm sure you could find one in Wimbledon Public Library. The main library, that is.' She smiled at him. 'They have to be kept up to date, because of the Poll Tax, you know.'

'Where'd I find Wimbledon? I thought they played tennis there.'

'That's correct, sir. But a lot of people also live there. Quite a nice area,' she said. And showed him the way on the map.

He took a cab straight there and spent the afternoon combing the lists they held. Street by street, name by name, electoral ward after ward. Again there were plenty of Powers, but only one place where the two names lived at the same address. Geoffrey Reginald Powers. Claire Cristobel Powers, at 11 Sunbury Avenue, Wimbledon, SW19.

He felt he was making progress.

14

When Freddie Godber went to church – at Upton Broome, a few miles south-east of Worcester, just off the Pershore Road – he let the press know in advance. Melanie liked the act too and lined up the children for him so that they looked ideal, trustworthy, breakfast-cereal good as he drove up in the Jag with the security men following in the second car. Of course the police had been warned, and as they drove the ten miles from his secluded manor he noted with some satisfaction the helmeted motor cyclists in their day-glo coats waiting at appropriate crossroads. The car purred smoothly through lanes full of new leaf and early flowering trees, hawthorn and chestnut and apple. High hedges on either side cut off his view of the orchards and rolling fields, but this was his England, he told himself, the very heart of the land, and no one would take it from him. It was going to have his name written all over it, for ever and ever, as soon as the present crisis was overcome, the Government reformed and the PM had gone. But it was no good waiting until it was too damned late, until they had lost the Election in a few months' time. That way would lie oblivion, for if he was part of the losing side who knew when they'd win again, and if the present leadership won – the polls were now evenly balanced – then Christ knows what they'd do with Freddie.

He rested a hand gently on Melanie's knee, a proprietorial hand, as if to say, 'I'm going to win this one, darling,' and

Melanie smiled that ever-so-slightly superior 'I know you're a clever bastard but I come from a better family' smile. Second daughter of a peer, after all that was pretty good, he told himself. As for himself, he had reached his moment of decision.

The countryside looked beautiful, he decided.

'Not many peasants about,' she said.

'They don't go to church, my dear.' After all he knew the people, he was their representative, had been voted in round here ever since he had greased his way into old Humphrey Shotton's seat with a fifteen thousand majority, nineteen years earlier.

Now he was starting his bid, and one part was a photo opportunity, arranged by that sprat of an agent, Peter Brocklehurst. In the rural heart of England, raw and beating.

The Jag came round the final bend into the village street, and he watched it all with satisfaction. He had picked this setting deliberately – the row of half-timbered houses, the village stores still functioning, the tiny pub called The Mitre, a school, a butcher, a basket weaver – although Lower Broome was nearer, and technically his address. The two TV crews were trailing cables from their vans, already set up on the corner by the lich-gate, and the curious crowd, intrigued by this burst of fame, murmured with excitement.

The car drew up and he helped Melanie out, then the two wholesome daughters of fifteen and eleven. Melanie, Lady Godber, resplendent in a hat that set off the heart-shaped face. Traditional virtues, he thought: women should be covered in church, not that they ever were, except in this kind of fairy-story.

He walked up the path beside them, his wife and children under the pealing bells, the vicar, primed, awaiting them at the door, the outdoor crews trotting behind them.

He turned and smiled at them.

'Please leave us alone now. To worship in peace.'

It was ham, pure ham, but it worked, and he would be shown on the news as a church-going statesman. Also he'd squared the vicar to let them into the balcony.

Only an hour of this, settling into his pew, carefully ignoring the eyes that were trained on them. Up from his knees he gazed along the roof of the fifteenth-century building: a mixture, of course, like the country, a rebuilt Victorian chancel and wooden roof, a battered medieval nave with later clerestory windows throwing sunlight on the spandrels. Coloured lights from the lower windows slanted across the walls, across the tombs, including that Elizabethan monster in the south transept, Sir Berkeley Tattershall, wife and kids round the periphery of the slab, hands folded in prayer. He wouldn't mind a tomb like that: the old boy resting on his back, complacent and broken-nosed, feet warmed by a small lion.

Freddie Godber came back to the present as the choir progressed down the aisle and the service began. Hymn Number 510.

'I know not what the future hath
Of marvel or surprise.'

Quite right, he didn't. But unless someone did something the whole bloody enterprise of HMS Great Britain would be taking on water badly, in his opinion. Melanie was touching his hand. 'Concentrate darling,' she whispered, head up in the pew. Good old Melanie, she knew how the system worked, probably more ambitious even than Freddie himself, but she had chosen him. He glanced at her and smiled. Two love-lines curved from her nose into the sides of her mouth, otherwise she looked pretty good. Melanie took care of herself, took care of him, and didn't ask any questions about what went on in London in St Ermin's Court when she was elsewhere.

The sermon wasn't up to much and Freddie Godber was restless. His thoughts began to wander again out to that photo call for which he had invited them down. The statement. The declaration. He had the notes in his pocket but he would not need them, he had it off by heart. The Cold War might be over, the Berlin Wall demolished, but let us not be deceived by reformist movements. The country must keep up its guard and nobody should imagine the spies would pack up and go home. Democracy a vulnerable plant. Running sores over Middle East oil. Watch for the neo-fascism filling the German vacuum. I'm warning you not to stand down . . .

'What?'

She was prodding him again, Melanie.

The vicar was crossing himself. They were led into the responses which she had learnt as a child at Bramlingham, but he had to read from the book. Not, thank God, that awful new Series 3 service but the traditional words, Melanie had seen to that. It was the whole point of the programme.

'O Lord, Save the Queen.'

'And mercifully hear us when we call upon thee.'

'Endue thy Ministers with righteousness.'

'And make thy chosen people joyful.'

That just about summed it up, he thought, filing out at the end of the Grace into the sunshine. The crowd had swelled by now, locals all down the pathway, drawn by the TV cameras. Godber held his wife's arm, pretended to point out the apple blossom on the trees around the churchyard. How idyllic, he thought, how bloody idyllic. You didn't get coverage like this by spending time in London. When he was in Number 10 he'd want to keep his roots down here and be seen to advantage. This blessed plot, this England.

Brocklehurst was waiting by the gate, his agent, the media man; better on PR than politics, but that's where it counted these days. The Party would have to choose someone, and if he could shoot up in the polls he reckoned he had the best chance. That was what they were all gambling on, Brocklehurst and Oliphant . . . and Landsdowne. A strong man who knew his own mind and hadn't licked his arse on the backbenches. Godber had stood up and been counted. He smiled at the lenses now.

'We're going back now, boys,' Brocklehurst said, a bounder really, brown hair groomed over well-fleshed forehead. A fixer, a wheeler-dealer. Worth his weight in share certificates.

The OB teams were winding up and jumping into vans, following him down the road and out of the village, the Jag gathering speed now. He realized he hadn't waited to shake hands with the vicar, had been too keen to let them take pics. Melanie would see to that and send him a note of apology. He relaxed in the back of the car and put his arm round her shoulders as they drove through the Vale of Evesham, orchards and sheep and hop poles. Quintessentially English. And three generations back the Godbers had been German-Dutch.

'Will Geoffrey Powers be there by now?'

'I bloody well hope so,' he said.

The house was set in fifty acres, a small parkland, its mellow stone gleaming in the sunshine. There was a gateway, a drive that was lined with lime trees, a circular path to the front, a modest Georgian façade. His money, and hers, an investment, a sanctuary, a statement. A statement of what he stood for – get that in camera please, as they posed outside the door, and he rested one hand on the urn – stability and common sense. He smiled that ridiculous, flatteringly sincere smile.

'Now, come inside, boys. Please.'

Inside was the local maid – nothing ostentatious there, and local employment – a black and white chequerboard hall, leading to a handsome staircase. Some chairs and cabinets and clocks. Melanie had seen to that. Melanie had traditional virtues, like taste and tact – enough taste and tact, he thought, to make sure her bit on the side was entirely private in London, and who could grudge her that – Melanie was now welcoming them in, the two TV crews, those loons in anorexic jeans and spotted leather anoraks, and the better-class reporters from a couple of the heavies.

'Where's Powers?' he asked.

As if to humour him the door to the sitting room opened and the young man came out, carrying the red despatch box, as arranged.

'I brought it straight down from London, Secretary of State.'

'Thank you.'

Christ, the nonsenses you had to go through for the sake of the PR, with Brocklehurst running behind them as if he'd wet his pants. But this was contemporary politics, the name of the game. He took the box from Powers and walked into the other corridor, towards the library-cum-study. A good place for a statement of faith, he thought, a mixture of old and new, let them note the Apple 204, and the satellite TV and photocopier as well as the leather-bound books inherited when he bought the house.

'I'll leave you to work on your papers,' Melanie said, on camera.

'Daddy, don't be long,' from the girls.

He smiled modestly. Pan to the opening door. 'Can you hold it, sir, and do that again?'

Patiently, they repeated the lines, then he was behind the desk, good profile to the light, opening the despatch box.

'Geoffrey, would you come over here . . . and take these papers.'

Powers nodded his head with no sign of apparent emotion, more like some waxwork version of the real thing. His dark eyes betrayed no secrets, gave nothing away about the relationship between them, that relationship foisted on Godber by his Permanent Secretary, Henry Burton, when the older man Greenland had pulled out. There was a limited choice, Burton had said, among the younger Grade 5s, not all of them willing to take on the kind of demands, the mix of hours, that Freddie Godber required. So he had settled for Powers, hard-working, conscientious Geoffrey, in spite of his hesitation about that closed-off, Welsh borders face. God dammit, Powers ought to have felt at home in country such as this; didn't he once say that his mother had been born in Uttoxeter? Looking at him now, as he repacked the papers that the Minister was signing, Godber thought how untelegenic the poor bugger was and hoped he would go off-camera. What was it about Geoffrey Powers that sent a chill down his spine? Not simply the narrow face, the pinched nostrils and deep-set eyes, nor that small head of neatly cropped hair, the white hands and the deference, no, it was something deeper, a feeling that he lacked a quality that Godber found hard to define: bottom or soul or emotion; none of them really fitted. He was a clever bastard, no doubt about that; priggish and serious and scathing, married to a much nicer girl, a man who wouldn't buy you a drink, a self-confessed workaholic, wrapped up and private and cold. Powers was pointing out something.

'Redeployment of NATO forces, sir. The new paper from the Secretary-General.'

Good. 'Ah yes, thank you, Geoffrey.' That smile.

Powers was clever, reliable, almost too good to be true. A loner, an introvert. A devoted husband, possibly, at home, but for all Godber knew he might have been an evangelist or a transvestite in his spare time. That was the trouble in fact. He lacked any kind of depth, Godber decided, a brain in a cardboard suit. In a word, Godber decided, he was a cut-out.

'Okay. That's enough, boys,' Brocklehurst was saying. 'Now let's get set up for the statement, after the break.'

He made it sound like a commercial.

They crowded round and had coffee and chocolate biscuits, brought in by the little maid. The sun shone through the window and illuminated the books of a past era that he'd never bothered to change: Surtees, Thackeray, E. Phillips Oppenheim. And the more up-to-date ones: his own *Call to the Future*, the recent political hagiographies, the series of strategic studies from Chatham House.

Godber put down his cup. Melanie came in the door to supervise the clearing away. She gave him a quick kiss to show how tight-knit they were.

'Right, gentlemen,' he said. 'Perhaps I can now go live.'

Against the backcloth of the books, he thrust his head forward, serious and positive.

'I have made a number of speeches inside and outside the House, over the last few months, about the future as I see it.' His face was unflinching but sensitive, the voice carefully modulated, classless and somehow sincere. 'Let there be no mistake. This country needs a Government concerned with the welfare of everyone, and that means a buoyant economy. It needs to maintain the progress made in the last ten years – ' not a word of criticism, they'd not be able to fault him on that – 'but at the same time I do not believe it would be either

83

wisdom or sense to lower our defensive guard below the point of no return.' Pause. 'People say to me – many people whom I meet in the street – that Russia now poses no threat, and what do we need the tanks for, or the submarines. It would be entirely logical to scrap them all, and put the money into hospitals or schools. Well, in a sense I agree.' Smile, frontal. 'Naturally, anyone would. Up to a point, but not the point of no return. That was the message of the Gulf crisis. That is the message of today. I am speaking of course solely as Secretary of State for Defence – ' note that, Number 10, treading a careful path between the present and future – 'and I do not know any more than others quite what the future will bring. But I do know this. We cannot afford to lower our guard against the possibility of a hard-line reaction in Moscow. Against the neo-fascist militants regrouping for a Greater Germany. Against the very real threat posed by resurgent Islam and Islamic fundamentalism.' Pause. 'And against the possibility that someone somewhere will try to push us around.'

The Times defence correspondent asked, 'Do you mean, Secretary of State, that you see threats on the horizon?'

Godber's hands were flat on the table. Nothing concealed except naked ambition.

'There are always areas of tension,' he said. 'The Middle East. Hong Kong. South and Central America. My intention is to make sure that this country stands strong on its own two feet, whatever the challenge . . .'

'Does that mean, if you become Prime Minister – '

Freddie Godber held up his hand. 'Read my book *Call to the Future*. We already have a Prime Minister. The best there is.' That should please 'em, he thought. 'When the time comes, if people want to support me, naturally I should not stand aside from what would be my duty.'

'Thank you, Secretary of State.'

The TV anchorman speaking into the camera.

'Well, we have seen a day in the life of the politician many would say is most likely to inherit Number 10, Frederick Godber, speaking in his Worcestershire home. But whether that call comes, and whether it comes before or after the impending Election which will be so crucial to this country's fortunes, that is a question that none of us can answer. Certainly not Freddie Godber.'

'Cut. Okay. Marvellous. Thank you, sir, for your cooperation.'

'Now come and have lunch,' he said. 'Cold buffet in the dining room. And some drinks.'

15

'Mrs Claire Powers?' Melrose said. 'I think we met a few days ago.' For a moment she failed to recognize him standing there on the front steps of 'The Wing', a neatly sliced-off half of what had once been a Victorian rectory, complete with its laurel bushes, in a quiet private road. Wimbledon, near the Common. This tall American Jake whom Billy had turned up with in Hereford. He had found out and tracked her down somehow. She smiled at him in her confusion.

'Oh,' she said. 'You'd better come in.' And laughed. 'How on earth did you manage to find me?'

He followed her into the hall, appraising the tumbled russet hair, naturally wavy, the slim figure, a blue denim skirt and smart brown flatties, as if she'd been going out. Library books on the table. Even with a few bruised ribs he had found her attractive before. Now she looked a real honey.

'Sorry to disturb you,' he said.

It drove from her head the thought of the shopping trip, and brought back that awkward evening when he had saved her from Billy, a commitment she should never have considered. He reminded her of Gary Cooper in an old black and white movie, 2.30 p.m. Channel 4. She flashed that terrific smile.

'That's all right.'

It was Monday afternoon. She'd seen him only five days back, but a lot of water had flowed under bridges since then, including her final rejection of Billy Vane's advances. 'Come on in,' she repeated, leading the American into a front room with its new suite of chairs, the bookcases and the fireplace, a screen of flowers in the grate, some birthday cards on the mantelpiece. Her birthday. He deduced she was under thirty: one of the cards said, 'A year to go. Don't forget to make the most of it,' and he saw love and crosses, Billy.

She turned round to face him, gesturing him to sit down. That smile again, embarrassment and sincerity mingling.

'How are you?' she asked, with what appeared genuine interest.

The young-old face looked at her, a face that seemed toughened by years of necessary caution, a keen face with bright blue eyes and a greying thatch of hair. She warmed to him.

'Fine,' he said. 'Better shape than when I last saw you.'

He wasn't bad-looking, she thought, then put it behind her. 'Look. Would you like a cup of tea?'

He hesitated. 'Okay. Great.' These British and their tea.

'It won't take a minute,' she said. 'If you'll excuse me.' She found herself suddenly unnecessarily flustered.

When she had gone he inspected the room carefully. Noted the telephone number. Noted the cards to 'My Darling Claire' from Geoffrey, and Mother and Dad. Another one from a sister. Several from aunts and cousins. One from the girls of 4B. So she was a teacher, and now was the middle of May. He'd been lucky to catch her in. The room was very much hers – a good selection of books, he thought, some of them in French and German. And pictures: old paintings of rustic scenes with little lights over the frames.

She called out to him from the kitchen.

'Do make yourself at home . . .'

'Sure thing.' Melrose was studying the place with an experienced eye. Circumstances told a lot. The big room was cream and white with splashes of colour from two vases of tulips. Cushioned window seats looked out over the drive where a new Volvo Estate was parked on the hard standing. Cherry red, current reg. Either this pair had money or they were living high. The books, the Bang and Olufsen hi-fi, and a flat

86

screen TV, gave an impression of leisure and – he groped for the word – sophistication, which made him feel slightly ham-fisted.

She was back with a tray of tea things: silver teapot and dainty little cups.

'Here we are.' She put the tray on a coffee table between them. 'I'm so glad that you weren't hurt.'

He got the impression she meant it.

'That's sure pretty china . . .'

'Oh. Glad you like it,' she said, pouring the tea. 'Milk and sugar?'

'Uh – huh. Please.' He watched her rattle the cups and checked out the maker's mark: Haddon Hall by Minton.

Sitting back on the opposite settee, her legs tucked into the side, her skirt pulled above the knee, she looked at him with schoolgirl curiosity. His relaxed interest in the domestic scene she found rather appealing and certainly a change from Geoffrey.

'How did you know where I live?'

Melrose grinned. 'Detective work. Found your name in a book. Found your address from the Electoral Register.'

Smart, she thought. Just like some kind of private eye. 'Ah. But why have you come to see me?'

'Well . . . Billy Vane warned me not to, for starters.'

'He warned you?' The eyes opened wider, frank and blue, a cornelian blue. But she was not annoyed.

'Came to see me. Told me that you weren't relevant.'

She smiled. 'So you usually don't take a hint?'

'Not from guys like him,' he said. 'Not until I know what you're relevant to.' He shook his head at her and grinned.

Claire stared at him, realizing he was serious. Something about him disturbed and pleased her at the same time.

'Look. What do you want?'

'I guess I'd like an explanation.' He sipped the tea, some kind of special brew, and nibbled a sweet biscuit.

'You're lucky to find me at home. I teach,' she said defensively. 'But it happens to be half-term.'

'Yeah.' Let 'em say what they want and lead 'em on, one

87

of the remembered notes from the Security Program, Interrogation of Suspects. That was the Firm in general: you threw money at training and sorted human nature by the book. He contrasted it in his mind with this little amateur set-up involving Vane and Godber and wondered why the hell had Wallace bothered. And grinned again at Claire, who sat there holding a tea cup.

'You weren't teaching back in Hereford.'

'No. I do supply,' she said. 'That means it's on demand. When somebody has a vacancy.'

Melrose glanced at the furnishings and the expense.

'Right. Now what made Billy clam up?'

'Clam up?'

'Sure. First he was going to talk. Then he comes to see me and tells me to forget it.'

She widened her eyes again.

'I don't understand . . .'

'Well. Let's start with a punch-up in Hereford. Maybe one meant for him. Would I be correct in that?' He spoke softly, sensing that she was retreating in confusion.

'I should think that's for him to say.'

'Aw, come on. Something's been fed to Billy Boy, no doubt starting from Godber. Something to do with security.'

He could see she was unnerved. He replaced his cup in the saucer carefully, his eyes fixed on her, and wondered what kind of guy Powers was to deserve a dame like her.

'What's the story, Mrs Powers?'

'Please call me Claire.' That smile was almost disarming. Melrose felt he could settle for a girl in a room such as this.

'Okay, Claire. And I'm Jake. James on the certificate, but everybody calls me Jake, ever since I was a kid.'

She found herself intrigued by that mixture of innocence and interest, but stubbornly determined not to admit what she knew, or at the least suspected. Nor to give in to him.

'I can't disclose official business.' It sounded so prissy. 'You know what I mean . . .'

'Sure.' So that was it. He said, 'Claire, a guy I know well was killed. Met with an accident in Regent's Park, London, the same night that I was in Hereford. A friend of mine. I want to know why, and whether there was some connection.'

'Oh my God,' she whispered. 'Is that why you disappeared afterwards? Billy said you ran away from the cottage.'

Melrose shook his head. 'No way.' She poured him some more tea. In time he could get to like the Goddam stuff, given a girl like Claire.

'I got the hell back because the US Embassy asked me. Because of what happened to this guy, Brendan Wallace.'

Just a flicker of recognition as quickly gone, he thought. She had heard or read the name, or maybe Vane had told her.

'Billy been back here?'

She was embarrassed now, and he saw a slight hesitation.

'Look, we're just friends . . . through my husband.' But she was on the defensive.

'So that was a real hotel? The Country Club?'

She nodded. 'I wasn't staying with him. I made that clear. And when he got back he told me you had gone.'

'Yeah. I had a problem in London. Big problem.'

Her eyes were wide open again, unblinking and alarmed. She seemed both flushed and nervous and he warmed to her.

'What happened?' Claire asked.

He drank the second cup and pushed it away. When he finished, he stretched out his long legs under the little low table, till they were almost touching hers.

'The guy who got a knife in his back first put me on to Billy Vane.'

She gave a tiny gasp. Again she said, 'I don't understand . . .'

'Nor do I, honey, but I intend to find out.'

He decided she was covering up now, back-pedalling hard.

'I'm sorry, but I really don't see . . .'

'No. But I guess we can work some things out. Between us, that is.' He didn't try to bully or hector, he was thinking aloud. 'Let's see. You spend a weekend with Billy – '

' – because Geoffrey was away. Billy invited me as an old friend. Nothing more than that,' she said hastily.

89

'And when you get there in the cottage, all tucked up with a cosy meal – '

'Look. Please,' she said. 'You've no right to interrogate me.'

'No. Okay. So in the middle of this meal, Billy suddenly shoots off back into town to find me. And rescue me. He tell you that?'

She nodded slowly. He wanted to encourage her, to get her on his side.

'Okay. Now you explain to me why.'

She hesitated, and then he knew she was honest. 'He had a phone call.'

'A phone call? Who from?'

Claire Powers flushed. 'I really ought not to tell you,' she said, biting her lip.

'Lady, come on. A friend of mine was killed. Knifed in cold blood. Who phoned Billy?'

'I don't know. A man with a funny accent. I don't know who he was.'

'Funny accent?'

'He was Irish,' she said. 'Billy called him an Irish bastard.'

Melrose digested that, along with a Rich Tea cookie. Biscuits for two.

'I think you can help me, Claire. I want to know what's going on, involving you and young Billy.'

Those blue eyes in the wide, sculpted face seemed to appeal to him to leave her alone.

'I can't tell you.'

Jesus. Keep on the point. Program basic Number 2: persistence pays.

'Just tell me one thing, honey . . . Come on. Please.'

She whispered 'What?' gripping her hands together.

He leaned towards her.

'Listen, Claire. What's so big about Spain, involving Freddie Godber? Big enough to make Billy Vane think that he's got a story the CIA would buy? Big enough to set some guys on me and warn him off? And maybe big enough to put a knife in the back of my old friend Brendan Wallace?'

'I don't know. I don't know. Please.' He felt the distress

was genuine, and would have liked to touch her, but this was a duty call.

'I think you do.'

She flared up. 'Who do you think you are, coming here asking questions? I'm not prepared to discuss it.'

'It?'

'Whatever it is.' She climbed up on her high horse, all British and we know best, and what the hell was it to do with him, but he could see her colouring and thought it suited her.

Melrose stood up. Uncoiled and hardened his tone.

'Claire. You just listen to me.' The earnest face stared into hers. 'There's been a murder. And something that you or your guy Geoffrey may have passed on to Billy Boy could have set it all up.'

Her eyes seemed wide as saucers. The American was looming over her, and in her way she wanted to help, in spite of protecting Geoffrey, and what she thought she knew. She was suddenly very frightened, as if she was in a car running out of control.

'Murder?'

'That's what it was, honey. And maybe you know why.'

'No. For God's sake, no. I swear it.' The room grew unnaturally quiet, the creams and golds washed out.

Jake Melrose felt angry. Nobody wasted his time and he came at her now with a low controlled voice, anger in its way about Brendan, and the unfairness of it.

'Then what the hell's going on? What has Billy Vane picked up with poison on it? Why don't you tell me that?'

Claire went cold, her stomach seemed to be clamped and he saw that she was trembling.

'I can't tell you.'

'But you know.'

She shook her head. 'Please. Don't.' She couldn't let Geoffrey down, yet she had done so already in taking up with Billy.

'Claire, this is very important. I'm on your side.' He spoke softly now, out of concern.

But whose side was she on, torn between two instincts, to

cover up for Geoffrey and to help the American, if what he said was true?

'I can't . . .' she began.

'Claire. What's going to happen? Where? What's Billy on about?'

She swallowed. He saw her shudder and blench, a whole mountain of worry and self-deception suddenly out in the open. She hated these secrets, these innuendoes between Geoffrey and Billy.

'Gibraltar,' she whispered.

Melrose stayed quiet. He smiled.

'Meaning?'

She refused to go on. Meaning, she told herself, that she had heard things said to Vane, when Geoffrey came back from that trip to Northern Ireland, that had made Godber's ambition plain. And later an Irish voice had warned Billy Vane to watch out: so much so that he had left her sitting there in the cottage and then returned with this American, picked up off the ground.

Melrose was staring at her, waiting for her thoughts to clear.

'Well . . .'

'Well, what?'

'Well, nothing. I don't know more than that.' And if she did she would not tell him. She still had some loyalty left, however much Billy Vane had aroused her instincts and tried to seduce her in Hereford. Before Melrose arrived. Before she knew about Wallace.

'I'm sorry. I can't help you,' she said. But he knew from her eyes that she was worried. Nothing in Claire's background, through school and university and a precipitate marriage, had prepared her for interviews with this kind of researcher.

'You can, Claire. You can and I guess you should. I just might be more use to you than Billy Vane.'

She flushed, then smiled again. She denied it within herself. She was a married woman who might have been sorely tempted, and might have strayed with Billy Vane if Melrose hadn't turned up.

'I think you should go now,' she said.

'Okay. I'm going. I'm leaving London. I'm based in Paris, but you can always reach me, if you want.'

Paris. He lived in Paris. The realization upset her.

'I don't suppose I will,' she said. He liked her for that stiff-upper-lippery, but, hell, what was she doing there wrapped up in a fancy box that seemed to deny her vitality?

'Your funeral. But here. In case you do – ' He gave her a card and a number as he shook hands, and said, 'Thank you for sparing the time.' He paused in the hall and admired the decor.

She watched him from the window as he drove away. He even turned turned round to wave.

16

When Melrose had left the house felt cold, and Claire found herself trembling. She wandered from room to room, and it seemed only big and empty, a place where they spent their money on material things. The walls were hung with Geoffrey's pictures, anaemic Victorian studio pieces that for some reason appealed to him. Alice in Wonderland, that's what she was, not knowing where she stood.

There was something about the American, an aura of quiet reserve, of competence, that made her increasingly guilty about time spent with Billy Vane. Worse, there now seemed a possibility that Billy and Geoffrey between them had set events in motion which they could not control, events that in Melrose's scenario could have included a murder.

She knew that what Geoffrey had stumbled on, and discussed with Billy Vane, was a political intrigue aimed at bringing Godber to power. Whether Geoffrey really wanted to stop him out of some misguided ambition or transferred anger, she was unable to decide. Geoffrey was deeply resentful of everything Godber stood for – his self-assurance, his success, his charisma – and yet he was bound to him, caught up in a careerist nightmare of work and pressure. She understood her husband in that, but increasingly in little else.

Left alone in the house, too late to go to the shops, she looked out over the garden, divided by a wooden fence from the other half of the building next door. There were kids' things in the garden there: a swing, some rusting toys. The Toveys had three young children, the youngest not yet at school, and what was she left with? Nothing. Geoffrey, his work and the house. Steamed up inside, she ran a bath to forget. That Jake. Why had he come, with that bone-hard honesty which pressed her to tell the truth?

She dressed again, and waited for Geoffrey. Dressed up for him in a smart partyish number, dark red and sleeveless, a touch of scent and paint. He'd got to notice. He must. But he was late.

She tried to read and failed. The television was a coloured wall. It told her nothing. Pictures of the PM speaking at a rally somewhere. She poured herself sherry and waited, feeling she was going bananas. She ate alone in the kitchen, an M and S frozen dinner, and laid one out ready for him. A lobster bisque and poulet au feu.

It was past nine o'clock when Geoffrey came back, delivered by one of the MoD cars, tumbling out with a briefcase and a bottle of wine. She hoped he would kiss her, but instead he merely nodded and walked straight past.

'Who gave you that wine?' she asked, following him into the kitchen. She was sure that he had not bought it: in any case he had no time.

'There was a party,' he said grumpily, 'in the Private Office. Somebody getting promoted. One of the clerks. I brought back a spare bottle.'

'You could have left it,' she told him. 'Given it away to somebody.' She disliked that streak of meanness. She wanted to make him laugh, relax, stop worrying about money and position.

He shrugged. 'If you don't want it – '

'No, I don't want it,' she said. 'Let's give it to your sister.' An abstemious, holier-than-thou bitch.

She knew she had drunk enough, waiting for him to come home: two gins on top of the sherry, and she did not trust her head.

'Suit yourself.' He turned away, unlocking his official brief-case, more papers being pulled out. A pocket recorder, more notes to put on tape. You poor devil, she thought, looking at his pallid face.

Godber is using you, Godber is using me because I'm yoked to you.

'I don't think you should talk to Billy about Godber any more,' she said.

'What?'

'I said, you shouldn't say anything more to Billy Vane about your work for Freddie Godber.'

He looked at her sharply as if he was going to complain, then sucked his teeth and said nothing. He spread out his papers on the kitchen table, almost ignoring her, getting ready to dictate. She decided to change the subject.

'Have you had a meal? Don't you want anything to eat?' She showed him the packaged dinner ready for the microwave.

'I'm not hungry.'

'Nothing at all?'

'No. All right. I'll just have the soup. Soup and some bread.'

'Is your stomach hurting again?'

'Yes,' he said in that clipped way.

She heated the soup, suggested he took the papers and worked in the dining area, had his meal with her in the kitchen.

'All right.'

'Geoffrey. What's on? What's cooking?'

'Nothing.'

'There must be. You're always late.'

'You've told me not to talk about it,' he retorted. 'I don't know what the bugger is up to. Phone calls and private meet-ings. Irishmen, and that creep Brocklehurst.'

In that case Melrose made sense, she thought. Godber and Geoffrey were an ill-assorted pair. How was it that Establish-ments didn't know, or didn't care about the yoking of opposites? It could be that Geoffrey was using Billy deliberately to keep his own hands clean, and Billy had gone in deeper than any of them thought. And been found out. She remembered the Irishman who had phoned Billy at the cottage and caused him to leave in a hurry, and shuddered.

She risked another G and T, and watched while he drank the soup and nibbled at a roll. Should she tell him about Melrose or not? Hell no, she kept her affairs to herself, including those with old school pals of Geoffrey.

'I'm tired,' he said. He had scarcely noticed her: she might have been dressed in a sack for all he cared.

At least it was a personal admission and she nodded in sympathy. Billy Vane, she thought, was different – what sort of school thing had there been between the two of them, she wondered – Billy who had taken to calling and tried to charm her. The start of the road to Hereford. Looking at Geoffrey's pale face, the skin tight under the eyes, she felt helplessly sorry for him.

'That American, Wallace,' she said quietly. 'The man who was knifed when jogging in Regent's Park. Was it . . . anything to do with Billy?'

'Billy?' Powers gave a snort. 'Don't be ridiculous. Of course not. What makes you say that?'

'Oh nothing.' She wouldn't say Melrose had been there.

'Why?' Powers stopped spooning the soup and broke up one of the rolls, one, two, three, four pieces placed methodically on the table. Like stepping stones. Then he gathered them up and crushed them into a ball in his hand. 'What put that idea in your head?'

She wouldn't tell him, so he guessed.

'Billy Vane? What kind of stupid story has he been telling you?' He sounded resentful and suspicious.

'Billy hasn't been telling me anything. I . . . just wondered . . . knowing the kind of thing he's involved with. Security, that sort of thing.'

'Look,' Powers said, reducing the bread ball to pulp, 'I think you should keep away from Billy. Completely.' He paused, then brought himself to ask, astonished, 'You're not . . . having some sort of affair with him?'

Claire smiled ruefully. 'Of course not. I've told you. He invited me down there to see his cottage while you were away with Freddie Godber. I'm not that sort of girl – ' She smiled again, feeling a fool, she nearly had been – 'and I told you exactly where I was going. I didn't even stay in the place. He booked me in to the White Horse Country Club. You can check if you like. It will be in the book.' She felt she had betrayed him in thought, if not in deed. And if that strange American had not appeared . . .

Powers was mollified. 'No. Forget it. Of course I believe you.'

'I had to get a break,' she said. 'It was half term and you weren't here. There was a lovely concert in the cathedral – '

'I know. I know. I'm sorry.'

She could see his nerves on edge.

'You should take time off. We need a holiday.' Though God knew he would only want to go to Scotland. The office had become his life.

'In due course,' Powers said. 'When all this business is over.'

'What business? What business, Geoffrey?' Her big eyes focused on him and she tucked her hands under her chin. But she felt she could have been stark naked and Geoffrey would hardly have noticed. He was looking away, dumped the bread ball like a bomb in the dish and pushed it over towards her. Hers, for the washing-up. Her heart was beating faster as she said, 'An Irishman phoned Billy while I was with him in Hereford, and something made him rush out . . .'

Powers had gone pale.

'There's something afoot,' she said, 'isn't there? Ever since you mentioned to Billy that Godber's been seeing an Ulster hit-man about something in Spain. Something involving Gib.'

Abruptly Powers said, 'Don't mention that place.'

But she persisted. 'Why not? Geoffrey, what's going on?' Gibraltar. The Rock. Claire had no service connections, her parents were teachers, but she had a mental picture of a great limestone fortress at the entrance to the Med, complete with British Bobbies and red pillar boxes. And apes. That was it. Barbary apes. She remembered a story that when there were none left British rule would end. Churchill had imported some more there, from North Africa during the war.

'How can anyone threaten Gibraltar in this day and age?' she said. 'Isn't Spain a part of NATO?'

'Oh shut up. Go away and read a book. I'm going to bed.'

He was angry at himself for confiding that far, for letting the cat out of the bag, and now he covered up. But there was something there, she saw with a flash of triumph as her eyes followed his back. Something he'd said to Billy had caused Vane to work on a story, and, knowing him, to try to make money from it, to sell it to the CIA: she was sure that's what it was. That was why the Yank had met him, perhaps why he was beaten up. But what really made her shudder was the thought that in some way it linked with Wallace's death.

She switched off the lights and walked upstairs behind Geoffrey. White doors, a balcony running round the bedroom floor. Four bedrooms, far more than they needed but the damned house was an investment, as Geoffrey said. What did he really want, this long-headed, careful, ambitious, mean-spirited man whom she had rashly married at twenty-one before she knew her own mind? Not children, that was for sure. Probably not even her. She listened to him in the bathroom, and half-undressed beside the bed. Half-undressed deliberately, and then waited.

He came back in pyjamas, silk pyjamas she had bought him, dark blue and edged with white. Geoffrey's eyes were half-closed, making him look Japanese. She softened the bedroom lights and watched him climb into bed without even glancing at her.

Claire wanted his attention as she began to disrobe.

'Billy Vane told me something in Hereford,'

She wouldn't mention the Yank. What was a little deceit between two people like them, living their separate lives . . .

'Billy?' Powers was low in the bed but he turned his eyes towards her. She unclipped her bra.

'Yes. Said a CIA man was attacked in the market there, a few days ago. Some bikers apparently. Four blokes in leather gear. Billy thinks they were looking for him.'

'What?' Powers shot up in the bed, staring at her. Not at her body, but her. She stepped out of the slip, then elegantly out of her tights, standing there in her knickers.

'Put something on,' he said. 'Who attacked him?'

She slipped on the silken nightdress with the décolleté bust, removed the wisp of panties and wriggled into bed beside him.

'He doesn't know. They jumped the man at night.'

'What? Was he hurt?'

'No. Billy came to the rescue.'

'Did he go to the police?'

'I don't think so.'

Geoffrey Powers didn't touch her, even when she rolled close, and tried to stroke his hair. He jerked his head away.

'Bastards,' he said. 'Bastards.'

'Who are, darling?'

'They're warning us,' Geoffrey muttered and the tone of his voice scared her. 'Claire?'

'Yes, darling?' Please, she thought, just for once give it a try. I loved you, admired you, once.

She could feel him tense in the bed, but not in the way she hoped for. Geoffrey Powers turned away. He didn't want her, he was too tired to kiss her, far too tired to make love. He turned his back on her and issued a warning.

'Listen. You understand? Keep away.'

'But why, Geoffrey? What's going on? Haven't I got a right to know?'

From the other side of the bed his voice sounded clouded and confused.

'No. Leave him alone for Christ's sake. Just keep out of his hair. And mine. I'm bloody tired. Billy is up to no good. He'll bugger everything up. I know him – he always did. Listen, Claire, that attack was deliberate, somebody out to stop leaks. That's why Billy's lying low. You follow me?'

'But what for, Geoffrey? How is it connected with Godber?'

Christ, how obtuse, he thought. Hadn't he told her enough? Too much, already.

'Forget Godber,' he said. 'Forget about Billy Vane. Just keep clear, okay? The less you know the better.'

For a moment she wondered if he knew how far she had gone in that weekend in Hereford, but then she dismissed the idea: he was too wrapped up in himself, in the pursuit of his career and in some kind of love-hate relationship with the Secretary of State.

'All right. But why?'

'I've told you to forget it, okay? Now shut up and let me go to sleep.'

She took her hands from her body and lay there quietly. She ached all over and could do nothing about it. The realization hurt her, but also she was elated. Well, well, well, she thought, the American was on to something.

17

They were flying Brendan Wallace's body back to Washington DC for burial at Arlington. He was a hero in the end, Jake Melrose reflected, as he comforted Angie following the short memorial service in St Mark's, North Audley Street. She was going home, on a USAF plane for the funeral, then returning for a few weeks to try and pick up the pieces. It was as if she couldn't yet face the house at Poquito Beach, Florida, just off Interstate 95, that they had brought years before, anticipating retirement.

Maybe Brendan liked the sunshine after a life in back rooms, but Angie's friends were now in London. No sooner settled, she said, than it was Berlin and Beirut, and finally London. London, where you thought you were safe after years under cover. She dried her tears.

'Ma'am, I'm sorry. Very sorry for you,' Melrose said,

quietly. 'But rest assured in this. I made a bargain with Brendan. And I'll stick to it.'

She sniffed and looked at him, pink-nosed in the sunshine, a widow – a widow who might try again, given six months, he speculated as he shook her hand and said goodbye.

Leibermann was standing in the porch with him while they watched the cars pull away. Arthur J. Kalthrop Leibermann, known to his friends as Harry – it sounded better that way – Deputy Chief of Mission and filling in. Three years older than Jake but not a grey hair on his head, just a little flab round the middle – he'd quit any jogging after what happened to Brendan, on the Ambassador's instructions; no way he'd jog in a threesome – sure of himself, growing pompous.

'You walking back to the Square?' he asked. The service had been short and informal, with only a handful there so as not to draw attention but Angie had felt she wanted something, some gesture near the office. Now Leibermann made a suggestion. 'Let's have a coffee, Jake.'

They went inside a patisserie, sitting at a marble-topped table where the sun could not quite penetrate the smoky plate glass of the window. Leibermann ordered two cappuccinos and selected a cream éclair. Melrose settled for the coffee.

Leibermann grinned. He was going to enjoy ordering other people about – it shone in his eyes and the butter-smooth face – and he hoped he could keep the Station.

'What you going to do now, Jake?'

Melrose measured him up. Not a hint of a smile.

'Not much I can do, Harry.' He reported again the little brawl in Hereford, and how Vane had come back and warned him off. He didn't mention Claire.

Leibermann was watching the waitress: dark haired in a tight brown tunic that was almost a mini, with golden shoes, hair cropped like an unruly schoolboy.

'Jeez,' he said. 'Look at that.' He noted Melrose didn't move. Straight-ass, he thought. 'Jake,' leaning closer over the table. 'You really think there's anything in this story of an adventure in Spain? To promote Freddie Godber?'

'Don't know,' Jake said.

'Okay. What the fuck does it matter? You know old Brendan was paranoid. Too many years away, too many deaths in Beirut. Shut up in some damned compound. He saw intrigues all around, trouble every goddam place, 'cos that was the way in Lebanon. But this country ain't the Lebanon, Jake, thank God for that. Leastways not yet, and no smart politician over here is gonna push his luck in Spain. It's a democracy, Jake. The Mother of Parliaments, huh? You know that. You don't get dirty tricks here.' He lowered his voice. 'Anyway who gives a toss about Gibraltar?'

'The Spanish,' Melrose said.

'Yeah. Maybe you're right.'

'Sure, I'm right.'

Leibermann was conspirational. 'Okay. So we'll have a word with Madrid. Listen, Jake. Back off and go home. Back to the grind in Paris. You got a job there, right? Lot of work in Eastern Europe, now that the Curtain's down. Okay, Jake, you get moving. Don't waste your time over here. This country's got clean politics, man. I guess you know – Christ look at those legs – and if anybody starts telling you they are going to put up with a megalomaniac like Freddie Godber, you tell 'em get screwed.'

'Yessir,' Jake said. 'Is that an order?'

Leibermann laughed. 'More coffee?'

Jake shook his head.

'We-ll, I reckon I'll have one. You in a hurry, Jake?'

'Nope.'

'Great.' He chatted up the waitress, who brought him a second cup. 'Believe me, Jake. You get the conspirators in public life. In all kinds of politics. I could name 'em in the States. Guys who encourage people to come up to them and say they could fix an election. Like Watergate for Tricky Dicky. Freddie Godber's one of those, but it don't add up to a row of beans.'

'He's got style.'

'Style, my ass. Got his wife's money and a good PR machine. That gets you a long way but it don't get you to the top. Not in a fuckin' Government that ain't managed the economy so good. So he's just pushing his luck. No plot, okay?'

'Okay. No plot,' Jake said.

Leibermann adjusted his belt and paid the check.

'You got it.'

'Not even with a knife in the back in Regent's Park; and four guys on a beat-up in Hereford?'

'Aw, come on, Jake. There's no connection, man. The police have got statements from guys near where Brendan was stabbed. An A-rab. Definitely an A-rab. We reckon some Shi'ite group, just like they said. Probably Said Hamid. Brendan had dealings with them, trying to get a hostage exchange and we reckon the bastards nailed him for trapping the Ankara hijack.'

'What about those guys who jumped me in the market?'

'Do me a favour, Jake.' Liebermann looked at the earnest, planed-down face, and thought he had probably asked for it. 'You get these things. Drunks. Punks just off the freeway. Birmingham hooligans. Forget it, Jake. Conspiracy theory don't wash. This is the UK, man.'

'Sure, Harry.'

18

The two key men in the next bid for power walked quickly and quietly along the corridors of the House of Commons, through the Central Lobby, up the stairs to the ministerial wing, along the end of the passage to Godber's room. Pickering and Drumblane. Philip Pickering, the grey man who chaired the influential '22 Committee of back-bench opinion and Duggie Drumblane, the leader in the Lords.

Freddie was waiting inside, together with Peter Brocklehurst, burning the oil late at his ministerial desk. The room was ill-lit and seemed dusty, so that the Secretary of State's face, illuminated by the green desk lamp, had a faintly forbidding air.

'Come in, boys,' Freddie Godber said, getting up and offering chairs, the squelchy red leather kind that Melanie had said he should have to brighten the place up a bit. 'You know Peter Brocklehurst, my agent? You can say what you want.'

Even so Pickering was looking around, as if he still expected a secretary, or at the least a witness.

'Powers has gone,' Godber said. 'I released him so we could talk in private.' It was ten past eleven, and the House was still sitting on the Northern Ireland Bill. He put away the papers on the desk.

'Well?' He looked at them, arms folded, the handsome head thrown back.

'It won't work,' Pickering said, his face as unemotional as if he was taking back a broken clock. 'I have to tell you it wouldn't work.'

'They wouldn't stand for it,' Duggie Drumblane added, his jaws wobbling. 'The Party. No good pretending.'

'Won't stand for what?' Godber asked quietly. Much as he disliked Pickering with all that Walsall greyness behind him, the man was a bloody genius at picking up opinions, just as he'd picked up a fortune out of scrap metal when the industries closed in the Midlands. He wielded internal influence, as chair of the '22, which Godber could not afford to ignore. Everything Godber disliked about contemporary politics he saw in Philip Pickering: the yes-men, the save-our-seaters, the free lunch brigade – but Pickering was the ring master who knew how to make them jump. He spent his time in the tearoom, this anonymous figure whom nobody bothered to hate, and chatting in the corridors, and working away with the Whips, and on the stump for by-elections, and helping out in hard cases until everyone owed him a crust, the hardest thing in politics. Now he was a surveyor who could tell the trees in the Cabinet exactly how tall they were in the eyes of the backwoods.

'Freddie, they liked your stuff. The weekend TV was great. But they won't buy a foreign adventure.'

Godber smiled, trying to put him at ease. What a narrow-minded runt, he decided.

104

'Foreign adventure? That's not at all what I mean.'

'Stirring up trouble with Spain. That's an adventure,' Drumblane burbled. 'We're both in NATO.'

Freddie Godber laughed and Brocklehurst followed suit.

'How you chaps get the wrong end of the stick. I hope you haven't suggested that I had such a thing in mind . . .'

'Of course not, Freddie,' Pickering replied. No, he wouldn't be such a fool. What he had done was simply to canvass opinion. Did they want Freddie or not, as leader of the Party within the next twelve months, before the next Election, if the PM stood down or was pushed? And if they weren't sure – and fifty-two per cent weren't sure – what could Freddie do to improve himself.

'Fifty-two per cent in the Party?'

'In the Party in the House.'

'About the same in the Lords,' Drumblane added.

'What about the constituencies? The feeling in the country?'

Pickering shrugged. 'Pretty good. High profile. Come over well on the telly. You're known. You get around. You'd be acceptable.'

'Acceptable. Christ's sake,' Godber said. 'That sounds like a bargain offer for a used three-piece suite.'

At last a small grave-yard smile on Pickering's bony face.

'There's nobody who stands any higher.'

'Humph.' Small comfort. He simply couldn't trust him, any more than he could trust Wainwright, the Chief Whip.

'Listen,' he said. 'All that has been suggested is bringing the overseas factor into play. It wouldn't cost any powder. It wouldn't cost any lives. I'm not asking for anyone's blood. All that I want to do is show I can answer the challenge, show that I can act decisively. Philip, you know that. The Party knows that. Okay, following the CFCE summit in Paris we've got arms reductions. I don't object to that, you know that, Phil. And you, Duggie. What we need now is a new style defence force with a balanced capability. I've got that, too, by George. I've secured it. Smaller but better equipped.' The lights shone in Freddie's eyes. 'It's been a management triumph. Fantastic. A small, hard force, capable of rapid deployment in Europe or elsewhere, as well as keeping the peace in Northern Ireland.'

'I know. I know . . .'

'No, you don't, Philip. None of them know. The country doesn't know. I've got to make it plain that I'm the man for the job. Think of it as a conglomerate, the UK plc, retooling and restructuring. That's what I want to manage, Duggie. I want to show what I can do. And the best way is to show what I have done with the armed forces, in spite of the economies. I want to show the results of my management.'

'Well, you can't do that for real, Freddie,' Pickering said bluntly. 'You can show 'em off on manoeuvres on Luneberg Heath, if anyone will watch.' He was a sod, a hard-headed Birmingham son of a bitch, Godber decided, who would sell his own daughter.

'You know bloody well, Philip – '

'Salisbury Plain, then.'

'Salisbury Plain is full of Greens. And there's no votes in manoeuvres, none at all. It has to be the real thing.'

'Well, it can't be war-mongering. The Party wouldn't stand for it.'

'Not even reaction against a hypothetical threat?'

There were times when Pickering had to browbeat Ministers, in the interests of the Party. He rather enjoyed it.

'No, Freddie. No.'

Left to themselves in the room, Brocklehurst and Godber looked at each other.

'I can't believe it,' Godber said. 'Scared. Namby-pamby. I wouldn't trust Pickering further than I could see him.'

'Do you think he'll split? Start circulating rumours?' The political agent was already manoeuvring out of that particular corner.

'No,' the Minister said. 'That's not his style.'

'And Duggie?'

'Duggie's on our side. He just daren't say so.'

'Okay, good. Then we'll go ahead,' Brocklehurst said.

The Secretary of State opened the door of his cupboard. 'Scotch?' Godber felt he could do with it.

The younger man nodded and Godber realized that he was now yoked in a conspiracy whether he liked it or not, tied to this Saatchi and Saatchi man with the red mouth and the bow tie, who was marketing him like a fruit juice. The uncertainty of back-bench opinion meant nothing to an advertising man working to a sales plan.

They clinked glasses and Freddie wished Melanie were there. She knew how to handle things better when the chips were down. Brocklehurst paused over his drink.

'Well? Will you see Landsdowne now?'

Godber breathed in hard, summoning his resolve. 'I think I'd better,' he said. 'Strictly in private.'

'Great.' Brocklehurst had been waiting for weeks to drive him to that point. The agent had no illusions about the need to strike now. Politics was public relations, timing, and what you made of the openings.

'Better leave the official car and take a cab. Less obvious,' Brocklehurst said.

They walked through the Lobby, towards the St Stephen's entrance and turned down Westminster Hall, past the brass plates commemorating the lyings-in state. George VI. Winston Churchill. Freddie Godber found a lump in his throat as their footsteps echoed under the hammerbeam roof still scarred by German incendiaries. He thrust his hands into the pockets of his blue double-breasted pinstripe, and nodded upwards.

'People forget . . .' he said.

Brocklehurst smiled. This was the stuff he would use. Might get a picture here sometime, Godber's little wallow in history. But his mind moved to other things, to the present, as they stood in Palace Yard while the light flashed for a taxi. How to present a politician who was frightened of losing. Ambitious but nervous, that was Godber's problem. The next couple of weeks would make or break them both. Even then Godber hesitated. He look round anxiously.

'I'm not sure how safe it is . . .'

'Don't worry,' Brocklehurst said.

The taxi came over the cobbles and they climbed in.

'Islington,' Brocklehurst instructed. '4 Pelham Street.'

Big Ben was striking midnight as they left the House of Commons.

'You told him we might be late?'

'I rang him earlier. Told him to wait till he heard. He's used to it.'

'You've got it buttoned up, haven't you?'

Brocklehurst caught the uncertainty in Godber's voice. Underneath the charm and self-confidence lurked a neurotic, an over-ambitious romantic who pushed himself to get to the top and would shit himself when he got there. Melanie had the real bloodstock, Brocklehurst thought. By Christ, he could have sold her.

They drew up in North London, outside a row of terraces with 1816 carved on the gable. The year after Waterloo, Godber noted. A black, anonymous door with a large bronze knocker. Brocklehurst touched a bell at the side and they were ushered into a half-panelled room with wing chairs, tall lampstands, carpets unrelated to the decor, a transient kind of room, with furniture that didn't quite match. Godber realized that it was rented at some exorbitant rate.

The figure emerging from the chair had been watching television, snapped off by the remote control in his left hand. In his right he held a glass of vodka, recharged from the bottle at his elbow.

'Landsdowne,' he said. 'Colin Landsdowne.'

Godber nodded, immediately remembering that nearly bald, frosty-haired skull, and the soft, careful Ulster voice. Landsdowne smiled and offered both of them drinks, but they refused. Landsdowne reseated himself and watched them with a told-you-so smirk.

'I'm not sure it would work,' Godber began.

'Of course it would work, sir. I would arrange it. Never you fear.' The Irishman brushed aside doubt.

'The Cabinet security people have already begun to ask questions. Someone has talked to the Yanks.'

'That's all right. I know. Don't worry.' Landsdowne waved

it away. 'There's a freelance called Billy Vane who's been trying to sell them a half-cock story, because of their bases in Spain. I've warned him to keep his mouth shut.'

Landsdowne's face was high-coloured. Blood pressure, Godber thought. The man needed to watch his drinking, or perhaps it was what kept him going in the psy-ops field. Landsdowne gestured with his glass to the Minister, deferential but cunning.

'I saw you on the television. You were brilliant. Now's the time to make your stand. Show them how smart you are.'

'Thank you. But I don't want any foul play.'

'Foul play?' Landsdowne was sweet puzzled innocence.

Brocklehurst put things more bluntly. 'There's a suggestion that the murder of Wallace and the American interest in Billy Vane's story might be in some way connected.'

Landsowne laughed. 'Ridiculous. Who said that?'

'A man called Frewin has been to see the Secretary of State. Cabinet Office security. On a tip off from the CIA.'

'Well, it's a nonsense. Wallace was done in by one of the PLO groups. The Yanks had a message from them, and an Arab was seen running away.'

Godber decided he needed that drink. When Landsdowne poured he said, 'If anything happens out there, it's got to be provocation. Pure Spanish provocation. No shooting. You understand me? Nothing like that security ambush on the Rock. Just something that I can respond to, a little local difficulty which I can scotch efficiently.'

'A TV event,' Brocklehurst added.

'Perfectly understood. Nothing went wrong last time.'

Godber frowned but seemed satisfied. He took a small sip of the vodka and twisted his face. It was one of those tinted vodkas the Russians liked, flavoured with catmint.

Brocklehurst said, 'It has got to be undercover. The Party won't stand for anything worked up in public.'

Landsdowne stretched out his legs and contemplated his shiny brown shoes.

'Goes without saying. I know what I'm doing,' he replied. Twenty years in covert operations, ten of them in Northern

Ireland, reporting directly to the GOC, Land Forces, there under cover of being a press man. His credentials, he reminded them, were impeccable.

'You tell me what you want,' he said. 'I'll lay it on.'

Godber was breathing heavily. 'First of all, I want no traces. No leads running back to me.'

'Done.'

'Secondly, I want something fast. Something to influence opinion in the Party before the October conference. I'm going to challenge as soon as the moment is ripe. If there are some Spaniards mad enough to give me a platform, I'll take that option, but only if it helps me to get on the front of the *Sun*, waving a Union Jack. And only if there's no risk.'

Landsdowne said, 'Understood. Just a token threat, right?'

'Enough to use the Rapid Deployment Force. The paras. Three light carriers. Two squadrons of jump jets, all there in twenty-four hours.'

'An international photo opportunity,' Brocklehurst grinned.

'Maybe a few explosions?'

'So long as no one gets hurt. Is that absolutely clear?'

Landsdowne said, 'No problem.'

'Nothing must rub off on me.'

Landsdowne finished the bottle, stood up and held out his hand.

'That's for sure. Have no fear.'

Godber said, 'You'll use the Countess of the Asturias?'

'Of course. The Falangists. The ones who want Carlos out. Franco's old guard.'

Godber said 'It must be secret. And it must be properly planned. Cooperation not conflict.'

It was then that Landsdowne offered his side of the bargain, still grasping Godber's hand.

'There's only one thing that can guarantee it completely. You know that?'

Brocklehurst knew but Godber didn't.

'What?'

'Gibraltar is expendable, Minister. Surplus to requirements, you might say.'

110

'I'm not giving it away,' Godber said.

'No, no. Of course not. But you make them think that you might. When you've got into power.'

19

It was raining when Melrose hit Paris, one of those freak storms that sent sheets of water out of a black and blue sky and drummed on the cobbles like bullets as he shook himself out in the stairway to his apartment in the rue de Miromesnil. And cold. Everything caught up with him there. He unlocked the door of the big, old-fashioned apartment, care of the US Embassy round the corner in the rue du Faubourg St Honoré, and thought, 'Hell!'

As he slipped into the hallway and retrieved mail from the floor, where the concierge left it whenever he was away, he found himself more and more thinking about the events in England that had led him to Claire. Above all, thinking of her. Circulars, bills, drinks invitation from the USIS, a letter from Joy in Denver – long time no see, kiddo – a card from Chuck Leeming stationed in Hawaii, grass skirts and waving palms, and an envelope stamped OECD. That was Marie-Louise: it brought him up with a jolt, it seemed that long ago.

Inside now, shaking off a wet coat, lights on in the big room, it was that dark. The rain was rattling the windows and he crossed to peer out, catching a glimpse of the car-tops, headlights on, creeping through the flooding in the Avenue de Marigny. Even the duty police had disappeared from the wall of the Elysée Palace on the opposite corner, and one lonely figure sheltered as best he could in the awning of the magazine stall. Melrose watched for a moment, never quite off his guard, that was the old philosophy, but the guy moved on after a while. Some poor devil without a raincoat, in down-at-heel shoes.

Okay, he thought, I'm back. Back in the too-big place fixed

up for the wife and family of a Political Officer, Grade 2, Victor and Annie Seymour and four young kids, now on six months' furlough in Long Beach, California. He didn't envy them, didn't know what it was to have that kind of complication. The apartment was still stuffed with their things: bedrooms full of her clothes and the kids' toys, a bathroom with plastic ducks and Tampax packets. Melrose switched on the fire to dry himself out: his pants and brogues were saturated, maybe he'd take a shower. But Marie-Louise's letter was sitting there staring at him, like a photograph from the past. He moved into the kitchen, which smelled damp from his absence, and plugged in the percolator.

While it was bubbling he opened Marie-Louise's envelope. A message on her office paper, 'Organization for Economic Co-operation and Development', 2, rue André Pascal: she had missed him. Jake, let me know when you're around and maybe we could meet again. His place, or hers at Rocquencourt, ten kilometres outside Paris. That was the offer, and he turned it over in his mind, drinking two cups of black coffee. Women. Some of them felt sorry for him, one or two tried to mother him, most wanted a good time. Melrose shifted uneasily, reading the invitation. He'd been in Paris five months, since he finished in Seoul, that ugly, stone-faced, hell-hole, and had met her almost at once, as soon as he was set up there in the Seymours' apartment. She'd not known they had gone and came to the door one day to ask about some report that Seymour was supposed to be writing. But Seymour had flown off with the wife and kids and taken the goddam thing with him, and there she was, standing in Jake's new doorway, a cute Parisienne in a white embroidered tunic and red track pants with hair clipped and contoured short. She'd taken one look at Jake and more or less declared an interest as soon as he invited her in, first to the apartment, then to his leisure life. And in between his trips round Europe checking on locks and fences, she had slipped into his bed, or rather the Seymours' bed, three or four times. She liked it, she liked Jake, and she gave as good as she got, leaving him pleased and grateful. She invited him to meet her friends, girls from the OECD and

112

the Ministry of European Affairs on the Quai d'Orsay from which she had been seconded, and now she was suggesting a weekend.

It gave Melrose pause. A casual affair was one thing, but not what he really wanted. It ought to go so far and no further. The girl in London, the girl in the Wimbledon house, she somehow seemed a different quality. Marie-Louise was still a kid. What kind of life did he offer, anyways, some bastard ex-Marine who shunted round the world for a living looking at US property, surveillance and security equipment. Moreover, he had fucked up lives, kids' lives in a chopper in 'Nam, and maybe Mary's too, in that short-lived and tragic marriage before she skidded in the Plymouth while he was stuck on base. Ended before they had kids, before they really had anything. He sniffed and climbed to his feet. When they told him he'd broken down. Some Marine.

Melrose walked back to the big room and punched the TV. Nothing worth watching. Marie-Louise's letter in his hand. He'd have to tell her no good; no way could he lead her on. Better to break it now, before the going got rough, one more of those small-time romances picked up along the way. Too many, looking back, but he was no pipe-and-slippers guy, they had to understand that. Better check on the planes to Warsaw, get back in line.

The street down below the Avenue de Marigny corner was coming alive again as the rain stopped. Smart girls high-stepping the pavement, the gendarme out in the car lanes caped like the Masked Crusader, and that scarecrow again, the drenched maybe spastic guy hanging about on the sidewalk next to the tabac stall. Nothing to him, he decided, but he gave it a careful check. Why was he running scared after the Hereford punch-up? He looked at himself in the mirror: the bruises had almost gone. That had been quite an evening, his meeting with Billy Vane, his meeting with Claire Powers. Claire. Not the gamine prettiness of sexy little Marie-Louise but something more secure and solid; one look from those wide blue eyes in the face framed by soft bronze hair had registered deep inside him. It was as if she was searching for

113

something, for a way out of a trap. And he reckoned the trap was her marriage. Well, that ought to be no business of Jake H. Melrose, but as he recrossed the room and slumped in the Seymours' chair, flicking through the *Herald Tribune*, Claire would not go away. Something else was his business: her relationship with Vane and maybe Vane's with Wallace's death. He remembered the scared look when he'd suggested it, and the confused way in which she had covered up for Geoffrey and refused to tell him anything. Claire knew what was going on, she was an interested party, aware of what Godber was up to with some kind of political Mafia over there in London. And if that Mafia got to realize as much . . . he pondered the attack in Hereford, which could have been meant for Vane. What had made Vane run scared when the phone call came through from the Irishman, scared enough to come and look for him? The thought tumbled out and he feared for Claire. Far more than his interest in sweet chestnut Marie-Louise, he found himself worrying about Claire.

Telephone. He could reach her by telephone – he'd noted the number when he visited the Wimbledon house. Wimbledon. Tennis and strawberry teas: he'd watched it on the television in London two years back. He grinned to himself in the big old room of that rather grand apartment handed around by the Embassy: compared with the glitter of Paris London seemed almost small-scale. You looked down on it from the top of a bus. What happens, he wondered, when a guy nearly over the hill, who thinks he's too old for marriage, meets a girl like Claire married to some die-cast Brit and maybe sleeping with another one?

He checked on the local time. Friday night, five o'clock, British Summer time, and she should be in that house with the grandfather clock and the pictures in gold frames. And the neatly mown lawn. Wimbledon. Geoffrey would still be at work, that was for sure. He dialled London.

Almost immediately he was through.

A man's voice, sounding guarded.

'Hullo?'

114

He was tempted to say wrong number, but something made him hang on.

'Hi. Is Mrs Claire Powers there?'

'Claire? No. Who is it calling?' Powers was scarcely inside his front door before the bloody phone rang. When he got off early for once – Godber had gone back to Worcestershire – Claire wasn't there, and some Yank was asking for her. 'Who's calling?' he repeated.

Melrose said, 'Just a friend in Paris.'

'Paris? She hasn't got any friends there.'

'Sure she has. She's got me. Is that Geoffrey Powers I'm calling?'

'Yes, it is.'

'Well, hello Geoffrey. She told me about you.' He could almost feel the suspicions mounting at the other end of the phone.

'Look, who the hell are you? What do you want?'

Melrose smiled to himself. Keep 'em talking, that was rule Number Three. Just keep the information flowing so they get interested but don't have too much time to think. Powers sounded clipped and nervous, a guy who would fall for the bullshit.

'Old friend of Claire's,' he said. 'We were at college together . . .' Don't ask me where, he thought, don't ask me where. 'Jake Melrose from Wisconsin.'

'I was at Exeter with Claire. I don't recall you.'

Nice one. He didn't recall him. He didn't fucking recall him. Melrose was hugging himself.

'Post-graduate year.' he said.

'Oh, I see.'

Got him. There had been the year, Powers remembered, when he had entered the civil service and was already living in London while Claire had stayed on for the teacher training diploma. He'd wanted her to qualify before they married: it gave her something to do and supplemented their income.

'Right. Nice to know you, Geoffrey.'

Powers disliked this American with his instant attempts at

rapport. 'What do you want?' he asked, ignoring the compliment.

'I guess just a chat,' he said. 'While I'm over in Europe.'

'Europe?'

'Yeah. I'm over on a job. Thought I'd give Claire a bell. Maybe you could pass on a message?'

'All right,' Powers said grudgingly.

'Great, Geoffrey. Tell her that Jake called, and could she give him a ring, for old times' sake. She going to be home soon?'

'I don't know.' He sounded as if he didn't care.

'Okay. Great talking to you, Geoffrey.'

He repeated the Paris number, and only when he had finished did he realize how badly he wanted Claire to make that connection.

Jake Melrose had a beer and a plain omelette in the Brasserie Niçoise round the corner. It was still raining, the kind of cold, grey evening when Parisian chic seemed to swirl down the drains and disappear in the honking traffic. He had to make up his mind, remembering what Leibermann said: Gibraltar, what the fuck did it matter? He had nothing to go on except the warning from Vane and the nervous reaction from Claire. As for Jake himself, he was safeguarding Uncle Sam's interests, and nobody else's. And don't confuse duty with pleasure. Try and forget the girl, Jake.

He downed a second beer and turned up his coat collar, tramping back to the rue de Miromesnil: cars parked on either side, a thin stream down the middle, a girl getting her legs wet in a short plastic mac. He dodged her and caught the perfume. A car on the opposite side with a guy sitting in it, two doors down from the apartment. Was he just getting paranoid or was some bastard watching? He felt like going across and asking what the hell he was doing sitting there on a wet Friday night, but instead he walked on past, to the corner and back again. The man did not look up: young, in his twenties, short hair, no raincoat. Could have been there some time, could be waiting for a girl, even a pick-up. He saw

116

the girl in the short shiny mac coming back down the street, stop by one of the cars and then move on.

Melrose keyed open the entrance to the apartment block and went upstairs. There might have been a message on the answerphone but the green light was unblinking. She hadn't called back from Wimbledon, or maybe Powers hadn't told her. He felt a strange disappointment, and told himself not to be stupid.

20

Powers had other things to do than worry about oddball callers: another bag of stuff to dictate after Godber's planning meetings on the Defence White Paper. He poured a glass of mineral water and wondered where the hell Claire was. He didn't much care what she did, but he liked to find her in the house. No note. No indication. He wondered if in spite of his warnings, loverboy Vane had been around again: she wouldn't have stayed late at school on a Friday afternoon.

He picked himself a frozen meal and slammed it in the microwave, sorting out his papers while he waited. Already two nights' work there, today and tomorrow. On Sunday he should be free. Maybe he should take her out, drive into the country somewhere, try to mend a few fences in the relationship. There wasn't much warmth in it now, and yet in a way he still needed her, part of the career image. One more year of Freddie Godber and Geoffrey would be pushing old Henry Burton to promote him into civil service Grade 3. That was the name of the game. That was why he hung on, if Godber lasted that long as Defence Minister in these changing times.

The lasagne was ready, piping hot, and he carried it through to the dining room. Cream walls, creamier evening light, the sun filtering through the curtains. He switched on the radio to catch the news. Speculation about the date of the leadership challenge, and whether the PM would stand down. Speculation about the succession and when Freddie would stand up. It sounded as if the troops were being rallied, but Powers had no idea how many supporters there were. It was comforting to be isolated from the realities of politics, the infighting on the back benches, and yet he was being drawn in, in ways that left him disturbed.

The Security man, Didsbury, ex-naval commander, had asked for a private word that very afternoon, soon after Godber had gone.

Powers had shown him into the Secretary of State's big room, leaving Bramley the APS and the duty clerks outside, so that they could have privacy. Malcolm Didsbury was older than he expected, stocky, with hair in small wavelets over a worldly face which when he smiled gave way in an attempt to ingratiate, as if he'd been hurt by past failures. Conservatively dressed, with a dark naval tie, and polished shoes, he seemed embarrassed at finding Powers so young.

'Afraid I have to ask you one or two personal questions, sir,' he muttered. 'Security check.'

Powers had nodded, sitting himself neatly behind Godber's big desk with the Commander in the interview chair. It gave him the advantage of position and of height. He looked like a City banker, Didsbury thought: small head, sharp eyes, a Welshness.

'Go ahead.' Thin smile.

'I'm attached to Cabinet Office Security.' MI5 was not mentioned.

'I understand.' Hands resting easily on the table. No nervous ticks or shuffles.

'We are conducting a periodic check into the general security position of . . . ah . . . senior Ministers.'

Powers had nodded again, knowing this wasn't routine.

'You will be aware, sir, of various rumours in the press of ambitious plans by Mr Godber to put himself forward to succeed the Prime Minister?'

'Can't miss them,' Powers replied coolly.

'Good. Well. It has come to our attention that Mr Godber may be in touch privately with one or two Ulster undercover agents. Psychological operations people who have been involved in dirty tricks in Northern Ireland. You follow me? I need hardly say that if there is any truth in our information – and, as I say, it is only if – it would be entirely contrary to the rules of conduct governing Cabinet Ministers.'

'Of course.'

Didsbury paused, delved into his briefcase and checked his references.

'Do you know Peter Brocklehurst?'

'Yes. I've met him, naturally,' Powers said. 'He's the Secretary of State's political agent.'

'Correct. Did you know that he has been meeting privately with a man called Landsdowne? Colin Landsdowne. Previously involved with undercover ops in Belfast?'

'Who?' Powers went cold at the memory of that conversation he had overheard at the airport.

'Landsdowne. Colin Landsdowne. Man about fifty, white-haired. Speaks with an Irish accent. Does it ring a bell?'

'No. 'Fraid not,' Powers had said. His advantage was in covering for Godber. There was nothing wrong in that.

'Ah. Well. Thank you.' Didsbury noted his book and seemed a little disappointed.

'Oh. One more thing, sir.'

'Yes.' Powers getting fretful now, as if his time was being wasted and he had a lot to do.

'I believe you know a man called Vane? Billy Vane. Ex-SAS.'

'He was at school with me.'

'Where was that, sir?'

'Wellington. Wellington College, in the '70s.'

'Ah. Thank you, sir. When did you last see him?'

Powers said, 'About a month back, I think. He came to dinner.'

Didsbury looked genuinely embarrassed.

'I'm sorry to have to go in to this, sir, but are you aware that he's been seeing your wife since?'

Powers went pale. These goons must have been trailing him: hanging around his house, tracking Claire down to that cottage.

'Yes,' he said, his fingers curling. 'I am aware.'

'He was seen with the lady in Hereford, while I believe you were away with Mr Godber, about two weeks ago.'

'Yes. I know.' There was a cold, hard look in Powers's eyes. 'A perfectly straightforward weekend.'

Poor devil, Didsbury thought, and who could blame her.

'Do you discuss any matters relating to security and Mr Godber's political plans with your wife, or with Mr Vane?'

'Of course not.'

'Are you aware of any undercover operations?'

'Certainly not.'

'You're quite sure, sir?'

'Yes. Quite sure.'

'You haven't mentioned any ideas Mr Godber may have for stirring up trouble so that he can demonstrate the Rapid Deployment Forces which he has built up?'

'No,' Powers said. 'What ideas, Commander?'

'That's what we're trying to find out,' Didsbury had said.

21

She had eased the cherry red Volvo out of the Sainsbury centre and manoeuvred it to set off home. Claire Powers liked driving, she was confident in the machinery: the car had a solid feel and was built like a tank. She felt secure coming back with the shopping.

Turning into Parkside, the big houses, the Common on the other side, she noticed the little Golf was still behind her. A dark blue VW, one of those anonymous cars you didn't look at much from a Volvo, somebody's runabout. She drove into Sunbury Avenue, the open, familiar gates. 'The Wing', the gravel, her own front door. Unlocking the door, then the tail, unstacking a week's groceries in carrier bags. Keeping up with the Joneses.

The little Golf was still there, a man in the driving seat

watching from the other side of the road. Ridiculous, she told herself, but a chill ran through her. She bent over to get the bags which had slid down inside the estate, then clasping a box of cereals and washing powders, the bulky stuff, she managed to turn round and get a better glimpse without appearing to stare. An oval face, almost as bald as an egg, framed by cropped silver hair. She found herself sighing with relief: he didn't look a mugger. But the man was still staring at her across the roadway, with pale unblinking eyes, as if he was not so much examining her as her circumstances: the big Victorian house with its gables and pitched roof, the three steps up to the porch, the central circle of grass in front of the drive. The house, the car and herself, dressed smartly in a shortish skirt and red and black Pringle sports top, all indicating a certain style and income. She felt he was weighing them up and sensed her mouth going dry.

She was half inclined to walk across and ask if he wanted something, he seemed so brazen sitting there, but that would be quite stupid. Perhaps he had a reason, was looking for a house to buy or waiting for someone in the villas along the road. She turned away and marched indoors, glad to have shut him out, becoming less charitable once her front door had slammed: a nutter, a gawper, a flasher.

From one of the front room windows she could see out between the gates and something made her go and watch, standing well back in the shadows. He waited twenty minutes, the man, and then climbed out of the VW. She saw him more clearly now: a nondescript middle-aged man in a careful grey suit, the silver hair almost stubble around the florid head, an oval head, like a rugby ball, but somehow the eyes were probing. He came and stood by the gate and looked up at her house.

Claire almost phoned the police but decided that would seem panicky. Anyway the fellow was going, eventually climbing into the car and driving off. She found her hand was shaking as she ran out to the Volvo again and drove away from the house, anywhere, in traffic, so as to feel safe, ending

121

up at Liz Formby's, a classroom colleague. Crack a bottle. Have a drink, and laugh about it.

When she came back a couple of hours later Geoffrey had already arrived and unfrozen a meal. He was working in the dining room and hardly seemed to notice she was flustered, as she tried to explain.

'Do you think he was following me or marking the house?' Powers was entirely unhelpful.

'Who'd want to stake you out?'

'I don't know. Perhaps somebody checking on the kind of life we lead. Don't they do that sometimes, the Security people? To see whether you live beyond your means. That sort of thing?'

'Forget it,' he said brutally. They would only do that, he knew, if he was under suspicion, and he did not see how that could be.

She was annoyed with him but tried not to show it. He resented suggestions that anyone should question his lifestyle: the big house, the big car, the *investments* as he liked to call them. He was a social climber, she admitted to herself. He thought money, position, a public status was everything. Geoffrey had moved a long way from the lean and hungry student that she had married. He was already talking about a place in the country near Tunbridge Wells or Lewes, where he could ride on a lawnmower, a conventional, commuter burial in coffee mornings and golf that she found herself dreading. But she let it pass.

'Been a bad day?' She wanted to share it with him, share information and gossip.

He grunted. 'Too much bloody work. The big chief wants a trip to the States: talks in the Pentagon.'

'That would be great for you.' She tried to get closer to him, to bridge the gap. 'When?'

'Probably some time next month. He's angling for a visit to the White House. Photo call with the President.'

'Oh. Can you go with him, Geoffrey?' She hoped he would enjoy it as a change from the pressure, and secretly told herself she wouldn't mind being alone.

'Nope. The less I see of Godber the better. He and Henry Burton and General Taylor are going with young Bramley.' Bramley was a year his junior. He could go as the bag-carrier.

'Why?'

'For God's sake, who knows how Freddie's mind works? He just wants the photographs. All he thinks of is publicity.' But privately Powers was glad that he could distance himself.

She led him back to the question that was so disturbing her. 'What is all this about Godber's schemes? What has set Billy going?'

'Forget Billy.'

'Well. Freddie Godber then: what's going on?'

'Mind your own business,' he said.

Claire suspected he was trapped, not knowing which way to turn. If he denounced Godber and got it wrong, it would be disastrous for him, yet if he stayed what kind of game was afoot? She wished he would understand her and offered an olive branch.

'Why don't you leave? Put in for a transfer from the Private Office. We can't go on like this. It's driving us mad.'

'Don't be stupid. It's my future.' He said it like a sentence, but was greedy for the next step up.

In her way she still admired him, admired that single-minded ambition. That night she wanted him, suddenly, surprisingly. But he turned away again and said he was too tired.

She taught at a school in Tooting, near the Broadway, where she was filling in, an old three-decker building on a pre-war campus, St Faith's Comprehensive, English and French on supply, three days a week. The kids were liquorish allsorts but she enjoyed it: a real United Nations. Like her they wanted stability and it was good to get out of the house, away from his mandarin presence.

She caught the bus as usual during the following week, got off by the school gate and strode across to the staff room.

'Ullo, miss,' they said, great grinning boys and noisy girls. She smiled.

'I fancy you,' she heard one of the kids say.

123

She didn't mind. It was life. Christ knows what Geoffrey would have said, but he lived increasingly in a world of his own, unaware of her needs. Perhaps that was why Godber obsessed him, she decided, these rumours and speculations about his future. In the staff room she read the *Guardian* during the mid-morning break.

'Rock seeks role in changing Europe.'

The headline drew her attention. The garrison was being withdrawn, leaving it without an operational force for the first time since 1713. She showed the piece to Liz Formby, the staff room Tory, and Liz only shook her head.

'Not much bloody use these days, having a base there.'

Perhaps it was all a joke then, these schemes of Godber's that Geoffrey would not or could not reveal. What the hell did it matter to her? She talked about exams instead.

At midday she went for a drink to the King's Head down the road, the favourite watering hole of the more lively members of staff. She didn't normally go, but this time it was a birthday – of 'Mad' Carew, the PE man, who fancied himself in his track-suit, pumping his pecs and delts.

Inside, at the snug corner of the bar, she caught a glimpse of the face. She could have sworn it was him, the man in the dark blue Golf; the same rugby-ball head and frosted coating of hair, the same build, same inquisitive, baleful blue eyes. She felt like asking his business, but he just drank up a short and left with a younger man, a punk by the look of him, his hair skinned off like a rabbit's, leaving a shiny blue pate, a jerkin, bovver-boy boots. Odd company, she thought, watching their backs. Who on earth wants to watch me?

'Drink up,' Carew said, giving her the heave-ho smile.

She realized that she was adrift.

Geoffrey would be late coming home, and she had hours to kill. When she came out of the school at four fifteen the whole of Boundary Road was deserted. She didn't drive the Volvo there in case it got damaged by the kids: there was a convenient bus that dropped her outside the main entrance, and anyway it was more egalitarian. No need to rub it in that

Geoffrey earned more than the Head, and that her earnings from teaching represented her clothing allowance.

She decided to go to the cinema. Branagh's *Henry V* was showing on a rerun at one of the multiplex screens and she wanted to compare it with the Olivier classic. She asked Liz Formby to come, but Liz had seen it, and anyway she had a hubby, as she said.

Claire caught the five fifteen showing.

The cinema was almost empty and she chose a seat at the back, losing herself in the rhetoric. A football supporters' campaign, it seemed to her, the blood and meanness of politics was up there on screen for real, and fully engrossed her.

Next, he was there beside her. The man. The menacing pale eyes, that egg-shaped and frosted head.

'Don't let me worry you,' he whispered. 'Please don't make a scene.'

She went rigid in the dark of the cinema. Menaces. Assault. Threats. She wanted to scream but the sounds froze in her throat into a tiny gurgle. She found he had touched her thigh, a gesture of intimacy neither invited nor deserved.

'Please, Mrs Powers. I'm not going to harm you.'

The voice was a soft Irish brogue, and she knew at once that this was the man who had telephoned Billy Vane. 'I need a word with yourself.'

As the lights went up she studied him more closely, unable to protest. He was not threatening her, close to he seemed harmless, and she nodded dumbly, following him out into the foyer, past the popcorn stall and the sweet bar and the queue for the evening showing. She could have protested, or run, or shouted, but she did nothing.

It was a relief to be outside in the street, to look at him face to face instead of those furtive sightings. Middle-aged, middle-height, grey, with those alarming eyes.

'Would you like a drink?' he said. 'I could buy you a drink?' He smiled, good dentistry on the teeth. 'I don't want to pick you up,' he added.

'I've got to go home,' she mumbled. 'My husband will be waiting.'

'Quite. Quite. It's him that I want to talk about. Privately. With you.'

Her heart began to thump heavily and she was chilled by his tone. It was as if he was pulling her into a net, while they stood by the bus-stop. Her bus-stop. Nobody else waiting. Why hadn't she brought the car? She felt exposed, nervous, but anxious to know what he was after, a bundle of contradictions.

'What do you want? Why are you following me?'

He smiled. 'Lady, I'm not following. I'm merely observing.'

Observing.

He leaned closer. Those eyes, those animal-like eyes, in their way hypnotizing.

'Is he with us or against us?' Landsdowne said.

She froze. 'What are you talking about?'

The eyes opened even wider, pale blue with a line round the iris.

'Mrs Powers, please don't fool about with me. It's Geoffrey I mean. He talks to you, I'm sure. How much does he tell you?'

She searched in vain for a bus. A taxi. Anything to get away. But if it came he could get in with her, with his fatherly air. She wondered if he was mad, but he didn't look mad. He looked intense.

'I don't know what you're talking about.' She tried to turn her back. 'I don't understand. Leave me alone.'

'Oh yes you do. He told Billy Vane. And he told you. Isn't that right, Mrs Powers?'

'Told him what?' Oh Christ. Melrose, she thought, the American. The other man killed in the Park. But Geoffrey had really told her nothing, he played his cards close to his chest. She was a wife kept in ignorance, but could not say so, the admission died on her lips.

'Listen,' the Irishman said, pressing his head closer. She could see the hairs on his nose. 'Is he with us or agin us? Which side is he on? Mis-ter Powers?'

'For God's sake, go away. You're talking in riddles,' she said. 'I want to go home. If you don't go I'll call the police.'

He smiled. His eyes were like two glass pebbles.

'I just want to warn you,' he said. 'You know nothing. You say nothing. To anyone at all. Is that understood? Otherwise people get hurt. Terribly hurt.'

She shook her head, her mouth dry.

'Don't try and pretend.'

She saw a passing bus and feebly tried to wave it down, even though it was not her route. It did not stop.

'Pretend what?' she stuttered.

'There are people who shop their friends,' Landsdowne said sweetly. 'But I hope that Geoffrey isn't one of them. I hope not, Mrs Powers. I've had to warn Mr Vane, and now I'm warning you.' The punk she had seen with him. Melrose's story about the punch-up in Hereford market, she thought, and she was shivering.

'I don't understand.' She was isolated at the bus-stop.

'I think you do, Mrs Powers. I'm British, through and through. We're all helping the right man to lead the nation. Are you with us Mrs Powers, or are you agin us? The way that young Mr Vane wanted to sell out . . . to spread disinformation . . . caused me a lot of concern. And when I get concerned, I act. You with me now?' His smile was the smile on a deathmask.

'No,' Claire said. 'Leave me alone, or I shall scream.'

'I don't think you will,' he said carefully. He looked up and down the road. 'Listen. People may come asking questions. They've been to see Geoffrey already. So-called Security people, from inside the Government.'

'I don't believe it – '

'Oh yes they have. You ask Geoffrey. We know,' he said. 'We watch. You ought to make sure that Mr Powers stays on the right side. And keeps his mouth shut, like you.'

'Please tell me what it's about,' she asked desperately.

'None of your business. Don't worry, Mrs Powers. And stay away from Billy Vane. No harm will come to you as long as you keep mum. Mum's the word, as they say.' He even laughed, a little throaty rattle. 'Because if you don't – '

'Don't what?' she asked feebly.

'If you say anything, anything at all, you or Mr Powers, that damages our prospects . . .'

'What prospects?'

'Don't be stupid now, please. I'm talking about the next Prime Minister.' He took his hands from his pockets and showed clenched fists. 'You keep quiet, Mrs Powers, or someone could be cut up rough.'

She thought she was going to faint and leaned against the bus-stop, holding it in a daze.

A young man was speaking to her.

'Excuse me, are you all right?'

She looked around. The genie had gone, slipping away between the cars.

'You look a bit pale,' he said. He was pushing a kid in a pram.

'Yes, thank you,' she said. 'I'm fine.'

When Geoffrey Powers came back, at half-past nine, she again tried to tell him.

'He threatened me,' she said.

'You should have called the police.'

'There was no one about. He frightened me, making threats like that.'

'A loony,' he said. 'Trying to extort some money. Forget him. Take the car next time.'

'He wasn't mad. He knew something.'

'I've got a lot to do,' he said.

'Look, Geoffrey. Listen. There is something going on, isn't there? Have you had somebody round about Security? Is there some sort of plot with Godber in it? How are you involved?' She felt like crying: he was so closed-up, evasive. He would not tell her anything. She realized he was running scared.

'Claire. It's none of your business.'

'That's what the Irishman said.'

But it had been Billy Vane's, and the American's, and possibly the business of the man who died.

Powers looked at her coolly and suspected she had slept with Vane.

'This isn't what I married you for,' she shrieked at him, banging her fist on the table. 'This secrecy. It's like talking to a brick wall.'

'You tart,' he said.

'What! What did you call me?'

Powers walked out of the room.

That night they slept in separate beds for the first time. She took her pillow and nightdress, and slept in the guest bedroom, crying herself to sleep.

In the morning they did not talk. He faced her with a skull of iron, thin-lipped and terrible, battened down as if he was prepared for a storm which did not come. Instead she felt weak and ashamed, scarcely able to look at him, let alone raise the issue of whether he was in possession of secrets, secrets that could ruin Godber or himself.

'I'll be late again,' he said.

Claire Powers went through the motions, the semblance of partnership. 'There'll be a meal,' she said. 'I will be here.' She would come straight back from school, straight back in the Volvo whether the kids scratched it or not, and whatever Liz Formby might think. She was running scared too.

'I don't know what Godber intends,' he said as he picked up his case. His mouth was a thin line, and she thought he had chickened out.

It was only when he had gone that she remembered the contact number left by the American. She found his card in the drawer of the bureau where she had put it, and turned it over and over. 'Jake H. Melrose, 17A rue de Miromesnil, Paris 8e arrondissement. 369.90.11.' Jake, who had made a bid for her support.

She hovered. If she phoned him it implied a contact, and perhaps they were bugging the lines, whoever they were. But this half-life couldn't go on. She needed to talk to someone.

It was a memory that held her: the way in which he'd turned to wave.

She dialled. There was no reply. Then a click on the answering machine. 'This is Jake Melrose. I'll be away for a while. If you would like me to contact, please leave a message after the dialling tone.' He said it in English and French, passable, nasal French. It made her smile.

She left a message, giving her number, asking him to call her between five and six London time. Long before Geoffrey got back.

22

From then on Claire drove to school. She felt safer in the big Volvo, less prone to attack once the doors had been centre locked. Less vulnerable. But there was no repetition of the warning from the Irishman and no more sign of his car. Once or twice on the way to school she saw a skinhead and wondered if they were still watching, those assistants he used, but she dismissed the idea. No good becoming paranoid, frightened of every stranger, every ring on the bell. Even the milkman. Terrifying.

She tried to telephone the American again. Still no reply, no indication of when he would be back. She wondered about telling the police, but could not face appearing to be silly, a nervous, fluttery woman with nothing but a pick-up story. No good either.

Relations with Geoffrey stayed formal: he seemed to have gone into a shell. She sometimes felt sorry for him as he came home at night, loaded with papers to read, committee notes awaiting dictation, which he would carry through to the dining-room table.

She brought him a cup of coffee and wished he would touch her.

'Why don't you pack it in? Have a break. Let's go out on the town?'

He did not even look up, his face drained a chalky white as if he had some sort of virus. He shook his head. She knew it was more than the work. It was not just the consequences of the build-up of meetings, it was something eating his mind.

Billy Vane had compromised her, and compromised Geoffrey's faith in her, and no way was Geoffrey going to help her. Or help himself.

She watched him becoming sick. Mentally sick. And stood helplessly by.

She had days when she was alone in the house, the days when she did not teach, and now she dreaded them. Every time the telephone rang, or somebody came to the door with the post or the milk, she felt her nerves wobbling. But the Irishman did not come back, even though she found herself watching the movements outside her front gate from behind the bedroom curtains.

In despair she rang Billy Vane, in spite of the warnings. Billy had not been around, Billy had not pursued her since that business with the Yank in Hereford, but perhaps he would tell her something. She couldn't believe Billy was frightened. She knew he had an office in Hereford, and in the end she tried it.

'Export Recruitment Services,' a girl's voice said, one of his various bimbos. She told Claire that Billy was abroad, in Tanzania. Anyway, how could she trust Billy after what the American had told her. Melrose. Jake Melrose. He had seemed honest enough, but why should she trust him either? She had put out a call for help to his number in Paris because of something in his face, yet that in itself seemed crazy. Cancel it. Stop the message that she had left. Her hand hovered on the telephone . . . and made no move.

She had one more try with Geoffrey, on the following Saturday. He'd been in Whitehall all morning, and she hoped he had finished work when he came home at two o'clock and said that he'd had some lunch.

'Oh. Where, darling?'

She feared he would snap her head off, and in a desperate attempt to mend bridges she was prepared to try anything, but he said quietly, 'With Peter Brocklehurst.'

That over-smooth political agent with the bow tie and the slick PR patter. She'd met him first at a cocktail party and

131

disliked him on sight. There was something about his sleek head and already paunchy charm that turned her off.

'Why don't you go and change now?' she said. He had on his customary suit of burnt ash grey. 'Slip into something casual.'

He glanced at her as if she was a camel. She wanted to say I'm sorry. Sorry. Sorry. Darling, let's have one more try to make this marriage work. But the words would not come. She felt that they had both deserved it: what they had got.

He sat in the Parker-Knoll chair with his feet up, reading the papers.

'I think I'll bath,' she said. 'Why not come and talk to me there?' An invitation, a hint of past glories when they had bathed together at the start of the marriage.

'No,' he said.

She turned, went over to him and sat on the edge of the chintz settee.

'Look, Geoffrey. I know I made a mistake. I was stupid . . . going off for that weekend with Billy Vane.'

'I know.'

'But I didn't sleep with him. I swear to you.'

Powers sat still and said nothing. He did not even look at her. He sat there staring at some official report as if it was about to fly away. In the end he got up, flinging the papers from him. 'Go away. Go to hell. I've got an engagement.'

He left her standing there.

After a few minutes he took the Volvo keys and drove away without telling her where. She saw the stare in his eyes, almost as if he was sleepwalking.

'Be careful,' she said. 'Geoffrey, please . . .'

But he ignored her and went off on his own.

In the end she phoned Paris again, but there was still the same message on the answerphone.

23

Powers drove back into Saturday afternoon London: heavy traffic, huge coaches from Bremen and Rome full of tourists, tipping them out in Millbank and all the way round Smith Square as he tried to nose through in the Volvo. Horseferry Road blocked: he had to go through the side streets and park half a mile from his rendezvous in the flat at the south side of Vincent Square. By the time that he had walked there his guts were wound up like elastic.

Number 4, Everton Mansions. A cricket match on the sports ground belonging to Westminster School; small boys enjoying themselves, shouting and clapping. How he disliked small boys.

The door opened almost at once. Peter Brocklehurst was smiling at him.

'So glad you decided to come, Geoffrey. We were just about to set off.' He was waiting with another man, middle-aged, middle height, red face set off by grey hair, round head bald at the crown. 'This is Colin Landsdowne,' Brocklehurst said. 'You may recall meeting in Belfast.'

'Yes,' Powers said. 'And I believe you have talked to my wife.'

The Irishman grinned. 'Don't worry. All for the best.' Landsdowne was in command, and Powers noted an air of authority, as if he had just made his fortune. He was tailored discreetly in blue, whereas Brocklehurst wore the street clothes of the up-and-coming entrepreneur: broad chalk double-breasted with a Jermyn Street shirt. Powers felt shabby beside them. Both of them exuded success and Powers felt the spell they cast.

'That's right. I had a word with your wife a few days ago,' Landsdowne added. 'Thought it advisable to ask for her understanding. We can't afford things to go wrong.' He handed across a whisky and soda in a good piece of cut glass. Powers looked round the room: expensive, well furnished in leather, with greenery in the window and a thick shaggy carpet. A bachelor's pad, in clubman decor.

'I'm sure you appreciate that we can't take any risks,' Brocklehurst said. Both men observed Powers closely. 'The politics and timing are tricky.'

'Certainly no disrespect intended to your wife,' the Irishman muttered.

If they had threatened his wife, she damned well deserved it, he thought. She had it coming. No wonder she had tried to suck up to him over the last few days. Nevertheless he did not want her harmed, or problems with his career. He hadn't crept up this far inside a competitive system to throw it all away.

'Okay.' Brocklehurst downed his whisky, and the Ulsterman smiled, a smile with a knife behind it. 'Let's go.'

On the way down the stairs Brocklehurst said, 'Glad you are with us, Geoff. You realize the rewards are enormous. Once Freddie is in power . . .' He looked behind him and grinned into Landsdowne's face. 'We keep our word you know. With those for . . . and those against us.'

Powers felt a tremor pass through him.

They piled into a BMW and fought their way across London, the traffic streaming round Hyde Park Corner, the West End, South Audley Street, Claridge's.

The hotel was an oasis after the bustle of the city, and Landsdowne showed a card at the desk with a Spanish name printed on it.

They purred up in a gilded lift to a suite on the fifth floor. Powers found himself impressed by the air of quiet money: flunkies and flowers in alcoves, a hushed air of wealth and excess.

'The Countess is waiting.'

Landsdowne knocked and ushered them in.

She was standing with her back to the windows in a room twice the size of Powers's best room in the Wimbledon house:

a forty-year-old, beautiful woman, dark-haired, dark-eyed and slim. She smiled at them.

'Mr Landsdowne, of course, I know. Come, and please sit down,' she said in clear accented English.

They were introduced in turn to the Countess of the Asturias. Brocklehurst had told Powers a little about her, but not what to expect. He realized that somehow Landsdowne was already on close terms with her, as if numerous trips to Madrid were all part of his trade. She had a pale oval face, framed by short, razor-cut hair which had the gleaming blue-blackness of a young crow's wing, and eyes as deep and lustrous as new berries, a dark mahogany brown; mischievous, scheming eyes, offset by a soft mouth. A slim and devastating woman in a pale green silky dress.

A bodyguard sat in the corner, a young man without an expression. Otherwise they were alone.

'Please,' she said. 'You will have refreshment?'

A form of command. It came almost at once, before they had even completed the introductory small-talk. Whisky and soda for the others, and tea for Powers. He began to feel the odd one out.

The Countess sat and watched them across a small coffee table. She had the most exquisite arms.

'Now. We are all friends?'

'That's very true,' Landsdowne murmured. 'Very true.'

'And you wish to talk to me . . . about a proposition?'

'In strict secrecy,' he added.

'Of course.' She inclined her neck.

'Countess,' Landsdowne said, 'I've come to offer you a bargain.'

Some bargain, Powers thought.

'A proposition involving a certain political gentleman, who shall be nameless in future references. But as you see we have here his Private Secretary, Mr Powers. You understand?'

'Yes.' She stroked her head and smiled at them in turn.

'And our friend needs his side of it quickly.'

The Countess of the Asturias nodded but made no comment.

'Countess,' Landsdowne began. 'We know your standing within the Falange.'

'The Falange is dead,' she said. 'It died with Franco.'

Landsdowne shook his head and complicity passed between them. The big room seemed hot and stuffy and Powers began to perspire, but Landsdowne was fully at ease.

'I think not, Countess, while you are alive. The daughter of Franco's key general, Vidal Villalba, the Count of the Asturias, the man who said Juan Carlos was soft. A lady who inherits a blood-line going back to José Antonio Primo de Rivera, and before him to his father.'

She looked at the Ulsterman and accepted the flattery. 'You have researched my history.'

Landsdowne was good at this, Powers thought. He wondered what Irish shenanigans had given him so much opportunity to ingratiate himself with her and practise his gift of the gab on Godber's behalf.

'I know, Countess, that you saw your father blown up by separatists in Madrid, when you were only a teenager. I know, Madame, that the Army has seen in you a symbol of the old authority, destroyed by the Socialists.'

The Countess smiled again.

'What do you really want from me, gentlemen?' There was a steel in her voice and the small frame seemed to stiffen.

'An agreement, Countess,' Landsdowne whispered, bending towards her. 'A private political agreement . . . over Gibraltar.'

The word hung between them like an unexploded bomb.

'Gibraltar is ours,' she said, 'a part of Spain.'

Powers sensed the frisson of excitement running through each of them.

'Accepted in principle, but not in practice,' Landsdowne said reassuringly.

A look almost of disbelief came into her face.

'So?'

'So. I want to offer you a new possibility. A political deal.'

'Go on,' she whispered, her face tense with emotion.

136

'British troops have now been withdrawn. You know that we now have no plans to maintain a garrison there.'

'I am aware.'

'But there is still a sensitivity. Underlying sensitivity, about the Rock. The population has declared for Britain.'

The Countess's lip curled. 'An ethnic mix,' she said. 'Moroccans, Genoese, Maltese, Portuguese, Jews. I do not count them as Spaniards. If they wish they can go elsewhere.'

'Precisely. I think we see eye to eye.'

She hesitated. 'What are you asking of me?'

'Cooperation,' he said, 'by your friends in the Army and the Air Force, the group that still owes its allegiance to Franco – and to you. The Falangist core. We want them to threaten Gibraltar.'

'Threaten?' The Countess sat very still.

'Air swoops over the Rock. Mobilization of one of the para battalions. No bloodshed, you understand. Mainly threats and sabre rattling. Maybe a few careful bombs, where they will do no harm. A plan can be worked out.'

'And then?' she asked coolly.

'And then the UK will respond. The British Rapid Deployment Force will mount a combined ops on the Rock. A show of strength. And Freddie Godber will be up there with them. You follow me?'

'A photo opportunity,' Brocklehurst said. He seemed unable to think in other than publicity terms.

She seemed to stare through the Irishman, whose ruddy face was beaming at her.

'And what exactly is your bargain?'

'Just this,' Landsdowne said. 'If you do what we propose, if the right groups in the Army and the Air Force, the key people in Madrid, can be mobilized to go that far and no further, so that they seem to suffer – shall we say – a rebuff, I guarantee, within three years of our friend being in power, Gibraltar will be negotiable.'

Jesus Christ, Powers thought. He saw Brocklehurst's little piggy eyes looking excited as if he had just brought off some

137

big advertising coup. And the flush mount in the Countess's cheeks.

'How?' she said. 'What guarantees can you give?'

'Two guarantees,' Landsdowne replied glibly. 'Nothing in writing of course. The first is our own assurance, our own word. You must know the score, Countess. Gibraltar is expendable. Hong Kong is going already.'

Powers felt mounting elation mixed with a certain panic deep inside. I've got him, I've got him, he thought. Godber would never be able to live with this disclosure. Selling out Gibraltar. And Brocklehurst sitting there smiling.

But the Countess was cautious. 'I think you have no more intention of handing back Gibraltar than handing over the Falklands.'

'Ah. The Falklands are more difficult. We fought and died there. We want no repetition with Spain. Public opinion counts. But Gibraltar – ' Landsdowne waved his hands – 'in three years time, who cares?'

The Countess moved to place her fingers on the onyx coffee table. Honed, clear-red nails.

'And the second guarantee?'

Landsdowne replied in that soft Irish whisper, 'I have no doubt, Countess, that the second will be the recording that you have made of this conversation with the three of us. You have that thing with our promises on it – ' and he pointed to the bodyguard in the corner with the small machine under his chair.

Powers's stomach seemed to be split by pain, sharp, shooting, ulcerated pain. He had been caught. They'd got him pinned down on a tape. Landsdowne may have conned the Spaniards, but the mere existence of such a tape could ruin Powers. Bastards. Bastards. Bastards, all of them, but no one seemed to notice. Brocklehurst and Landsdowne were pure adventurers. If they failed they would disappear. If Freddie failed he might even brush it off: a dirty tricks campaign by Landsdowne, its authenticity denied. They could not guarantee Gibraltar in three years time or ever. But he was tied hand and foot: his career hung on whether that recording ever got near Henry Burton and the Official Secrets Act boys such as Didsbury.

And the Countess of the Asturias merely held out her hand. 'Mr Landsdowne. Mr Brock-le-hurst. Mr Powers.' She smiled. 'I am tempted . . . Very tempted.'

They were slapping and congratulating each other, the three of them, Powers putting a brave face on it as the meeting broke up. The Countess called for more drinks and this time he felt he needed one to quell the stabs in his stomach and in his mind.

He drank a double whisky to kill the agony of indecision.

They tumbled down in the lift in high excitement.

'Whew!' Brocklehurst said like a schoolboy, grinning at them. 'What a stunner.' The important thing to the political agent was that he had made a sale.

'She's got a reputation, I believe,' Landsdowne muttered, loosening his tie as if he'd just finished an interview.

Powers felt cold as Brocklehurst slapped him on the back with ad-man bonhomie.

'Well. What do you think, Geoff? One of us now, eh sunshine?'

He decided that he'd been driven to it by the state of his marriage, that rootless unreal cohabiting for which he blamed her – Claire, the bitch – and by his own ambition. To succeed he now had to be part of this right-wing wheeler-dealing in the clubs and corridors of power. Whether he liked it or not, he had been drawn in and was now part of the bid. He said, 'It's got to be kept very quiet.'

'Don't you worry, Geoff. We'll see to that.'

'No problem,' Landsdowne added. Life to him was like that. 'I shall be going to Madrid. Make sure she keeps her word. I speak a pretty good Spanish.'

They burst out into the street, dazzled by the afternoon sunshine and by what they had done, but Landsdowne was aware of the doubts in Geoffrey Powers's eyes. As they climbed into the BMW, he said, 'I'll sit behind with you, Geoffrey.'

They moved off into Davies Street and down past the US

Embassy, where if they'd only known, Leibermann was still working on the death of Brendan Wallace, down towards Piccadilly.

'Don't worry, Geoff,' he said again. 'There'll be plenty of pickings for you, once this thing's done. Principal Private Secretary at Number 10 for a start.'

And then he'd be tied for ever, an endless grind, on his way up to the top. Powers both loved and hated the very prospect, but Landsdowne misread his hesitation. 'Show him,' he said to Brocklehurst.

The political agent opened his black leather case and took out the second tape, which Powers saw to his horror had been picking up through a mike disguised as a central name tag.

'Just in case there's any misunderstandings,' Brocklehurst grinned.

Powers went pale. 'What are you going to do with that?'

'I'll keep it in my little safe, in Worcester,' Brocklehurst said. 'Wouldn't want those security bastards knowing about it. That bloke Didsbury, for instance. Or friend Frewin.'

The knives were back in Powers's belly.

When he came home he was in a furious temper. Claire had bathed and changed, trying to calm her own nerves, and now she stood before him, in heels and the little flame dress that did so much for her figure, but he ignored her. He stalked right through to the lounge and poured himself another drink. She saw that he was breaking his habits, turning into a drinker through some internal crisis which could only be her fault, and she began to cry.

'Oh go to hell,' he said.

He would not say where he had been, or what he had done, and in a burst of confusion she wondered if he'd found a woman, or had some pro in the West End. But looking at his drawn features and haggard face she was forced to dismiss it. Some canker was destroying him.

At eight o'clock he went to bed. She heard him in his room, their room, and knocked on the door.

'Geoffrey, darling. Are you all right?'

She heard him moving about there.

'Yes. Go away,' he shouted. 'Get away from me.'

She went downstairs, tried to watch television, tried to savour a gin and tonic, but none of it drove out her fears. There was a crisis on and she was part of it, although she did not know what it was. She kicked off her shoes to curl up in misery on the settee and noticed his jacket lying there, crumpled, where he had thrown it. She retrieved it to find a hanger and saw in his breast pocket the card he had retained, standing at Claridge's reception, when Landsdowne had passed it to him as a kind of souvenir.

'Julia Maria Robles Villalba, Condesa de Asturias.'

24

'Jake!' she said. 'Jake Melrose. Thank God.' Claire found her hand was shaking as she caught the American voice.

It was five o'clock when he came through after a week's absence, timing the call carefully to pick her up when she returned from the classroom and well before Geoffrey appeared.

'I got your message,' he said calmly, pleased that she'd come to him and called him Jake. 'I've been away.'

'Jake. Where have you been? Why didn't you say?' A sense of relief swept through her, as she heard him respond.

'Honey, I didn't know you called until I got back to Paris. I got other work, Claire. I been in Poland.'

'Poland?'

'Right. A little job on there. I kept putting it off. It's over now.' Poland had an austerity which in a way appealed after the consumer excesses of the West. It brought out the puritan in him, and the empty countryside reminded him of Wisconsin, long before the Marine Corps, and combat and killing and then the CIA with its layers of duplicity. Warsaw, Gdansk, Cracow. Two days in each was sufficient, time enough to

141

glimpse the down-at-heel shops and the desperate flea markets on street pitches, the queues for some over-priced necessity. He came back to Paris tired, more tired than he expected after the bumpy LOT flights and the poorly surfaced roads. A string of messages, including a call from Leibermann asking if there was any news, and the call from Claire Powers. No word from Marie-Louise.

Claire's voice was low and confused.

'It's just that . . . I don't know . . . Are you coming back to London?'

'London. I wasn't planning, honey – '

'I think we should talk,' she mumbled. 'I think so. I'm not sure.'

'Not sure?'

'No. I need to talk,' she said. 'About the thing you mentioned. I'm scared, Jake.' She had to sit on a chair.

It was her fear that triggered him.

'Okay,' he said. Nothing over the telephone. 'Where do I pick you up?'

She hesitated as if she thought someone was listening.

'Give me a call,' she said, 'as soon as you arrive.'

When he had rung off she felt pulped. All she had to go on was the address card and Geoffrey's half-admissions, and the threat from the Irishman. But between them they confirmed the story which had interested Billy Vane. Well, she could let them all stew but she was alarmed by Geoffrey, and she also had her own politics. She saw the kids in school, starved of new books and equipment and the two empty classrooms where water had come through the roof; she saw the runaways and derelicts in the cardboard city at the Waterloo underpass; and the needs in the old people's home she visited now and again. Now there was some kind of plot to keep Godber's people in power. New privilege and fast money. She could not get through to Geoffrey with the old radical talk, he wasn't changing society as he once said, he was lying down with it, and some of its material values had rubbed off on his shoulders and showed themselves in his face. It frightened her.

Melrose touched down at Heathrow and checked into a small hotel, the Malvern, off the Cromwell Road. He never used the same one twice, as the field rule said, but it meant that he lived his life out of a series of suitcases in a succession of rooms. Paris was a lucky break. Home was a locked-up apartment in Reston, Virginia, bought five years ago when he was stationed in Washington, and rarely used since. Home was where the suitcase was, he thought grimly, surveying the scuffed room at sixty-five pounds a night: single bed against the wall, a box with a shower cabinet and separate toilet carved off from some grand bedroom of a Victorian town house. Brown carpet, plastic settee pretending it was leather, TV, no remote control, room service up to midnight, please don't flush ST's down the pan. A Cypriot-run boarding house.

He reported first to Leibermann, taking a cab to the Embassy in Grosvenor Square: Harry Leibermann still sweating it out as acting Head of Mission, sitting behind Wallace's desk. He'd changed the furniture round; now had it arranged in a kind of V, with the screen table at the side, so that when Melrose walked in Harry seemed to be at the prow of a ship. He pumped Melrose's flesh and sat down in his shirt sleeves, a puffy forty-five-year-old sweating on an in-post promotion. The last time that they had met he'd been dismissing the conspiracy theory.

'You got my call, Jake?'

'Sure. Sure. I been in Poland.'

Melrose gave him state-of-the-art about the security there on US Government property and Leibermann nodded wisely, searching for some piece of paper, while Melrose thought, 'You bum. Get off your theoretical backside, and think about why Wallace was killed. And how it was arranged.'

Leibermann found his reference. It was a newspaper clipping, an article in the *New Statesman*, savaging Freddie Godber, 'The man who will stop at nothing.' Naked ambition, he read, was the spur to his political career, but he had to move fast if he was going to dissociate himself from the end of the Government. He was looking for a cause. Likely to play risky games.

Leibermann had been asked to comment and he waved the piece at Melrose.

'What d'ya make of that, Jake?'

Jake said, 'That's what Brendan thought.'

'Brendan's dead, for Christ's sakes. We know that. Some fuckin' A-rab. Nothing to do with this.'

'You sure?'

'Yeah. We're sure. The British cops are sure. And Special Branch. The bastard Shi'ites are sure. They issued a press release, Beirut: "The traitor gets his reward".' He offered another cutting, from the file. In Arabic, with a typed translation.

'Okay. So what's the hassle?'

'The hassle, Jake, is this – ' he scratched his pork belly through the buttons on his shirt – 'we got a lead from Madrid that trouble's brewing over Gibraltar. We got to stop it, Jake.'

'Stop what, Harry?'

Christ, the man was obtuse, sitting there unsmiling in Harry's interview chair like some hick hill farmer who just rode into town, asking the price of feed.

'Listen, Jake. Somebody oughta tell the Fa-langists not to start being fuckin' difficult. Know who's been over in London, seeing some guy who's up-to-the-eyeballs trouble? Little Miss Franco, the Countess of the Asturias. Know who she is, Jake?'

'Nope.'

Leibermann shook his head. If it weren't for Wallace, he seemed to imply, I'd tell you to get back in your saddle and ride off into the sunset.

'Okay. Don't matter.' He sighed. 'Listen to this, Jake . . .' He was reading from the Madrid report. 'The Countess is a young and forceful beauty infused by passion. Her speeches incite those factions in the military which still feel they owe allegiance to the former dictator. In a country where the Virgin has a special place in religion the concept of a dedicated and beautiful young woman who calls for a return to the old authoritarian values has a strong appeal in some quarters . . .'

'Huh,' Melrose said. 'You mean she's dangerous?'

144

Leibermann grinned like a schoolboy. 'Number One with the Army. The Franco Generals.'

'Who's the guy been talking to her?' Melrose said.

'Ulster Protestant hit-man called Landsdowne. The Brits been watching him visit her hotel.'

The Irishman, Melrose thought. Billy Vane's Irish bastard. 'On the line, Harry. What you want me to do?'

'Well. That rumour Brendan Wallace was on to. You keep tracking it, Jake.'

Melrose nodded. 'Okay with me. Expenses paid?'

'On the firm, Jake. You got a month.'

25

Melrose called Claire from the hotel, sitting on the side of the bed, at the same time next day, and knew she'd been waiting for him. Suddenly it was desperately important that he should see her, and not just because of Harry Leibermann.

'Oh, Jake. Where are you? I must talk to you.' She seemed to respond in kind, a mutual anxiety conveyed over the phone.

He told her the place: the Malvern, near Cromwell Road.

'I'll find it. I'll be there in half an hour.' She sounded both relieved and scared.

'Honey. Listen. No need to come here. Let's meet someplace else,' he said. But Claire said 'No'. She wanted to see him in private.

She was waiting in the lobby when he went down, a slim girl dressed in a caramel sweater and grey slacks, her hair blown by the wind. He thought she was looking older and felt his heart go fast forward. Then his pleasure stalled at the anxiety written on her face. He took her by the arms for a moment: someone else's wife. But he need not have worried.

She glanced around nervously, clinging to him.

'I think I've been followed.'

Melrose tightened his grip, remembering Leibermann's briefing. 'Is it some Irish guy?'

Claire felt reassured simply by having him there.

'No. I mean by a skinhead.'

Hereford, here we go, he thought.

He took her up the staircase, a carpet spotted with grease, and into the dark little bedroom.

'Don't switch the light on.'

'Okay.'

He sat on the plastic settee and gave her the rather grand chair, a wing-back that would have been at home in Windsor Castle.

'Jake, listen to me . . . I'm scared,' she began. 'I think there is some kind of plot organized by Freddie Godber, involving a threat to Gibraltar. Geoffrey has been drawn in, and now I'm being threatened.'

'What kind of threat?' he asked calmly.

She shook her head. 'I'm not sure.' She told him everything she knew, from Billy Vane's half hints to Geoffrey's refusal to talk and the warning from the Irishman. Then she produced the calling card from the Condesa following the Saturday visit that had so upset Powers.

Melrose at last saw the pieces coming together, but he was cautious, so cautious she feared he was disengaging. And in a way he was, telling himself it was crazy to become involved.

'Why doesn't Geoffrey report it all to his Security people? He could just do that, right?'

'Geoffrey is going to pieces. He's implicated and wants to keep his hands clean. He doesn't know how to play it.'

'Well, honey, you could tell your Security guys. See what they say.' In his heart he wanted to say, 'Dump that Geoffrey guy before he hits the skids.'

She hesitated, breathing heavily. 'I can't do that to him.'

But she had trusted Jake. Melrose put his hand on her arm and said quietly, 'What you want me to do about it?'

'I don't know,' she whispered. Then, 'Geoffrey needs help. He's in trouble.'

'I'm just a freelance, honey: It's not my patch.' Not tangling with other men's wives.

Her big eyes were earnest like a child's. 'You said that Brendan Wallace was a friend.'

'Kind of . . .'

'Well, the Irishman who threatened me said that people could get hurt.'

'That don't prove he killed Wallace.' But now he knew from Leibermann that the Irishman was called Landsdowne, and Landsdowne was in deep, with connections to the Falange, and the Northern Ireland Loyalists.

Melrose limbered to his feet, hands in his pockets, and crossed to the window. She watched his back.

'Where's this guy who was following?'

She peered cautiously through the net curtains and saw him parked almost opposite, in a souped-up Mini Cooper.

'That one. The man in the blue Mini.'

All he could see was an outline, a shaved head reading a paper.

'Can't you do something to stop them? Can't you warn people in Spain?' she asked desperately.

'Okay. Don't worry.' He put his arm around her, an automatic, almost fatherly gesture to smooth her nerves, and she was drawn in towards him. 'The trouble is, kiddo, I don't even speak Spanish.'

'But you will help? You will?' she pleaded.

He grinned at her. 'Sure. Okay.'

She stared into his face, her eyes moist with tears.

'But Jake, for God's sake be careful.'

'Sure, honey, sure.'

'Take Billy with you,' she whispered. 'He knows his way around.'

He gave her a long glance.

'Would he go?' The last twice that he and Vane had met it hadn't exactly been a close working relationship. The last time that they had talked, when the Englishman had appeared in Bayswater, something had given Vane cold feet. Now she was asking Jake to trust him, and that was not something he found easy. The guy might have his merits but Melrose didn't fancy going to Madrid with some fancy little womanizer, especially one interested in Claire.

But Claire said, 'Yes.' Vane was the one with the story, and Vane was a Brit. And Billy Vane was close to telling him at the start of all this.

Melrose did not move his arm, and she made no effort to disengage.

'Okay, I'll look him up again,' Melrose said reluctantly.

'He's in Tanzania,' she said. 'I phoned his office.'

And Melrose laughed, remembering the call sign that Brendan Wallace had given him at the same beginning. 'Uncle William.'

'They wouldn't let Billy in there unless he blacked his face and took a shoe-shine kit. No, that little guy's still around; just lying low. Landsdowne has warned him off.'

'Please keep Geoffrey out of trouble . . .'

She felt happier but also sad, aware of the mess she was making of what was still a marriage. The tears were close to the surface.

'Hey, come on, honey,' he said. 'Sit down, and I'll fix you a drink.'

He found a mini-gin in the room fridge, and a can of orange juice, and mini-bourbon but no ice. He parked Claire on the settee and sat on the bed opposite.

'Cheers!'

'Cheers,' she sniffled, and suddenly she cried.

'Oh, Jake. Jake, what have I done?'

He swallowed the slug of rye and smiled across the room towards her.

'Nothing. Nothing, honey. You just done the right thing.'

She realized she didn't really know what his position was, or whether he would tell the British, via the CIA. Didn't even know how much time Melrose had.

'A month. I got a month. On expenses,' he grinned.

'Then you go home?' she asked. 'To Paris?'

Home. He shook his head. Not sure about home. It was hardly the locked-up apartment in a condominium in Virginia.

Some day he would have to face it, and what then? But not yet. He put the question aside and found she was standing up, she was walking towards him, her eyes wide, as if waking from a dream or nightmare, unblinking, magnified, so close to him now he could smell the faint drift of perfume.

'Claire,' he said. 'It's going to be fine.'

And then her arms were round his neck and he was holding her.

'We-ell.' He kept her at arm's length and smiled into her face. Her cheeks were streaked with tears.

'I guess we got a deal. Me and Billy.'

'Be careful,' she cried.

He nodded. 'You said it. You look after Geoffrey, lady.' One girl between two men was no way to start a relationship. 'Leave Billy Vane to me.'

'What will you do?' she whispered.

He touched her face gently, then pulled away.

'If he says we go, we go.'

'If not?'

He smiled. 'I reckon I'll go anyways.' He was slipping on a lightweight jacket, a dark navy-style coat, and stood looking out the window as if making up his mind. In his hand was a heavy metal ashtray.

She glanced at him anxiously.

'Jake? Jake?'

'Wait here,' he said.

She saw Melrose walk out of the hotel and cross the road. The guy in the Mini saw him coming out but shifted gear too late. She saw the skinhead's arm lock the door on the offside and start the engine, a puff of smoke from the exhaust. She saw Melrose move so fast he might have got up from the blocks, saw him standing beside the car, saw rather than heard the shatter of the offside glass as he smashed it with the ashtray.

Melrose was inside the car, sitting in the passenger seat, and the other guy staring at him, pop-eyed as Jake squeezed him.

'Ow-Jesus.'

The skinhead's hands left the wheel and scrambled at his groin. Just to make sure, Melrose encircled his neck. He was tough, this young guy, and strong, but not that tough when his scrotum was pulped. Leather jacket, jeans, late twenties, his head not quite shaved, just stubbly, like iron filings over a boulder.

'I think we've met before.'

The skinhead gurgled a curse. Melrose tightened his grip as the other man flailed helplessly.

Somebody was shouting, banging on the roof of the car. Broken glass on the road.

'Hey – what's going on?'

'Get stuffed,' Melrose said. Then to the guy, 'Let's go.'

Three blocks further on, the Mini pulled up and stopped. The other guy still seemed shaken. Melrose grinned.

'Tingling a bit?'

'You bastard.'

'Okay. Cut out the compliments. Tell me what you're doing following the lady?'

'It's none of your fuckin' – Ow! Jesus!'

'That's better,' Melrose whispered alongside his ear. 'Now then. Who's paying you?'

'Don't know.'

'Oh yes you do. Who recruited you?'

'An Irishman,' the man groaned. 'A fucking Irish bastard.'

'Come on. You don't know the name, huh? You really don't?' The hand on his neck tightened.

'N . . . no.'

'Well, I'll do a deal. You tell me what he wanted you for, and I'll let you off names.'

'This Irish guy. We done jobs for him before. In Northern Ireland.'

'Uh huh. What sort of jobs?'

'Undercover stuff. Dirty jobs an' that.'

'Hence the gear?'

The skinhead swore.

'Okay. So you did some dirty jobs for this Irish guy with

no name. What'd he want from you next: beat up some Yank in Hereford, right?'

And the man shook his head.

'No. Aw, Jesus, my balls. Honest. We just done what we was told.'

'Like knifing a guy in the Park?'

'What? We ain't done no one in.'

Melrose relaxed his grip, now that they were really friends. 'Go on.'

'We was just told to rough up this bloke who was meeting Vane.'

'And then?' The arm was still round his neck; Melrose gave him a final windpipe squeeze that left him coughing.

'Give over, squire. Then I had to come to London and stake out this guy in Wimbledon, and his missus. Hang around, see what they're up to.'

'Still with this Irish guy?'

'Right.'

'I'd like to meet him,' Melrose said. 'How does he pay you?'

'Notes through the post.'

Undercover in London. Powers was tied to Godber and had started the leak. One more link in the chain. Shit, Melrose thought.

'Okay. Well, you take an order from me. You leave the girl alone. No more snooping, feller. On me, or her. You got that, man? Because if I find you around again – ' his voice took on new menace – 'next time I won't squash your nuts. Next time I'll break your neck.'

The skinhead cursed him.

'Good. Now drive me back to the lady in the hotel, and then you can go clean up the car.'

Claire saw the Mini return and the Yank climb out. Unhurried and unharmed. The Mini shot off like a rocket.

In the frowsy bedroom she clung to him with relief.

'Jake. Jake. Don't take risks like that. Don't. Don't frighten me.'

'Honey, you're kidding.'

151

Melrose didn't count the risks. He said. 'Don't you worry, Claire. Just you get back home. That jerk won't come around again. Leave Spain to me.'

26

'For Christ's sake, don't keep coming back to me,' Leibermann said when Melrose told him as much as he knew from Claire. 'Get some evidence; or tell the Brits.'

'Don't you want to find who got Brendan?'

'Brendan, for Christ's sakes, ain't nothing to do with this. The bastards from Beirut got him. I keep telling you, Jake. Your business ain't murder. It's putting a spoke in the wheel of a guy who may be in league with a load of maniacs in Spain. You got that, Jake?'

'Yeah. I read you, Harry.'

'Okay. Well, get on with it, man. Go ahead, tell the Brits what you know.'

So Melrose was hanging around, waiting for an appointment with the contact Leibermann suggested: somebody called Lionel Frewin. Commodore Frewin, RNR, who seemed an over-busy man and lived, when he was around, in an office off Victoria Street. When Melrose finally got through Frewin offered a slot in the diary two days later.

It turned out to be a wet morning and the office was high up the stairs in a Victorian Building with a security grille.

Melrose checked in with a secretary who looked competent enough to body search.

'The Commodore will be with you shortly.'

He was left kicking his heels in an outer office like a dentist's waiting room. He watched the girl go in. He watched two young men come out carrying thin buff folders. They glanced at him suspiciously. He had the distinct impression that he wasn't being given priority.

'Do come in,' the girl said, re-emerging.

Frewin rose to shake hands: a white-haired man with a wisp of white moustache, a superannuated Captain Kettle, in a dark single-breasted suit. He sat at a large wooden desk in a room that was almost bare, apart from six filing cabinets and a small vase of freesias on a side table. The one window looked down to a well.

Frewin smiled politely.

'You've come with a good set of credentials from our friends in Grosvenor Square,' he muttered, staring at Harry Leibermann's letter as if Melrose was seeking a job. Once again Jake found these formalities difficult to understand.

'Yeah. I came because Harry told me you were interested in this story about trouble brewing in Gibraltar.'

'Trouble, Mr Melrose?' Frewin said. 'Suppose you put your cards on the table.'

Jake felt he might have been consulting him about an ingrowing toenail, but he held his peace.

'The story I got is this,' he said. 'One of your politicians is running for the top job. Right? Freddie Godber, your Secretary of State for Defence. It ain't exactly pole position for an ambitious politico who wants to be next in Downing Street, so he has to work up a lather. Get himself to be man of the moment. So it's Happy Hour for the plotters, and some Irish Prod called Landsdowne, one of their dirty tricks brigade, has sold our friend a scheme involving the Spanish Falangists in some kind of threat to the Rock. You with me, Commodore?'

Frewin put his fingers together and stared at the American.

'Go on,' he said.

'We . . . ell. I guess our boy Landsdowne is known to you.'

Frewin smiled. 'Very well known.'

'Okay. So this guy Landsdowne has sold our man Godber some kind of proposition. What exactly I don't know, and anyways that's for you guys. But it's a proposition that got to the ears of a jerk called Billy Vane, by way of Godber's private secretary, Powers. Vane wants to earn some kudos and some cash, and offers it to the CIA. My old buddy Brendan Wallace happens to be Head of Mission and calls me over. Then wham-bang, you know the rest. Brendan gets a knife in the back and the Arabs claim responsibility.'

Frewin nodded, his sparse white hair glinting in the artificial light. It had begun to rain heavily and not for the first time in an English summer Melrose felt cold.

'Do you have any evidence?' he asked.

Melrose thought Christ, that's for you, but he said, 'I been talking to the wife of Powers. She's real scared. Reckons that her man's implicated and doesn't know how to pull out. Shit-scared for his career, clinging on to Godber's tails. And now I got evidence that this guy Landsdowne has got wind of a leak and is sealing it up. He's warned off Billy Vane; he tried to warn me off; and he's been marking Powers. So Lands-downe's a dangerous guy and he could have done in Wallace.'

Frewin became agitated and started looking at his watch.

'It's an interesting theory. But it doesn't quite fit with the facts. Brendan Wallace was most definitely murdered by an Arab hit-man. He was seen running away, together with a companion. Very much the Arab cast of feature, all the witnesses agree. We even have the note from the Said Hamid group, claiming responsibility. And, as you know, Wallace was a long time in Beirut. So that part must be discounted. Scotland Yard are quite clear about that, and so are your people.'

He made it sound as if Leibermann and Pallett and the boys were some kind of supporting cast.

'Okay,' Melrose said. 'Have it your way. But that don't account for Billy Vane's story, and the guy shadowing Claire Powers.'

Commodore Frewin rose. He had the irritating habit of addressing an unseen audience over Melrose's shoulder, just outside on the window ledge.

'I'm very grateful to you. It's an interesting hypothesis.' He felt the side of his face. 'As a matter of fact, I've already questioned Godber,' he said.

'You questioned him?'

'Yes. Of course. Following the earlier story that came

154

through from your people.' He referred to his notes. 'Christopher Pallett.'

Melrose gritted his teeth and nodded. 'What did Godber say?'

Frewin held out his hand. 'Mr Melrose, I'm afraid that I can't disclose a confidential discussion with a member of the Government. But I am extremely grateful to you for your information. Rest assured that we are watching the situation . . .' he paused, then added 'very carefully indeed.'

As far as Frewin was concerned the interview was over, and Melrose came away frustrated. It appeared on the surface that MI5 didn't care. They didn't fucking care: or, if they did, they didn't want to be upstaged by some interfering Yank. He told Harry Leibermann as much, and Harry said, 'Forget it, Jake. Go and get hold of Vane, like Brendan said.'

But Frewin sought another meeting with the Secretary of State, this time late at night in the St Ermin's Court flat, in order to keep it private. And he took his sidekick, Didsbury.

They were shown into a large, cream-panelled room awash with discreet lights. A set of comfortable chairs was ranged round a coffee table in front of an expensive oil-painting of the S S *Great Britain*, Brunel's great ship, adrift in a rough sea.

'Wonderful picture that,' Godber purred as they admired it. 'Worth rather a lot of money these days.'

'Quite,' Frewin said.

'Drinks?'

'No, thank you, Secretary of State. We really don't want to keep you, at this time of night.'

Godber smiled. 'No problem. Tell me what's worrying you.'

He sat there silently while they explained; explained about Wallace's death, and the continuing rumours about some trouble over Gib.

'My dear fellows,' Godber said. 'I really have never heard such nonsense, but you have to remember that in this hot-house political atmosphere all kinds of smears are used to try and discredit people. I just have to get used to it.'

Didsbury did not mention that he had interviewed Powers.

155

He simply asked, 'Have you had dealings with Colin Landsdowne?'

Equally calmly, Godber without hesitation answered, 'Of course.' He leaned forward confidentially. 'But I must ask you not to disclose it. Landsdowne is our key psy-ops man in Northern Ireland. You understand? Absolutely brilliant at undercover work against the IRA. So he has to be very careful. And so do we. Landsdowne is a marked man, and he has to move very quietly but there is no doubt that he has been . . . of enormous value in the Army's operations there. Irreplaceable. So of course I've seen him, in that context. But I must stress this, gentlemen, he must be kept out of trouble. I do not want the connection mentioned. Do you understand?' He smiled.

Frewin asked, 'Has he any connection with Gibraltar?'

'Gibraltar?' Godber laughed. 'Are you joking, Commodore?'

And Frewin blushed like a schoolboy as Godber added, 'You appreciate the seriousness of what I'm saying. Landsdowne is working for us in Northern Ireland, a key man who must be safeguarded. I want no misunderstandings.'

They looked at each other, and nodded.

Coming out into the night air, Frewin listened to the notes of Big Ben dying away and offered Didsbury a lift.

'These bloody Yanks,' he said. 'They panic.'

Didsbury said, 'And Powers lied.'

'What?'

'Powers, Godber's secretary, lied. He told me he didn't know of any connection between Godber and Landsdowne. That's scarcely conceivable for a Private Secretary as close to Godber as he is.'

Frewin watched late-night London and told the driver to drop Didsbury off in Bromley on his way home to Sanderstead.

'But if Landsdowne is hush-hush on anti-terrorist work in Ulster, it's not surprising.'

'Do you believe that?'

'Yes. But we'll check it out.'

Didsbury said, 'Mind if I smoke?'

Frewin wrinkled his nose. 'No.'

Over his first cigarette of the evening, his nerves shredded, the younger man added, 'I don't trust Powers. He lied. He's also a security risk who's been gossiping to this man Vane.'

Frewin was inclined to agree. 'I'll warn Sir Henry Burton.' He yawned.

Too complacent, Didsbury thought.

'Maybe you should go further.'

Frewin waved away the acrid smoke.

'What do you mean?'

'Warn him about Godber too. And Landsdowne.'

Frewin turned round in the car, almost angrily. 'Look. I'm in charge of political security. I also know the problems in Northern Ireland. If Godber says we keep Landsdowne clean, we keep him clean. Is that clear?'

'Yes,' Didsbury said reluctantly. 'But this bloke Geoffrey Powers . . .'

'Ah. Powers is a different matter. Powers, if you ask me, is the weak link. A civil servant who gossips. A P S who spreads stories about his political boss.' Frewin smiled grimly, and made a cutting motion with his hands. 'It could be Powers is our man. Mister Powers, chop chop.'

27

Melrose changed his hire-car again. Always cover your tracks, and anyway he was sick of other people's transport, so he picked up a Budget Cavalier and bombed down on the M4, over the Severn Bridge and up the beautiful road from Chepstow to Monmouth, through the Wye Valley. Coming into Hereford this way from the south over the small hills and neat farmland, it was an easy detour to find the village of Coombe Whitbourne where Vane had the gingerbread cottage.

He arrived after lunch, in the somnolence of a June afternoon when nothing seemed to happen. It could have been a ghost town as the sunshine wrapped the deserted churchyard, the twin row of white stone houses, the closed-up post office-cum-shop. Not even a dog moved as he rolled down the single street and turned into the gravelled lane up which he remembered walking towards the main road, his ribs hurting like crazy, that night when he had first met Vane.

- He found the picket fence, white-painted (he recalled how it shone in the moonlight), the indeterminate rose bushes, the small untidy front lawn, some hollyhocks round the windows that he hadn't noticed before. No wheelbarrow: that had gone, so somebody had been around. He unlatched the gate and went in. He didn't expect Vane to be there but there were signs of his presence. Peering through the front window into the living-room-office he saw that the VDU was plugged in and moved from the table on to a side desk. Papers were scattered about. Somebody was working there. And on the other side, in the low-beamed kitchen, signs of a recent meal: frying pan on the stove, milk carton on the table. Walking round the back he found two garden chairs, white-painted, under a furled umbrella, close to an iron-work table and a half empty can of Bulmer's cider wedged against the wall. Billy was in residence all right. He picked up the can and stowed it neatly away in the trash bin.

He climbed back into the car and drove on into Hereford, over the railway lines, along Commercial Road, towards the hotel he'd checked into when he first met up with Billy. For old times' sake he detoured round the market, but no sign of bikers now: just the bustle of clearance at the end of the cattle sales. He nosed his way through, following the street map, and came out into Widemarsh Street. Houses, small shops, a school, and then the anonymous shop front proclaiming ERS, Export Recruitment Services in smaller type. He parked and walked back on foot.

It was an old-fashioned shop, converted into a bureau, a cross between a recruitment office and a Chinese take-away. There seemed no one around, only an empty counter with a few plasticated signs: 'Want a job with excitement: try ERS' and 'If you've got what it takes, we will take what you've got'.

158

Melrose's eyes wandered to the easy chairs round small tables, designed for waiting, the posters on the walls advertising South African Airways, Borneo, Malaysia, then to the girl who came forward, out of an inner office. He smiled that confidential smile that could light up his face as if from some hidden battery.

'Uncle William? Tell him Jake's here to see him.'

She turned without a word and went through to the rear, then came out again and said, 'Will you come through?'

He found himself in an extended office occupied by two more girls, reading papers, making notes. Then there was another door, leading to an inner sanctum, with a double lock and metal frame. Vane must have had that put in, a kind of strong room.

Billy Vane was watching TV, a cricket match on the box in the corner. He switched it off and smiled, but did not offer to shake hands. They looked at each other warily.

'What brings you here, Jake? Thought I had warned you off.'

'Figured we needed another word. You've been quite hard to find, Billy. Claire thought you'd gone away. She sends her regards,' he said.

That sudden flashpoint of anger came into Billy Vane's eyes, then was quickly disguised. He seemed to size up the American and then relax.

'Listen, old boy. I told you not to meddle.' He motioned to a chair and Melrose sat down, so that they fronted each other beside the blind TV screen. There was a desk, uncluttered, a single telephone, three locked steel presses. The room must once have been a kitchen, with a door out to a yard where Melrose could see the parked Bristol through a barred window.

'Maybe you should have taken time to say that to other people. Such as the guys bugging Claire.'

Vane's urbanity vanished. His schoolboyish face went hot. He brushed his hand over the neat, straight brown hair.

'Who's bugging Claire?' His voice was tight with concern.

'Skinheads. Like the guys came for me.'

159

Vane stared at Melrose. 'Go on.'

'That why you went quiet? Scare you off?'

Vane said softly, 'Don't be so bloody stupid. Just keep your nose out, that's all.' If this Yank thought he would rile him, Billy would prove him wrong.

'I was minding my business until somebody got Wallace. I guess you weren't around that time . . .'

Vane swore softly. Melrose could sense the short fuse, screwed down, under control.

'I'm around when I want to be,' he said.

'Sure. Appreciated. Now listen, pal. You're sitting on quite a story. This guy Godber wants to show that he's tough, that he can hold it. So he plots a phoney war about a lump of rock called Gib. And Powers knows and tells you, and you want to cash the cheque, then an Irish bastard shuts you up. And you tell me to shut up, so we can all go away. That right, Uncle William? Billy Boy?'

Vane turned to him furiously, his caution gone.

'You hear me, Jake, old son. Stay out. Stay out for Claire's sake. I don't want Claire to get hurt. That clear? You think they scare me?' He laughed. 'No way, old son. But Claire is another matter, and that's where I come unstuck. They've warned me, and they've warned her, as well as you.'

'Who is they?'

'That bastard Landsdowne.' He hammered his fist into his hand, his compact body tight as a spring.

'Landsdowne?'

'A bloody Mick operative for the Army.'

'Right.' Melrose traced a finger across the silent TV screen. 'Well, your Irish guy is still after Claire. He'll set the dogs onto her, and onto Geoffrey Powers, just to make sure they play ball. I had a heart-to-heart talk with one of his supporters the other day: met him down here a couple of weeks back and got to know him then.'

For the second time, Billy Vane saw he had guts. Maybe they could do business after all.

'That fucking Irishman.'

160

'Yeah. Somebody ought to put the skids under his little scheme. Starting with the Spanish end.'

'That's my story,' Billy Vane said. 'And it's not for sale.'

'Listen, Billy. You ain't got a story left. We know it all. We've been piecing it together, alongside the Brits. Landsdowne's the start of it, along with the old Franco hard-core, the Falangists, and a woman called the Condesa de Asturias, right? Countess of the Asturias, some goddam coal-mining area in North Spain where she gets her money from. They've been meeting in London: the Brits've been watching. Somebody ought to find out what's in it for her, before anybody starts shooting. Madrid. That's where we ought to look.'

Vane said, 'We? You telling me how I can play my hand?'

'I'm telling you we need a bit more evidence and then we hit the headlines.'

'Look. I run a business,' Vane said. 'Hiring and firing guys to do jobs abroad, Africa, South America, Arabia, the Far East. I don't piss about with some game of political musical chairs. I just want the cash.'

'You mean you do what this guy Landsdowne says?'

The younger man half rose. 'You dare say that!'

'I'm telling you Claire wants someone to stop Godber and get her Geoffrey off the hook. That means someone else has to stand up and spill the beans. Like me and you.'

'Say that again?'

Melrose smiled. 'How's about coming in with me? A trip to Spain?'

'Why me?'

'You speak Spanish. And I know a chicken from an egg. This thing's at the egg stage, Billy. In another month it could be fully hatched.' Melrose put the proposition that he had been mulling over. 'What say we make a team?'

'A team?' Vane was amused and intrigued at the suggestion that they should work together. 'What's in it for you, old boy?'

'Billy. I got to find out if this guy Landsdowne killed Wallace. You get these crazy men and next thing you get is big trouble, like a guy whose life I once saved, knifed in the back. That's bad, Billy. That really upsets me, talking to the guy's

161

widow. Goddam stupid, but it does. Let's get this straight, Billy. Between us we might clear Powers, and that's what the lady wants. On my own, I'm looking for evidence about who killed Brendan Wallace.'

Angrily Vane said, 'I told you to lay off, you nosy bugger. It's my story, old man. Geoffrey Powers told me, I told the CIA. Nobody would believe me. Then they send you.' He looked at the American as if he saw over-ripe cheese.

'Yeah. And then somebody does in Brendan Wallace.'

'That's not my business, Jake.'

'No, bud, but it's mine.'

They glared at each other. Slowly, Vane said, 'All I need to do is go to MI5. British Security. They're smelling round it, but can't quite believe their ears.'

'I tried them already.'

Vane's eyes widened. This guy was not so slow.

'Yeah. We got contacts. I've seen a guy called Frewin. He gave me the brush-off. "Thanks very much, old bean. We're keeping the situation under review." '

'So. Maybe they'll cross-question Godber, and pull in Landsdowne.' Billy Vane put his hands in his pockets.

Melrose stared at him. 'Don't kid yourself, Billy Boy. Godber can say this Landsdowne is a hot-shot in Ulster security. Keep off, he'll say. No way. We got to deal with Landsdowne in private.'

The telephone rang and Vane killed it. 'No. I'll ring you back.' He stood up and stared from the window, back to the American, weighing up what he thought about Claire Powers. It was a difficult admission, even to himself, let alone to this beanpole Yank.

'Listen, old man. Believe me, the only reason I held off from spilling the Gibraltar story was to safeguard Claire. Not that shit of a husband, though she still wants to let him off. You with me, Jake? It wasn't because I wanted more cash. It wasn't because Landsdowne's thugs had given me the yellow card.' He swung round and confronted Melrose, breathing heavily. 'It was because I was scared about Claire. And when I told her, she worried about Geoffrey. That was when I warned you.'

Melrose realized.

Now she had come to him. In those stumbling messages left on his machine in Paris, and in their meeting in London only days before, she had asked for his help. She was singling him out. She was preferring him.

And Billy Vane feared as much.

'Look. Don't get involved. I can give this Godber story to the press without asking for a penny. Without implicating Powers. Tell them Landsdowne set it up.'

'Okay. You go ahead.'

Vane hesitated, and Melrose knew he was caught. The Englishman shuddered. 'Damn it. You know I can't,' he said. 'God dammit I can't make it stick. Landsdowne's as thick as thieves with the Security Services. And Claire would be at risk.' He shook his head. 'I can't do it.'

Melrose shrugged. Love was one of those things hard-bitten field agents were never advised to shack up with. A fling, a bit of ass, that was part of the rule book, but no way a full-blown affair, turning you up at the ends. That was some girl, he thought. As for himself, he could tell Leibermann, hand him the half-finished story, but what good would that do? Godber would deny it, of course, just as he would deny anything that got in the press. Perhaps it might stop one scheme, but with a guy like Landsdowne, there would be some other wheeze, some other murderous venture. No. Landsdowne must be investigated, and if Vane wouldn't do it, he would.

Melrose stood up.

'Well. I guess it was worth a try. Just stand clear of the fall-out and maybe you can pick her up, Powers or no Powers.'

'I told you to keep your nose out . . .'

The American hesitated; a spark of understanding between them.

'You know, if we could find some evidence in Spain implicating Landsdowne in a plot to threaten Gibraltar and give Godber a cause, you could get your story, and I could maybe sort out Landsdowne.'

163

'And keep Powers out of it?'

'Right,' Melrose said. He looked steadily at Billy Vane and wondered if they could ever get an act together.

Billy Vane weighed up the odds. All he could raise in England at the moment would be some kind of interest from the scandal sheets: lurid stuff about Godber's ambition. But they ran that line already, whereas out there in Madrid there might be some real action. Even some jobs on the run-in for the kind of men he employed. And he couldn't risk leaving it to the Yank with his cowboy behaviour.

'Don't go,' he said. He held out his hand. Something about the Yank enticed him. 'You're on.'

28

Vane suggested a meal in a restaurant picked from a good food guide.

'You've got to eat. You've got to live.'

'Right,' Melrose said. He took food as it came, a can of beans or venison, but this was good, Vane had the style, the polish, and laughed at the Yank.

'Jake, stop taking life so seriously.' Billy Vane rarely had in the years when he had organised sweepstakes from school, and had his first girl in the bushes, and built up a reputation as a mad dog in the Greenjackets, and then in the SAS, until an Argentine splinter took a bite out of his quadriceps and just missed the femoral artery. After that he had set up in business, he told Melrose, supplying the world's hot trades with a source of trained men looking for constant excitement, and with anything else that was needed.

'Such as the Godber story?'

Vane shrugged, and offered more wine but the Yank shook his head. Booze didn't go with the job.

'We're going to work together, we've got to drink together.'

'It doesn't follow,' Melrose said.

'Jesus. You are a straight-arse.'

'Way I was brought up,' Melrose said. 'I ain't no plaster saint, though.'

In spite of their uneasy alliance, Billy Vane found the Yank hard going. Melrose kept his thoughts to himself. He wouldn't talk about 'Nam, blotting out in his mind the terrible mistakes in his life, the reason he was there at all, the falling 'copter and the black smoke in the trees.

'You've gone quiet,' Billy said, ordering coffee and brandies.

'Yeah. We got a job on. And I don't drink brandy.'

Vane sighed. 'I've got a good deal then. Double cognac for one.'

'Look. This is a business arrangement. A professional job. We go to Spain. We check out on this Condesa, and then we go public. And maybe I get Landsdowne. Right? If you want to back off, you back off, but don't fuck me around when we're there.'

Vane's eyes narrowed. Jesus, the man was a lunatic.

'I've given my word, Jake. And that's as good as they come.' He twirled the brandy in the balloon glass and sniffed it like a connoisseur. 'Okay?'

'Okay.'

They walked out and stood in the air; soft, warm, inland air with midges whirling in thousands.

'Where are you heading?'

'London,' Melrose said.

'Stay clear of Claire.'

'You told me that before.'

'I'll ring her. Tell her we're both going.'

'Suit yourself.' It occurred to him then that she had a choice between them, if she wanted to choose, and the thought troubled him.

'Alternatively,' Vane said, 'you could come back with me. I've got a room in the cottage.'

Melrose grinned. 'Yeah. I tried the bed. Remember?' No way was he going back there.

In the end it was Melrose, not Vane, who tried the press: a

165

phone call to a couple of tabloids, and he found himself talking to some young guy from the *Mirror*.

'You been running stories about Godber's chances . . .'

'Yup. Ambitious bugger,' Askey said. He wore a kind of clown's suit, baggy all over.

Melrose sat over a coffee in a café in High Holborn. They weren't giving him the expense account treatment: maybe he should have insisted on a fee.

'Well, I reckon you should check out whether any guys in Spain are being encouraged to flex their muscles over Gibraltar . . .'

'A flare-up with the Spics?' It seemed so improbable to young Askey that he laughed. 'You got any evidence?'

'Nope. Only hearsay.'

Jesus, this guy was wasting time. Askey had two more stories to cover that day, one about the trade in dogs for vivisection in French laboratories – that was a real winner.

'Come on,' he said.

'I'm telling you. There's a story in Godber's ambition. He's got contacts with guys in Spain. The Spanish Falangists. A woman called Condesa de Asturias.'

'Come again?'

'Countess of the Asturias.'

'Who's she when she's at home?'

'Leader of the right-wing mafia.'

'Oh, come on. Nobody risks his neck on that kind of throw. We don't have Irangates here.'

Melrose shrugged.

'You ain't going to follow it up?'

Askey laughed. 'It's not sexy enough.'

But when the American had gone, he checked up with the horse's mouth, and got through to John O'Brien, Godber's Chief Press Officer.

'We've had a suggestion that the Secretary of State is antici-pating some kind of threat to Gibraltar,' Askey said.

'You're off your rocker. We own it.'

'Well, somebody is in play. The Spanish right wing? And that you know all about it and Godber's going to use it as an excuse to show the flag, get public opinion behind him just as he makes his bid.'

'Oh for Christ's sake,' O'Brien said. 'When are you press boys going to grow up and stop inventing stories.'

'Is that a comment?'

'The comment is rubbish,' O'Brien said. 'And if you start printing crap like that about the Minister, I'll see you in hell, next time there's a real break.'

'But there must be something in it? Otherwise why should this bloke . . . ?'

'Who?' O'Brien enquired.

'Some American.'

'Oh Jesus. A trouble-maker.'

29

There was a lean and hungry look about Madrid in the early morning. They rendezvoused in the dining room of the hotel that Vane had chosen, the Alameda in the Calle de Alfonso XII, overlooking the Retiro Park; the English adventurer and the American one, Billy Vane and Jake Melrose, linked in a queasy partnership. The place seemed to echo with money, frequented by tour groups of Germans and Spanish business-men escorting well-painted mistresses. Such obvious displays of wealth among the black glass and chrome of the hotel held no great appeal for Melrose, the more so when his stroll out-side – before Billy Vane appeared, dressed in a cream linen suit and some kind of old school tie – had run him straight into the beggars crowding the opposite railings, ancient black crows with claws, sitting in the shade of the trees, and kids with cardboard boxes, one of them pencilled in English: 'Help Pedro. 100 pesetas to eat. God bless you.' Melrose was dis-turbed by poverty more than he liked to admit, more than by violence or crime, and came back to give him five francs, a French coin left in his pocket. The kid chewed on it and put it away nimbly inside his rags. *'Dios te bendiga,'* he whispered to the sucker. Only then did Melrose realize that the kid's fingers were missing.

He walked back into the four-star hotel clutching the Madrid paper that he was unable to read, and found Vane already at breakfast, eggs and bacon, coffee and toast, English style.

The Englishman looked up and grinned. 'No kippers,' he said.

'Hell, no. Nothing for the kids outside, neither.'

Vane glanced at him sharply, then resumed the cooked meal. Melrose had rolls and coffee.

'You mustn't be so damned sensitive. Wrong line of business for that, Jake.'

'Too public here,' Melrose said. 'And too fancy. That makes me sensitive.'

'Just put it down to expenses, and forget it.' Vane brushed the hair from his forehead where it fell in a neat fringe, the same style that he'd worn since schooldays. 'Anyway, we're well placed for the Prado.'

'The what?'

'Prado.' The cold blue eyes smiled with contempt. 'The art gallery. One of the best there is.'

'Like the hotel?'

'That's right, old man. Always go for the best.' He began on the toast, unwrapped it from a linen napkin and turned up his nose at the marmalade. 'They just don't know how to make this stuff. All they can do is to grow the bloody oranges.'

Okay, Melrose thought, looking at that almost cherubic face, tell me when we get going. I'm not here for the pictures. And he had the uneasy feeling that among the faces in the foyer there might be others who knew that.

'El Greco,' Vane said. 'Velasquez. Goya. Murillo. You heard of those? They've got some marvellous paintings here, Jake lad.'

'Nope.'

'Well, I ought to take you round, old son. You look an arty kind of chap. And then there's Bosch.'

'Who?'

'Bosch. *The Garden of Delights*. One of the masterpieces, Jake.'

'Yeah. Look – '

Vane held up his hands. 'Okay, okay. Don't push me. Life's not like that. You know your trouble, Jake? You're too damned earnest. You've got to be doing things all the time. It's not good for you, old man. Sit back and relax. Have some of this local marmalade.'

But Melrose rode doggedly on.

'I came here to do a job. Not to look – ' he leaned forward to speak softly – 'not to look at Goddam pictures.'

'Well, you should, Jake. You should. Good for the soul.'

This was a different Vane, Melrose decided, from the short-fused bastard who blew up when he was crossed, more like the Billy Vane who had swung that pole in Hereford cattle market without hesitating, cool and composed. A connoisseur, he asked himself, of brandy, art and women and what else besides? Of ruthlessness? The cold light of Vane's eyes still did not appeal. On the way over on the Iberia flight the evening before, Vane had refused to talk about how they would make contact here. He had turned his head casually over the in-flight drinks, when Melrose came back to the subject. 'All in good time, old man. All in good time. We've got the main name. What more do you want?' But Melrose was floundering in a country he couldn't understand, in the down-wind position, relying on Billy's good offices for translation and it didn't sit easy on him.

'Billy, listen. I'm not here for the ride, or the tourist sights. I want some evidence of a plot going on. It's called Intelligence, Billy. I want a line on Landsdowne. Not looking at some damned pictures.'

Billy Vane smiled. He folded the napkin neatly, nodded his thanks to the waiter and said, 'Okay. Let's walk.'

They came out into the street, a Mexican snarl-up of traffic, the fumes hanging in the air like teargas.

'Buy you a coffee,' Vane said.

'Don't want another coffee, Billy.'

169

'Jake, this is Spain. Madrid. We've got to be friends. Relax. Look at those guys over there.'

Young men hand-in-hand. Jesus. Sick, Melrose thought. What was this Brit suggesting: that he put a hand through his arm? He strode away, leaving Vane laughing beside him.

'Jake, act natural, for Christ's sake. Not as if you had the shits. I'll buy you a soft drink.'

'A what?'

'Fresh lemon,' he said, 'with sugar.'

They came to the Paseo del Prado and found tables in the sun at one of the tourist-trap cafés just getting into its stride: a group of blond Nordics, two coachloads of Spanish kids.

'This'll do,' Vane said. He elbowed his way through to one of the inside tables, where it was dark and sober; a long polished bar top, pinball machines, a sleepy, sullen waitress.

'*Dos zumos de limón, por favor.*' He grinned at Melrose. 'How about that, old man?'

Melrose sat with him in silence, while the waitress prepared the drinks.

'Billy –'

'Okay, okay.' Again that superficial grin as Melrose stared round the café.

'I just got a hunch somebody knows we're around.'

'Don't tell me my business, Jake.'

Melrose was silent.

'Right. Then we understand each other. Excuse me while I make a call.'

Vane disappeared into the phone booth in the corner of the room, a squalid mahogany box, and Melrose watched him dialling, then heard him speaking fluently in Spanish.

When he returned the smile had spread even wider. 'No problem, old sunshine. She'd just love to see us. Happens to be in residence tomorrow.'

Melrose felt he had drawn an ace. His face cracked into that slow smile, eyebrows raised at Vane.

'The countess?'

'The same.'

They looked at each other and laughed. Maybe not such a

170

bad guy after all, Melrose thought. And Vane wondered if the steady hand and eye of the Yankee greaseball stood for an inner calm, or covered up a fear he was fighting, some locked-in and private secret.

Melrose stared at this playboy in the tropical suit and desert boots with something like respect.

'How d'you manage it, Billy? How d'you manage to persuade them?' Melrose knew damned well that you didn't ring out of the blue and get an instant appointment with the leader of the Spanish Fascists. They would be smarter than that.

Vane sipped the cold lemonade, swirling the ice round the glass. 'I just mentioned that Landsdowne had sent us. Colin Landsdowne, from Ulster, on behalf of Freddie Godber. They seemed quite keen.'

30

The estate was seventy miles south of Madrid, and Vane drove there in the hot afternoon in a hired Mercedes. Even with the windows down, the oven-heated air seemed to grill them, but Vane appeared impervious to it. He drove with the practised skill of a rally driver, slipping in and out of the traffic on the dangerous three-lane highway, airily pointing out landmarks.

'That's the road to Toledo. You been there?'

'Nope. Never been over here before.'

Vane turned his head and smiled without losing concentration. He squeezed past a TIR juggernaut with three inches to spare and hurled the big car round a bend.

'Great country,' he said, 'for hard-liners.'

'Yeah?'

'Yup. Franco showed them a thing or two. How to keep out of the war, for starters.'

'Watch that guy on the bike . . .' weaving like some drunk in the middle of the road.

Vane overtook without effort.

171

'Don't worry, Jake. By three o'clock half the bloody country's like that. Either asleep or dead drunk. Nobody cares.'

That effortless prejudice, the assured and in-built superiority: Melrose couldn't take those jokes. They weren't particularly funny. He wanted this business over.

'How much further?'

Vane waved vaguely.

'Must be almost there, old boy.'

Melrose bit back his resentment and stayed silent.

The rolling hills gave way to fields, large farms, a countryside of vineyards on either side of the road, and then the marker posts of an entrance. 'Finca de los Caidos': a sign swung between the posts suspended from a bracket as Vane turned the car and they bounced up an unmade track with dust trailing behind them. The road seemed to stretch for miles between long ridges of vines, unfenced, unworked except for a few lonely figures in straw hats in the distance.

'See that,' Vane said, pointing out the sign board. ' "Estate of the Fallen Ones".'

'Yeah. Funny sort of name.'

'Some name old Franco gave to his civil war morgue. The Valley of the Fallen, outside Madrid. Take you there one day, old man, if we have time.'

They came to a wall now, a flint and stone boundary marking an enclosure. Trees: pine forest smelling of resin, where deer bounded away. *'Reservas de caza'*. Vane grinned. 'Reserved for the hunting,' he said. 'So long as they don't hunt us.'

They drove through a funnel of rocks, outhouses, big dogs running free: black and golden Labradors panting with effort in the heat, but friendly, wagging their tails. Vane slowed the car and rolled slowly up to the house, a huge, ornate, peach-coloured house with figs growing over one wall, and, as they stopped, a woman came forward to meet them.

The woman, the Countess of the Asturias, a supple, slender woman of indeterminate age. She held out her hand in greeting as Vane scrambled from the car.

172

'Welcome,' she said in English.

Melrose saw there were three men following her, and a servant carrying chairs on to the wide terrace which stretched along one flank of the house, commanding a view of the farmland on that side: more terraces of vines, and orchards, espaliered peach trees across a sheltering wall watered by whirls of spray, and blue-green woodland shimmering into the distance. An inland sea.

The Countess turned her head and talked in Spanish to Vane, leaving Melrose standing there as the others came up, full-bodied conquistadors in sporting clothing: Miguel Luis Quintilla, a grizzled head flecked with silver, General of the Army, and two senior Air Force men, General Jesus Antonio Ossorio and Colonel Francisco Lopez, all of them in hunting boots.

The Countess clapped hands for drinks under the trailing grapevines on the terrace, while the dogs lolled underfoot. The great house was eighteenth century, Lopez, who was friendly, explained, a converted monastery which had retained its grounds. They were lapped by a vast estate of growing vines, with the cellarage to match, and sitting out on that patio, queen of all she surveyed, the Countess was the spiritual heir of the great dukes of Spain, the old Monarchists, the Falange. The Generals paid court at her feet, this small, dark, pale-skinned woman in a cool, lime-green dress, as petite as a couturier's model. Melrose guessed that she was ruthless in diet as well as politics.

'I was in London only two weeks ago,' she said, standing in the shadows. 'Your Mr Landsdowne came to see me then with two other young men. An interesting conversation. We discussed a proposition,' she added, beating at gnats in the air.

'Right,' Vane said. 'The others. Who would they be?'

She frowned. 'A Mr Brocklehurst. The other, I forget his name. He did not say much. No. I remember. Mr Powis.'

'Snap,' Billy Vane added. 'Great pals of mine.' His eyes never left her face, as if he was paying homage, while Melrose made a note to check out Brocklehurst's name. Nothing

173

seemed to worry Vane now, he could feel his luck sailing with him, ignoring the cautious Generals who wished she had said much less. The hauteur of her bearing did not encourage them to challenge her.

'Perhaps we should sit,' she said. The dogs were moved to one side, and they reclined in basketwork chairs, waiting to be served with drinks, long, cool, gin-based orangeade.

'My dear Countess,' Vane said as if he had known her for years, with that air of in-bred authority which Melrose found so irksome, 'you sit here like a bird of Paradise.' He waved airily towards the view, the blue-green lines of the vineyards, and they could see she was flattered. She fluttered her eyes towards the Englishman. The talk drifted on and off, with Melrose an outsider to the charmed circle, which increasingly talked Spanish, unintelligible to his ear.

Colonel Lopez turned to the American. 'Come. I will show you the house.' Taking Melrose away, he led him through the great rooms that had once been dormitories, the solarium, library, chapel, the individual cells now knocked into a long gallery. At the end he paused, a confident, good-looking man with a military moustache.

'Señor Melrose. I hope you do not play games with us, coming here like this?' His eyes glittered.

'Games, Colonel? What the heck makes you say that?' Melrose could ride the enquiry, but Billy Vane was too damned loquacious with the hot little Countess.

Lopez nodded. 'It is just as well to be clear.'

They returned to the dark, high rooms of the interior and the Countess showed them the new library, the officers trailing behind. One of the white-coated retainers served them with lemon tea. Vane stood with her by the bookcase, absorbed and self-confident.

'Now tell me about England,' she said in English. 'What is happening in politics?'

Billy Vane's eye caught Melrose's. The Englishman was far too smooth, sucking up to the woman like that, Jake decided.

'Election coming up,' Vane declared.

'And a bid to replace your Prime Minister?' Her hands

played cautiously with the edge of a great case of parchment maps, relics of Spain's golden age.

'Chaos and old night, I reckon,' Vane responded grandly, trailing his coat, 'unless Freddie Godber takes over.'

In the shadows of the room Melrose sensed a gathering suspicion to which Billy Vane seemed oblivious; or maybe he just didn't care. Billy thought he was so goddam clever.

'So Mr Landsdowne has told me.' She paused, seeking out the American. 'And, as an outsider, do you think he will?'

'I guess I don't know,' Melrose said. Landsdowne. Landsdowne. What was that bastard up to, in addition?

Billy Vane moved in smartly. 'Depends on who helps him.'

The military looked at each other. Quintilla walked away, as if it was of no importance, but it crossed Melrose's mind that he wasn't sure of their credentials.

'Do you know what you are saying, Mr Vane?' General Ossorio asked.

Melrose saw him visibly stiffen, but Billy Vane hardly noticed.

'Sure. I got it from the horse's mouth.'

'The horse's mouth?' A furrow of uncertainty appeared in the Countess's forehead.

'From Freddie Godber's office,' Vane said. 'The other man you met, Countess. His secretary, Geoffrey Powers.'

'Oh. But he said so little.'

'Yup. But he knows the score. Like you, Jake, right?' He seemed to take a pleasure in needling the American.

Melrose was non-committal, thinking very much of Claire, and what Powers had done to deserve her.

'Gibraltar,' Vane said. 'That's the deal, I think.'

Suddenly the Countess clammed up. She waved her hands to deny it. General Quintilla stepped in angrily. He imposed his thick-chested bulk, in a white cotton polo-neck, between Vane and the Countess.

'My friend, I advise you not to think,' Quintilla said threateningly. He was a big, potentially violent man. 'We are concerned with Spain, and not with British political manoeuvres.'

Vane coloured. Melrose could see him fighting to stop a flare-up.

'I got that,' Melrose said, calming the waters.

'As long as that is understood,' the General said. 'I shall be explaining as much to your friend, Mr Landsdowne.'

And that seemed as far as they were prepared to go. Melrose was disappointed but Vane had the instant ability to brush off any setback. Almost as if he assumed that the point of the visit had been made, he concentrated on the Countess with his slightly raffish charm, and Melrose watched her responding as she suggested they viewed the estate.

He found himself left again with Lopez as Vane and the Countess, with the dogs gambolling around them, walked down the steps of the terrace to inspect the formal garden.

Lopez at his elbow said, 'You are staying?' He had taken a shine to the American.

Melrose shook his head. 'Got to make it back to Madrid.'

The little Air Force Colonel smiled. 'I think you will travel alone, the way your friend talks to the Condesa.'

Jake Melrose didn't need telling. Some guys could make eyes at women and other guys couldn't, he thought, watching them in the distance.

'It appears Mr Vane will be staying at the Condesa's request,' Lopez muttered with a sidelong grin. 'You have transport back to Madrid?'

Melrose gazed stolidly ahead.

'He drove me down.'

The Colonel smiled. 'Then let's forget him. One day perhaps you will be my guest.' There was some warmth in the offer. He hesitated, then added, 'Other people, other plans.'

Vane was walking down the rows with her, watching her as she instructed the supervisor, an old man in blue dungarees and a ragged straw hat. The air seemed sleepy with warmth. Billy Vane, the potential lover-boy, resplendent in his cream suit and faultlessly cut shirt, washed and ironed overnight. She seemed small and cool beside him, friendly and harmless.

In the middle of the vines she stopped.

176

'What do you want?' she asked. Her small, dark, suspicious head turned towards him.

'To talk to you, Countess' he said, chancing his luck.

She dismissed the supervisor. They stood alone between the rows of vines, small, green clusters of grapes, powdery earth, scorching sun overhead.

'You were stupid to come,' she said. 'You and the American.'

He grinned, full of confidence, but watched her eyes. 'Nonsense.'

'No. I think you try to infiltrate.'

'Rubbish, Countess. Jake Melrose comes from Landsdowne. I came to see you. I was told you were the most beautiful woman in Spain. And now I know.'

Vane was self-confident. He was beginning to feel he made headway under those searching eyes.

'You infiltrate,' she said again.

'Countess. Infiltrate what?' he protested.

The Countess brushed her clothes. Flies hovered round the vines. Her composure had gone.

'Gibraltar is Spanish,' she said. 'And you are seeking to betray us. You are from British Security.'

'For God's sake! Nonsense. Let's discuss something else,' he said glibly, 'out of the sun.'

They walked back through the rows of vines and up the long fields to the house, climbed up the steps to the terrace, and the Countess clapped her hands.

'Iced tea,' she snapped.

Billy Vane drank it with her, eyeing that flawless beauty in spite of the dust in her hair and on her clothes. He could not believe that she would be ruthless with him.

'You mustn't think,' he said, 'that I have any interest in politics. I don't give a toss. All that I want is company such as this – ' he smiled at her again. 'I leave the ideas to Melrose.'
It seemed a neat little joke.

She looked at him in amazement.

'I do not believe you. I think you are British Intelligence. What makes you think I will not arrest you? I have guns in the house. Plenty of guns. I could ask one of the servants to bring me one.'

'You could, but I don't think you will.' He grinned.

She stared at him. After a while she said, 'I am hot. I must go and change for dinner.'

'May I come with you?' he asked.

She found his directness confusing.

'If you wish.'

He assumed he was winning then, as she took him upstairs to her rooms on the first floor looking out over those endless hectares of ripening grapes: a huge, white-and-gold panelled bedroom with a canopied bed, and cut flowers in vases, everywhere; a room for lovers. She went through into a drawing room and he heard the noise of doors.

He waited, then he went forward.

'May I come in?' Vane said.

'Yes.'

She was waiting there fully dressed, together with General of the Army Quintilla, who had changed into full service uniform with crossed swords on his epaulets.

'Mr Vane,' she said, 'don't come here and try to fool me.'

The General stood by the doors, a bull of a man in a sand-coloured uniform, and Vane knew he had an enemy. A challenge hung unspoken between the two men and seemed to rustle with the draperies drawn across the windows of the salon. The Countess looked from one to the other with an enigmatic smile and Billy Vane turned on the charm.

'My dear Countess. Don't confuse me with Jake.'

31

'I guess I ought to wait for Billy Vane,' Melrose said half-heartedly. The Englishman had gone to earth leaving him adrift with these Spaniards. Vane, with his eye on the Countess, clearly had ideas of his own.

178

Colonel Lopez, showing him to a BMW parked at the rear of the buildings, laughed. The terrace had been deserted, beaching Melrose high and dry until Lopez returned.

'In that case you wait for ever, my friend.' The Colonel invited him into the sleek new machine.

'How come?' That was what Melrose feared, isolated, lacking the language.

Lopez's glance told him. 'The Countess has her own way with men. Take my advice and leave them alone. Come. I am going back to Madrid.'

Without Vane, and without the interpreter, Melrose had small chance to argue. Vane must know his way around. He could see no one else about as he climbed in beside the colonel: the Countess, Quintilla and Ossorio, together with Billy himself, all seemed to have vanished. And Billy wouldn't want Jake in the way. Vane was a puzzle to him. What kind of guy was it who could chicken out on a story because of threats from the Irishman? And then come and make eyes at the Countess? Melrose didn't care a spit in the bucket about Billy Boy, but Claire was a different matter, and Vane was a complication. He was beginning to regret that he had ever enlisted him, and, shit, if the guy went after skirt that was his own funeral. Let him stew.

Lopez shot out on to the highway and headed back to Madrid. The sun slanted through the windscreen and he pulled the visors down low but did not slacken speed. They were whirling back through the traffic like a stick down the rapids, and Melrose felt Lopez was waiting to be told that he was going too fast. The speed took his words away as he shouted over the wind-drag.

'Have you met this man called Landsdowne? Colin Landsdowne, the Irishman?'

Lopez smiled. 'That is a matter for the Countess.'

Melrose was silent, feeling increasing unease. He watched the shadows stretching over the central *meseta*, pressed down the window and caught the tangy fragrance of thyme and fresh lavender. The rocky ledges strewn with boulders stretched away on either side, a fierce, bleached, parched

179

landscape. It reminded him of the Old West: rancher country, and these guys were some kind of cowboys.

'Don't mess me around, Lopez.'

'I'm not thinking of doing that, señor.'

Melrose said, 'So long as we understand each other.' In his mind he was still thinking about who killed Brendan Wallace. He saw again the anguish in Angie Wallace's face. He bit his lip. Why was he so determined to finish the job he'd been given: Angie, or Claire, he wondered? Certainly not Harry Leibermann.

Lopez slowed down. He had begun to respect the silent American, but could not fully read him.

'Señor Melrose, I advise you not to make enquiries.'

'Okay, I understand,' Melrose said doggedly. 'Billy Vane is the guy for enquiries.'

The car eased into a steady seventy along a treacherous road. Spaniards lived dangerously and liked to set up challenges, Melrose decided. He looked at the compact, swarthy figure beside him and concluded that he was the action man among the plotters.

He said, 'That invitation of yours still stand?'

'Sure.' Lopez hammered the horn and zipped past a labouring truck. He shot a quizzical glance at the American. 'I could show you all you need to know.'

Melrose knew he didn't mean it. Maybe he read too much into Lopez's voice but he seemed to catch an edge of complacency that could be useful. What they needed was evidence, not a tumble around with the Countess. Billy was a liability, and the Irishman was a danger. He pushed up the visor again and watched the needle hover on eight-five.

'You aiming to get back to Madrid in one piece?'

Lopez took a hand from the wheel and waved it expansively. His tone was almost confiding, now they had left the estate.

'You are best away from that house.'

Melrose began to fear bad vibes about Billy Vane, but he could not pin them down. If Vane went off on his own he could make his own bed. Jake would report on the Countess.

'Maybe someday I'll come visit you,' he said. 'Where did you say you're stationed?'

'Pinaflores airbase,' the little colonel said. 'Home of the Africanistas. Number one secure base.'

'I just might take that up,' Melrose said.

There was a smile of improbability on Lopez's face.

A stone village up in the hills. Clumps of limestone like fortresses. Bandit country. Lopez was signalling friendship across the language barrier.

'Stay away from the Countess.'

'Why?'

'She is . . . like a wild animal. Underneath.'

The American was silent again; concerned and silent. He hoped to God that Billy Vane knew what he was doing.

He wished he spoke the damned language, he wished there was some other way than letting Vane go off on his own to try to lay the Countess.

Lopez caught his thoughts. 'The Englishman. He chases the Countess. He will be disappointed.'

'Not my business,' he replied.

'No offence meant.' Then the Spaniard carefully added, 'He should not upset General Quintilla.'

Melrose gazed straight ahead at the unwinding road, the first straggle of houses coming into the Madrid periphery. The telegraph poles changed to concrete. The sun was a red ball in the haze of pollution.

'Not my business either,' he said.

Lopez shifted down, a racing change. He seemed satisfied. 'Good. But there is something else? Something that brings you here?'

And Melrose could not disclose. He found he could not articulate. It was nothing to do with the Countess. It did not even concern Landsdowne. In his heart he was longing for Claire.

'I don't think so,' he growled, his eyes narrowing against the evening sun until they were slits. 'But I'd sure like to visit that airbase.'

Colonel Francisco Lopez braked, weaving between the

buses, the start of the Madrid tailback. He became more realistic.

'That would be difficult, my friend.'

32

That night Vane did not come back, and Melrose felt angry and slighted. He had rushed into a relationship with the Englishman and now found Vane had abandoned him in favour of the Countess. In spite of their agreement in England he was no nearer the truth about Landsdowne, while fresh-faced Billy had gone chasing a woman.

Jake Melrose walked the streets, screwed up and on his own, along the Paseo del Prado and the Calle de las Heurtas, where the girls were parading in short black skirts. He was tempted, Jesus wept, tempted, by the thought of what Vane was up to, and it made him want to talk to Claire.

A telephone booth, but the instructions in Spanish. Shit, it was worth a try. If Powers answered he could ring off, wrong number. He stood in the booth and dialled her number in Wimbledon, hoping against hope. The line to England buzzed and freaked. Sweat ran down his face in the closeness of the glass box.

'Hullo?'

A woman's voice that sent him spinning.

'Claire. It's Jake.'

He was sure he heard her gasp. 'Where are you?' she said hurriedly.

'I'm in Madrid, honey. Claire, are you okay?'

'Yes. I'm fine. Oh Jake, it's good to hear you.'

'Where's Geoffrey?'

'He's in the next room. So we'd better be quick.'

'Claire, are those guys still following you?'

'No,' she said. 'Not as far as I can tell.' She had picked up the phone in the kitchen, pure chance that she was out there, on her way to the garden to get away from Geoffrey, brooding in the lounge over his overnight papers, get away, get some air; and as she crossed to the door, Jake's call had come through.

'What's happening?' he said.

'Happening?'

'With Godber?'

She put her hand over the telephone, anxious that Geoffrey might hear, might stir himself to ask what the hell she was doing; but no one moved. On the table were the weekend papers, the *Sunday Times* and the *Mail on Sunday* that she had been reading there to keep out of Geoffrey's hair. 'Government on a tightrope' one said, with a lead about the state of the economy. The other one said 'Rebel without a cause,' with a photograph of that head, the confident, curly-haired smiler.

'Lot of talk and no action,' she said. 'Not yet.'

'You reckon?'

'Yes. Oh Jake, take care.'

That was why he had telephoned, he realized then. She wanted him to take care. She was concerned for him. He felt a glow of happiness, a sudden lurch of the heart. It was good to be working for her, as well as paying off Brendan Wallace.

'Okay, honey, I will.'

'I can't stop,' she said, thinking she heard a movement in the next room. A door opening. 'When will you be back?'

'Two or three days, I guess.' Enough time to talk to Lopez before Vane made fools of them both, before Quintilla checked with Landsdowne.

Claire was signing off hastily as Powers came through to find her.

'Take care,' she said again.

He heard the receiver replaced.

'Who was that?' Powers asked.

'Oh, just my friend Susan Aldridge.' Long-distance, up in Cumbria, not likely to be found out.

'What did she want?'

'Nothing much. Just keeping in touch.' These small lies that papered over. He seemed satisfied.

In the morning Jake skipped breakfast and found Vane still hadn't come back. The bastard had holed up there with the Countess, he decided, and that made Melrose pretty sick. Billy Vane had left him Lopez.

33

It was thirty miles south-east of Madrid, and clearly sign-posted: Pinaflores, a detour off the road to Valencia. He drove there in a hired SEAT and reconnoitred in a heatwave through which the base shimmered like a mirage. It was much the same as every other airbase he'd seen, from San Diego and Edwards to Nha Trang and Frankfurt and Mildenhall and Hawaii, the same wired-off perimeter with the howl of engines somewhere over the horizon, then the entry barriers and the first sight of camp roads, stretching to olive-green huts and the bustle of operations, military phenomena that he understood instinctively.

He drove up to the gate and climbed out. An airman or para-military, he couldn't be sure which, in greeny-brown camouflage patches and a grey beret, cradling a carbine, walked across and told him to mind his own business; a chin twice the width of his forehead which peaked in a sprout of hair pushing through the front of his cap, a really tough look-ing animal with a badge saying 'Guarda'. His watch said two o'clock, and the heat was a steady oven, time for siesta. Beyond the pole barrier he could see the trucks and tankers of an operational base, just as Lopez had said, and smell the fumes of kerosene. There was a sign at the gate with a large coat of arms and a long inscription in Spanish. More briefly, it said in English, 'Home of the 4th Parachute Battalion, formed out of the Africanistas, the old guard who served in Morocco under the Caudillo.'

The sentry flicked the catch off his rifle, motioning with his head to piss off. Melrose grinned and restarted the car, coasting back down the road for a couple of miles and pulling in by the shade of a barn. 'Wait on' was an old Corps saying, and one thing Jake Melrose knew was how to work access to an airbase. He unplugged a pack of gum and waited for the traffic to resume.

They began again around three thirty, the military trucks and buses carrying paratroopers, their insignia painted alongside. A trailer with a museum helicopter, a Sikorsky S–61, old-fashioned but effective. He grinned to himself again – 'take off weight 22,000 lbs, 62 feet rotors' – remembering when he had crouched in those rattly old washtubs way back in '72.

Wait on. At four thirty the private cars started to trickle away, day shift workers heading home, some other guys driving in, together with some service trucks: refrigerated food vans, aviation fuel tankers. Not quite yet what he needed. He stretched out the gum and stayed there, prepared to wait for ever.

And then he saw the vehicle he wanted, a blue-painted service coach with a civilian driver, returning to the base empty. He tailed it for fifty yards, then shot in front, swinging across the road with his headlights on, forcing it to brake and stop.

The driver didn't stand much chance as Melrose hit him hard twice and said, 'Sorry, I'm gonna borrow your machine.' He trussed him up like a chicken with the tow rope left in the car and drove him back to the barn.

The driver had a coat and a pass, and he didn't look much like Melrose, but Jake guessed they wouldn't check. A bus was a bus was a bus, the same bus they saw every day, going in and out of the base, a big, rough-riding Renault diesel, with the steering wheel and drive left side, unlike in crazy England. He restarted and headed back up the road.

The sun was lower by now, right in their eyes on the gate, and the big guard had gone, replaced by two conscript guys who weren't inclined to argue when they saw him thundering towards them. He waved the pass and waited. The check was perfunctory, and he was under the raised barrier, up and away inside.

He reckoned there would be one place where Lopez would have kept his tricks, the central admin building, and he went looking for it, driving round the rows of barracks, then the communal centre with its cinema and tin chapel, and the inner rows of repair shops, hangars, vehicle bays and stores. He could have walked it blindfold, right out to the far dispersal strips, but it was quicker in a bus that nobody stopped to look at.

The admin building was next to the officers' mess and he noted with approval the bearing of the guys going in there, tough-looking youngsters in combat kit. It was time to take a look.

He was dressed in lightweight pants and an open-neck shirt with two pockets, more like an officer in mufti than some of those guys themselves, and he guessed, rightly, that there were groups in training and visitors to the base, which made identification difficult. Some of them carried name tags, a few sported photo passes, but most of them were anonymous. Melrose left the bus and walked in, carrying his driver's pass.

It was a building with a plain portico and round-headed windows. Inside was a hall of white marble with trophies, flags, cases of souvenirs and inscribed guns on the walls. His footsteps echoed.

He saw stairs and a reception desk, empty, standing at the bottom. A civilian came out of a door and said something in unintelligible Spanish. Melrose flashed the pass and nodded, walking up the stairs without looking, as if he knew the way.

Upstairs, corridors, doors. A few of them were open, giving on to desks and work surfaces, most of them by now deserted, the rest of them locked and shut. Melrose walked back down the corridor. He couldn't search the goddam building. He needed help.

He found it in the form of a girl, a clerk or typist coming out of one of the pool rooms, a tiny, dark-haired woman immediately intrigued by the American who smiled and said, 'Colonel Lopez?'

She struggled to understand.

Jesus, he thought. To come this far and not make it.

Then he added, 'Lopez. Secreto,' and a smile broke out on her face.

She led the way to the second floor, to a cold concrete corridor which looked half-finished. He was being taken to a security checkpoint.

There was another guard there, a bored conscript sitting on a chair by a table, reading a magazine. But he had a rifle with him.

'Americano,' Melrose said. 'See Colonel Lopez.'

The guard shook his head, held out his hand for the pass. Melrose pretended not to understand. The nice girl had gone.

'Listen,' Melrose said in English. 'I came here to see Colonel Lopez. You got that? Lopez. Telephone. Call the guy up. Telefono.'

The youngster was doubtful but Melrose was insistent. He thumbed through a register and found a number, then made a call, signing to Jake Melrose to wait.

Melrose sat on a chair and waited, breaking out a fresh stick of gum, oozing confidence. Nobody asked any more about his pass, he was so far in they all assumed he was serious. He offered a stick to the kid with the gun.

When they spoke to him in Spanish he just shook his head, cursing that Billy Vane hadn't bothered to come along with him. 'Melrose,' he repeated. 'To see Lop-ez. Lopez.' He sat there half an hour.

'I can't wait,' he said, 'all night.' He walked to the end of the corridor ignoring the guard, and counted ten big Chinooks, the standard medium transport helicopter of the US Army, lined up on the horizon.

And then eventually he saw Lopez, an angry little fellow buckling on a side-arm, who'd been roused from married quarters somewhere and came trotting towards him.

'Hi, Lopez,' he said, as the Spaniard emerged at the head of the stairs. 'Glad you could make it.'

187

The Colonel's head turned and he came at a run, breathless. He looked at the lanky American as if he could not be sure whether he was there by magic, incompetence or a joke.

Melrose greeted him warmly.

'How did you get here?' Lopez asked. 'This is a top-security base.'

Melrose looked surprised.

'Came in at the gate,' he said. 'Just asked to see you. You ain't got no secrets here, have you?' He grinned.

Lopez said, 'What do you want?'

'I want to know what you meant. Remember? Other people, other plans. The ones you offered to show me.'

Lopez stared at him. They were standing in the corridor arguing, with the conscript kid watching open-mouthed, a kind of duel between the dapper Colonel and the persistent American.

'You'd better come with me,' Lopez said.

He signed a book and beckoned Melrose past the last barrier.

'You have a nerve,' he said.

'Why? I ain't on anybody's side. Just interested in what you said.'

Lopez led him to a room at the end which he unlocked. Melrose saw the Colonel's name on the door, and oblique signs which he presumed were a high-security level, but his luck seemed to be holding.

'Sit down, please,' Lopez said.

It was an office much like the others, with a desk fan which Lopez switched on, blowing dust in the air. He noted there were shutters on the windows and Lopez switched on a light.

'You should not have come. I don't know how you got past security. You could have been arrested,' Lopez said.

'Aw come on, Colonel. You more or less invited me, so as I was coming this way, I just called in.'

Lopez sat in a basket chair at a plain wooden desk.

'Now.' He repeated the question that he had put to Melrose before, on the Countess's estate. 'Why do you come?'

'I told you I don't play games,' Melrose said. 'You told me you had some plans. You said you'd show me.' That was the

Latin promise on which he'd picked Lopez up, and Lopez felt his honour at stake. Melrose was going to keep him that way.

Lopez's brown face looked at him steadily. He liked him, he admired his nerve, but he wanted some other answers.

'I mean, why do you come to Spain? To the Condesa?'

And Melrose told him. 'You know a guy called Landsdowne? Right?'

The Colonel frowned, then nodded.

'Okay. One of my friends was killed. Knifed in the back in London, because he was following a story started by Landsdowne. The other half of that story is here.'

The Colonel's lips pursed. 'There can be no connection between Landsdowne and the killing.'

'I figure there is.'

Lopez had taken the bait. He put his hands together and worried.

'Captain Melrose. Are you saying we can't trust Landsdowne?'

'You show me your plan for Gibraltar, and I'll tell you.'

'Is that a deal or a threat?'

'A bit of both, I guess.'

The Colonel thought about it. Melrose had come a long way; and he was a long way inside, almost as if it was official. And he wanted to know. He smiled, at ease, confiding.

'All right,' he said.

'Gibraltar first,' Melrose replied.

Lopez was on his feet, unlocking a second door to an inner room which was curtained and dark.

Lopez switched on the lights.

Melrose saw a model of the whole of Gibraltar, the size of a billiard table: the harbour and its moles, the town at the foot of the Rock facing the Bay of Algeciras, the highest point at the Pan de Azucar, the forts now largely abandoned, the Playa de los Catalanes on the sheer, inaccessible side, the airstrip jutting into the sea across the main road, the narrow isthmus of sand joining the great limestone crag to the mainland at La Linea. The drop zones marked by red flags.

Melrose pointed to them. 'What is all this for, Colonel?'

'A training scheme,' Lopez replied.

Melrose studied it carefully. 'Training scheme, huh?'

Lopez said, 'What right have the British there, except by conquest? And what is it now? Not even a strategic base; a haven for easy money: drug traffic, laundered funds. We cannot control them from Spain, with that Achilles heel. Now, are you satisfied?'

'But just a training scheme, that so?'

The Colonel smiled.

Melrose kept his silence, thinking, Jesus, the thing was on. Either Godber set it up for his own glory and moved the Brits back in, the paras and the Navy, the Rapid Deployment Force, or the Spaniards took him at his word and these guys dropped in first, now that the garrison had gone, and occupied the fucking island. Either way it spelled big trouble. No wonder Landsdowne didn't want his version leaked. No wonder Wallace was killed.

'Sure,' Lopez said.

The Colonel doused the lights and ushered him from the room. There was a cockiness in his voice as he added, 'So you see, the schemes of this Colin Landsdowne will very soon be irrelevant. Either they give it to us, or we shall take what is ours.'

Melrose said, 'Okay, Colonel. Now I said I'd tell you something about Landsdowne.'

Lopez was thoughtful. 'He has offered us a deal.'

'Yeah. Some deal,' As they stood on the steps together Melrose added, 'From a dangerous, double-crossing skunk.'

34

Billy Vane stood by the pool and watched the Countess swimming. The pool was at the far side of the house, sheltered by an umbrella of pines, interspersed with ancient olive trees, relics of the monastery garden. But there was very little monasticism about the Countess now, he thought, once she had him alone on the following afternoon. She swam like an eel across the blue tiles of the pool, her sleek head bobbing in the water, and clambered up the steps on the far side. She waved to him. He hitched up the string of his borrowed bathing drawers and dived in. He felt confident after a night there, his fences mended with the Countess, Jake seen off the premises. Ready to wait his turn.

He cut across the blue-green water with a slow crawl and shook his head on the other side. The Countess had called for drinks and was reclining in a long, low chair that more than displayed her figure. She was wearing a black bikini which was little more than an apology. He saw it drying out on her pale brown skin, and she watched him looking and laughed, turning over to expose her buttocks.

Billy Vane stood alongside. He noted the smooth hillocks, he followed the long legs down to the elegant feet. He felt he was on to a winner.

'Well,' she said, her face pressed into the chair. 'Where is your American friend today? What have you done with him?'

He put a glass of champagne into her outstretched hand. 'Gone back to see Madrid.'

The Countess giggled. 'He is on duty, that one.'

'That's right,' Vane said. The poor bugger didn't know how to enjoy himself. He slipped a hand on to the Countess's warm back. A jar of lotion stood on the little table. 'Would you like me to oil your back?'

She buried her head in her arms without looking round. The servants had disappeared: they knew their place.

He began to unstopper the oil, which was perfumed and smelt of sandalwood. The Countess stretched languorously and he found the signals encouraging. He moved to unclip the bra.

'No,' she snapped. 'Don't touch me.' She sat up and pushed him away. 'I don't trust you.'

He was caught off balance by the sharpness of her refusal and suddenly felt his leg give way: a spasm where the muscle had been shot away at the back of his left thigh. It didn't

191

trouble him much, most times no one would notice. He only limped under pressure, like when he carried a pack or became over-tired or sometimes turned over in bed, but Christ it pulled him now and he winced with the pain.

'What is the matter?' she said, suspiciously. At first she thought he was fooling.

'Nothing,' Vane said, but he had to twist away.

'Yes, there is.' She noticed for the first time that the back of one thigh was mangled, a strip from the buttock to just above the back of the knee, discoloured, sewn up, a different colour of flesh. It was a weaker leg.

'What happened?' she said.

'A little bit of trouble that I ran into once.'

'Where?' But she knew. She seemed to understand that it had been a war. Vane did not want to remember: invalided from the Army, that had been the end of his fighting – and the end of his youth. Since then he'd been pretty cynical about calls to honour and glory.

The spasm had come and gone, and he relaxed. The Countess looked up at him thoughtfully. One of the maids reappeared and she slipped on a towelling robe. Somebody brought him one too. Now she was consulting her watch.

'Come inside. There is someone who wants to meet you.'

She was leading him through to the library, the big room he had seen before, when he had talked to Quintilla on the previous evening, but now the General was sitting there in uniform with a companion: a middle-aged balding man with a soft Ulster voice, the man whom he knew was the Irishman.

'Well, well, well,' Landsdowne said. 'You don't take a hint, do you? It's stupid to run up expenses staying at the best hotels. Much too public.'

The General had drawn his heavy-duty revolver and it lay on the table in front of them, Quintilla's fingers playing with the butt. The Countess crossed and sat with them, three heads like some Inquisition made more real by her own robe on the other side of the table. Her eyes seemed as dark as sloes in the silence of the library.

She came back to the charge she had levelled at him on the

previous afternoon during their walk in the vines. 'You have come here to spy.'

'I don't know what you're talking about,' Vane countered.

But Landsdowne intervened in that soft, murderous voice.

'I think you do, Captain Vane. I think you want to sell a story. Isn't that right? To make a lot of money by blocking a deal on Gibraltar?'

'Don't believe him,' Vane said. 'The man's a crook.'

'Really?' Landsdowne purred, knowing that one or the other had to go to the wall. 'Really? Is that what you would be saying about Secretary of State Godber?'

'I wouldn't trust you further than I could throw you,' Billy Vane snapped, conscious of the concentration on the countess's face. Vane was ten feet from her, on the other side of the table, clad only in a towelling robe like some prisoner-of-war. There was no way he could jump that table but he wanted to wipe the grin off the Irishman's pink face. Instead he smiled, seeking to exert his charm. He smoothed his hair with his palm, a gesture Quintilla misinterpreted.

'Stay where you are.' The gun was tipped towards him.

'What do you really want?' the Countess insisted.

Vane found he had no answer, apart from the flattery which he had tried on her before. Melrose had led him there with some half-crazy notion of exposing the Irishman and finding out whether he had killed Wallace. But now Melrose had disappeared, gone back on his own to Madrid and left Billy in the lurch. He began to hate Melrose's guts.

And Landsdowne seized his chance. 'I tell you he's working for British Intelligence in cahoots with the CIA. He runs a recruitment agency as a cover.'

'It's a lie. It's not true.'

'You see, General, I've warned you. They are out to stop us. The man's a congenital liar. He said he had come from me. He runs an agency in Hereford.'

Vane felt his chances slipping. 'Don't trust the man,' he croaked.

He saw Quintilla growling. 'One of you must be a liar.'

'Listen, Countess,' Landsdowne said. 'You've been to London. You've heard what's on offer.'

'Don't trust him,' Vane shouted.

'Shut up. Remember it's all on the record, Countess, that conversation,' Landsdowne whispered. 'Our guarantee is a tape: your tape and our own version.'

It was the first that Vane had heard about the existence of a tape, and even at that stage he reckoned it would give him the evidence that he would need.

'Don't let him fool you. You can't have guarantees . . .'

But Vane's words seemed empty in front of the tribunal, with Landsdowne on the attack.

'If this boy gets back to England, Countess, he'll blow the whistle on the whole damned scheme . . . and you know what that means for you.'

And the Countess nodded. Vane saw Quintilla's hand tighten.

'I don't think he's going back,' Quintilla said.

Bastards, Vane thought. They really assumed that he was some undercover man for Military Intelligence. He swallowed and said 'Look. Believe me – '

But the Countess cut him short.

'Where is the American now? He also must be stopped.' She turned to Quintilla. 'Where is he?'

The General said, 'He went back with Lopez yesterday.'

The news stung Landsdowne too. He realized he had taken him too lightly.

'Lopez is unreliable,' she said. 'He cannot stop himself boasting.'

Vane saw the anxious look pass between the two Spaniards.

'We'll pick up the American,' Quintilla said, 'and have both birds in the cage.'

35

But Jake Melrose had learned one thing in a lifetime of dealings, and that was to cover his back. What Lopez had shown
him with that combination of pride and confidence, misread-
ing him as a neutral, told him it was time to go before the Air
Force came looking. Or the police. He had waited long enough
for Billy, and Billy could look after himself, that was for sure.

Leaving the Pinaflores base, he felt he'd been hit by the
heat. Lopez had wished him goodbye and waved him off
down the road as if the whole thing was assured, as if they'd
been friends for years. Maybe he thought he would scare the
shit out of some oddball Yank. Melrose found himself swearing, a kind of indecent fury at the way the world ordered
itself, and he could do nothing about it. Nothing. Any more
than he could have decided, actually decided, why he'd pulled
Brendan Wallace back from that goddam dead CH 53C all
those years ago.

Once out of Lopez's sight he climbed back on the bus and
drove it out through the gate. He'd been gone nearly two
hours but the bus guy was still there in the corner of the barn,
close by the parked car. He untied him and apologized, trying
to calm him down. He could see the man was terrified; not
much he could do to smooth him, but a handful of dollar bills
helped. Melrose kept the keys to the bus. He didn't want the
base alerted too quick.

Melrose was hammering the hire-car, determined to get
out of Spain; straight to the airport that evening, but no late
international flights, except to Paris, they told him.

'Okay. Okay,' he said. 'I'll take that.' And left the car there
and ran.

By the time that he landed at de Gaulle he had begun to
cool down. He reckoned, hell, Vane had jettisoned him and
any teamwork between them was broken.

He spent the night at his place in the rue de Miromesnil, and waded through the junk mail, grabbed a beer and a sandwich in the brasserie round the corner and tried to get through to Leibermann. But it was late and, unlike Wallace, Leibermann didn't take deals at home. At the Grosvenor Square Embassy all that the duty clerk would say was that he could leave a message and Harry would get back to him sometime on the following morning. Otherwise, if Jake came over, the acting Head of Station could maybe give him five minutes at round about four thirty. So Melrose sat down in the flat and wrote out the facts as he knew them, set down on two sides of report pad, to be delivered by hand.

He flew into London next morning and tried again from the airport.

'Harry, I got to see you.'

'Sure, Jake, sure. but I guess maybe they told you, I'm pretty damn busy.' He could sense Leibermann smiling, probably resuming his talks with Chris Pallett and the FS3s and 4s that he was now in charge of. Jesus, he would be telling them, hand over the mouthpiece, these contract men, they think they got instant access to the Acting Head. Let old Jake kick his heels a while.

So he was back in London, minus Vane, back in grubby old London awash with tourists and noise, and looking for another hotel room, another anonymous box, this time just off Earl's Court: the Redstone Private Hotel. He humped his case on to a chair and threw himself on the bed. These European affairs: headlines on Godber's speech defending his new White Paper; defence cuts, a claw-back in Europe. These European affairs in which Wallace had tried to meddle and got a knife for his pains. That fact still worried Melrose, along with the quiet warnings that Landsdowne had troubled to deliver. He couldn't pin the bastard down.

Yet there was something else. There was the woman called Claire who had asked him to keep her husband out of whatever political scandal should creep out of the woodwork. He saw her appealing eyes the last time that they had met, prompting him to enlist Billy. Find out what's afoot in Spain and keep Geoffrey out of trouble. Well, it had turned out to be more complicated than that. There was some kind of a deal that Landsdowne and his pals thought they had worked out with the Countess, a deal that had sparked off Vane. But those military guys like Quintilla and Lopez appeared to have gone one stage further. Whether or not the Countess knew, it was clear from what Lopez had shown him that they were now quite ready to jump the gun. It could be they would pitch in first. It was a monstrous scenario. Melrose had seen the model, the red flags marking the drop points, the choppers lined up on the apron. He got up and walked to the window and let up the blind for sunlight to spread into the fusty room. The window wouldn't budge.

Jake Melrose beat his sides in sheer frustration, trying to see through a situation which still didn't bring down the Ulsterman. And Harry fucking Leibermann was busy until four thirty.

He tried to phone Claire Powers, but of course there was no hope, only a muddle-headed answer after a while from some elderly cleaning woman. Mrs Powers wasn't in, she was teaching at her school. When he rang off he realized that he didn't even know where the damned place was.

Harry Leibermann had moved offices, just down the corridor, out of Wallace's old room. This one was bigger, wood-panelled.

'Welcome home, Jake.' He held out his hand and said, 'Coffee?'

'No, thanks.'

Leibermann offered a chair: a new suite of delicate leather, not like the battered set that he'd inherited from Brendan. He noticed it registered with Melrose.

'Well, Jake. We're moving on, I guess. Don't want too many associations with the past.' He sat heavily in the big chair, hands on his growing paunch, an inflatable man, full of his own importance. 'What's cooking in Madrid?' he asked.

Melrose told him. Told him all that he knew, from Claire's accusations about Godber and the lead to the Countess, through to their visit to Spain, Melrose and Vane together. Told him he didn't trust Vane, who went off the rails with women and was smitten by the Countess. Told him there was a double-cross in the wind; Godber had set up the Spaniards for some kind of phoney threat and he could end up with a real one, a para drop on the Rock.

'Baby!' Leibermann whistled. Melrose handed him the report that he'd written out in Paris, and the expenses claim. 'Two weeks, Harry,' he said. 'Air fares. Hotels. Cars. I'm out of pocket right now.'

And Leibermann looked at the claim form before counter-signing.

'Christ, Jake. That hotel in Madrid? You take the bridal suite or something?'

'Billy Vane booked it,' he said. He hated Vane: the bastard was trouble, even when he claimed expenses.

'Okay,' Leibermann said, 'I got the picture.'

Melrose looked tired.

'You'd better get a rest, Jake. Maybe take a vacation. You due to go back to the States? Going home?'

'The States?' Melrose was hardly sure whether he counted them home; whether he would ever get a thrill at unlocking the door into that disused apartment in the Reston condo, with joint rights to the lawns. A sunset home. 'No. I'm not going back yet, Harry. Listen.' His face had a kind of despair. He couldn't quite sign off. 'It ain't my business, Harry, what the Firm makes of this stuff. You got a political alliance to see to, I know that. NATO. That crap. But if you kind of spill the story – ' he could see the way Leibermann's mind went – 'I want to ask one favour. Try and keep this guy Powers out of it.'

'Powers? Why Powers?'

Leibermann toyed with his desk set. Very fancy, he thought. Like he was Head of the Firm. Now was the chance to make it.

'Geoffrey Powers is secretary to the Minister. Private Secretary. Implicated because he's gone along. He should have reported it, but, no sir, he kept his head down. I said I wouldn't get him hurt, Harry. I promised his wife, Okay? You cut him out of the story.'

And Leibermann gave Melrose a very sharp look. Well, well, the old bastard had a soft heart. He nodded in sympathy.

'Sure, Jake. Sure. Do what we can.'

Melrose stood up. 'Well. I guess that's it, Harry. My part of the job. You'll get the expenses through quick?'

Leibermann was busy, busy. He indicated his in-tray. 'Soon as I can, Jake. Just look at this lot. Withdrawals from Air Force bases. Visit of Congressmen. Some girl from Ohio falls under a train. You name it, Jake – '

'Okay.'

Leibermann held out a hand again.

'Well done, Jake. When you leaving the UK?'

Melrose really hadn't thought. He knew he wanted to see Claire before that happened, wanted it bad.

'Aw. Few days, I guess.'

Leibermann's eyes were cunning. 'If I were you, Jake. I'd get out pretty soon.'

36

The Countess was no longer a prospect, Vane had begun to realize. Whether Quintilla was her protector, uncle or sugar daddy, neither of them ever made clear, but he knew he had drawn the short straw between the General and the Irishman.

'Come with me,' the General had said, and he found himself bundled into a car, a military, khaki car with four stars and a black and red pennant. The Condesa had disappeared with Landsdowne.

He was driven, he reckoned, thirty miles further south into a country of scrub and stunted thorn trees, ending up at a camp in the hills. A grid of prefabricated huts behind a chain-link fence and recruit boys kicking up the dust, running across the exercise pitches in canvas shoes. Whether they were train-

ing for something, or whether it was just routine Billy Vane
could not be sure.

'Get in there,' Quintilla said, and handed him to a sardonic
lieutenant with a gleam in his eye, scuffed brown boots, an
Armalite on his shoulder.

'Listen,' Vane protested. 'I came here to see the Countess.
Spot of private business. You've no right to detain me.'

They locked him in one of the huts, a detention centre: a
barred window high on the door, a light from a single bulb,
a plank bed hanging from chains, two blankets, a chair, a
bucket. By climbing on the chair he could see the end of the
world from the tiny head-high window, also barred, on the
other side of the cell. Blue mountains in the distance, the bald
plain of Castile, somewhere beyond Toledo.

'Bastards,' he said.

He waited a long time, growing intensely hungry, before
the door opened again. It was dark now as they pushed him,
handcuffed, across the camp, sandwiched between two
guards.

'You can't do this – ' he began.

'Shut up,' they said.

He was led to a large room, a desk, three officers, Quintilla
in the middle. Another General. Another Colonel, with para
flashes: the 4th Parachute Battalion, the Africanistas, he read.
Well, well, he thought, a relic of Franco's Iron Guard. He
saw a flag with battle honours from the Civil War: Navarre,
Granada, Seville, Valladolid, Madrid.

'Name?'

'You've got my details,' he said.

The other General flicked the pages of his passport and
looked through his wallet. In contrast with Quintilla he was
dark and slender, distinguished by wings of white on the side
of his black hair. A bit of a ladies man, Vane thought, dismissing him. He concentrated on Quintilla.

'Occupation?'

He stared at them. 'Businessman.'

'What sort of business?' Quintilla snapped. He came round

the desk to loom in front of Vane, who was sitting facing them in a chair, his wrists now handcuffed behind him.

'I want these off,' he said. 'You've no right to arrest me. I demand legal representation.'

Quintilla hit him, slapped him with the palm of his hand, a heavy fist with a signet ring that drew blood from the side of Vane's mouth.

'Damn you,' Vane said.

'What sort of business?' he shouted.

Vane wondered how much they knew about his way of life. Surely they wouldn't have time to have his record checked out?

'Export recruitment services.'

'Liar.'

'No.'

The hand slapped his face again. Vane's cheek was angry and red and his mouth was bleeding.

'I have spoken to London. So has the Condesa. You recruit mercenaries. Landsdowne has confirmed it.'

'Export them,' Vane said. His eyes blazed and he held his head high.

'Mercenaries!'

'It's not illegal. Ex-servicemen.'

Quintilla put his hands on his hips. 'Trouble-makers. Ex-Special Air Services riff-raff.'

'Guardians of the peace,' Vane said.

Crack. Another blow across his face. He licked the blood from his lips. He did not whimper.

'I demand to see a lawyer. Put me in touch with the British Embassy.'

Quintilla laughed. The thin General smiled sourly. 'All in good time,' he said. 'They may not want to know you.'

The room was an ugly place, Vane realized. He was confronting the Army across a wooden floor, the bare boards of an interrogation room, shuttered and soundproofed: cork tiles on the walls and ceiling, an open door to a second room with an iron-framed single bed visible through the door.

'You are recruiting mercenaries for Gibraltar.'

'What?' Vane could hardly believe they had got it so wrong.

'You are a spy.'

'Ridiculous. Why should I spy?' Vane asked. But he cursed Melrose for persuading him to come and then deserting him.

Quintilla breathed into his face: he saw the man's pouchy eyes and heavy jaw-line: a thug, a pugilist in his youth, judging by the slant of his nose.

'I'll tell you why, Captain Vane. Because you are trying to find out our plans for Gibraltar.'

Their plans. 'What should I do that for?'

Crack. Another blow to the face that sent his senses reeling, though he pulled away from the worst of it.

'You come, you and your stupid American, because you have heard that we have plans for the Rock.'

'Rubbish.'

'Don't fool with me, Captain.' Quintilla dropped his voice until it was almost a growl. 'What is the British idea? How will they double-cross us?'

'For Christ's sake, General, watch that Irishman.'

They stared at him, the three men who themselves, he realized, had some kind of plan for that ancient and now redundant fortress. Gibraltar. He never wanted to hear the name again.

'Why are you here? Why did you come?'

His head was ringing and he found concentration impossible.

Why, why, why, they shouted at him. How could he say because of Melrose, because of Claire. He tried to tough it out on the one thing they seemed unsure of.

'Landsdowne,' he said.

'Landsdowne?' the General repeated. 'Why did you want to see him?'

'About a murder,' he said. His arms chafed, he was losing the argument. He wondered if they would take him through to the bed in the other room, a bare bedframe, no mattress, and set up electric goads. He'd seen it done himself, but could not tell them. He could not tell them anything. Billy Vane felt exhausted.

Quintilla smiled.

'I warn you, Vane. It is not necessary to lie. Your so-called friend Landsdowne, he has already told us. Told us that you are a cheap spy. An *agent provocateur*. You understand me?'

Crack! Another blow on the side of his face.

Quintilla was boiling with rage. 'You do not fool me, Captain. I want to know why you have come. Why you pursue the Condesa? What are your plans for mercenaries?'

Vane looked at them steadily. Quintilla was standing over him drawing blood with the signet ring, the other two impassive behind the wooden desk, like counter clerks. His head hurt like hell.

'I don't know what you're talking about.'

'All right. Why has the American disappeared? Disappeared leaving you here?'

'How the fuck do I know?' Melrose had run, the bastard.

The General loomed over him again, threateningly. 'Then you'd better sit down and think. Unless you do, you'll be hungry. And thirsty,' he said grimly. 'Or dead.'

The next night they brought him back, after a day in the cooler. Billy Vane was sore and sobered, with nothing to eat and, much worse, a raging thirst in that stifling cell. The sun seemed to beat on the roof, which he realized was corrugated iron and turned it into an oven. He was like some fried chicken, stripped down to his underpants, rubbing a swollen tongue on equally swollen lips, a bruise slowly hardening on the side of his face. Through the tiny window on the back wall the distant range of mountains outside shimmered in a blue mist. Unreachable as the moon.

Vane had a chance to think in between sweating it out in the fly-infested misery of that stinking cell, his slop bucket like a sewer. Had a chance to think it right through, from the first chance hint dropped by Powers, to the Yank who'd been sent to pay him and had done nothing of the fucking kind. Melrose had loused it up: loused it up all the way, first because of that guy Wallace, and now because he wanted Claire. The bastard wanted Powers's woman, Billy was sure about that.

He tried to lick his lips, moistened them with his own sweat dripping from his chest and armpits. Melrose was after Claire. Well, he wasn't going to have her. That cunt wasn't going to win. Not over Billy Vane.

Where the hell was Jake, to bail him out of this mess: Jake who had fixed himself up with that little arse-licker Lopez, got his story and vanished. Lopez. That little runt of a colonel with the Air Force. Melrose wasn't coming for him. Melrose had left him to stew in his own juice, while he ran back to London. Jake Melrose wasn't coming to help him. Jake had dropped him in the shit. Jake had sold him out in order to save his own skin.

The facts became confused in his mind. He stumbled as they led him back, across the deserted parade ground, into the same cruel room. His legs weren't so good any more, especially the bad one. Maybe they would notice soon and start to play on it. He tried to keep going, tried, but his mouth was so swollen that he could hardly speak. Twenty-four hours in this pen, thirty since he'd last had liquid, didn't do the mind much good, and he knew his reserves were going. He had to do something quickly.

Quintilla was there again, with the badger-head General. A different supporting Colonel, this one as swarthy as a Moroccan. There must be a real gang of them: para flashes, hard-line faces.

'I hope you've had a good rest,' Quintilla said.

Vane did not respond. This time he hung his head. He didn't want more rough stuff; he had to show them that wouldn't get them anywhere.

They nailed him to the chair again, a bright light in his eyes, handcuffed hands behind his back.

'Why have you come?' Quintilla repeated. He strode across the room, jack-booted, in battle fatigues, a pistol clamped to his side like some South American dictator.

'I told you. To talk to Landsdowne.'

Crack! They started on him again. His head swung bowed and bloody.

'You don't help yourself,' the second General said.

He knew he couldn't last much longer, else it would all go; the pride and self-assurance already stretched paper thin. The pain in his head, his leg, the unbearable dryness.

'I came to help the American,' he whispered between bloody teeth. 'The American Melrose. The CIA.'

'Ah.'

Quintilla stopped his mad bull pacing. 'Why?'

'To find out about Gibraltar.'

'Where is Melrose?'

So Jake had not been traced. The bastard had already pulled out. 'Back in London, I should think.'

Quintilla looked at the others.

'Get Lopez,' one of them said.

They took Billy Vane through and tied him on the iron bedstead. Naked. An electric prod on his genitals. And hurt his leg. Just as he expected. And feared.

37

Leibermann didn't handle it himself. He used Chris Pallett: Chris who knew Melrose of old and thought himself too clever by half, Chris who had handled the Brendan Wallace story with the press. Chris who hoped for Harry's job, and now felt disappointed. He called him from along the corridor, one floor down. Pallett's plain face, Leibermann thought, as Chris sat in the chair Jake Melrose had occupied an hour or so before, Pallett's face had no distinguishing features. It might have been a photo-fit it was so bland. The fellow now had his big opportunity.

'Chris, I got a great story for you. I want it in the British press. Unattributable. You know those shite-hawks have been jumping up and down trying to get a lead on Godber. Well, now's their chance. Give it to 'em hard, Chris. No bullshit. Mister Goddam Secretary of State Godber is planning a little war with Spain, to show off his mini-Navy. And the goddam Spaniards are taking him at his word.'

'Jesus Christ.'

'I'll give you all the dope. Just get it across in private. You know the drill. You handled 'em well over Brendan. Use the same guys. Unattributable briefing.'

'What have I got as evidence, Harry? Credibility?'

'Oh for Christ's sakes, Chris. Here – ' And he handed over a copy of Jake Melrose's report.

'Do you want me to name Jake?'

'If you have to,' Leibermann said.

Pallett skimmed through it quickly, so excited that his glasses slipped down his nose. He was sweating with pleasure. If he picked this up right and stopped an international incident, that would be a big credit in his investigation report. He nearly wet himself.

'It'll damage Godber,' he warned.

'Damage? It'll sink the bastard,' Leibermann said. 'He's never been reliable. A Mister Big-mouth. Wanted Yanks out of Europe last year: all that "We can handle it" stuff. Chris, the important thing is that we drop a hint about talks on selling out Gibraltar that will blow this little macho confrontation idea right out of the water. Okay?' He paused, then added, 'I guess that's the line Brendan was after . . .'

'Okay by me,' Pallett said.

That evening he called the first of several groups of pressmen to briefings at various bars and hotels. Anonymous tip-offs, source unidentified. Told them that reports received showed that there was collusion between a British Cabinet Minister and the Spanish Falange. Named the man as Freddie Godber, strictly off the record.

'He'll deny it,' they said, grinning. 'Freddie's a slippery customer.'

Told them they could check with the Countess of the Asturias.

'Come on,' they said. 'Some crackpot Spanish madonna! Who you going to put up front? Who is that making the story? We've got to have a face.'

At first Pallett tried to hedge. He didn't particularly want to name a guy that he'd known in a small way over nearly twenty years. He didn't want to cut Jake's throat and he knew the poor devil felt bad about a life in the field while Chris had climbed, if not high, at least a decent few rungs up the internal ladder. The Firm looked after its own, but Jake, after all, had left the Firm and set up on contract. A freelance had to take his chances. A freelance was fair game.

'Guy called Jake Melrose,' he said.

'Where do we talk to him?'

'You could try the Redstone Hotel. Earl's Court,' he said. You could wash your hands of responsibility for a guy on a temporary contract.

38

There was a call from the press office at seven fifty-five p.m. Friday evening, just as Geoffrey Powers was leaving, after a long hot week.

Keith Bramley, Godber's assistant private secretary, took it, then handed it over.

'It's John O'Brien. Says it's urgent. Wants you.'

It was unusual for the Chief Press Officer to come through as late as that, normally he pushed off home by half past five, but O'Brien sounded distraught. Bramley switched the intercom through.

'I've just had *The Times* on, and the bloody *Sun*. What's all this about Freddie organizing a threat to Gibraltar?'

Powers's face whitened. He looked across the desk at the APS and denied all knowledge.

'I don't understand,' he said. But he did; and Bramley saw it in his eyes, and thought back to what Geoffrey had said about Godber in private, behind his back. The big head, the liar, the megalomaniac.

'I can't hold them,' O'Brien squealed. 'They've got this

story, says Godber's running an ego trip to show how tough he is. Sets up the Spanish looney Right to make a claim on Gib, and then moves in with the Rapid Development Force. Paras, the Navy, the lot.'

'Where . . . where did it come from, John?' Powers's throat had gone dry. A clerk came in with some papers and he pushed them away.

'Don't bother me. What?'

'I said that's not all. According to this source, some bloody Yank, the Spaniards are double-crossing Freddie, using it as an excuse to mount the real thing now that the garrison's gone.'

'What Yank?'

'A guy called Melrose.'

Powers felt cold. Jake Melrose, who had phoned him up asking for Claire. Then he recovered himself and smiled at Bramley on the other side of the office.

'It's absurd. A pack of lies. Tell them to boil their heads.' He replaced the phone and found that he was shaking.

Two minutes later O'Brien was on again.

'They're after a statement,' he said. 'A denial. Where's Freddie?'

'Gone off to Worcestershire. He won't be back till Monday. He's incommunicado.'

'Jesus Christ, they've all got it now,' O'Brien said. 'The whole bloody Lobby is buzzing. It'll be all over the ten o'clock news. ITN want an interview.'

'Well, they can't. He can make a statement on Monday.'

'The weekend press will crucify him unless they get a firm denial. Jesus . . .' Powers heard the telephones ringing in the background of O'Brien's call. 'What about Brocklehurst?'

'For God's sake, no.'

Powers's thin face snapped shut, remembering the tape that the political agent had secreted somewhere after they had met the Countess. He couldn't use Brocklehurst who had him by the short and curlies.

O'Brien came back again. Panic. More telephones. One of

them got straight past the switchboard somehow, and knew his name.

'Mr Powers? Could you comment on the suggestion – '

'No. I can't.' He rang off. But that was worse than a quick denial, he realized. It encouraged speculation.

He got through to O'Brien.

'Tell them it's rubbish. Crap.'

'Is it?' O'Brien asked. Bramley thought Powers looked ill: the peakiness made him seem yellow, almost Chinese in the evening light.

'Yes.'

'Okay, you talk to them. You tell 'em Geoffrey.'

O'Brien gave way to the pressure. Six lines, all of them used. No prospect of an instant denial, no way to kill it off unless the Private Secretary acted firmly on Godber's behalf.

He put the *Sunday Times* through. Safe pair of hands. 'Don't mince words, Geoffrey,' he said.

'Mr Powers, we have a story that the Secretary of State intends to secure his position by a demonstration of strength in response to a threat to Gibraltar. That he's been involved in discussions, secret discussions, with the Spanish Falangists, through intermediaries. True or false, Mr Powers?'

'Utterly false,' Powers said between clenched teeth.

'That's very strange, Mr Powers,' the *Sunday Times* man said, 'because you have been named as one of those involved in the discussions, in London recently.'

Powers touched incoherence. 'What?'

'A meeting took place in London, didn't it? A couple of weeks ago. At Claridge's Hotel. To discuss some kind of deal with the Countess of the Asturias. You are named as being present, together with Mr Brocklehurst and somebody called Colin Landsdowne. Who is Landsdowne?'

Powers felt his stomach contract, as the ulcer peppered his guts. Somebody knew. Somebody had got an account. It couldn't be Brocklehurst or Landsdowne, they were committed to Godber. He hadn't said anything to anyone, least of all Claire. Oh God. Oh Christ. Some bastard had been talking in Spain. He wanted to sit there and die.

'Mr Powers? Are you still there?'

'Who . . .' he said, 'who gave you this story?'

'The source is an American. A freelance called Melrose is named, Mr Powers. Have you ever heard of him?'

'No,' Power shouted. 'For God's sake go away. No.'

But he remembered with horror the American who had called from Paris, one wet afternoon. Jake Melrose.

Melanie Godber took the first warning of trouble in the study at Lower Broome, nine thirty that night, and Freddie relaxing with a drink on the terrace, thinking how nice the roses were, and the formal garden, and the lattice-work in the arbour dappled with evening light. His, all his, and still on the way. She had to call him upstairs.

'It's Geoffrey Powers. Says there's some kind of story. A leak about you and Gibraltar.'

She looked at him: the firm head, the Roman curls and full sensuous lips. She never asked what he was up to so long as she was given free rides, a mutually beneficial arrangement.

On the phone Powers said, 'It's going to be all over the papers. That you've been having private talks with the Countess of the Asturias, using Landsdowne as a go-between. The whole damned business. It'll be on the ITV news. They want a statement now.'

'Tell them it's nonsense.' He sat down at his large ornate desk with the group Cabinet photo and the signed smile by the PM mocking him behind the pen tray.

'Secretary of State, it won't wash. They're accusing you of setting up an incident.'

'They're bluffing,' Godber snapped. 'Speculation and smears.'

'Unfortunately not.' Powers's voice sounded betrayed. 'They've got the names of Brocklehurst and Landsdowne, and the date of the meeting at Claridge's. They've got me.'

'Deny it. Deny everything.' Godber knew he would get through. These little flurries, these antics, they were the stuff of politics. Publicity never did harm.

'They want to interview you for the main news.'

'No,' he said. 'No. Impossible. My weekends are sacrosanct.' He would be seen in church, playing the country gentleman, not dragged in the mud by rumours and speculation. 'I'll say something in the House.'

'We won't be able to hold that line. If you're not available they want to talk to me.'

'You? Why you?' Surely not the little official who organized his office?

'They know I was at the meeting.'

It dawned on Godber that if one of them squealed – Brocklehurst, or Landsdowne or Powers – he would be deep in trouble. Where had the leak come from?

'Ring Brocklehurst,' he said. 'Tell him to get up here fast. And Landsdowne.'

'I don't think Landsdowne's in the country.'

'Oh, for Christ's sake! Brocklehurst must get hold of him. Get them back here at once.'

'It's late, Secretary of State.'

Godber looked at his watch. He had to watch the ten o'clock news.

'All right. Get Peter first thing tomorrow morning. It'll blow over,' he said, with more confidence than he felt. 'Just say it's not worth a comment. And keep out of the way.' He stopped to consider, having secured his flank. 'Where do these stories originate?'

'Apparently an American called Melrose, who seems to have nosed around in Spain, and talked to the Countess.'

'Jesus Christ! And who's he?'

Powers bit back the admission that there might have been a chain: Claire to Billy, Vane to the Yank.

'I don't know.'

'All right,' Godber said. 'We must rubbish him. Now get on with it, man.'

He had no sooner signed off than Number 10 came on the scrambler. An angry voice.

'Freddie, what is all this?'

'Nothing, Prime Minister. Some kind of press fantasy.'

211

'Freddie, is anything going on behind my back? Anything at all?'

'Of course not,' he said smoothly.

'No talks with the Spaniards?'

'No.'

A pause. He could almost feel the eyes.

'All right. Then you'd better say so on Monday. In the House.'

'Yes, Prime Minister.'

But they wouldn't go away. He was pestered by several more calls. He saw some fool on 'Newsnight' speculating on the chances of 'playing the Jingo card'; somebody asking a general if there was any sense in it; and an ITV Special about a crisis in relations with Spain. The bloody Rock; he wished he had never heard of it and never heard the name of Landsdowne.

39

They brought Billy Vane back with blood between his legs, a beaten, shaking wreck, on the verge of unconsciousness, one eye already closed, mumbling through his swollen mouth.

Quintilla had him tied to the chair again; tied so he could not fall. They splashed his face with water, the first he'd had for three days, in that heat, in that choking, fear-laden, blood-streaked, murderous three days of solitary.

'Listen, Captain,' Quintilla said. 'We have been in touch with Colonel Lopez. You remember Lopez, my friend?'

He held his hand under Vane's chin and breathed fumes into his face. Hot brandy-breath.

Vane nodded.

'So. Your American hero has left you in the lurch. He has abused your friendship and told lies. He comes here, he asks our plans, as if he is a friend. He goes to Pinaflores. You know that, eh? You understand, eh? And he sees certain things.

212

And he goes. He flees. He leaves you in the lurch. That is not right.'

The blood came and went in Vane's mouth as he struggled to understand. Jake Melrose, who wanted Claire.

Quintilla stood back. 'Melrose is back in London. He tries to sell a story to the press. He is quoted on the television. He thinks he is some kind of smart guy. You follow me?'

He lifted Vane's head again, staring into the fuddled eyes. 'You have been betrayed. And he goes round telling lies.'

Billy Vane groaned as the fingers pinched his face, the bruises on his mouth and jaw.

The General jerked Vane's head to stop it falling. A trickle of blood and perspiration ran down the left side of his mouth.

'I could kill you,' he said, 'and nobody would know the difference. Except that you can help us.'

Vane had gone. Switched off.

'More water,' Quintilla bawled.

They brought a bucket and tipped it over the thin figure strapped on the chair. The water swilled down his bare chest, down the blood-soaked trousers, and ran to waste on the floor.

'You make such a mess,' the General said. 'Useless mercenary trash.'

Billy Vane had nearly reached the end of the road. But not quite. He raised his head and tried to spit. A thin slobber of bile eased from the swollen lips.

Quintilla laughed, a raucous bellowing laugh.

'We won't kill you,' he said. 'I am sending you home. No doubt he will name you, too, this Melrose. Then you can accuse him. Brand him as a liar, this man who said he was your friend. This criminal who has deserted you.' He squatted down eyeball-to-eyeball in the squalid room. 'I think he is your enemy.'

The powerful head leered at Vane. 'Your enemy, eh? You follow me? What is he?'

'A bastard, like you,' Vane groaned.

40

Peter Brocklehurst drove to the house at Lower Broome next morning, when the story was all over the papers: 'Crisis over Gib', 'Godber defends the Rock', 'Spanish threat to NATO security', 'Hands off: it's ours'. Stupid bloody stories about secret talks with the Falangists, and even more crazy suggestions that they would jump the gun now that Godber had removed the garrison. Freddie, for Christ's sake, as if it was his decision, and not the Cabinet's.

The Secretary of State found himself growing angry as he shouted at Brocklehurst. Everybody damned well knew that if it hadn't been for the mismanagement of the economy there would have been no need to count the candle-ends. One thousand five hundred British servicemen, that's all they had bloody well saved; and lost a base in the Med and handed it over on a plate. All that he was trying to do was make the best of a bad job – couldn't they damned well see that? The local Gibraltar Regiment, a glorified Territorial Army Unit without even a field battery or anti-aircraft guns? It was a bloody disgrace, he told Brocklehurst. And now that fool Gervase Taylor was getting cold feet about a military exercise which he said would be politically motivated. The CIGS would have to go.

The agent agreed. His fresh-complexioned face – as cheerful as a bookie about to make a run, Godber thought – nodded assent. Within themselves both men were less sure.

'It'll blow over,' Brocklehurst said.

Godber handed him a gin and tonic.

'Who is this wretched man Melrose?'

'Some snooper from the CIA. Doesn't know his arse from his elbow.'

'Get me the American Ambassador – '

Brocklehurst waved him down. 'I wouldn't, Freddie. It only

adds fuel to the flames. We've got to drop it now. Drop the whole damned idea once it's out in the open. Damage limitation exercise.'

Godber saw that. He walked out on to the terrace and calmed down. His roses, his estate. On the way to the top there must be no suggestion of falsehood, no murmurs of foul play. He hadn't liked the tone of the PM's voice. He could hear the knives sharpening in the political air, but they mustn't be in his back. He realized he was running scared: he could only make one mistake.

Brocklehurst came out beside him. Christ, Godber wondered, why had he risked his future on such a chancy proposition? He had let himself be led by the nose by this bumped-up PR man out of Saatchi and Saatchi, for the sake of ambition. 'Vaulting ambition,' Shakespeare said somewhere, 'which o'erleaps itself.' His resentment was bitter and deep. He feared that his less sincere friends would murmur that he'd sounded them out about some such crazy adventure. But they would all deny even considering it: that cold fish Philip Pickering, Duggie Drumblane and the rest – fair weather sailors with the guts of a louse. He jutted his chin out towards the Malvern hills. 'Bugger them,' he said.

Melanie appeared, looking elegant and he took comfort from her. He held her hand, his peach, his honey-dew, his most secure supporter. Lady Godber. What if she did her own thing? She kept it entirely private, as befitted her background. Why couldn't they do the same with a little bit of political intrigue?

'I've cancelled the calls, darling. They're giving "line unobtainable".'

'Good.'

'Is Mr Brocklehurst staying for lunch?'

'No.' Godber said. 'I think not.' He turned his ineffable public smile on the younger man. Brocklehurst had caused enough trouble, and Freddie was still wanting him to sew up the defensive line. Privately he vowed that Brocklehurst would also go as soon as the dust settled.

'Where's Landsdowne? About time he showed up.'

Brocklehurst shuffled his feet. 'I'm afraid he's not coming, Freddie.'

Don't keep calling me Freddie, Godber thought. I've let this young Turk get too big for his boots, and too familiar.

'Not coming? Why not?'

'I gather he's being questioned in Spain.'

It was Monday afternoon when he rose to make a statement after Questions: a packed House, a murmur of tension on the green benches. Godber began to realize he might have more enemies than friends in the massed ranks behind him, let alone the Opposition.

Best suit, small rose in the buttonhole, smooth front for the cameras.

'Mr Speaker, with permission, I wish to make a short statement. Allegations have been made in the press, and in certain other quarters, that private discussions have been conducted with certain interests in Spain concerning the future of Gibraltar. I wish to make it absolutely clear – absolutely clear – that no such discussions have taken place. The rumours are false and totally without foundation. The future of Gibraltar remains a matter entirely for the British Government and the wishes of the residents of the Rock.'

Godber sat down to muted murmurs of support, and the House moved on to fresh business.

Powers heard him and shuddered, but Godber was all over him, as soon as he came out of the Chamber.

'Well? How did that go?'

Geoffrey smiled like the sun on a razor-blade. 'I only hope it's enough.'

Godber drew him aside. 'What do you mean, enough? Let's go back to my room.'

They marched along the corridors and up the narrow stairs. Once inside, Godber said, 'I don't want a word, from now on, about Gib. Another word. You understand?'

Powers was very white, a muddy, chalky white, thinking of his voice on the tapes. He stood on the other side of the Secretary of State's desk, rigid, almost to attention, and handed over a paper: an Immediate telegram, from the British Embassy, Madrid.

'The trouble is, Landsdowne's been traced in Spain and questioned by the police. He says discussions have taken place, and that someone authorized them.'

Silence.

Godber read it three times. Landsdowne had sold a discredited idea. Landsdowne was now deserting the ship. Under interrogation. He got a grip on himself, his mind boiling. If the Irishman was believed, he would be accused of lying to the House of Commons, an offence the House would not forgive, and neither would the PM or the Party. He saw his whole career, the years of effort, crumble on two men's assertions, that Ulster dirty tricks man, Colin Landsdowne, and the unknown American working for the CIA. Jesus Christ. The colour flamed in his cheeks. He saw Powers watching him like a snake in the grass.

'Get out. Leave me alone.'

Powers went without a word and Godber sat down to think. If the chickens came home to roost as close as that there was only one hope he had of extricating himself from the chicken-shit. He needed a scapegoat. And the more he thought about it, the more obvious it seemed. Three men had been party to talks: Landsdowne, Brocklehurst and Powers. Three men had been named in the press, but only one could be publicly tainted by the accusation of ambition, a naked lust for preferment that might have led him on, led him to unauthorized actions. That man was was Geoffrey Powers.

41

Chris Pallett phoned through to Jake, now under an assumed name, Roberts, at another hotel. Next rule in the book: keep moving around, easy in the UK, nobody asked for credentials. You could sign in as Adolf Hitler and nobody wanted to know, but Melrose had kept the Firm informed. A hotel along the road, close by the Albert Hall. With that lean and hungry look he might have been a musician.

'Jake? You creeping out on the press?'

'Yeah. Publicity wasn't part of the deal.'

'But you got real coverage, Jake. You seen the stories?' Pallett sounded pleased with himself.

'Sure. I seen 'em. What d'you think I had to move base for?'

'Aw, come on, man. Had to get you on record. It's blown the thing wide open. I'm gonna write a citation.'

'Citation? I just want my expenses.'

'Sure, Jake, sure. They're going through okay. Paid over to you in Paris. Reckon soon you can get back there, out of the limelight.'

'I'm not in the limelight now, Chris. You're the only guy knows I'm here.'

'Well, I have to say, Jake, I don't think we can hold that.'

'What's that mean?' Melrose was tired of dissembling. He just wanted to see Claire, tell her how it had come out, explain that he hadn't named Geoffrey and then . . . and then . . . He hadn't worked further than that. He too was in a turmoil, but he wouldn't go until he'd seen her, that much was clear.

'They want to talk to you, Jake. The press boys. You heard Freddie Godber's denial?'

'I heard. I seen it on TV.' He felt less compunction now, knowing the man was a dissembler.

'Christ knows where they got your name from.'

You bastard, Melrose thought.

'You shouldn't push 'em away, Jake. They scent blood, Jake. Those guys are closing in for a kill.'

'I don't want to drop anybody in the shit, Chris.'

Pretty damn late now, Pallett thought. 'Of course not,' he said. 'We just want you to talk to a few of 'em. Really explain what happened: like how you talked to this Countess and stumbled on a highball. Act some kind of Deep Throat.'

Melrose seemed to find that hard. He was not a man who liked talking, least of all about himself.

'No way.'

'Listen, Jake. It's an order. Part of the Wallace deal.'

'Not part of any deal, Chris. You know that.'

Jesus, the man was obtuse. Patiently, Pallett said, 'You want your expenses paid? Okay. You finish the job.'

'I'm sorry, Chris. No way.'

'Extra three grand . . .' Pallett was sticking his neck out, but Leibermann had given him carte blanche.

'Work off, Chris.'

'Okay. Okay. I know. You feel sore. You feel used. But it ain't like that, Jake. Godber's on the record now, man, in the House of Commons, denying he had any dealings with the Spaniards. That's crap and you know it. All you got to do is say so. Back up this guy Landsdowne who's selling out for big money in Spain, and we've got him sewn up.'

'I think Landsdowne had a hand in killing Wallace,' he said.

'Jake, you got any evidence?'

'Nope.' Fuck them, he decided, these flies round the dung-hill. Even if he didn't get paid. Fuck them. He wasn't going to be interviewed. 'Go wash a shirt,' he said.

And Pallett bounced back to him, before he could say more. 'Well now. Sorry about that Jake. Sorry you feel that way, 'cos we've already told the press guys. Told them where you're hanging out, name of Roberts. You'll find them around there any time now. The rat pack.'

Melrose had packed his bag again, the one and only Kluge suitcase, his portable home: two suits, four shirts, two pairs of shoes, a tie, toiletries, some papers, some money, and the pocket Testament given him by his mother, the only thing left from the past; he carried it like an icon, or a St Christopher charm, although he never read it.

He phoned the reception desk and told them to get the account ready. He wanted out. But he was already too late.

'There's some gentlemen to see you, sir,' the receptionist said.

'Tell them I'm not at home.'

'They know you're here, sir.'

He looked round the room, his loaded case on the bed.

219

Sneaking away, another place, maybe go back to Paris, maybe not. In the end, better not to see Claire. Let them all stew. Hell, no, he wasn't sneaking away. He'd face them out.

He left the case and walked downstairs.

There was already a mob in the lobby: ten, fifteen, twenty guys with cameras. Pallett had been too damned smart putting them on the trail. The Embassy wanted this. They wanted to body-bag Godber. None of that phoney crap about not interfering with other people's domestic affairs, not when they were upsetting your interests. The special relationship, shit. Okay. He confronted them, and the receptionist nodded them through to the hotel lounge, disturbing the payroll cat. They perched on the chairs, in the windows, an unruly gang of anoraks and sneakers and jeans, the gentlemen and ladies of the media, in this great democratic world of ours, he thought grimly.

'You Jake Melrose?'

He nodded, standing tall. They noted a square-jawed face, tanned, sharp-looking eyes, grey hair, lightweight jacket.

'Yup.'

'What do you do for a living, Mr Melrose?'

'I'm freelance,' he said.

'Freelance what, Mr Melrose?'

'No comment.'

A frisson of excitement. One of the girls, face like a tapir, said. 'Mr Melrose, we have it on record that Freddie Godber, Secretary of State for Defence, has been having private talks about the future of Gibraltar. Yet he denied it in the House of Commons yesterday. Maybe you heard? True or false?'

'No comment.'

'What do you mean, no comment?'

'Not my business. I got to go . . .'

'Where?'

'Well . . .' he hesitated.

'Have you just come from Spain, Mr Melrose?'

'Yeah. A few days ago.'

'Did you see the Countess of the Asturias?'

'Did you know about a plot?'

220

'Has the Minister been in touch with you?'

'Are you a member of the CIA?'

'One question at a time, please.'

'Come on, Mr Melrose, how'd they get your name?'

'Who?'

'The guy who told us. Unattributable.'

Yeah. And he knew who that was. 'You mean the US Embassy?'

'You said it, Jake.'

'Okay, Jake. What's the story? Godber trying to set himself up as Numero Uno? Some big deal on Gib? What's going on? What have you been finding out?'

'No comment.'

'Of course there's a comment, Mr Melrose. It's your word against his. You going to be called a liar?'

'I'm not a liar.'

'Okay, right. Now what's this about the Spaniards having got some other plan? Parachute drop on the Rock? Somebody saw a model, Mr Melrose.'

He tried to push through them, but more hounds had arrived and he was wedged in the room.

'No comment.'

'Did you see a model, Mr Melrose? If not, why did some-body say so?'

'It was a training scheme.'

'Oh. A training scheme to airdrop the Rock? That really so, Jake?'

'Look, I'm telling you guys, I got nothing to say. If some other bastard says it, that ain't my business. Okay?'

'What about this Irishman, Landsdowne, who's been sound-ing off in Madrid? He says that talks have taken place.'

'No comment.'

'Do you know Landsdowne, Mr Melrose?'

'Not personally,' he said.

'Have you met him?'

'Nope. Come on now. I got to go . . .'

'Wait a minute, Mr Melrose. Do you deny these reports are said to have come from you?'

'I said no comment.'

'That means you don't deny them.'

They goaded him. Angrily he snapped out, 'Why don't you ask Landsdowne?'

'Who is Colin Landsdowne, Mr Melrose?'

'I know who Landsdowne is,' said a guy in a leather jerkin. 'He was involved in the Lebanon affair, trying to get hostages out of Beirut.'

'That's right. Same deal as Brendan Wallace . . .'

'Okay,' Melrose said. 'Now you know. Go ask him, let me alone.'

'Where is Landsdowne now, Mr Melrose?'

'Your problem,' Melrose replied. He would have liked to know but some things had to be left.

He managed to get through them then, retrieved his bag and called a cab, still pursued into the street.

'Just drive,' he said. Drive, while he tried to think.

The taxi took him down Knightsbridge, the traffic swirl of Hyde Park Corner, down towards Buckingham Palace. The Guards in their red coats, toy soldiers with real guns. He'd lived with that world too long, it seemed he could never escape it. At Waterloo Station he said, 'Okay, stop off.'

At least they weren't following him now, hounding him, those jackals. He carried his suitcase into the station and saw on the departure board the times of trains to Wimbledon. For one moment he contemplated going there, but that would be crazy too. She wouldn't be at home, and what would he say to her? Maybe he would apologize, say that he loused it up, he and Billy between them. The thought of Billy worried him. They were going to go public between them, when they had all the facts. That had been his original idea. Instead he'd left Billy there and garbled his piece to Leibermann, and his own people had opened the bag.

Billy wouldn't like that.

Where was Billy, he wondered?

He sat in the station buffet drinking coffee, while the world rushed for trains, and realized he had nowhere to go. In a way nowhere to hide. And in his heart he knew why he

222

stayed, why he didn't get the hell out and go back to Paris and start on the contract job, the security of Uncle Sam's property in Budapest, Prague, Bucharest. In his heart he knew that he coveted another man's wife.

None of them let Godber go. Freddie Godber heard to his horror that the American had been tracked down and had refused to deny the story. An ex-Marine Corps Captain on some kind of surveillance job. Just like that devil Landsdowne, now selling his story in Madrid, according to Brocklehurst.

He tried to hold the line. He issued a further denial and referred to his Commons statement. No Minister misled the House, why didn't they damned well believe him.

The *Standard* came out with pictures of the Countess of the Asturias, glamorous in a low-cut black dress.

He got on the phone again to Brocklehurst.

'This has got to stop. That meeting you had with the Countess? Did you keep any record?'

'No, Freddie, but she did,' Brocklehurst lied, thinking of the tape recording securely in his safe: enough to keep Powers onside if he thought of running for cover.

'It's got to be destroyed.'

'Don't worry,' his agent said. 'She won't want to disclose it. It'll all blow over in a couple of days.'

But Godber was not so sure.

42

Powers steamed home to Wimbledon that day, his face chilling those who saw him in the train, a mask of hate and fear. Godber, the bastard he had tied himself to, would let him down. He knew it, he could see it coming in the curve of the politician's lips, the way his eyes were shifting. Freddie Godber with his back to the wall was a very dangerous animal, and he'd be looking for a scapegoat: unstable advisers, acting without his authority; that would be the last-ditch line.

He got in just as Claire came back from the afternoon's school. She was surprised to see him there, and shocked at the way he looked.

'Are you all right? Why back so early?'

He followed her through to the lounge, where she put her legs up on the settee. She was perturbed by the way he stood there, clenching and unclenching his hands. She couldn't stand the look on his face and found herself sitting tensely, as if he was interviewing her. Geoffrey had not said a word, just stared at her wild-eyed.

'Are you feeling all right? These stories on the news . . .' she ventured. 'Shall I get you a drink?' She was scared for him and for their future.

He shook his head in a distracted way.

'Say something,' she said. 'Geoffrey what's happened?'

He was breathing heavily, rocking in the middle of the room, blank-eyed. It occurred to her that he was ill, that he might have had a brainstorm, a stroke, brought on by overwork.

'It's Godber, isn't it?' she said. 'I wish to God you'd leave that job . . .' but her voice trailed away. The intensity of his eyes disturbed her. She seemed to see contempt in them, contempt directed at her.

'Say something, Geoffrey . . . Don't stare at me like that.'

But he walked slowly across, and one look embodied his bitterness as she confronted him. At that moment he hated her, holding her somehow responsible, hating even her prettiness in the neat summer dress. Worse, he knew she wanted to touch him and could not bear it. He froze her so she could not move. And then his hands reached out towards her, as if he was managing to respond, reached out and felt the collar, then the bones of her neck. His fingers were icy cold. For one awful moment she thought he would put them round it, tighten them on the throat. She tried not to back away. She caught the sourness of his breath, saw the pores of his skin as he stood inches from her, and the inflammation in his eyes. His

224

hands moved down and tore at the front of her dress. The stitching gave way and he pulled it half off her shoulders.

'Geoffrey! Don't! Geoffrey – ' Tears streamed down her face.

He ripped at the dress again, pulling it further down on her arms, ruining it.

'Geoffrey, no!' She tried to run but could not. She seemed rooted to the spot, almost powerless, horrified at the repressions that she had only guessed at which now boiled up within him.

She tried to pull up the dress without attempting to fight him. He pushed her towards the settee.

'Geoffrey! For God's sake . . .'

'You've sold me out. Sold me to Billy Vane.'

'Geoffrey. No. You did it yourself. I'm sorry. So sorry for you, darling.' Feeling humiliated, she cowered on the cushion, away from him as he leaned over. Christ knows she had played a role, that was the thing that appalled her: in the end he had driven her into Billy Vane's arms. She saw the danger too late.

He slapped her. He hit her, and she was unable to move. She crouched with her back towards him, hardly feeling the blows.

'You little bitch.'

'I'm sorry, Geoffrey. Oh God, I'm sorry.' But she could no longer even pretend that she loved him. Geoffrey Powers did not want her, except as a means of abuse, of taking out some demon that was eating his being.

At last he stopped. She heard him gasping for breath: he wasn't even fit.

'You've sold yourself,' he said. 'Sold yourself and sold me.'

'Geoffrey, that's not true . . .'

'Billy Vane? Where is he?' Worse, he had once been a friend, a friend he had formerly admired, and even envied.

'Billy?' She dried her tears. 'I don't know. I haven't seen him for weeks.'

Powers was calming down and she ventured to turn round. There were marks on her arms: perhaps she had deserved

them. She felt oddly stirred, and yet she couldn't stand him.
She began to resettle the dress, to retrieve a scrap of dignity.

'Stay still,' he said. She thought he would hit her again.

'Geoffrey, I've had enough. This can't go on.'

'You told Billy Vane. You told him, you told him, you told
him,' he repeated. Not that she'd gone away for that fatal
weekend. Not that Billy might have persuaded her to spend
the night with him. Geoffrey was now shifting the guilt by
blaming her for the leak.

'No. You told him yourself,' she said, and saw him flinch.
'Billy picked it up here.'

Geoffrey Powers stared at her; the fight had been drained
from him, only the misery remained. He told her that he'd
been named, that he was going to be the fall-guy, Godber's
word against his. She murmured her sympathy.

'Go to hell,' he said. He walked slowly from the room, his
stomach shooting with pain.

She gathered her clothes from the floor and cried at the
wrecked room, the bitterness that had come between them,
the parting of the ways.

43

This time Graham Didsbury insisted on seeing Freddie Godber
himself. In person, in private, on Frewin's instructions, as he
said to Geoffrey Powers, noting how eaten up the civil servant
seemed.

They came in the evening, Didsbury with another man,
introduced as Bloomfield. Didsbury was short and dark, neat
as a tailor, with a naval crest on his tie. Bloomfield wore a
plain grey suit and ungentlemanly shoes.

Geoffrey Powers showed them in to the Secretary of State's
room in the ministerial corridor of the House of Commons.
Godber had been awkward – always a sign of trouble – and
insisted on seeing them there instead of in the MoD. It was

almost as if he felt the Gothic room was a talisman, a guarantee against harm, or at least against unwelcome intruders from the outer space of the Department who might have insisted on sitting in – such as Sir Henry Burton.

Didsbury displayed an identity card. A card stamped 'Cabinet Office', justifying his existence, even giving his date of birth, marital status and previous rank: a married man of forty-eight, formerly in naval Intelligence. The look in his eyes seemed to expect a confession, and Bloomfield said, 'I hope you don't mind my taking notes.'

Godber thrust forward that well-photographed head, wanting to be taller and stronger. Haircut by Trumper of Curzon Street, suit by Airdey and Strawson. A clever, prosperous bastard running for the Leadership, Didsbury decided, and with a dose of the shits.

'Of course not. May I offer you a drink?'

They both declined politely, but Godber helped himself to whisky: another sign of pressure, they thought.

He sipped it cautiously, nosing at them over the glass. 'It's been a long and tiring day, gentlemen.'

'Lot of pressure,' Didsbury said.

'Well . . . yes. You get used to it.'

'That's what we've come about. Previously we talked with your Private Secretary.'

'Oh, really?'

'Yes.' You play ball with us, Didsbury thought, and we might, just might, begin to play ball with you.

'I've already made a statement to the House.' The big bland face smiled at them.

'Of course, sir. It isn't that. We would like to enquire what kind of discussions you've had with this gentleman, Colin Landsdowne, who is making statements in Madrid.'

Godber frowned. 'Landsdowne? I've already emphasized to you and Commodore Frewin the confidential nature of meetings on Ulster . . .'

'Let me refresh your memory perhaps, sir. Mr Landsdowne says that you had a private meeting with him at his flat in Pelham Street, Islington, a couple of weeks ago. I have here

227

a transcript of an article in the magazine *La España*.' He pushed across the glossy *Time*-style publication. On the cover was a photograph of the Ulsterman, looking plausible.

'Oh yes. I remember now. I met him once at Belfast airport. We were delayed on take-off. He mumbled something about contacts in Madrid. I gave him short shrift. I'd completely forgotten. One gets so many loony propositions.'

'But he offered to talk again?'

Godber paused, aware they were digging a pit, uncertain where the edges began. He felt like a blind man. 'Er. Yes. I believe so.'

'So you did meet him in North London, at his private address? Mr Landsdowne is correct in that?'

'Yes.'

'Let me quote to you from the article, sir. It says "I was recruited" – recruited is the word he uses, he implies by you – "to plan a Spanish threat to Gibraltar. It was to be an undercover operation, but if necessary," – if necessary, sir – "some incidents were to be staged, such as a few explosions. I was instructed to contact the Spanish right wing, through certain known Falangists . . ." '

'That's total rubbish,' Godber exploded. 'Absolute balls. The man's a pathological liar.'

'Possibly, sir. It's your word against his.'

'Ask Brocklehurst,' he yelled. 'Ask Peter Brocklehurst. He was there. He will confirm it's rubbish.'

'We have, sir. He confirms your view.'

'Good.'

'But it doesn't altogether explain why the Americans are so concerned. Concerned enough to send this man Melrose on an assignment – '

'I've never met Melrose. Never heard of him'.

'Quite so, sir. An assignment with an English operator called Billy Vane. Ex-SAS Captain William Vane. Have you ever met him, sir?'

'No, I've never heard of him either.'

'Interesting, sir. You see he was at school with your Private Secretary, Geoffrey Powers. Quite an old friend it seems. Even to the point of taking if you'll pardon the expression what appears to be a dirty weekend with his wife.'

It came as a shock to Godber to realize how much they had found, and also how little he cared about sacrificing Powers. Powers was a dog anyway, an efficient number-crunching dog who wagged his tail when you trod on him. He seized the explanation that Didsbury on behalf of the Government, a Government already in trouble and looking for one less problem, was now half-offering.

'I've long suspected Geoffrey Powers. He's not the right man for my office. I believe his views are left-wing.'

'Yes sir . . . ?'

And Godber blundered on. 'I think you may have put your finger on the reality, gentlemen: an attempt by Powers to discredit me, for political reasons. That must have been his motive. Powers must have traded on his contacts with this man Vane. One of them must have talked to Landsdowne – Powers could get the address from my confidential files – and between them they dreamt up this story about Gibraltar. A deliberate attempt to discredit me, at a time when it is – ah – common speculation in the press that I may be making certain political moves.'

'Is that so, sir?' Didsbury's unyielding glance told him they didn't believe him. They didn't believe anyone.

'Absolutely. Yes. The more I think of it, the more I realize there have been odd quirks in Powers's behaviour. The man is morose. Unstable.'

'Yet you had him appointed?'

'I had very little choice. My Permanent Secretary, Henry Burton, decides that sort of thing.' He smiled that warm, dangerous smile.

'You're under a lot of pressure, sir, as you said. Lots of people believe the rumours. There's a good deal of circumstantial evidence, you might say. Statements by this fellow Landsdowne and the American, Melrose. Nasty position, sir, especially when you haven't been involved.'

'Yes.' Another false smile.

'Did you know,' Didsbury added, 'that Billy Vane has come

229

back to this country? Thrown out of Spain, declared persona non grata. Claims he was badly beaten up, almost emasculated, by some General at an Army base. Been showing his scars to the FCO. Spitting blood, your Mr Vane. A dangerous chap when wounded, by all accounts.'

Godber wasn't smiling now. 'What makes you say that?'

'We think Mr Vane may try to exact revenge on the people he holds responsible for setting him up in Spain, such as our American friend. Possibly such as Mr Powers, sir.'

'Revenge?' Godber stared at them.

'People in that position don't always act entirely logically, sir. Not if they feel badly treated.'

Godber nodded, hoping they had finished with him.

'By the way, Minister,' Didsbury closed his eyes and rubbed them behind his glasses. 'I was asked to give you one other piece of advice from the same quarter.' What that quarter was he seemed unwilling to say, but Godber knew.

'Well?'

'If you want to keep your nose clean, sir, someone may have to be thrown overboard, so to speak. Made responsible for all this trouble, so to say.'

Godber said softly, 'I have come to the same conclusion myself.'

The Secretary of State for Defence, the Rt. Hon. Frederick Godber, made a telephone call that night to Henry Burton, instructing him to stand down Powers, and a further statement in the House at ten o'clock, with the hounds yapping at his heels.

'It has come to my attention,' he read out, 'that certain serious misrepresentations of Her Majesty's Government's position over the future of Gibraltar have been traced to clandestine meetings in which my Principal Private Secretary has been involved, without my permission.' Against the hubbub on the Opposition benches he gritted his teeth and repeated, 'Without my authority.'

'Resign. Resign.'

'Liar.' The shouts echoed round the chamber.

The Speaker called them to order, pretending he had not heard.

'The Secretary of State for Defence . . .'

'I have already assured this House that I have entered into no discussions about the position of Gibraltar, on which the views of the Government have been plainly stated. I have been most disturbed to find that allegations have been made – allegations without foundation – and statements apparently attributed to me which have no basis in fact. These misrepresentations have stemmed from unauthorized actions by a senior official, my Principal Private Secretary, Mr Geoffrey Powers, who has been suspended forthwith, pending a full enquiry.'

He sat down to open hostility and little support behind him, clinging on by his fingernails.

Sir Henry Burton was waiting when he returned at midnight to the big barracks in Whitehall housing the MoD. Lights burned late in the top-floor rooms.

'Well, how has he taken it?' Godber enquired.

'I don't know. I've just told him not to come in tomorrow. Didsbury will see him at home and then report to me. Avoids embarrassment.' He cast a beady eye over the tall, dark-haired Minister with the matinee-idol profile, as much as to say, 'On the level Freddie, what the hell's going on? I was there when you talked to Letwine and Gervase Taylor. I know what's been going through your mind, you devious bastard. The question is how far did you push your luck?'

And Godber merely smiled, that urbane and affable lady-killer flash that got him on the TV chat shows.

'It'll blow over, Henry. It's got to,' he said.

'I'm afraid that's not quite all,' the Perm Sec said. He was sweaty, embarrassed: one rogue flushing out another, slippery Snakes and Ladders on a professional board.

'We've had the *Sun* on. Landsdowne now says that when he first warned you that there'd been a leak through this man Billy Vane, you authorized him to put the dogs on. That was when the American apparently got beaten up for his pains.'

'Absolute nonsense,' Godber said. He sat at the big desk,

glaring at the trappings of office: the pile of letters for signature, the redraft of the White Paper, the incoming telegrams, all bleeding away.

'Listen, Minister,' Burton said. 'Let me say something man to man.' In his contorted way he loved the big buck bastard. It was exciting to serve a rogue who might still climb up the greasy pole, better a buccaneer than a nonentity. And if Godber went, Burton might fall too. They clung to each other in the storm. 'Listen. Landsdowne can be bought off. He's had his moment of glory. The papers here will pay fifty thousand pounds: top that and you're home.'

Godber stared aghast. 'Fifty thousand pounds?'

'Everyone has a price. For a political future.'

Fifty thousand pounds was peanuts if Landsdowne played ball. Godber began to see daylight. He looked at Henry Burton with a renewed respect, one card-sharper to another. Who would have thought that the old careerist had so much blood in him. He nodded.

'I'll keep Colin Landsdowne onside,' he said.

'Good.' The Perm Sec warmed to his task. 'And I can take care of Powers. Brocklehurst is presumably safe?'

'Yes.'

'Right. That really only leaves two people that you might have to fear: Vane himself and the American.'

Their eyes met. Burton sat himself in the big chair, his pink head level with the top, a clubman in in a club armchair. 'I've had a quiet word with Leibermann, the new CIA man, acting Head of London Station. As usual they've pushed their big noses in where they shouldn't have done. His predecessor, Brendan Wallace, the fellow who was knifed in Regent's Park, set Melrose going. Leibermann says they're sorry. Sorry, for Christ's sake! But anyway they're satisfied now that there's not going to be a diplomatic incident. You'll have to come off the Gib factor, Freddie, but there it is. Better to save your skin.'

Godber said humbly, 'What about the Yank himself? Melrose? Apparently he's talked to the Spaniards.'

Sir Henry Burton rubbed his hands. Nothing that he liked

232

more than a good intrigue: it was in his blood, from thirty-five years of service to the Establishment; manipulating people; economical with the facts.

'Don't worry about him. I'm going to have lunch with Leibermann at the Reform. They love that sort of thing, Americans. Melrose is employed on contract, security officer for US Embassy premises in Europe. Happened to be a friend of Brendan Wallace. He's going back to Paris. May have already gone. All he wants is his expenses.'

And that left Billy Vane, the last counter on the board. Ex-Captain William Vane, Export Recruitment Services, who'd tried to sell a story and stopped, for reasons unknown. The two men weighed him up, wondering how much he'd discovered through his talks in Madrid, and what had got him conveyed in a hurry from Spain. Burton pointed to an FCO telegram in the Minister's in-tray.

'William Vane, alleged undercover agent, given immediate deportation order Madrid airport. Seems to have suffered considerable physical assault.'

Burton relaxed. Godber was in his hands now: his political future hung on a decent cover-up.

'Tea?' he enquired. 'Cup of tea?'

Godber tried to keep calm. 'No, thanks. What about this man Vane? Will he keep quiet?'

'I think so,' Burton said. You scratch my back, I'll scratch yours was the unspoken message as he smiled at the Defence Minister. 'He uses ex-SAS men. We could put him out of business.'

A long, slow sigh of relief from his political boss, Burton noted, confirmed the suspicions that he had put together, carefully and cautiously, over the last few weeks. Either he played along in the attempt to save Godber's skin, and profited if he succeeded, or Godber fell, with all the turmoil that meant, even if Henry Burton's own head stayed on. Looking at Godber, a relationship this side of idolatry, Burton nevertheless knew which option he preferred.

'Splendid,' Godber said. 'Well done, Henry.'

What neither of them knew was Billy Vane's state of mind as he flew back from Spain with murder in his heart.

44

Billy Vane had hobbled off the Iberia flight after five days in hell. The air crew thought he had been in an accident, the young man with the bruised face. He walked down the steps in pain. A raw red weal just outside the line of the eye ran down one side of his cheekbone. His normally smooth brown hair was matted with dried blood, but it was his groin that hurt. They had taken his testicles and mangled them until he screamed; it hurt to urinate and he feared the damage they'd done, those sadists led by Quintilla in the punishment room. But worse, they had rubbed in salt, as he twisted and turned on the bedframe, trying to stop the agony. They had told him Jake Melrose had split. Had named him, had blown him, and run. Nobody did that kind of thing to Billy Vane and got away with it.

He staggered through Immigration and Customs, feeling on fire with every moment. He needed a check-up, a doctor, but even more he needed revenge.

In the phone booth by the baggage reclaim he dialled Powers in Wimbledon. On the plane coming over he had read about the political fall-out.

'Who is it speaking?' It was Claire who replied, unable to recognize the voice. Geoffrey was in the house, sullen, brooding, sent home to await his fate.

'Where's Melrose?' Vane asked, his mouth swollen on one side.

He heard her catch her breath. The indicator over the baggage carousels clocked up his flight number. A surge of people went past him. Emotionally he was alone in the airport, nursing a hatred.

'Melrose? I don't know. Who's that calling?' There had been

so many calls, even anonymous breathers, that she hesitated, even when she recognized Billy – a strange and muted Billy.

'I want him,' he said. 'I want him.'

'Look,' she said. 'I don't know. Leave me alone, Billy. I don't want you to come here.'

Billy, the would-be seducer, who had pushed his luck with her in Hereford. She was washed up with him. Through. Two men to be cut from her life, Geoffrey and Billy Boy, that was what she intended. For him it was a further blow.

'You know where he is all right. Jake Melrose, the bastard.'

His tone was stronger, a bark, a note of wounded pain. He clung to the side of the booth, feeling the swelling in his groin. They'd nearly killed him, those sadists Jake Melrose had led him to. Now he was going to get Jake.

'I don't know. I haven't seen him.'

'He's been in London, talking to the press. They've named me. Me.' Vane had seen it in the papers in Spain and on the aircraft. That morning's London press. The gutter press.

'Look. Go away, Billy. There's been a fearful row. Geoffrey has been suspended,' she whispered down the phone. 'You've stirred up a hornet's nest.'

He couldn't care. He focused only on a terrible and final repayment, for which he wanted Jake Melrose.

'Where's Jake?' he repeated.

'I tell you I don't know.'

She could hear Geoffrey moving about upstairs. At any moment he might come down. She wanted to run away, run away anywhere so long as she left this house, the bright and false promises of Geoffrey's fancy career, respectability, preferment, that had lured a schoolteacher's daughter caught up in student radical chic, before she knew her own mind. Before the ideals had faded. Get away, she told herself, away from this narrow-eyed bitterness, the insults and the physical threats.

And Vane on the end of the line, swaying in an airport phone booth – she could hear the racket beyond – was issuing an ultimatum, whether she knew or not.

'Tell him he's finished, will you?'

'What?'

'Tell him he's finished. Washed up. I'm coming to get him, wherever he is, if I have to go to the ends of the earth.'

'Billy – '

'You heard. Tell him.' His voice was much stronger now, almost a screech.

She heard the receiver replaced, leaving her numb. She looked round the room, the house, as if she expected ghosts, but the only ghost was Geoffrey, coming downstairs.

'Who was that?'

'Billy Vane,' she said.

His eyes seemed emotionless. 'That bastard,' he said calmly, as if it was irrelevent to his own state of mind. 'I suppose he still wants you.'

'No. I told him to go away.'

'Go with him, for all I care.'

She looked at him: round-shouldered, whey-faced, he seemed ten years older after Henry Burton's call, the death knell to his hopes. Even if he cleared his name – and Brocklehurst had the damned tape – he knew it would make no difference, their trust and respect was gone. He faced a broken career, a wife who had drifted away.

'Geoffrey – '

'Go to hell. Leave me alone.'

And Vane's warning in her ears.

She feared for Jake Melrose.

She feared for herself.

45

Half a marriage, half ended. Claire didn't care any more. She had had enough of the insults, and the half life.

'I'm leaving,' she told him. 'I can't stay here.'

She was really going. Geoffrey Powers looked as if he'd misheard. It hit him like a blow in the face. He'd never believed it, never. Thought she was bound to him by some sort of ultimate contract. Now she was hitting him, hitting a man when he was down.

'You can't – '

'I can. I will.' Her face was inflamed with misery. Tears welled in her eyes.

'Look . . .' but his voice trailed off. He stood in the middle of the living room, almost a stranger, watching her. He had no words to placate her, her future was not in his hands, his future first and last was the only thing he could think of, the knowledge that Godber would shop him to save his own career. His fists clenched in helpless anger. He heard her run upstairs.

She was abandoning the house. A suitcase, money, some clothes. She tore into the wardrobe, hurling out coats and dresses, underwear, personal things, piling them in the Revelation case. Her cheeks were streaked with tears and she could not be bothered to stop them, her breath coming in great gulps. This was the end of the road. She had to get away from him.

When the case was ready she had calmed down. She sat on the end of the bed, exhausted. Their bed. Perhaps he would come and see her, give some sort of grovelling apology.

Instead, she heard him go out, slamming the door behind him. From the bedroom window she saw him walk down the drive and turn the corner.

She carried the big case downstairs, lugged it into the lounge and stared round the familiar room. It sickened her now, those careful cream settees, the ghastly Victorian oils he was so keen on, the photographs of Geoffrey with Godber on some freebie abroad. She wanted to be sick, but all she could think of to do was to throw the frames in the fireplace. A tinkle of broken glass.

'Oh Christ. Oh Christ,' she moaned.

She went in to the kitchen to telephone.

She had to warn Jake Melrose. She had to leave this place. But where the hell was Jake: all she had seen were the reports in the paper that he'd been implicated. Now Vane was out for

237

blood and the tone of his voice told her that he wasn't joking. Whatever had happened between them, the American was in dead trouble.

She had only one address: Jake's apartment in Paris, and she knew somehow before she tried that he wouldn't answer. She rang, but the line was dead.

Maybe the Embassy, she thought. The US Embassy in Grosvenor Square. But why the hell should they help out – except that he'd done them a favour? He was still on their payroll. At least she could give them a warning.

She got through to the switchboard, asked to be put through to somebody dealing with the Brendan Wallace case. Information, she said.

After a while she was connected.

'Who is it speaking?' Chris Pallett said.

She gave him her name, explained her contact with Melrose, told him, gabbling away, that she'd had a call from Vane, who was threatening revenge.

'What for?' Pallett asked. 'Take it slowly, lady.'

'I don't know. Oh, for Christ's sake, listen. I know this man Billy Vane. When he's upset he's dangerous. He's like so many people who seem so smooth on top. Underneath they're compensating for something. Some insecurity. You've got to believe me.'

Gee. Amateur psychology from a kind of nutcase, Pallett thought.

'Well, where is this guy, Billy Vane?'

'I keep telling you, I don't know,' she screamed at him. 'But I think you should warn Jake Melrose. Just warn him, PLEASE,' she said.

'Warn him, huh?' On the strength of a phone call.

'Just tell me where he is. I'll talk to him. On the phone.'

'You ain't got an address for Melrose?'

'I've got his address in Paris, but he's not there.'

'No. Well, I figure he's still in the UK, but I'm afraid we don't disclose addresses. Maybe you could come round here and talk – '

'You're useless' she screamed. 'Useless.'

When he realized that she'd rung off, Pallett called in his team.

'Some woman called. Said she had a message about this guy who was in Spain with Jake. Billy Vane. Now Billy's back in London and breathing fire. He say's he wants Jake's guts.'

'Better warn Jake,' Kingsley Manning volunteered.

Pallett agreed. 'You got an address in London?'

'Not since he checked out of that crummy little hotel in Knightsbridge, after you put the press on. He ain't telling us any more.'

'I know he's not telling us. Don't give me that. I want to know how the hell we get in touch now.'

They looked at each other.

'Jake can take care of himself.'

'Sure . . . but where is he?'

'Well, we could drop him a warning in Paris.'

'He ain't in residence. And his phone's off the hook.'

'Send the embassy round to leave a message for when he turns up.'

'Okay.'

'And check up on this guy Vane. Maybe we should warn the Brits. Melrose's report said he was difficult.'

Pallett hesitated. Something about the woman's call had made him nervous. He was glad of his own higher security after Brendan Wallace got that knife in his back.

'And circulate a warning through our European stations, Kingsley. Melrose has still got a contract to check the buildings in Hungary, Czechoslovakia, Rumania. Tell 'em to look out for him,' he said.

Claire had set it in train, and now she could only hope. Suddenly she realized how badly she wanted to talk to him.

But it was no good crying.

She was a married woman. She couldn't just freak out on Geoffrey, let alone take another man. The pangs of conscience began like hunger, rumbling and growing.

In the end she sat down at the table and left Geoffrey a note. It can't go on, she wrote. I know you're in trouble but this kind of relationship simply cannot go on. I need time to think it over. And left him the address in Scotland.

It was their shared bolthole, the cottage above Loch Tay that they had seen one summer and fallen in love with and bought. An investment, he said. An idyll, she preferred to call it. 'Braewean'. The little cottage on the hill underneath Ben Lawers overlooking the long water.

They had planned to go there in August this year, like the previous four, when Geoffrey at last got away and Parliament closed down for the summer recess. Exhausted, frayed at the edges, he could sit and read while Claire did old-fashioned things, walking and sketching and browsing in the shops at Crieff and Pitlochry. Nothing ever happened there. Nothing. It reminded her of Yeats's poem about the Isle of Innisfree, where peace came dropping slow. Sometimes she had regretted it, asking why he had wanted a place so isolated, so remote, but it appealed to him, he had a need to escape, and she had gone along. Now it seemed to her a necessity, somewhere to go and hide.

She walked out to the Volvo and put the suitcase in the back. No one else needed to know. They were shut up in themselves, too shut up, she realized, with no children, no pets, no close neighbours to bother them, her parents elderly, his already dead. The alarming narrowness of lives spent too much with each other, while the American – why did she keep thinking of Jake – went freelance round the world.

Damn Godber, damn Geoffrey, damn Billy.

She hammered the starter and set off for central London, Park Lane and the Finchley Road, Brent Cross and the M1, heading north, heading to Scotland.

So that when Jake phoned, nobody was there to answer. He missed her by a couple of hours. He called again in the evening, from the Heathrow terminal that Vane had come through the other way only a few hours before.

Powers answered the call. He sounded drunk or ill.

'Who the hell are you?' he demanded, his head seeming full of pressure, as if it might explode. He suspected some other bastard from Burton's office, or some stringer from the papers newly supplied by the press office with his ex-directory number, even some obscene caller, some joker . . . but it was the voice of the American.

'Is Claire around?' he said.

'No, she's bloody well not. And who the hell are you?'

'An old friend. We spoke before.'

'Well, she's gone. She's gone, and good riddance,' he said, and slammed the phone down.

Leaving Melrose whispering to himself, 'Gone?'

Powers read all the papers, watched all the TV news, and shut himself back in the house in an agony of despair. He was being pilloried by Godber as the man who was too big for his boots, the career civil servant trying to manipulate strings for his political boss. A shyster, a Johnnie-come-lately, a fool deceived by his own ambition. He could see all Godber's own weaknesses impersonated in him. He even recognized that in their different ways they both shared that sinister obsession with naked self-preferment, ambition writ large. Well. He wouldn't let a smear campaign pass: he'd take the whole apparatus of the civil service to the cleaners before that happened.

Geoffrey Powers opened the briefcase that he'd brought home and wondered if he could find in there something to incriminate Godber. But Godber held the upper hand, and what really scared Powers was the record of a taped conversation with the Countess of the Asturias.

Even so he phoned his legal representative in the civil service union. He mentioned unlawful dismissal.

46

Melrose stood empty-handed in London airport, checking in for the Air France plane to Charles de Gaulle. It might have worked out but it hadn't. Or maybe it had in a way: at least

he'd honoured Brendan Wallace's summons and been led to
the Countess. It was splashed all over the tabloids that he'd
bought at the bookstall: 'Minister Exposed', 'Godber's plan for
Gib', 'Rocked by the Rock'. Well, the Government was in dead
trouble. Exposure was what Leibermann and the Agency had
wanted. It didn't justify Brendan's death and it didn't explain
it, but he'd done what he could, and that was always something.

He shuffled towards the check-in, in the never-never land
of Number 1 terminal, on his way to Paris and Budapest, and
perhaps Marie-Louise and the life he had left when Brendan
asked him to come over: Brendan picked off a chopper that
they should both have been on, years and years before. They
shouldn't have made old bones, and he should by rights . . .
he shook his head. Something was buzzing round and round
there, and he couldn't swat it down.

The girl at the desk was asking him for his ticket: club class
to Airport Charles de Gaulle. One lesson he'd learned from
Billy was always to travel first class, but no first class on the
airbus. First class travel: Billy Vane. This wasn't running away.
No sir. Brendan had asked him to come and he'd done his
duty by Brendan, exposed the whole wretched story.

But not why Brendan had died. How Wallace had come to
be killed.

He pulled back from the desk and the girl looked up in
surprise: wide-set eyes, blue mascara, the cheeky scarf of Air
France.

'Sorry, ma'am. I'm not flying.'

He saw the panic in her eyes; fear, alarm, terror. This man
had a bomb in the baggage hold.

'Have you checked in your luggage, sir?'

'Nope. Not yet. I ain't going, that's all.'

She pressed a buzzer on the desk. He was now a security
risk. 'Would you mind standing aside, sir?'

'I ain't flying, that's all.'

'All right, sir, if you wouldn't mind waiting.'

They took him back and worked through his suitcase, two
security guards and a policeman cradling a semi-automatic.

He was clean, they were sorry to trouble him. It was just that most people didn't change their minds at the desk suddenly like that. Last minute. Unless something occurred to them.

Melrose took a taxi straight from Heathrow to the Victorian house in St John's Wood. No sign of a police guard now. Presumably they thought she was safe once the killing was over, and were concentrating their energies on the mysterious Arab.

He rang the bell. A maid. A Filipino.

'Is Mrs Wallace still home?'

She nodded and invited him in, and he found Angie reading the papers in that big square upstairs lounge, looking out onto the plane trees: a green sea of summer leaves.

Angie Wallace looked frailer, stained by grief. She stared at him as if to say, 'why have you bothered to come', and then with a sort of hope that perhaps he had some news.

'Angie,' he said. 'I can't answer your questions. I know. I'm sorry. But I want to ask you something. I want you to cast your mind back . . .'

She blinked at him, a middle-aged woman in glasses, a little plump, a little worn. She needed to remake her life with a new home, and new emotions. He couldn't give her that, but he wanted her to know he cared.

'I don't want to remember . . .'

'Angie, sweetie, you must. Remember the guy you said telephoned and didn't give a name, trying to get hold of Brendan, before he went out that night?'

He sat there and held her hand, urging her on.

She nodded.

'You told me he telephoned a couple of times?'

'Yes.'

'Same evening that Brendan was killed?'

'Yes,' she said slowly.

The day when he'd gone to Hereford at Brendan's request, crawling through the English countryside in a series of traffic queues, time enough to shoot rabbits. He'd got there late and

243

had dinner, then found himself in trouble. And later found Brendan was dead.

'What times did he call, Angie? Think hard, please.'

She tried to remember and couldn't.

'Listen, honey. Six o'clock? Eight o'clock?'

'Six o'clock,' she said. 'And maybe again around seven.'

'Ah! Tell me again what he said.'

'He didn't say too much. Just could he speak to Brendan. And when would he be back.'

'Yeah? And what did you say?'

'I told him he'd better call back when Brendan was home. He said, "Maybe around eight?" And I said make it later, because he'd be running then . . .' her voice trailed off.

'In Regent's Park?'

She was crying.

'Listen,' he said. 'Angie, please. What kind of voice? Was it British or Irish? Like this – ' And he made a passable shot at a soft Ulster brogue.

She stared at him, horrified.

'Yes . . . I think so,' she whispered.

And he knew now that Landsdowne had been mixed up with Brendan's deals in Beirut, trying to rescue hostages, Landsdowne, who had contacts with both sides. It was Landsdowne who could have given Brendan away, simply by one more phonecall to the Said Hamid people.

Melrose could never prove it but in his heart he was sure. He felt a great weight had lifted, as if he had solved a problem, or completed an experiment. It wouldn't bring Wallace back, any more than he could bring the others back, the ones who had died on that aircraft, but it explained a death, and that was something. Landsdowne had had his own contacts with the CIA, and learned of Wallace's interference, Landsdowne had tipped off the Arabs. And Brendan's luck had run out. It didn't make Melrose feel good, it left a shit taste in his mouth, but at least he knew how it had happened. And in knowing he felt better and happier that he, Jake, had fucked up Landsdowne's plans, blown them into small pieces to the point

244

where the Irishman had now had to break cover and tell part of the story. The two-faced, treacherous bastard.

He put his arm round Angie and felt her tremble.

'Honey, don't cry any more.'

The only thing anyone could do was put the past behind them. He would stay with the living; and maybe one day get even.

47

Billy Vane hired a car with a driver. Always travel first class, irrespective of cost. One hundred and sixty pounds was a small price so far as he was concerned, nursing the ache in his groin, feeling his weakened leg was going to give out on him. He gritted his teeth to continue, full of a black rage. The limousine driver found him a pain in the arse, slumped in the back, silent, whatever he tried to say. An uncommunicative bastard. He wouldn't even stop for a break when the driver said he wanted one, and sat in the back, eyes closed.

The driver returned, a middle-aged man with a family, wanting the money, but scared – scared by the look on his passenger's face, which was the look of a killer. A young man bottling up fury through the pain.

'Are you all right, sir?'

'Don't talk to me. Just get on.'

They drove down the M4, across the Severn Bridge, watching the yachts below blown across the water like feathers, and storm clouds darkening the Black Mountains as they took the road up the Wye Valley towards Hereford. Its beauty made no appeal to the young man in the back, who seemed to be nodding to sleep.

'Where to now, sir?' the driver asked on the outskirts.

'Bradbury Lines Camp,' Vane muttered. 'I'll tell you.'

He began to give directions and the chauffeur found the road, nosed past the gate. Barbed wire and bare brick. Vane showed a pass. It had been seven years since he had left the service, but they knew Billy there.

A row of huts. The memorial that always stirred him.

> We are the Pilgrims, Master:
> We shall always go a little further
> It may be beyond that last blue mountain barr'd
>   with snow
> Across that angry or that glimmering sea.

They were coming in from exercise now, those tough, hard, fit men he had once been so proud to command, the élite that there had to be in every country. Billy Vane summoned a weak smile, and knew that he could never rejoin them.

'Okay,' he said. 'This will do.'

They stood around for a moment and watched him, these youngsters to whom he meant nothing. A veteran, or maybe an undercover man hobbling back from some job.

He paid the driver and crawled into the sickbay, the hospital.

'Jesus,' the duty doctor said. He was young, untried RAMC stock. He looked at the mangled groin, the blood-soaked scrotum. 'How did you get that?'

'Friends of mine.'

They began to clean him gently, his mouth rigid with pain. 'The leg's bad. But it'll mend.'

'I know. But what about the rest . . . ?'

The doctor shook his head. 'I don't know. Time will tell. A severe beating like that can lead to shock throughout the system. May cause symptoms of impotence, but only temporarily. You've got an effusion of blood into the tunica vaginalis. We'll see if we can drain some off . . . We'll have to give you a local.'

He waited while they syphoned off the fluid in the membrane surrounding the testes by inserting a hollow needle. He felt no pain, only a weariness and a grinding anger against one man in particular.

The doctor stood back at last. 'You had a tough trip.'

Billy Vane said nothing.

'Will I need any more treatment?'

'The main thing you need is rest. We'll have another look in a week. Especially at that leg. When you feel better. You want a bed here?'

He glared at them. 'I've got a bed of my own,' he said. 'I'll feel better when I've settled a score.'

They ran him back in one of their private cars to the hide-out at Coombe Whitbourne. He walked stiffly down the lane, through the gate, across the path and circumnavigated the cottage. It hit him that someone had been nosing around there: round at the rear of the cottage somebody had moved the can, the half empty can of cider that he always left there carefully wedged against the ironwork table. It hadn't blown over. Nobody had cut the grass. Nobody came in to clean, he was too self-contained. Yet somebody had nosed around shortly before or just after he had set off for Spain. He swore to himself grimly. Some tidy bastard with big feet and an American accent.

Vane limped through his own front door. It hadn't been touched inside. The papers were as he had left them, the VDU still plugged in, the milk had gone sour in the fridge. It was as if nine days had never happened, nine days in the limbo of time. A postbox full of old circulars.

He telephoned through to the shop, the anonymous shopfront in the cathedral city. The take-way of ERS.

'I'm back,' he said.

The girls were devoted to him. He was someone to admire. He paid them to keep it going, not very much but enough, whenever he was away on one of his 'assignments'. Something he never disclosed.

'It's been very quiet,' Karen said. She gave him the latest details: a call for more recruits for the South African Police, a job somewhere up-country in Zaire. He could pick it all up again. He would be in there soon.

He loped back to the rear of the house, to the wrought-iron table and chairs positioned outside on the patio, positioned over the flagstones that led into the cellar. He found the cider can tucked away in the outside trash-bin, then he eased away the heavy iron table, wincing with the effort, to get at the cellar entrance.

The central stone came up on its ring, and he peered down. He had had it converted, this cellar, originally a coal store leading under the kitchen. Now there were six steps down on a wooden ladder, a light switch, a bare bulb. It gave him a certain satisfaction to know that whoever was calling had not disturbed his private store.

He went down slowly and gingerly, in pain but feeling better, now that he had his toys, his private assortment: four wooden ammo boxes, raised on planks from the brick floor. He unlocked them, one by one, and looked at the cache of weapons, oiled and wrapped in cotton, then in waterproof bags. He wasn't sure what he would want, but in the end he selected three thin layers of Semtex, a blasting cap and a timer; a Kalashnikov AK47 and his own favourite, a German Army pistol, the Walther P38.

Cradling this little stockpile he felt his strength coming back, but desperately tired. It was as much as he could do to haul the table and chairs back into place and carry the guns indoors. Upstairs. On the bed where he'd laid the American when he had rescued him from a beating that he should have allowed to continue, and introduced him to Claire. Jake Melrose, who had deceived him.

He stretched himself out on the bed and let the waves of tiredness flow over him. There was no one to bother him, no one for that matter to care, now she had gone for the Yank. He knew it, he was sure, he swore it and was filled with a great black void of bitterness, empty, wounded, alone.

He had food. He had treatment. The doctors had told him to rest. He slipped his clothes off slowly and looked at the padding on his body, swore vengeance, and went to sleep.

48

The gaudy tourist buses round the Minster made the stonework seem dull, verdigrised, when Claire stopped for the night at York, in a bed and breakfast hotel. There was even a street called the Shambles, reflecting her own frame of mind. She thought about phoning Geoffrey, and decided against. He had brought this on – he could suffer. Perhaps he would come to the cottage seeking some kind of reconciliation, but she very much doubted it. As far as she knew, as far as she could feel, it was all over between them.

The old buildings of the city now held no charm for her, it was just another noisy settlement full of visitors queuing for heritage museums, toilets and fish and chips. She was glad to leave in the morning, after a restless night, continuing the journey north. She took the empty road over the Cheviots to Jedburgh, the sun lighting up patches on the bleak, bare hills, then Edinburgh and Stirling. She did not stop.

At last she was winding down the deep gorge of Glen Ogle, as rugged as somewhere in India, and turning into the valley of the Dochart. At the little town of Killin, where the water creamed through the Falls, she breathed in the slow pace of rural life before the holiday season, as people gossiped in the road. The air was crisp and clean as new bed linen. She stopped off and bought provisions, milk and tea, bacon and bread and canned beans, in one of the little stores in the main street. The Tay, a blue-green curtain of water, was stretching in front of her now, its ripples reflecting the sun; a loch that was almost deserted. Then she set the car towards the hills in the shadow of Ben Lawers, the peak invisible under its mist cap.

The cottage was high on a bank, surrounded by woodland, with a stream trickling down from the hill. The burn at

Braewean. It stood on the flank of the mountain, isolated, at peace, an old stone croft that someone had enlarged and improved as a holiday home. They'd bought it from a doctor in Glasgow who was off to Madeira in search of more permanent sun, bought it complete and modernized, with the long see-through lounge looking down over the drop in the garden, rockery more like, to the road and the loch. At night they could see the lights of the fishing hotel, the Lindsay Arms, on the far bank. Now it was hers, alone.

The place struck her as chill, disused like all those holiday homes inhabited for only a few weeks a year. She had suggested to Geoffrey that they should rent it out but he always refused, climbing onto that high horse of behaviour, regarding her with contempt. 'We don't need the money,' he said. 'It's ours, whenever we want it.' Well, now it was hers.

She unlocked the door, carried in the provisions and switched on the heating. In an hour the house would be warm, a home where she could think, decide about the rest of her life. It was as good a place as any in which to do so, a haven under the hill. Claire felt at ease there, more so than in the big rooms of the Wimbledon house, rooms which echoed her emptiness. There was a neat comfort in the armchairs left by the doctor, and his pale biscuit carpets and curtains, and the soft double bed, and the books. She wanted to curl up there, in front of a log fire, pretend she was never married, curl up and forget.

But of course it was impossible. There was too much at stake. One flick of the TV button brought the harsh world home: Godber was being hounded now because he had sacrificed Geoffrey. There was an emergency debate, and she caught a glimpse of his face, defending his innocence. He had not lied to the House. There had been no collusion with the Spanish Right. Landsdowne was simply a liar, a dirty-tricks man, and Powers had set up the contacts, if contacts they were, without his permission or authority. She watched them howling him down, a 'Godber must go' campaign. Geoffrey had become a celebrity.

She felt that she had to phone him, exposed to that kind of publicity. In a small way she also was sorry.

Geoffrey answered at once. She pictured him sitting there, taking the call in his study, compiling some volume of memoirs, exposure or riposte.

'Geoffrey. I've seen the debate on TV. It's not true is it, what Freddie Godber says?'

'Of course it's not true. I'm a scapegoat.' But he had also swum with the tide when they went to see the Countess at Claridge's, Brocklehurst and he with the Ulsterman; and kept his mouth shut.

'What are you going to do?'

He seemed mollified by her call, and she was glad now that she'd made it; but his voice sounded strange.

'Where are you?'

'You know where. I'm in the cottage. Braewean,' she said, and half-hoped for an apology, some feeling of sympathy towards her.

Instead he said, 'I had your latest damned fancy man on the phone.'

'Fancy man?'

'The American.'

At first she could only repeat 'The American?' as her heart lurched.

'You heard. That Yank who telephoned before.'

'What did he say?' she whispered.

'I put the phone down,' he said.

She could have cried. Jake Melrose, be careful. She feared for him, remembering the wounded bark when Billy Vane had called her to issue his warning.

Jake was alive and well, and presumably somewhere in England. He hadn't gone back. It gave her a boost to realize that he still wanted to see her. Find her. And she wanted to warn him, had to, about that soured relationship between the three men: Geoffrey and Billy and Jake. He was a walking target, Jake on his own. Too open, too naive; she hesitated, then said to herself, too vulnerable.

'Geoffrey, do you know where he is? The American?'

Powers exploded. 'For God's sake, why the hell ask me? I've never even met the bastard.' He was thinking about his own future, wondering how to trump Godber, one last card, one disclosure that would bring it all down. The tape cassette Brocklehurst held could expose Godber as well.

'What are you doing?' she said.

'Mind your own business.'

He was addressing a problem, not his wife. The problem was his career, the means to reinstatement which had become a fresh obsession, a challenge to his ingenuity. The union people had been down there to discuss his options, a small dapper man called Wilcox, legal secretary.

'What you need, old chap, is hard evidence,' Wilcox said. 'Hard evidence of Godber's involvement.'

And Powers knew where that was: the cassette in Brocklehurst's safe.

So that when Billy Vane came through, a call that was half expected, there was a meeting of minds. Billy Vane, nursing his grievances in the Hereford cottage, was feeling stronger, wanting to settle the score.

'Where's Jake?' he said.

Powers leapt at the contact. He wanted help too. 'Jake?'

'The American bastard. Melrose from the CIA.'

It fell into place. Jake from Wisconsin for some reason had crossed Billy.

'I don't know. Where are you Billy? I need you.'

Vane groaned. He couldn't use Powers, or could he?

'No good, old man. No more bloody politics.'

'Not politics, Billy. It's for me. I want someone to bust a safe.'

Vane listened and wondered. This fellow called Brocklehurst, Powers was gabbling, had a tape somewhere in Worcester, probably in his office, of the whole conversation on Freddie Godber's behalf with the Countess. Get that and he would screw Godber, even if he sank with him.

Billy Vane grinned to himself, and remembered what Landsdowne had said about guarantees on such a tape at that

252

first interrogation in Spain. Also he could see a prize. He gathered that Claire had left: he reckoned that Powers was wavering about whether to go for divorce or try and patch the thing up. He knew that Jake fancied Claire.

'Okay,' he said. 'On condition.'

'What condition?'

Billy Vane nursed his wounds. His leg was no longer hurting, the weakened muscles were healing, his potency – well, that needed testing.

'On condition you help me find Jake.'

'Melrose? How?'

'Easy. We offer Claire as a bait.'

'Claire?' Powers had tried to cut her out of his mind, but one part of him felt guilty, a sense of failure. He had wanted to let it blow over, to let things take their course while he waited for the political fall-out from Godber's panic. But events were pressing him.

'We're having time apart, Claire and I.' He explained that she was in Scotland and he didn't know what was happening between them.

'That's no problem, Geoffrey. You and I will go up and see her.'

'I don't think that's wise. I've got enough on my plate . . .' The union were coming back to him about proceedings for wrongful dismissal and in his heart he still hoped for a call from Burton, a reinstatement or an apology.

'Listen, sunshine,' Vane said. 'I'm going to insist.'

He arrived in the afternoon, feeling better for the thought of action as he wheeled the big old Bristol through the gates of the Wimbledon house.

Powers came out to meet him. Vane looked thinner, more worn, not quite the old dare-devil of their dinners together. Something had aged him, as if he'd been through the mill. He appeared to be limping more heavily.

'Are you all right?' Powers asked.

'I will be when I've done what I want.'

They walked into the house and Billy asked Powers for whisky. Powers was still sticking to tea. He also seemed pale, the ex-SAS man thought, almost lethargic, like a plant that was drying out. Well, Billy was not going to dry.

It took Vane some time to get through: Powers was withdrawn and damaged, not like the old Svengali; but in the end he opened up. He told Billy about the marriage, the fact that it hadn't worked.

'You mean it never really got going?' Billy said calmly.

Powers flushed and dipped his head.

'Don't worry. Just tell me about this call from Melrose.'

It had only been yesterday. The bastard must still be around, odds on he was still in London. And Billy was used to chances and setting traps.

'I'll show you how to get him,' he said, without explaining why.

It was a lousy day. Dull, rain on the windows. More whining about the way Godber had shuffled the blame on to his suspended aide-de-camp. Powers felt sick, but was led along by Billy; Billy was regaining his composure with every move.

'What do you want him for?'

Billy Vane felt his sores again. 'I've got a score to settle with that old turkey, Geoffrey.' He did not say the prize was Claire.

He took another slug of whisky.

'How?' Powers asked. He sipped Earl Grey, one finger curled at the edge: his little finger.

'Through Claire. He'll come wherever she is. Sooner or later. We'll leave a bait,' he said. 'Several baits, to make sure . . .'

Vane was as good as his word. A message on the answerphone. A note for the cleaning woman telling her if someone called – tall grey-haired American, or someone on the telephone with that kind of accent – she was to give the address, a cottage on the shores of Loch Tay. 'Braewean.' Mrs Powers had gone there on her own. And just to reinsure he typed out a letter to Leibermann, to be passed on to Jake Melrose, care of the London Station, a letter signed by Billy Vane, the man who'd approached Brendan Wallace – a letter saying that Claire wanted to talk to Jake, wherever he was.

He grinned at Powers's uncertainty. 'Don't you worry, old son. Always worried too much, Geoff. Even at school.'

Powers just stared at him.

49

That night there was an unexplained break-in at the constituency offices of Freddie Godber in Worcester. The entry was made from the yard, so the police said later, by someone who knew his business, someone who forced the locks and knew how to scale a ten-foot back wall, someone who left no marks, but eased up the lavatory window above the outhouse and wriggled in like a snake.

Nothing of value was taken, so it appeared. There was eighty pounds of small change in a portable cash-box in the drawer of the desk. The desk had been forced but the cash-box left. The two steel presses were also forced but untouched. And the wall safe was blown by a small amount of plastic explosive, probably Semtex. It hung on its hinges, burnt black.

The anti-terrorist squad checked it over, and Brocklehurst came down in a hurry from his London flat.

Were there any documents missing?

Peter Brocklehurst knew what he had: it was all there.

Would the Secretary of State have kept any secret material in his constituency safe?

Of course not.

Inspector Andrews rubbed the back of his neck, a gesture from years of policing with sweat down the back of his helmet.

'Well, sir, it has all the hallmarks of an IRA bust-in. No fingerprints. Expert explosives. You sure nothing's been taken?' He thought from the other man's eyes that he could have been lying, but presumably the poor devil had something to cover up. Godber was in enough trouble.

'Quite sure,' Brocklehurst said.

When the police had gone he helped to clear up the wreckage. Then he called the Minister and told him it was all okay, nothing to worry about. A new safe was needed but no other

255

damage. Hadn't Didsbury warned him that security needed to be checked. Be on your guard, he'd said.

He walked to the local pub and listened to them in the bar: the pundits. Nothing much happened in Worcester unless the cricket ground flooded or somebody murdered his wife. Now there was some excitement.

'If you ask me,' the barman said, 'they were after Freddie himself. Wanted to pin something on him. That bloke's more slippery than eels.'

But Brocklehurst knew better. He knew there was something inside there that concerned only two other people, the ones that were on the recording as well as himself. Landsdowne the Ulsterman, who had set up the Countess and then disappeared in Spain; who had taken the money and run. And that runt of a civil servant, Geoffrey Powers. He kicked himself for ever believing that they could have dealt him in, but at that time it had seemed important to avoid the risk of a spillage from Godber's office. All Powers needs now, Brocklehurst thought grimly, is one fucking tape to show that the negotiations were on Godber's behalf from the start. If his bloody lawyers found that, it would be curtains for Godber. And curtains for me.

He went back to the constituency offices. They'd just finished replacing the glass in the back room and putting new locks on the doors. The telephone had not been touched.

He rang the MoD. Powers was still suspended, and on holiday so far as they knew.

He rang Spain to warn the Countess.

He rang the Wimbledon house, but there was no reply, apart from a recorded message saying that Claire Powers had left, and could be reached at Braewean, Tayside.

It was that message to the Countess that Colin Landsdowne picked up. The Irishman had sold a story but not severed his connections. He had sold a story but he didn't want a tape released, a tape which would make it clear how much of the detailed planning was his.

He drove to the 'Finca de los Caidos', and found the Countess in the large drawing room, with a servant whom she dismissed with a flick of the head.

She looked at him with contempt, standing in front of the empty fireplace, a small figure in a dark dress.

'I'm surprised that you dare to come.'

The Irishman grinned. 'I have to make a living, Countess. There were opportunities that could not be missed.'

She stamped her foot. 'The opportunities have been missed.'

'No. No. Just one set of plans, that's all. Obviously I couldn't deliver once the balloon went up. But there will be other times—'

She cut him short. 'I don't care about your stupid schemes. I'm talking about the way it has dragged into the open our own plans.'

Even then he wasn't discountenanced. The pink head gleamed at her, and his eyes were like two glass beads in the oval face.

'That wasn't my doing. It was Lopez.'

'Lopez is a fool,' she said angrily, resting a hand on the chair back. 'And so are you.'

'I don't think so, Countess. I'm simply an operator.' He looked slyly over her shoulder to the panelling and the paintings that must have been worth millions.

'In my opinion,' he said, 'it is best now to treat the whole matter as fiction. I sold a story without going into details, without incriminating you. Popular stuff, blaming the English.'

The Countess looked at him sharply. 'What do you want now?'

Landsdowne sat down in one of the old leather chairs which smelt of dust and polish, a heady mixture. He sniffed. 'I suggest we destroy the evidence. The evidence of collusion between us. Just in case there are further enquiries.' He hesitated. 'Criminal enquiries, you follow me?'

She walked to the long window and gazed out between the leaded panes at the terrace and the vineyards beyond where she had talked with the English, and lured on Billy Vane.

'There is no evidence,' she snapped.

The Irishman spoke softly. 'No evidence on paper, Countess. But you have a tape of promises. And so do we. I suggest they are both destroyed.'

The Countess did not move. She continued looking over the vineyards of her estate, an estate which had once been forfeit, and could be again. The stakes that she had played for were high.

'It's of no advantage now,' he pleaded, 'to have something like that on record. Think of the impression if it got into the wrong hands.'

He waited.

'It is a hold that I have on you English.'

'I'm not English.'

'Nevertheless it is a weapon. A statement of intention.'

'You're wrong,' he argued. 'It's a liability. A dangerous piece of evidence.'

'So?'

'So I suggest you destroy it.'

She continued looking through the window for what seemed to him an age, then finally turned round. Without a word she unlocked a drawer in the small cabinet by the fireplace. In her hand was the tape.

'Forget it, and start again,' he said.

She said slowly, 'I will destroy it, on one condition.'

Landsdowne smiled. 'Name your poison.'

The Countess of the Asturias said, 'On condition you find and destroy the version in England.'

'Done,' he said.

It was only then that she had told him of the warning from Peter Brocklehurst that the second tape was already missing.

It caused the Irishman to fly to London as furtively and unobtrusively as he had slipped out, and begin a round of visits. He consulted Brocklehurst and learned about the Worcester break-in.

Brocklehurst said, 'Whoever has that recording could sink Godber and the lot of us.'

'It crossed my mind,' Landsdowne said, 'that such must be the intention.'

'Don't try and be funny.' The pained look on the agent's face left him no doubt of the agony.

'As a matter of fact,' Landsdowne added, 'I've no particular wish to hear it on the BBC, or in front of a select committee. I like to keep myself private, if you know what I mean. I don't want that kind of linen washed in public places.'

Brocklehurst could not agree more. 'Then you'd better bloody find it.'

Almost immediately the Irishman began a second round of enquiries, which led him to the information that Powers was unexpectedly absent and thus to the answerphone message that Claire Powers was in Scotland. It was a message which the cleaning woman confirmed when she explained there was a cottage somewhere up on Loch Tay, with an address she was asked to give by Mr Vane, who was expecting a call from an American.

Landsdowne had a drink with Brocklehurst, very quietly in a neutral bar.

'Have you got any news,' he asked, 'about that tape?'

The agent shook his head. 'No. Have you?'

The Ulsterman grinned again. 'Nothing definite. But I'm beginning to put things together.'

50

Angie Wallace had asked Melrose to stay. He had sat on the settee with her, holding her hand, a plump, warm hand. A lonely, middle-aged woman.

'Don't go,' she said. 'Talk to me.'

He hadn't anywhere to go, except a job in Paris. He knew how the Irishman was responsible, indirectly if not directly, for Brendan Wallace's death. Landsdowne, who tried too many tricks, Landsdowne who had stopped Wallace because

259

he was on to one of his schemes, Landsdowne who knew that the Said Hamid Shi'ites had old scores to settle with Brendan Wallace, dating back to Beirut. He wondered how much they had paid for a single piece of information, the time of Brendan's last run. The Irishman was a murderer, as far as Melrose was concerned.

'Sure,' he said to Wallace's widow.

They sat together, the two of them, over the dining table in the upstairs room, served by the Filipino maid. Angie insisted on candles, a brave face to cheer things up.

I bought a few years, he thought, seventeen years for Wallace and me, by pulling him off that chopper. He found no comfort in knowing who had set up the killing. He drank most of the wine.

The candles flickered and guttered. It began to grow dark. Her hand crept across towards him seeking reassurance.

'What'll you do?' he asked.

She sighed. 'Go home, I guess.'

'To Florida? Poquito Beach?'

She shook her head. 'Brendan liked that. Not me. My folks come from Virginia. I'm going back there.'

He smiled. 'I got a place in Virginia. Condo in Reston.'

Her hand searched his. 'You from there?'

'Nope. Wisconsin. Little place called Appeldoren, near Milwaukee. Nobody left there now.'

'Never been there.'

'Nor've most folks. Bit out of the way, honey.'

She laughed. He was glad he had made her laugh.

'Jake . . . I'll sell up in Florida, buy some place in Virginia . . . Richmond. I've always liked Richmond. Or maybe nearer to Williamsburg . . . or Jamestown . . .'

'Sure. There's plenty of time. Angie. Come on, don't cry.'

'Maybe we could visit with . . . each other.'

'That would be great.' He moved to pour her more coffee. She asked him to have a brandy but he refused.

'When you going home, Angie?'

'I don't know. Soon. I just want to put it behind me. Brendan's death. Everything.'

He understood. He knew. And he knew you could never do it as completely as that, any more than he could blank out the memory of the luck that saved Brendan, nearly twenty years back. Any more than he could forget Claire.

Angie was looking at him, but she reminded him of a different woman, somebody else's wife. And that was hell.

He changed the subject. 'You going to miss England?'

She pursed her lips, then smiled, fingers playing with a coffee spoon. The dusk came in over the trees and he could hear the swish of London traffic along the road by the Park. The Park where Brendan had died.

'Guess not. I shall miss a few things. The concerts. The flower gardens, maybe a bit of the Royalty. But on the whole not much. I've had enough,' she said. 'Enough of being pushed around the world for the sake of Uncle Sam. Bangkok, Beirut. London. What about you?'

He hesitated. 'Me too.' How did he explain his life, or apologize for it: the effort to live on his own. That terrible feeling that there was always another job, one more hill to climb. The suitcases, the hotel rooms, the borrowed apartments. The compulsion to prove himself. It suddenly seemed quite inexplicable.

She was looking at him with those eyes.

He drew away. 'Honey, can I use your phone?'

She said 'Sure,' and he walked over to the window, where the phone sat on a ledge. He looked out as he dialled. It didn't matter if he got Geoffrey, he didn't goddam care, but he had to speak to her somehow. It was almost dark now, and he saw the lights of Baker Street across the Park: the white lights in the buildings, the yellow sodium street lights, the red flares where the cars braked. And the trees, the great dark masses of trees; and somewhere there Brendan had bought it.

Jake Melrose felt lucky. Lucky to have the chance.

It wasn't Powers. It was an answerphone, in Geoffrey's voice, telling him that Claire Powers was not available but staying at some place called 'Braewean', Tayside.

He replaced the receiver and turned to Angie. She got up from the table and was moving closer.

'Honey. You got a map?'

'A map?'

'Of Scotland,' he said.

51

The Bristol rattled through the night, the big old engine hammering like a diesel in a motor boat. Vane's hands were clenched on the wheel as he pushed the big car at eighty up the M5. They joined the M6 north of Birmingham, then halted at a service station in the wasteland somewhere east of Crewe.

Billy Vane took on petrol. 'This thing eats the juice.' He hummed to himself, exhilarated. Some quick sums on a pocket calculator: he reckoned they could be there mid-morning. 'Time enough for breakfast,' he said.

Powers sat and looked at him across their plastic trays in the cafeteria. He found that his hands were shaking and his ears still ringing from the controlled explosion that had ripped open the safe, even though he'd run back to the car and let Vane take the real risk. He remembered Billy scrambling back grinning, just as he grinned now, waving the tape recording, which they had listened to on the cassette player in the car coming up.

'Two guarantees . . .' Landsdowne said on the tape. 'Nothing in writing of course. The first is our own assurance, our own word. You must know the score, Countess. Gibraltar is expendable. Hong Kong is going already . . .' The voice was lilting and clear, the voice of the Irishman, selling the future. And Powers saying it was correct.

And the second guarantee, in Landsdowne's soft voice, would be the Countess's recording of that same conversation. Now no doubt lodged in the 'Finca de los Caidos'. Unobtainable.

Powers felt fate in his hands: the fate to ruin Godber; and he was scared. He wanted to go back to London, to hole up

262

there and wait for the lawyers, Wilcox and the CS union people fighting for his reinstatement. In his heart he didn't want trouble, he would loathe the publicity of a full-scale scandal, especially one involving a burglary in Godber's constituency premises. He just wanted to get hold of that tape and destroy it, junk it. Leave it somewhere in a dustbin.

But Vane was waving it at him and wouldn't let him have it.

'You come with me first, old boy. Do what we have to do.'

'Why are we going to Scotland?'

'Don't you want to see Claire? She is your missus, old man.'

'I don't know. I don't think it wise . . .'

'Oh, come on,' Vane felt stronger all the time with that tape in his pocket, and his guns in the back of the car. He limped across the counter and ordered two more teas.

Powers saw his back and shuddered. The sports jacket, the grey trousers, the brothel-creepers; a slight limp, that smooth brown hair. How had he ever loved Billy Vane, whispered to him of rumours, put his own head on a plate? The bright but tawdry setting of the cafeteria, largely empty at four in the morning, with two tired girls manning the hot plates, struck him as right for Billy: flashy and slick and cheap. He wanted to run away.

Instead he forced a smile as Vane came back with the cups.

'Billy, that tape . . .'

'Shut up about the tape, Geoff. It's safe with me.'

A frown clouded Vane's eyes. When he began to look like that, few people challenged him. And nobody was going to know how badly he'd been hurt, until he tested himself.

Had he slept with Claire, Powers wondered? Have you really slept with my wife? And how many times? What do you want her for now – is it just to trap the American? Or do you want her again?

'Ready?' Vane said. 'Looks like a nice day.'

They walked out on to the forecourt. Big trucks were drawing in but there were few other cars. A police Rover was parked on the far bay, having an early break and for a moment

Powers was tempted to run across and ask their help. Vane must have read his mind. 'I wouldn't if I were you.'

Powers felt a long way from home, from the certainties of Godber's office which had given him status, from the ordered life of suburban Wimbledon. Instead he looked at a car park where the wind blew scraps of old plastic into the threadbare trees, and thought he'd come to the end of his luck.

'Let's press on, Geoff.'

He climbed into the car and Vane swung out again into the motorway. As the dawn came up he watched the changing skies, grey and then pearl and silver, pink, bronze and violet-blue. A stormy day ahead, as they headed round Preston and skirted the Lakes. The Pennines were hidden in mist, the road gleamed with overnight rain.

'You want some music?' Vane asked, as if anxious to show off his machine. He thumbed an old push-button radio and got a scrambled mixture of pop tunes: Boris Gardiner, 'I want to wake up with you'.

Jesus Christ, Powers wondered, who was going to wake up.

Perhaps, it's not me, Claire thought. Perhaps it's not me sitting here, in the cottage at the foot of Ben Lawers with the deer coming down to browse on the backyard grass in the early morning, shy, timid creatures, that ducked their heads and bobbed away at the first sound, as she opened the windows and breathed in the misty air. When the sun cleared the clouds after breakfast she could see the loch in the distance, like a huge streak of silver. Perhaps it's not me doing this, running away from Geoffrey, abandoning an empty relationship, hoping the telephone might ring and waiting . . . waiting.

She tried to put her life in perspective, from the little girl who had dreamed of romance to the Exeter student who had thought Geoffrey sophisticated and married him on the rebound from her first undergraduate affair. Politics and love in a tangle, when they wanted to reform the world. But Geoffrey had joined the system and she had watched him conform, down to the suits and the watch chain; an awful watchchain

264

worn from his left lapel. It made her weep as she sat in the kitchen and read about the row over Godber. That liar. That prick.

She needed to shake out of herself. She ran a bath, washed her hair, put on a fresh dress and stared at herself in the mirror. Not wearing badly, she thought. Those lines about the mouth had always been there, and surely they added character? Good firm figure, she'd always had a good figure. Geoffrey had withered away, an undertaker to the Establishment. What was left in it for him now once the cards had been marked? She knew enough to realize that even if he got reinstatement his prospects would not be the same. Geoffrey would draw the short straw the next time that postings came round. There were plenty more fish in the sea where that one came from, as her mother always said.

She was just about to go for a walk down the drive to the road, along the road to the village on the banks of the Tay, when she heard the sound of the car; a big, heavy, noisy car, nosing its way uncertainly along the lane, finding the gatepost 'Braewean', turning, grinding in bottom gear up the 1 in 2 slope to the house. It was eleven o'clock, a bright morning on the hills with racing patterns of sunshine and shadow over the higher slopes where sheep searched after the sweeter grasses.

She went out to the patio to see the grey submarine shape of Billy Vane's Bristol 603. Two heads, one of them Geoffrey. Her stomach contracted. The clouds shut down on the mountains and she felt her mouth go dry.

Billy Vane was getting out, limping, looking tired. They both looked tired, she thought, unshaven, as if they'd been driving all night.

She tried a smile, a weak, half-hearted greeting.

'Hullo. What on earth – '

'Get back inside,' Vane said. 'Get back inside the house.' His voice was angry. She saw Geoffrey white as chalk. 'Do as I say,' Vane added, the smoothness gone. She saw he was limping badly.

'Tell me what's wrong – '

'Better do as he says,' Geoffrey muttered.

265

She turned and entered the cottage through the patio doors. She looked round to find him behind her: Billy Vane carrying a gun, a pistol in his hand.

'For God's sake – '

'Shut up. Is he here?'

'Who?' But she already knew.

'That bastard Melrose.'

'Jake . . . ?' she whispered. 'He's not here. Of course not. What's he done?'

Vane wouldn't or couldn't tell her. He motioned her to sit down on the settee facing the windows, looking out over the garden, which dropped steeply towards the lane. She realized how isolated she was, at the mercy of these two men, and looked to Geoffrey for help. But Geoffrey seemed dazed.

'Do what he says,' he whispered.

'Geoffrey, tell me what's going on . . .'

Her hand went towards the telephone. 'Keep away from that,' Vane said. He moved round, light on his feet, cat-like, ripping the cable from the wall. Now he was standing over her, his face thinner than she remembered, no longer the dapper lover who had dined at their table and tried to lay her in Hereford.

'Has he been here? Melrose?'

'Jake? No.'

'Has he been in touch? Telephoned?'

'No,' she said. 'For God's sake what's got into you?'

A thin, acid smile split his features, just for a second. 'He'll come. The fucker will come.'

'Why. What's he done?' she asked.

'Sit there. Shut up. Done? I'll tell you what he's done – ' She thought from his eyes he was mad, almost deranged. 'He's run. Left me to the bastards in Spain. Do you know what they've done?' He cocked the gun at her. 'We'll see who's got the guts, when the time comes.'

She found her head spinning. Jake. Oh Christ. She wanted Jake, and wanted him alive.

She looked at Geoffrey, who seemed to be an automaton,

scarcely breathing. As if she wasn't his wife. As if she wasn't anything.

'Geoffrey, stop this.'

'I can't,' he said. She saw the pistol covered him too.

'Sit over there . . .'

They crouched together on the settee, and Claire reached out a hand to touch him for some kind of security. But Geoffrey drew apart, as if she would give him a virus. She saw the line of his lips, the blue stubble of chin, the sleepless eyes staring at something internal, the wreckage of his own hopes.

'Okay, just keep it cool,' Vane said. He backed through the doors, leaving them sitting there.

'Geoffrey . . .' she began.

'Keep quiet. He's crazy,' Powers said, but still without looking at her.

'Why?'

'Something that happened in Spain.'

'Because of Jake?'

'I don't know.'

Billy Vane was coming back, lugging a suitcase from the boot of the car, and something she knew was a rifle. Semi-automatic Kalashnikov. He put the pistol on the table and fixed the Kalashnikov. She heard the rattle of the magazine, the click of the safety catch. She saw him fiddle with her black plastic stereo radio, take out the cassette, insert a new tape from his pocket, close the thing, put it back, smiling, on the table.

'That's better,' he said. 'Someone might like to listen to the news. The latest news on Freddie . . .'

'What are you going to do?' she whispered, her heart hammering.

The blue eyes were hard as marbles, staring at her. 'Wait for him,' he said.

'With a gun?'

He laid the rifle on the table and picked up the pistol again. 'Nobody shops Billy Vane without running that risk.'

She suddenly thought about the death of the American, Wallace, and she sat very quiet.

267

52

Melrose didn't stay the night. Though Angie would clearly have liked it, she didn't say so.

'I got to go,' he said. 'Sorry, Angie.'

She had smiled, knowing there was someone else. 'That's okay. Maybe sometime . . .'

'Sure. Maybe sometime, honey.'

He had shaken her hand and left, upright as a board fence, and her heart bled for him.

He had walked up Avenue Road and checked in to the Holiday Inn at Swiss Cottage. He had swum in the pool, and been cocooned in the standard hotel room once again, a little piece of nowhere.

In the morning he drove north, the same route that Claire had taken, if he had known it, a couple of days before, but he was diverted by road works, then an accident near Newcastle. By a call-box on the A1, on the hills outside Morpeth, he stopped to get her number from Directory Inquiries, to tell her he was on his way, to explain that he would be late; but when he dialled her there was no reply, no connection.

It was a long hard drive in the rented Cavalier and by the time he hit the outskirts of Edinburgh he had nearly had enough. It was six thirteen p.m. by his watch and he reckoned he had another sixty, maybe seventy miles to go. Jake, no big eater, pulled in for coffee and rolls, realized he didn't feel hungry, just kind of tense about what he'd say to her, about what was happening to him.

He'd come over as a favour to Brendan, and Brendan had got mixed up with some game of Brit politics that Jake couldn't care a monkey's toss about. But Brendan had been killed and Jake felt he owed him something, him and Angie. What Landsdowne did was pig-shit so far as he could see, but it mattered that it might have been disastrous, and it mattered more that in consequence Claire had split up from Powers; split up and gone away. As for the Irishman's guilt, well that was unproven, just a supposition based on what Angie had said. But he would like to meet him in the dark someplace.

He drank the coffee, swallowed something called a jam do'nut and turned back on the road. The last seventy miles.

Billy talked to them during the afternoon, a mixture of sanity and a peculiar madness. Told them that shits made money by selling rumours picked up from bigger shits. Asked Geoffrey if that was right, and Geoffrey, paralysed, said nothing.

'Investigation,' Vane explained. 'That's what they want from me. Investigation. That's what Jake was paid for too. We teamed up, you know. A little trip to Spain to find out what was going on. How far would Godber go. To stitch things up. And then what has Jake gone and done?'

'I don't know,' she whispered.

'Jake got his arse out,' he said, 'and shopped me.'

'I don't believe it.'

'You wouldn't, you little minx, would you?'

His eyes frowned and narrowed.

'Aren't you hungry?' she said. 'I could make tea. Get a meal. You need to rest, Billy. You're overtired. Unwell.'

But he laughed at her. 'Get in the bedroom,' he said.

'No.'

'Get in the bedroom. You too.' He motioned at Powers with the Walther.

'It's loaded. I don't miss,' he said.

He forced her through to the bed, with Geoffrey following. A wide room, a double bed, their bed, an armchair, a built-in wardrobe.

He limped over to the window and pulled the blinds. They stood in a chilling semi-darkness.

'Sit in the chair, Geoffrey. Sit in the chair and watch.'

'You're ill, Billy.'

'Am I? Take off the dress, Claire.'

He was still holding the pistol, but she refused.

269

'All right. You take your trousers down, Geoffrey. And your pants. Show us. Good boy.'

He stood there, bottom naked, his underpants around his ankles. Ashamed.

'Geoffrey,' she screamed. 'Stop him.'

And Vane laughed. 'You couldn't manage it, could you, Geoffrey?'

She covered her face with her hands. 'Billy. For God's sake, please.'

And Billy Vane laughed louder. 'Claire, my dear. You think I'm going to rape you? You think I could – '

And suddenly he showed her, the swollen, padded groin, the marks of his beating by Quintilla.

He picked up the gun again. 'Jake Melrose caused that. That's why I'm waiting for him.'

It was nearly ten o'clock when Melrose turned the Cavalier through the street of closed shops in Killin and over the little river Lochay, up the hill towards the Tay, a long, deserted road with a few houses here and there offering bed and breakfast for the summer tourist. On his left the peak of Ben Lawers, 1200 metres on the Survey map, the sixth highest mountain in Scotland, already lost in cloud, great sweeping mist-clouds, creeping down to the road as the sun faded. Without the map he would never have made it, but 'Braewean' was identified on the Landranger series, 1:50,000, three or four scattered cottages on a track marked as Shielings.

He was coming into range at last. A signpost directed him left, leaving the metalled road. On his right the silvery waters of the fifteen-mile-long loch, 'Braewean' ahead now, locked in the mist from the shoulders of the mountain.

Jesus, he thought, what a place. But it was where she was.

He slowed down to pick his way along a pot-holed road, past one empty cottage, then two. There was no settlement here, it seemed a God-awful remoteness; it was something against nature for her to want to be there. But above all he needed to see her, not so much to explain, to try and articulate, but simply to be there, to share.

Running into the mist now, creeping and swirling like chiffon across the hood of the car, across the road: Melrose switched on his headlights and found the last pair of gateposts marking the end of the track. Some kind of farmhouse up there, some kind of modernized croft. He could see the lights in the house, high up over a bank. Then they went out.

Billy Vane picked up the headlights, the sign of the car below them on the road. He gave a shout of glee and switched off the lights in the lounge, dowsing the house in darkness except for the porch outside. He put the Walther pistol on the table and picked up the Kalashnikov.

'What are you going to do, Billy?' Claire whispered.

'Shut up.' He swung round and splayed the gun at them, finger cocked on the trigger, his face alive with excitement. 'I'll show you who is a man.'

'Billy, you're crazy. Sick.'

But he ignored her and stood just inside the curtains to the French windows. Seated behind him she could not see the road, only some trees and the distant grey-gold outline of the loch, with lights twinkling on the water. There was a terrifying quiet as they heard the car coming closer.

Billy Vane cocked the gun.

It was a blue saloon. She saw it roll to a stop in front of the house and park next to Billy's Bristol. She could see Jake getting out, peering into the shadows inside that blanked-off cottage, a white croft with a glass extension, a sun lounge looking over the water.

Jake Melrose was standing there like a cardboard cutout against the fading light. And she was afraid to shout. The words died in her throat.

Vane's hand was on the trigger.

It was Geoffrey who screamed. 'Get out. Get back in the car and run. He's got a gun.'

Vane fired. The bullet clipped the windscreen of the hire-car, parked nose in front of the Bristol, missing Melrose in the half light, scattering dust and glass chips that ran down the hill.

Vane fired again, but he'd gone.

Melrose, instinctively, ran, ran for cover round the cars, across the yard, into the bushes.

Vane fired five or six shots.

'No,' she screamed. 'Billy, no.'

But he was past hearing. He ran after the American, the limp gone as if by magic.

'Jake. Come and get it. Come and see what you did to me.'

Another volley into the bushes.

She rushed to the open glass doors. The chill night wind blew in from the loch.

'Billy! Jake! No!'

Billy Vane was running round the back of the house. She heard the noise of someone stumbling, bushes being trampled. There was a track there, an old sheep trail up the hill, the trail that the deer used when they came down to feed, overgrown with brambles and bracken, and Melrose had gone up high, seeking cover.

She heard Billy laughing and cursing.

'Come on, Jake. Come on and get me . . .'

She ran after them both, she and Geoffrey, screeching, 'This is madness, Billy. Billy, stop it . . . Billy, you're sick.'

Vane fired a series of shots, deliberately into the bushes. She heard some rocks tumble as Jake scrambled away.

'Come back.'

But Jake Melrose had gone, and Billy went after him.

53

Jake heard the shots and kept low. He didn't argue with guns. He didn't stop to wonder, instinctively he just ran. He heard the skitter of broken branches as bullets hit the bushes. One of them kicked up beside him, too damned close, and he jigged away, blundering into brambles that seemed to mark a kind of path, a sheep path, he guessed, and up there was the mountain, where he would have the advantage. Billy had a bad leg, he'd noticed that when they first met.

Crack. Crack. Crack. Assault rifle. Semi-automatic. He must have it on single shot. Playing some kind of game.

He stopped. Listened. Silence. Just the wind through the branches of the last stunted trees on the hill. He was getting higher.

'Jake! Come on.'

Billy Vane was somewhere below him. Melrose picked up a rock and threw it to his right. Billy didn't take the bait.

'Billy!' he yelled. 'Don't be stupid. I ain't done nothing.' The words fell away down the hill.

Silence. Then a sighting shot towards him, dangerously close, Billy firing into the wind.

Melrose scrambled away, then realized he was at the end of the cover. Only the thin skeins of mist and the moonlit semi-darkness stood between him and Billy.

There was a gully, with boulders on both sides, worn smooth and damp in the middle, one of the various footpaths up to the mountain; getting steeper. The ground dipped and climbed in the small hips of the mountain: light gorse, yellow at night, almost iridescent. Melrose glanced back. He could see distant lights down on the main road 2000 feet below, slow-moving lights on the water, green and red navigation lights. Something nearer: lights on the edge of the mountain, maybe a mile away. Hard to be sure in the dark, but a building there somewhere.

Crack – whee – ang. Another bullet ricocheted off a boulder somewhere above him. Vane had got him in line.

Melrose went flat, then crawled into cover. He heard people shouting below them, but could not hear what they said.

He needed to get round Billy, to get some help. No arguing with a nutcase. But Billy had thought of that too, and was driving him upwards. Okay. So it was up, and up there was plenty of cloud hanging on the top of the mountain.

Melrose took himself out of the line of the gully and made for a series of rocks. There was no more firing. He began to be chilled, colder in the high air, dressed only in the suit and sweater in which he'd driven up. His hands and face were dirty where he had clawed and crawled through the undergrowth.

And Vane saw him; saw him edge over the scrub, up towards the ridges which in high summer would be covered by saxifrage and bilberries and gentians. Saw him and followed.

He tucked the assault rifle under his arm, shouting, 'What did you leave me for, Jake?'

The figure had gone into the mist.

'Jesus Christ,' Melrose thought, and paused for breath, listening.

A slither somewhere that could be Vane missing a foothold. Could be sheep.

Jake hunkered down to keep still. Give Billy ten minutes, he could lose him, then get down the slope, pick up Claire, call the police. They'd got a guy gone head-funny. Berserk. He found his heart was still thumping. Calm down, Jake, otherwise you wouldn't live long. Calm down like the time you helped Brendan. Oh Christ, that chopper, falling from a height like this . . .

He waited, not caring to think, not daring to wonder what had turned Billy on. He'd never much liked the guy – too slick by half. Never. The whole lot a can of worms. Excepting Claire.

And Billy knew where he was. Billy was sure he was there, up on the final shoulder. Billy crept closer.

The cloud was breaking up. A stiffer breeze blew it sideways, towards Loch Rannoch, away from the top, exposing the ridges in the moonlight.

He saw him. He saw him crouched against a raw boulder, almost a part of the landscape. But not quite. Billy's eyes had trained for this, long ago. South Atlantic, hunting some other bastards, the ones who gave him the leg. But the leg had held up. He would hold up. He would show them.

The figure did not move, just crouched there, looking, straining, watching the other way. Billy had worked round behind him. Billy saw him. Billy had won.

Billy lay prone on the scree, levelled the Kalashikov on hold, random shot, range only 200 yards, uphill, into the wind. Fixed him. Fixed the bastard. Fired.

Then silence. Jake Melrose heard nothing more.

Silence. You could hear the wind on the mountain.

Then he came down.

Jesus. Jesus.

He saw Billy standing over the body, holding the rifle.

He scrambled down.

Geoffrey Powers, standing beside him, rocking on his feet, whispered, 'Is he dead?'

Melrose looked at the back of the head, then turned the body over. He'd seen them like that before, the blood leeching out, congealing, eyes open, face growing grey. Landsdowne, the Irishman.

'You said it.'

Vane put up the safety catch and slowly walked away without a further word.

Powers began to shake and tremble. 'He came out of the bushes. I saw him running up the hill . . . I shouted out . . .'

'Take it easy, man.' Melrose straightened up. They could do nothing there. He needed to sort out Vane. But Powers was rooted to the spot.

'The tape, the tape . . .' Powers was mumbling.

'Aw, come on. What tape, man? I'm cold. He's dead. Billy's come to his senses. Let's get the hell down.'

But Powers went through the Irishman's pockets desperately searching: a wallet, a notebook, a comb. He laid them out on the quilt of heather. It was too dark to see the contents.

'It's not here,' he said.

Melrose grabbed him by the shoulders. 'Pull yourself together, man. Where's Claire? Is she all right?'

Powers said something incomprehensible and retrieved the pistol, Billy Vane's Walther P38 which the Irishman had taken from the house.

'Come on,' Melrose said. 'Let's go talk to Billy.'

For a moment Powers stood there as if he could not believe it. 'There was a tape . . . Billy took it. Billy blew the safe.'

275

'What tape, for Christ's sake? Come on, let's go find Claire.'

'Landsdowne. I saw him. Landsdowne came to the cottage. I saw him searching for it.'

'Sure, you saw him. Come on, kid.' Landsdowne must have wanted something real bad, to trail them all the way to Scotland and follow Billy up a mountain.

He half pushed, half pulled Powers down the gully towards the house. They were coming out of the thick mist and he could see the house lights. She must have switched them back on. And then he heard a car start up, the unmistakable beat of the old Bristol engine. His senses relaxed. Nothing he could do for Billy Boy. Billy had driven off somewhere; pick him up in the daylight.

The gully was longer than he had thought, helping Powers down. And rougher. Christ, he must have had the shits to get up there that fast. Powers was skinny as a rabbit, trembling with shock or cold, he had to jolly him along. They would need mountain rescue to get Landsdowne's body down, or maybe a chopper. No, Christ, not a chopper. He must be getting out, getting back. He was James K. Melrose, ex-US Marine Corps, and he had a job to do, a living to make. What would Leibermann say . . .? They were slipping and sliding towards the lights at the rear of the house.

What had blown Billy's top, he wondered, and then brought him round? Something had made him see sense. It was as if he had to get his own back and suddenly saw Landsdowne there. Hell, what did it matter, for God's sake? It was all over now, and Claire was waiting.

'Claire!'

Beside him Powers stumbled and had to be held. He was no mountain goat.

'There was a tape . . .'

'Come on, Geoff. Nearly home.'

They entered the deer track between the two lines of bushes, birch thickets tangled by blackberries that tore their legs, and emerged at the back of the house, Melrose supporting Powers.

And she was running to him. Claire, running to Jake. 'Oh Jake! Jake? Are you all right?'

'Sure, honey. No problem.'

She saw Powers's hunted look. 'Geoffrey. What happened? Where's Billy?'

'Billy's gone home,' Jake said. 'There's a guy lying up there called Landsdowne, the Irishman who started all this and set up Brendan Wallace.'

His jinx with Brendan Wallace from all those years before. But in the end it was over.

'Billy shot him,' Geoffrey said; no emotion, just a statement of fact, as if he was telling Godber he'd answered a Question well. Chilling.

She threw a hand over her mouth. 'Oh, no. He came to the house. Then he heard the shooting and followed it up the mountain, and Geoffrey went with him . . .'

Melrose said, 'Something got into him, sent him chasing up here. I guess he was looking for something.'

Powers pushed past them.

'We've got to get some help,' Melrose added. 'He's lying up there under a rock, shot in the head.'

'Geoffrey!' she called.

'He needs a brandy or something. First time he's seen a guy killed. It's never pretty,' Melrose said.

'Oh Jake. Oh Jake.' She was clinging to him. 'How did you know – ?'

He began to explain the trail that had led him North into the middle of Scotland, the same that Billy had followed. And Colin Landsdowne.

Powers had stumbled into the cottage.

'Geoffrey, wait – ' she cried, standing there.

Melrose knew she was someone's wife.

There was a code in place. He wanted to hold her, kiss her, give her all the love in the world, and knew it couldn't happen. It never did.

He said, 'Go on, look after Geoffrey. He saved my hide, but all he wants is some tape – '

'A tape? What for?'

'I don't know. He searched Landsdowne's body, looking for some damned tape.'

'Oh my God – '

She saw Geoffrey's head in the kitchen, through the lighted window; saw him move into the lounge.

'Geoffrey – ' she screamed.

That radio that Billy had fiddled with. He had inserted the tape. He had hidden it there, and Geoffrey had remembered, paralysed and numb with shock.

'Geoffrey – no!'

The single shot echoed from the house and cracked through the open air. It stunned and drained her, almost knocking her down. She screamed again, covering her face.

Melrose heard the cassette playing. They were left in the darkness, holding on to each other.

'Stay here,' he said.

She saw him walk into the kitchen and close the door behind him carefully, as if in church, going through into the lounge. She sank down on to the grass.

After a minute he returned, and took her in his arms. 'Honey, let's go. There's nothing for you in there.'

They set off in the hire-car after wiping the glass from the bonnet. Dust, debris, broken glass. The wreckage of two lives.

Driving down the track to the road, calling for help, they saw the loch ahead, a sullen grey under the moon.

'Don't think about it,' he said.

'There's a Rescue Centre,' she whispered, 'along the road. Mountain rescue, Ben Lawers.'

'Okay,' he said.

He pulled out on to the Tay Road, then up another trail. His lights picked up a signpost for the National Trust of Scotland. Cattlegrids, a single-track road curving towards the lights on the edge of the mountain that he had noticed going up the slope. In high summer, he knew, this place would be full of tourists, car parks, picnic groups, but that night it was dead, wrapped in a cloak of silence. Only the lights remained. They drove up and clambered out.

'You okay, honey?'

She nodded, grimly.

278

He was banging on the door of a heavy timber building with a low hanging roof, like a Swiss barn. He put his arm round the girl. The darkness enfolded them.

There was a warden in residence. He looked as if he'd been asleep.

'Man, didn't you hear the shooting: and the shouting?'

The warden shook his head. 'I hur'rd sommat. But I've been watching the television.' He peered more closely. 'What's the matter with ye?'

They must have looked an odd couple, the beanpole American, grubby, grey-haired, holding the English girl who had seen Landsdowne go up the mountain after Melrose and Vane.

They were led into a display space, full of facts about screes and trees, then through to the warden's cabin. A camp bed, a colour TV.

'Wha-hey! Ye look all in . . .'

Slowly Melrose explained. This time he would try the whisky, and so would Claire. They needed it. A man had been shot on the mountain, another one had shot himself rather than face the enquiry.

'What the hell for?' the stunned warden asked, as he made the various calls.

Melrose pieced it together as he held Claire's hand at last. He realized that Landsdowne's scheming had started Godber running, then Powers to Vane to Wallace, who had called Melrose in. But something had happened to Billy – Claire whispered of the state he was in – and maybe, just maybe, Billy had saved Jake's own life.

Jake Melrose sipped the neat Scotch.

'Ye need it . . .' the man said.

Melrose smiled, lighting up his face. 'Two drinks under par,' he said.

The soundless television was flickering away in the corner, a late night news programme. Suddenly Claire jumped across to turn it up.

'Godber resigns,' the headlines said, 'following the continuing allegations over Gibraltar.'

279

A picture of him leaving the House. The Jaguar scurrying away. She switched it off.

'Too late for Geoffrey.' In a way she felt happy for him; in a way he had cleared the record.

Jake Melrose said, 'Honey, what good would it have done?'

Claire broke down in tears. 'I know. I know.'

He was looking at her as if his eyes would bore through her and could never see too much. Inarticulate, tough, tired-looking under the strip light and yellow pine in the cabin.

'Honey . . . I got a job. I ain't exactly got a home,' he said, thinking of the borrowed apartment, and the empty pad in Virginia. 'Not yet . . .'

He held out his arms, and she was moving towards him, out of the nightmare, into the kind of happiness she thought she would never have.

'I know,' she said. 'Not yet . . . but soon.'

A Selected List of Fiction Available from Mandarin

While every effort is made to keep prices low, it is sometimes necessary to increase prices at short notice. Mandarin Paperbacks reserves the right to show new retail prices on covers which may differ from those previously advertised in the text or elsewhere.

The prices shown below were correct at the time of going to press.

☐	7493 1352 8	**The Queen and I**	Sue Townsend	£4.99
☐	7493 0540 1	**The Liar**	Stephen Fry	£4.99
☐	7493 1132 0	**Arrivals and Departures**	Lesley Thomas	£4.99
☐	7493 0381 6	**Loves and Journeys of Revolving Jones**	Leslie Thomas	£4.99
☐	7493 0942 3	**Silence of the Lambs**	Thomas Harris	£4.99
☐	7493 0946 6	**The Godfather**	Mario Puzo	£4.99
☐	7493 1561 X	**Fear of Flying**	Erica Jong	£4.99
☐	7493 1221 1	**The Power of One**	Bryce Courtney	£4.99
☐	7493 0576 2	**Tandia**	Bryce Courtney	£5.99
☐	7493 0563 0	**Kill the Lights**	Simon Williams	£4.99
☐	7493 1319 6	**Air and Angels**	Susan Hill	£4.99
☐	7493 1477 X	**The Name of the Rose**	Umberto Eco	£4.99
☐	7493 0896 6	**The Stand-in**	Deborah Moggach	£4.99
☐	7493 0581 9	**Daddy's Girls**	Zoe Fairbairns	£4.99

All these books are available at your bookshop or newsagent, or can be ordered direct from the address below. Just tick the titles you want and fill in the form below.

Cash Sales Department, PO Box 5, Rushden, Northants NN10 6YX.
Fax: 0933 410321 : Phone 0933 410511.

Please send cheque, payable to 'Reed Book Services Ltd.', or postal order for purchase price quoted and allow the following for postage and packing:

£1.00 for the first book, 50p for the second; **FREE POSTAGE AND PACKING FOR THREE BOOKS OR MORE PER ORDER.**

NAME (Block letters) ....

ADDRESS ....

....

☐ I enclose my remittance for ....

☐ I wish to pay by Access/Visa Card Number

Expiry Date

Signature ....

Please quote our reference: MAND